INTRODUCING DISCWORLD

The Discworld series is a continuous history of a world not totally unlike our own, except that it is a flat disc carried on the backs of four elephants astride a giant turtle floating through space, and that it is peopled by, among others, wizards, dwarfs, policemen, thieves, beggars, vampires and witches. Within the history of Discworld there are many individual stories, which can be read in any order, but reading them in sequence can increase your enjoyment through the accumulation of all the fine detail that contributes to the teeming imaginative complexity of this brilliantly conceived world.

BOOKS BY TERRY PRATCHETT

The Discworld® series

————— **Other books about Discworld** —————

TURTLE RECALL: THE DISCWORLD COMPANION . . . SO FAR
(with Stephen Briggs)

NANNY OGG'S COOKBOOK
(with Stephen Briggs, Tina Hannan and Paul Kidby)

THE PRATCHETT PORTFOLIO
(with Paul Kidby)

THE DISCWORLD ALMANAK
(with Bernard Pearson)

THE UNSEEN UNIVERSITY CUT-OUT BOOK
(with Alan Batley and Bernard Pearson)

WHERE'S MY COW?
(illustrated by Melvyn Grant)

THE ART OF DISCWORLD
(with Paul Kidby)

THE WIT AND WISDOM OF DISCWORLD
(compiled by Stephen Briggs)

THE FOLKLORE OF DISCWORLD
(with Jacqueline Simpson)

THE WORLD OF POO
(with the Discworld Emporium)

MRS BRADSHAW'S HANDBOOK
(with the Discworld Emporium)

THE COMPLEAT ANKH-MORPORK
(with the Discworld Emporium)

THE STREETS OF ANKH-MORPORK
(with Stephen Briggs, painted by Stephen Player)

THE DISCWORLD MAPP
(with Stephen Briggs, painted by Stephen Player)

A TOURIST GUIDE TO LANCRE – A DISCWORLD MAPP
(with Stephen Briggs, illustrated by Paul Kidby)

DEATH'S DOMAIN (with Paul Kidby)

THE DISCWORLD ATLAS
(with the Discworld Emporium)

A complete list of Terry Pratchett ebooks and audio books as well as other books based on the Discworld series – illustrated screenplays, graphic novels, comics and plays – can be found on
www.terrypratchett.co.uk

―――――――――――― **Non-Discworld books** ――――――――――――

THE DARK SIDE OF THE SUN

STRATA

THE UNADULTERATED CAT (illustrated by Gray Jolliffe)

GOOD OMENS (with Neil Gaiman)

―――――――――――― **Shorter Writing** ――――――――――――

A BLINK OF THE SCREEN

A SLIP OF THE KEYBOARD

SHAKING HANDS WITH DEATH

―――――――――――― **With Stephen Baxter** ――――――――――――

THE LONG EARTH

THE LONG WAR

THE LONG MARS

THE LONG UTOPIA

THE LONG COSMOS

―――――――――――― **Non-Discworld books for young adults** ――――――――――――

THE CARPET PEOPLE

TRUCKERS

DIGGERS

WINGS

ONLY YOU CAN SAVE MANKIND

JOHNNY AND THE DEAD

JOHNNY AND THE BOMB

NATION

DODGER

JACK DODGER'S GUIDE TO LONDON

DRAGONS AT CRUMBLING CASTLE

THE WITCH'S VACUUM CLEANER

WITCHES ABROAD

A DISCWORLD® NOVEL

Terry Pratchett

CORGI BOOKS

TRANSWORLD PUBLISHERS
61-63 Uxbridge Road, London W5 5SA
A Random House Group Company
www.transworldbooks.co.uk

WITCHES ABROAD
A CORGI BOOK: 9780552167505

First published in Great Britain
in 1991 by Victor Gollancz Ltd
Corgi edition published 1992
Corgi edition reissued 2005
Corgi edition reissued 2013

Addresses for Random House Group Ltd companies outside the UK
can be found at: www.randomhouse.co.uk
The Random House Group Ltd Reg. No. 954009.

Pengui   for
our bus   rom

Print   lc

Dedicated to all those people – and why not? – who, after the publication of *Wyrd Sisters*, deluged the author with their version of the words of 'The Hedgehog Song'.

Deary deary me . . .

WITCHES ABROAD

This is the Discworld, which travels through space on the back of four elephants which themselves stand on the shell of Great A'Tuin, the sky turtle.

Once upon a time such a universe was considered unusual and, possibly, impossible.

But then . . . it used to be so simple, once upon a time.

Because the universe was full of ignorance all around and the scientist panned through it like a prospector crouched over a mountain stream, looking for the gold of knowledge among the gravel of unreason, the sand of uncertainty and the little whiskery eight-legged swimming things of superstition.

Occasionally he would straighten up and say things like 'Hurrah, I've discovered Boyle's Third Law.' And everyone knew where they stood. But the trouble was that ignorance became more interesting, especially big fascinating ignorance about huge and important things like matter and creation, and people stopped patiently building their little houses of rational sticks in the chaos of the universe and started getting interested in the chaos itself – partly because it was a lot easier to be an expert on chaos, but mostly because it made really good patterns that you could put on a t-shirt.

And instead of getting on with proper science* scientists suddenly went around saying how impossible it was to know anything, and that there wasn't really anything you could call reality to know anything about, and how all this was tremendously exciting, and incidentally did you know there were possibly all these little universes all over the place but no one can see them because they are all curved in on themselves? Incidentally, don't you think this is a rather good t-shirt?

Compared to all this, a large turtle with a world on its back is practically mundane. At least it doesn't pretend it doesn't exist, and no one on the Discworld ever tried to *prove* it didn't exist in case they turned out to be right and found themselves suddenly floating in empty space. This is because the Discworld exists right on the edge of reality. The least little things can break through to the other side. So, on the Discworld, people take things seriously.

Like stories.

Because stories are important.

People think that stories are shaped by people. In fact, it's the other way around.

Stories exist independently of their players. If you know that, the knowledge is power.

---

*Like finding that bloody butterfly whose flapping wings cause all these storms we've been having lately and getting it to stop.

Stories, great flapping ribbons of shaped space-time, have been blowing and uncoiling around the universe since the beginning of time. And they have evolved. The weakest have died and the strongest have survived and they have grown fat on the re-telling . . . stories, twisting and blowing through the darkness.

And their very existence overlays a faint but insistent pattern on the chaos that is history. Stories etch grooves deep enough for people to follow in the same way that water follows certain paths down a mountainside. And every time fresh actors tread the path of the story, the groove runs deeper.

This is called the theory of narrative causality and it means that a story, once started, *takes a shape.* It picks up all the vibrations of all the other workings of that story that have ever been.

This is why history keeps on repeating all the time.

So a thousand heroes have stolen fire from the gods. A thousand wolves have eaten grandmother, a thousand princesses have been kissed. A million unknowing actors have moved, unknowing, through the pathways of story.

It is now *impossible* for the third and youngest son of any king, if he should embark on a quest which has so far claimed his older brothers, *not* to succeed.

Stories don't care who takes part in them. All that matters is that the story gets told, that the story repeats. Or, if you prefer to think of it like this:

stories are a parasitical life form, warping lives in the service only of the story itself.*

It takes a special kind of person to fight back, and become the bicarbonate of history.

Once upon a time . . .

Grey hands gripped the hammer and swung it, striking the post so hard that it sank a foot into the soft earth.

Two more blows and it was fixed immovably.

From the trees around the clearing the snakes and birds watched silently. In the swamp the alligators drifted like patches of bad-assed water.

Grey hands took up the crosspiece and fixed it in place, tying it with creepers, pulling them so tight that they creaked.

She watched him. And then she took up a fragment of mirror and tied it to the top of the post.

'The coat,' she said.

He took up the coat and fitted it over the crosspiece.

---

*And people are wrong about urban myths. Logic and reason say that these are fictional creations, retold again and again by people who are hungry for evidence of weird coincidence, natural justice and so on. They aren't. *They keep on happening all the time, everywhere,* as the stories bounce back and forth across the universe. At any one time hundreds of dead grandmothers are being whisked away on the roof-racks of stolen cars and loyal alsatians are choking on the fingers of midnight burglars. And they're not confined to any one world. Hundreds of female Mercurian *jivpts* turn four tiny eyes on their rescuers and say, 'My brood-husband will be livid – it was *his* travel module.' Urban myths are alive.

The pole wasn't long enough, so that the last few inches of sleeve draped emptily.

'And the hat,' she said.

It was tall, and round, and black. It glistened.

The piece of mirror gleamed between the darkness of the hat and the coat.

'Will it work?' he said.

'Yes,' she said. 'Even mirrors have their reflection. We got to fight mirrors with mirrors.' She glared up through the trees to a slim white tower in the distance. 'We've got to find *her* reflection.'

'It'll have to reach out a long way, then.'

'Yes. We need all the help we can get.'

She looked around the clearing.

She had called upon Mister Safe Way, Lady Bon Anna, Hotaloga Andrews and Stride Wide Man. They probably weren't very good gods.

But they were the best she'd been able to make.

This is a story about stories.

Or what it really means to be a fairy godmother.

But it's also, particularly, about reflections and mirrors.

All across the multiverse there are backward tribes* who distrust mirrors and images because, they say, they steal a bit of a person's soul and there's only so much of a person to go around. And the

---

*Considered backward, that is, by people who wear more clothes than they do.

people who wear more clothes say this is just superstition, despite the fact that other people who
spend their lives appearing in images of one sort
or another seem to develop a *thin* quality. It's put
down to over-work and, tellingly, *over-exposure* instead.

Just superstition. But a superstition doesn't have
to be wrong.

A mirror can suck up a piece of soul. A mirror can
contain the reflection of the whole universe, a whole
skyful of stars in a piece of silvered glass no thicker
than a breath.

Know about mirrors and you nearly know everything.

Look into the mirror . . .

. . . further. . .

. . . to an orange light on a cold mountaintop,
thousands of miles from the vegetable warmth of
that swamp . . .

Local people called it the Bear Mountain. This was
because it was a *bare* mountain, not because it had a
lot of bears on it. This caused a certain amount
of profitable confusion, though; people often strode
into the nearest village with heavy duty crossbows,
traps and nets and called haughtily for native guides
to lead them to the bears. Since everyone locally
was making quite a good living out of this, what
with the sale of guide books, maps of bear caves,
ornamental cuckoo-clocks with bears on them, bear
walking-sticks and cakes baked in the shape of a

bear, somehow no one had time to go and correct the spelling.*

It was about as bare as a mountain could be.

Most of the trees gave out about halfway to the top, only a few pines hanging on to give an effect very similar to the couple of pathetic strands teased across his scalp by a baldie who won't own up.

It was a place where witches met.

Tonight a fire gleamed on the very crest of the hill. Dark figures moved in the flickering light.

The moon coasted across a lacework of clouds.

Finally, a tall, pointy-hatted figure said, 'You mean *everyone* brought potato salad?'

There was one Ramtop witch who was not attending the sabbat. Witches like a night out as much as anyone else but, in this case, she had a more pressing appointment. And it wasn't the kind of appointment you can put off easily.

Desiderata Hollow was making her will.

When Desiderata Hollow was a girl, her grandmother had given her four important pieces of advice to guide her young footsteps on the unexpectedly twisting pathway of life.

---

*Bad spelling can be lethal. For example, the greedy Seriph of Al-Ybi was once cursed by a badly-educated deity and for some days everything he touched turned to Glod, which happened to be the name of a small dwarf from a mountain community hundreds of miles away who found himself magically dragged to the kingdom and relentlessly duplicated. Some two thousand Glods later the spell wore off. These days, the people of Al-Ybi are renowned for being unusually short and bad-tempered.

They were:

Never trust a dog with orange eyebrows,

Always get the young man's name and address,

Never get between two mirrors,

And always wear completely clean underwear every day because you never knew when you were going to be knocked down and killed by a runaway horse and if people found you had unsatisfactory underwear on, you'd die of shame.

And then Desiderata grew up to become a witch. And one of the minor benefits of being a witch is that you know exactly when you're going to die and can wear what underwear you like.*

That had been eighty years earlier, when the idea of knowing exactly when you were going to die had seemed quite attractive because secretly, of course, you knew you were going to live forever.

That was then.

And this was now.

Forever didn't seem to last as long these days as once it did.

Another log crumbled to ash in the fireplace. Desiderata hadn't bothered to order any fuel for the winter. Not much point, really.

And then, of course, there was this other thing . . .

She'd wrapped it up carefully into a long, slim package. Now she folded up the letter, addressed it, and pushed it under the string. Job done.

She looked up. Desiderata had been blind for thirty years, but this hadn't been a problem. She'd

---

*Which explains a lot about witches.

always been blessed, if that was the word, with second sight. So when the ordinary eyes gave out you just trained yourself to see into the present, which anyway was easier than the future. And since the eyeball of the occult didn't depend on light, you saved on candles. There was always a silver lining, if you knew where to look. In a manner of speaking.

There was a mirror on the wall in front of her.

The face in it was not her own, which was round and pink.

It was the face of a woman who was used to giving orders. Desiderata wasn't the sort to give orders. Quite the reverse, in fact.

The woman said, 'You are dying, Desiderata.'

'I am that, too.'

'You've grown old. Your sort always do. Your power is nearly gone.'

'That's a fact, Lilith,' said Desiderata mildly.

'So your protection is withdrawing from her.'

''Fraid so,' said Desiderata.

'So now it's just me and the evil swamp woman. And I will win.'

'That's how it seems, I'm afraid.'

'You should have found a successor.'

'Never had the time. I'm not the planning sort, you know.'

The face in the mirror got closer, as if the figure had moved a little nearer to its side of the mirror.

'You've *lost*, Desiderata Hollow.'

'So it goes.' Desiderata got to her feet, a little unsteadily, and picked up a cloth.

The figure seemed to be getting angry. It clearly

felt that people who had lost ought to look downcast, and not as if they were enjoying a joke at your expense.

'Don't you understand what losing *means*?'

'Some people are very clear about that,' said Desiderata. 'Goodbye, m'lady.' She hung the cloth over the mirror.

There was an angry intake of breath, and then silence.

Desiderata stood as if lost in thought.

Then she raised her head, and said: 'Kettle boiled just now. Would you like a cup of tea?'

NO, THANK YOU, said a voice right behind her.

'How long have you been waiting?'

FOREVER.

'Not keeping you, am I?'

IT'S A QUIET NIGHT.

'I'm making a cup of tea. I think there's one biscuit left.'

NO, THANK YOU.

'If you feel peckish, it's in the jar on the mantel-piece. That's genuine Klatchian pottery, you know. Made by a genuine Klatchian craftsman. From Klatch,' she added.

INDEED?

'I used to get about a lot in my younger days.'

YES?

'Great times.' Desiderata poked the fire. 'It was the job, you see. Of course, I expect it's very much the same for you.'

YES.

'I never knew when I was going to be called out.

Well, of course you'd know about that, wouldn't you. Kitchens, mainly. It always seemed to be kitchens. Balls sometimes, but generally it was kitchens.' She picked up the kettle and poured the boiling water into the teapot on the hearth.

Indeed.

'I used to grant their wishes.'

Death looked puzzled.

What? You mean like . . . fitted cupboards? New sinks? That kind of thing?

'No, no. The *people*.' Desiderata sighed. 'It's a big responsibility, fairy godmothering. Knowing when to stop, I mean. People whose wishes get granted often don't turn out to be very nice people. So should you give them what they want – or what they *need*?'

Death nodded politely. From his point of view, people got what they were given.

'Like this Genua thing—' Desiderata began.

Death looked up sharply.

Genua?

'You know it? Well, of course you would.'

I . . . know everywhere, of course.

Desiderata's expression softened. Her inner eyes were looking elsewhere.

'There were two of us. Godmothers go in twos, you know. Me and Lady Lilith? There's a lot of power in godmothering. It's like being part of history. Anyway, the girl was born, out of wedlock but none the worse for that, it wasn't as if they couldn't have married, they just never got round to it . . . and Lilith wished for her to have beauty and power and marry a prince. Hah! And she's been working on that ever since. What could I do? You can't argue with wishes like that. Lilith knows the power of a story. I've done the best I could, but Lilith's got the power. I hear she runs the city now. Changing a whole country just to make a story work! And now it's too late anyway. For me. So I'm handing on the responsibility. That's how it goes, with fairy godmothering. No one ever *wants* to be a fairy godmother. Except Lilith, of course. Got a bee in her bonnet about it. So I'm sending someone else. I may have left things too late.'

Desiderata was a kindly soul. Fairy godmothers develop a very deep understanding about human nature, which makes the good ones kind and the bad ones powerful. She was not someone to use extreme language, but it was possible to be sure that when she deployed a mild term like 'a bee in her bonnet' she was using it to define someone whom she believed to be several miles over the madness horizon and accelerating.

She poured out the tea.

'That's the trouble with second sight,' she said. 'You can *see* what's happenin', but you don't know what it *means.* I've seen the future. There's a coach made out of a pumpkin. And that's impossible. And there's coachmen made out of mice, which is unlikely. And there's a clock striking midnight, and something about a glass slipper. And it's all going to happen. Because that's how stories have to work. And then I thought: I knows some people who make stories work *their* way.'

She sighed again. 'Wish *I* was going to Genua,'

she said. 'I could do with the warmth. And it's Fat Tuesday coming up. Always went to Genua for Fat Tuesday in the old days.'

There was an expectant silence.

Then Death said, YOU SURELY ARE NOT ASKING ME TO GRANT A WISH?

'Hah! *No one* grants a fairy godmother's wishes.' Desiderata had that inward look again, her voice talking to herself. 'See? I got to get the three of them to Genua. Got to get 'em there because I've *seen* 'em there. Got to be all three. And that ain't easy, with people like them. Got to use headology. Got to make 'em send 'emselves. Tell Esme Weatherwax she's got to go somewhere and she won't go out of contrariness, so tell her she's not to go and she'll run there over broken glass. That's the thing about the Weatherwaxes, see. They don't know how to be beaten.'

Something seemed to strike her as funny.

'But *one* of 'em's going to have to *learn*.'

Death said nothing. From where he sat, Desiderata reflected, losing was something that everyone learned.

She drained her tea. Then she stood up, put on her pointy hat with a certain amount of ceremony, and hobbled out of the back door.

There was a deep trench dug under the trees a little way from the house, down into which someone had thoughtfully put a short ladder. She climbed in and, with some difficulty, heaved the ladder on to the leaves. Then she lay down. She sat up.

'Mr Chert the troll down at the sawmill does

23

a very good deal on coffins, if you don't mind pine.'

I SHALL DEFINITELY BEAR IT IN MIND.

'I got Hurker the poacher to dig the hole out for me,' she said conversationally, 'and he's goin' to come along and fill it in on his way home. I believe in being neat. Take it away, maestro.'

WHAT? OH. A FIGURE OF SPEECH.

He raised his scythe.

Desiderata Hollow went to her rest.

'Well,' she said, 'that was easy. What happens now?'

And this *is* Genua. The magical kingdom. The diamond city. The fortunate country.

In the centre of the city a woman stood between two mirrors, watching herself reflected all the way to infinity.

The mirrors were themselves in the centre of an octagon of mirrors, open to the sky on the highest tower of the palace. There were so many reflections, in fact, that it was only with extreme difficulty that you could tell where the mirrors ended and the real person began.

Her name was Lady Lilith de Tempscire, although she had answered to many others in the course of a long and eventful life. And that was something you learned to do early on, she'd found. If you wanted to get anywhere in this world – and she'd decided, right at the start, that she wanted to get as far as it was possible to go – you wore names lightly, and you took power anywhere you found it. She had buried three husbands, and at least two of them had been already dead.

And you moved around a lot. Because most people *didn't* move around much. Change countries and your name and, if you had the right manner, the world was your mollusc. For example, she'd had to go a mere hundred miles to become a Lady.

She'd go to any lengths now . . .

The two main mirrors were set almost, but not quite, facing one another, so that Lilith could see over her shoulder and watch her images curve away around the universe inside the mirror.

She could feel *herself* pouring into *herself,* multiplying itself via the endless reflections.

When Lilith sighed and strode out from the space between the mirrors the effect was startling. Images of Lilith hung in the air behind her for a moment, like three-dimensional shadows, before fading.

So . . . Desiderata was dying. Interfering old baggage. She deserved death. She'd never understood the kind of power she'd had. She was one of those people afraid to do good for fear of doing harm, who took it all so seriously that they'd constipate themselves with moral anguish before granting the wish of a single ant.

Lilith looked down and out over the city. Well, there were no barriers now. The stupid voodoo woman in the swamp was a mere distraction, with no understanding.

Nothing stood in the way of what Lilith liked more than anything else.

A happy ending.

*　　*　　*

Up on the mountain, the sabbat had settled down a bit. Artists and writers have always had a rather exaggerated idea about what goes on at a witches' sabbat. This comes from spending too much time in small rooms with the curtains drawn, instead of getting out in the healthy fresh air.

For example, there's the dancing around naked. In the average temperate climate there are very few nights when anyone would dance around at midnight with no clothes on, quite apart from the question of stones, thistles, and sudden hedgehogs.

Then there's all that business with goat-headed gods. Most witches don't believe in gods. They know that the gods exist, of course. They even deal with them occasionally. But they don't believe in them. They know them too well. It would be like believing in the postman.

And there's the food and drink – the bits of reptile and so on. In fact, witches don't go for that sort of thing. The worst you can say about the eating habits of the older type of witch is that they tend to like ginger biscuits dipped in tea with so much sugar in it that the spoon won't move *and* will drink it out of the saucer if they think it's too hot. And do so with appreciative noises more generally associated with the cheaper type of plumbing system. Legs of toad and so on might be better than this.

Then there's the mystic ointments. By sheer luck, the artists and writers are on firmer ground here. Most witches are elderly, which is when ointments start to have an attraction, and at least two of those present tonight were wearing Granny Weatherwax's famous goose-grease-and-sage chest liniment. This didn't make you fly and see visions, but it *did* prevent colds, if only because the distressing smell that developed around about the second week kept everyone else so far away you couldn't catch anything from them.

And finally there's sabbats themselves. Your average witch is not, by nature, a social animal as far as other witches are concerned. There's a conflict of dominant personalities. There's a group of ringleaders without a ring. There's the basic unwritten rule of witchcraft, which is 'Don't do what you will, do what I say.' The natural size of a coven is one. Witches only get together when they can't avoid it.

Like now.

The conversation, given Desiderata's absence, had naturally turned to the increasing shortage of witches.*

'What, no one?' said Granny Weatherwax.

'No one,' said Gammer Brevis.

'I call that terrible,' said Granny. 'That's disgustin'.'

'Eh?' said Old Mother Dismass.

'She calls it disgusting!' shouted Gammer Brevis.

'Eh?'

'There's no girl to put forward! To take Desiderata's place!'

---

*Desiderata had sent a note via Old Mother Dismass asking to be excused on account of being dead. Second sight enables you to keep a very tight rein on your social engagements.

'Oh.'

The implications of this sank in.

'If anyone doesn't want their crusts I'll 'ave 'em,' said Nanny Ogg.

'We never had this sort of thing in my young days,' said Granny. 'There was a dozen witches this side of the mountain alone. Of course, that was before all this' – she made a face – 'making your own entertainment. There's far too much of this making your own entertainment these days. We never made our own entertainment when I was a girl. We never had time.'

'Tempers fuggit,' said Nanny Ogg.

'What?'

'Tempers fuggit. Means that was then and this is now,' said Nanny.

'I don't need no one to tell me that, Gytha Ogg. I know when now is.'

'You got to move with the times.'

'I don't see why. Don't see why we—'

'So I reckon we got to shift the boundaries again,' said Gammer Brevis.

'Can't do that,' said Granny Weatherwax promptly. 'I'm doing four villages already. The broomstick hardly has time to cool down.'

'Well, with Mother Hollow passing on, we're definitely short handed,' said Gammer Brevis. 'I know she didn't do a lot, what with her other work, but she was there. That's what it's all about. Being there. There's got to be a local witch.'

The four witches stared gloomily at the fire. Well, three of them did. Nanny Ogg, who tended to look on the cheerful side, made toast.

'They've got a wizard in, down in Creel Springs,' said Gammer Brevis. 'There wasn't anyone to take over when old Granny Hopliss passed on, so they sent off to Ankh-Morpork for a wizard. An actual wizard. With a staff. He's got a shop there and everything, with a brass sign on the door. It says "Wizard".'

The witches sighed.

'Mrs Singe passed on,' said Gammer Brevis. 'And Gammer Peavey passed on.'

'Did she? Old Mabel Peavey?' said Nanny Ogg, through a shower of crumbs. 'How old was she?'

'One hundred and nineteen,' said Gammer Brevis. 'I said to her, "You don't want to go climbing mountains at your age" but she wouldn't listen.'

'Some people are like that,' said Granny. 'Stubborn as mules. Tell them they mustn't do something and they won't stop till they've tried it.'

'I actually heard her very last words,' said Gammer.

'What did she say?' said Granny.

'As I recall, "oh bugger",' said Gammer.

'It's the way she would have wanted to go,' said Nanny Ogg. The other witches nodded.

'You know . . . we could be looking at the end of witchcraft in these parts,' said Gammer Brevis.

They stared at the fire again.

'I don't 'spect anyone's brought any marsh-mallows?' said Nanny Ogg, hopefully.

Granny Weatherwax looked at her sister witches. Gammer Brevis she couldn't stand; the old woman taught school on the other side of the mountain, and had a nasty habit of being reasonable when provoked. And Old Mother Dismass was possibly the most useless sibyl in the history of oracular revelation. And Granny really couldn't be having at all with Nanny Ogg, who was her best friend.

'What about young Magrat?' said Old Mother Dismass innocently. 'Her patch runs right alongside Desiderata's. Maybe she could take on a bit extra?'

Granny Weatherwax and Nanny Ogg exchanged glances.

'She's gone funny in the head,' said Granny.

'Now, come on, Esme,' said Nanny Ogg.

'Well, *I* call it funny,' said Granny. 'You can't tell me that saying all that stuff about relatives isn't going funny in the head.'

'She didn't say that,' said Nanny. 'She said she wanted to relate to herself.'

'That's what I said,' said Granny Weatherwax. 'I told her: Simplicity Garlick was your mother, Araminta Garlick was your granny. Yolande Garlick is your aunt and you're your . . . you're your *me*.'

She sat back with the satisfied look of someone who has solved everything anyone could ever want to know about a personal identity crisis.

'She wouldn't listen,' she added.

Gammer Brevis wrinkled her forehead.

'Magrat?' she said. She tried to get a mental picture of the Ramtops' youngest witch and recalled – well, not a face, just a slightly watery-eyed expression of hopeless goodwill wedged between a body like a maypole and hair like a haystack after a gale. A relentless doer of good works. A worrier. The kind of person who rescued small lost baby birds and cried when they died, which is the function kind old Mother Nature usually reserves for small lost baby birds.

'Doesn't sound like her,' she said.

'And she said she wanted to be more self-assertive,' said Granny.

'Nothing wrong with being self-assertive,' said Nanny. 'Self-asserting's what witching's all about.'

'I never said there was anything wrong with it,' said Granny. 'I told her there was nothing wrong with it. You can be as self-assertive as you like, I said, just so long as you do what you're told.'

'Rub this on and it'll clear up in a week or two,' said Old Mother Dismass.

The other three witches watched her expectantly, in case there was going to be anything else. It became clear that there wasn't.

'And she's running – what's that she's running, Gytha?' said Granny.

'Self-defence classes,' said Nanny.

'But she's a witch,' Gammer Brevis pointed out.

'I told her that,' said Granny Weatherwax, who had walked nightly without fear in the bandit-haunted forests of the mountains all her life in the certain knowledge that the darkness held nothing more terrible than she was. 'She said that wasn't the point. *Wasn't the point.* That's what she said.'

'No one goes to them, anyway,' said Nanny Ogg.

'*I* thought she was going to get married to the king,' said Gammer Brevis.

'Everyone did,' said Nanny. 'But you know Magrat. She tends to be open to Ideas. Now she says she refuses to be a sex object.'

They all thought about this. Finally Gammer Brevis said, slowly, in the manner of one surfacing from the depths of fascinated cogitation, 'But she's never *been* a sex object.'

'I'm pleased to say I don't even know what a sex object *is*,' said Granny Weatherwax firmly.

'I do,' said Nanny Ogg.

They looked at her.

'Our Shane brought one home from foreign parts once.'

They carried on looking at her.

'It was brown and fat and had beads on and a face and two holes for the string.'

This didn't seem to avert their gaze.

'Well, that's what he said it was,' said Nanny.

'I think you're talking about a fertility idol,' said Gammer Brevis helpfully.

Granny shook her head.

'Doesn't sound much like Magrat to me—' she began.

'You can't tell me that's worth tuppence,' said Old Mother Dismass, from whatever moment of time she was currently occupying.

No one was ever quite sure which it was.

It was an occupational hazard for those gifted with second sight. The human mind isn't really designed to be sent rocketing backwards and forwards along the great freeway of time and can become, as it were, detached from its anchorage, seeing randomly into the past and the future and only occasionally into the present. Old Mother Dismass was temporally unfocused. This meant that if you spoke to her in August she was probably listening to you in March. It was best just to say something now and hope she'd pick it up next time her mind was passing through.

Granny waved her hands experimentally in front of Old Mother Dismass's unseeing eyes.

'She's gone again,' she said.

'Well, if Magrat can't take it on there's Millie Hopgood from over Slice way,' said Gammer Brevis. 'She's a hardworking girl. Mind you, she's got a worse squint than Magrat.'

'Nothing wrong with that. A squint looks good on a witch,' said Granny Weatherwax.

'But you have to know how to use it,' said Nanny Ogg. 'Old Gertie Simmons used to have a squint and she was always putting the evil influence on the end of her own nose. We can't have people thinkin' that if you upsets a witch she curses and mutters and then her own nose drops off.'

They all stared at the fire again.

'I suppose Desiderata wouldn't have chosen her own successor?' said Gammer Brevis.

'Can't go doin' that,' said Granny Weatherwax. 'That's not how we do things in these parts.'

'Yes, but Desiderata didn't spend much time in these parts. It was the job. She was always going off to foreign parts.'

'I can't be having with foreign parts,' said Granny Weatherwax.

'You've been to Ankh-Morpork,' said Nanny mildly. 'That's foreign.'

'No it's not. It's just a long way off. That's not the same as foreign. Foreign's where they gabble at you in heathen lingo and eat foreign muck and worship, you know, *objects*,' said Granny Weatherwax, goodwill diplomat. 'Foreign can be quite close to, if you're not careful. Huh,' she added witheringly. 'Yes, she could bring back just about anything from foreign parts.'

'She brought me back a nice blue and white plate once,' said Nanny Ogg.

'That's a point,' said Gammer Brevis. 'Someone'd better go and see to her cottage. She had quite a lot of good stuff there. It'd be dreadful to think of some thief getting in there and having a rummage.'

'Can't imagine any thief'd want to break into a witch's—' Granny began, and then stopped abruptly.

'Yes,' she said meekly. 'Good idea. I'll see to it directly.'

'No, I'll see to it,' said Nanny Ogg, who'd also had time to work something out. 'It's right on my way home. No problem.'

'No, you'll be wanting to get home early,' said Granny. 'Don't you bother yourself. It'd be no trouble.'

'Oh, it won't be any trouble at all,' said Nanny.

'You don't want to go tiring yourself out at your age,' said Granny Weatherwax.

They glared at one another.

'I really don't see that it matters,' said Gammer Brevis. 'You might as well go together rather than fight about it.'

'I'm a bit busy tomorrow,' said Granny. 'How about after lunch?'

'Right,' said Nanny Ogg. 'We'll meet at her cottage. Right after lunch.'

'We had one once but the bit you unscrew fell off and got lost,' said Old Mother Dismass.

Hurker the poacher shovelled the last of the earth into the hole. He felt he ought to say a few words.

'Well, that's about it, then,' he said.

She'd definitely been one of the better witches, he thought, as he wandered back to the cottage in the pre-dawn gloom. Some of the other ones – while of course being wonderful human beings, he added to himself hurriedly, as fine a bunch of women as you could ever hope to avoid – were just a bit over-powering. Mistress Hollow had been a listening kind of person.

On the kitchen table was a long package, a small pile of coins, and an envelope.

He opened the envelope, although it was not addressed to him.

Inside was a smaller envelope, and a note.

The note said: I'm watching you, Albert Hurker. Deliver the packige and the envlope and if you dare take a peek inside something dretful will happen to you. As a profesional Good Farey Godmother I aint allowed to curse anyone but I Predict it would probly involve bein bittern by an enraged wolf and your leg going green and runny and dropping off, dont arsk me how I know anyway you carnt because, I am dead. All the best, Desiderata.

He picked up the package with his eyes shut.

Light travels slowly in the Discworld's vast magical field, which means that time does too. As Nanny Ogg would put it, when it's teatime in Genua it's Tuesday over here . . .

In fact it was dawn in Genua. Lilith sat in her tower, using a mirror, sending her own image out to scan the world. She was searching.

Wherever there was a sparkle on a wave crest, wherever there was a sheet of ice, wherever there was a mirror or a reflection then Lilith knew she could see out. You didn't need a magic mirror. Any mirror would do, if you knew how to use it. And Lilith, crackling with the power of a million images, knew that very well.

There was just a nagging doubt. Presumably Desiderata would have got rid of *it*. Her sort were like that. Conscientious. And presumably it would be to that stupid girl with the watery eyes who sometimes visited the cottage, the one with all the cheap jewellery and the bad taste in clothes. She looked just the type.

But Lilith wanted to be sure. She hadn't got where she was today without being sure.

In puddles and windows all over Lancre, the face of Lilith appeared momentarily and then moved on . . .

And now it was dawn in Lancre. Autumn mists rolled through the forest.

Granny Weatherwax pushed open the cottage

door. It wasn't locked. The only visitor Desiderata had been expecting wasn't the sort to be put off by locks.

'She's had herself buried round the back,' said a voice behind her. It was Nanny Ogg.

Granny considered her next move. To point out that Nanny had deliberately come early, so as to search the cottage by herself, then raised questions about Granny's own presence. She could undoubtedly answer them, given enough time. On the whole, it was probably best just to get on with things.

'Ah,' she said, nodding. 'Always very neat in her ways, was Desiderata.'

'Well, it was the job,' said Nanny Ogg, pushing past her and eyeing the room's contents speculatively. 'You got to be able to keep track of things, in a job like hers. By gor', that's a bloody enormous cat.'

'It's a lion,' said Granny Weatherwax, looking at the stuffed head over the fireplace.

'Must've hit the wall at a hell of a speed, whatever it was,' said Nanny Ogg.

'Someone killed it,' said Granny Weatherwax, surveying the room.

'Should think so,' said Nanny. 'If I'd seen something like that eatin' its way through the wall I'd of hit it myself with the poker.'

There was of course no such thing as a typical witch's cottage, but if there was such a thing as a non-typical witch's cottage, then this was certainly it. Apart from various glassy-eyed animal heads, the walls were covered in bookshelves and water-colour pictures. There was a spear in the umbrella stand.

Instead of the more usual earthenware and china on the dresser there were foreign-looking brass pots and fine blue porcelain. There wasn't a dried herb anywhere in the place but there were a great many books, most of them filled with Desiderata's small, neat handwriting. A whole table was covered with what were probably maps, meticulously drawn.

Granny Weatherwax didn't like maps. She felt instinctively that they sold the landscape short.

'She certainly got about a bit,' said Nanny Ogg, picking up a carved ivory fan and flirting coquettishly.*

'Well, it was easy for her,' said Granny, opening a few drawers. She ran her fingers along the top of the mantelpiece and looked at them critically.

'She could have found time to go over the place with a duster,' she said vaguely. 'I wouldn't go and die and leave my place in this state.'

'I wonder where she left . . . you know . . . *it*?' said Nanny, opening the door of the grandfather clock and peering inside.

'Shame on you, Gytha Ogg,' said Granny. 'We're not here to look for *that*.'

'Of course not. I was just wondering . . .' Nanny Ogg tried to stand on tiptoe surreptitiously, in order to see on top of the dresser.

'Gytha! For shame! Go and make us a cup of tea!'

'Oh, all right.'

---

*Nanny Ogg didn't know what a coquette was, although she could probably hazard a guess.

Nanny Ogg disappeared, muttering, into the scullery. After a few seconds there came the creaking of a pump handle.

Granny Weatherwax sidled towards a chair and felt quickly under the cushion.

There was a clatter from the next room. She straightened up hurriedly.

'I shouldn't think it'd be under the sink, neither,' she shouted.

Nanny Ogg's reply was inaudible.

Granny waited a moment, and then crept rapidly over to the big chimney. She reached up and felt cautiously around.

'Looking for something, Esme?' said Nanny Ogg behind her.

'The soot up here is terrible,' said Granny, standing up quickly. 'Terrible soot there is.'

'*It's* not up there, then?' said Nanny Ogg sweetly.

'Don't know what you're talking about.'

'You don't have to pretend. Everyone knows she must have had one,' said Nanny Ogg. 'It goes with the job. It practic'ly *is* the job.'

'Well . . . maybe I just wanted a look at it,' Granny admitted. 'Just hold it a while. Not *use* it. You wouldn't catch me using one of those things. I only ever saw it once or twice. There ain't many of 'em around these days.'

Nanny Ogg nodded. 'You can't get the wood,' she said.

'You don't think she's been buried with it, do you?'

'Shouldn't think so. I wouldn't want to be

buried with it. Thing like that, it's a bit of a responsibility. Anyway, it wouldn't stay buried. A thing like that wants to be used. It'd be rattling around your coffin the whole time. You know the trouble they are.'

She relaxed a bit. 'I'll sort out the tea things,' she said. 'You light the fire.'

She wandered back into the scullery.

Granny Weatherwax reached along the mantelpiece for the matches, and then realized that there wouldn't be any. Desiderata had always said she was much too busy not to use magic around the house. Even her laundry did itself.

Granny disapproved of magic for domestic purposes, but she was annoyed. She also wanted her tea.

She threw a couple of logs into the fireplace and glared at them until they burst into flame out of sheer embarrassment.

It was then that her eye was caught by the shrouded mirror.

'Coverin' it over?' she murmured. 'I didn't know old Desiderata was frightened of thunderstorms.'

She twitched aside the cloth.

She stared.

Very few people in the world had more self-control than Granny Weatherwax. It was as rigid as a bar of cast iron. And about as flexible.

She smashed the mirror.

Lilith sat bolt upright in her tower of mirrors.

Her?

40

The face was different, of course. Older. It had been a long time. But eyes don't change, and witches always look at the eyes.

Her!

Magrat Garlick, witch, was also standing in front of a mirror. In her case it was totally unmagical. It was also still in one piece, but there had been one or two close calls.

She frowned at her reflection, and then consulted the small, cheaply-woodcut leaflet that had arrived the previous day.

She mouthed a few words under her breath, straightened up, extended her hands in front of her, punched the air vigorously and said: 'HAAAA-iiiiieeeeeeehgh! Um.'

Magrat would be the first to admit that she had an open mind. It was as open as a field, as open as the sky. No mind could be more open without special surgical implements. And she was always waiting for something to fill it up.

What it was currently filling up with was the search for inner peace and cosmic harmony and the true essence of Being.

When people say 'An idea came to me' it isn't just a metaphor. Raw inspirations, tiny particles of self-contained thought, are sleeting through the cosmos all the time. They get drawn to heads like Magrat's in the same way that water runs into a hole in the desert.

It was all due to her mother's lack of attention to spelling, she speculated. A caring parent would have spelled Margaret correctly. And then she could have been a Peggy, or a Maggie – big, robust names, full of reliability. There wasn't much you could do with a Magrat. It sounded like something that lived in a hole in a river bank and was always getting flooded out.

She considered changing it, but knew in her secret heart that this would not work. Even if she became a Chloe or an Isobel on top she'd still be a Magrat underneath. But it would be nice to try. It'd be nice not to be a Magrat, even for a few hours.

It's thoughts like this that start people on the road to Finding Themselves. And one of the earliest things Magrat had learned was that anyone Finding Themselves would be unwise to tell Granny Weather-wax, who thought that female emancipation was a women's complaint that shouldn't be discussed in front of men.

Nanny Ogg was more sympathetic but had a tendency to come out with what Magrat thought of as double-intenders, although in Nanny Ogg's case they were generally single entendres and proud of it.

In short, Magrat had despaired of learning anything at all from her senior witches, and was casting her net further afield. Much further afield. About as far afield as a field could be.

It's a strange thing about determined seekers-after-wisdom that, no matter where they happen to be, they'll always seek that wisdom which is a long way off. Wisdom is one of the few things that looks bigger the further away it is.*

Currently Magrat was finding herself through the Path of The Scorpion, which offered cosmic harmony, inner one-ness and the possibility of knocking an attacker's kidneys out through his ears. She'd sent off for it.

There were problems. The author, Grand Master Lobsang Dibbler, had an address in Ankh-Morpork. This did not seem like a likely seat of cosmic wisdom. Also, although he'd put in lots of stuff about the Way not being used for aggression and only to be used for cosmic wisdom, this was in quite small print between enthusiastic drawings of people hitting one another with rice flails and going 'Hai!' Later on you learned how to cut bricks in half with your hand and walk over red hot coals and other cosmic things.

---

*Hence, for example, the Way of Mrs Cosmopolite, very popular among young people who live in the hidden valleys above the snowline in the high Ramtops. Disdaining the utterances of their own saffron-clad, prayer-wheel-spinning elders, they occasionally travel all the way to No. 3 Quirm Street in flat and foggy Ankh-Morpork, to seek wisdom at the feet of Mrs Marietta Cosmopolite, a seamstress. No one knows the reason for this apart from the aforesaid attractiveness of distant wisdom, since they can't understand a word she says or, more usually, screams at them. Many a bald young monk returns to his high fastness to meditate on the strange mantra vouchsafed to him, such as 'Push off you!' and 'If I see *one more* of you little orange devils peering in at me he'll feel the edge of my hand, all right?' and 'Why are you buggers all coming round here staring at my feet?' They have even developed a special branch of martial arts based on their experiences, where they shout incomprehensibly at one another and then hit their opponent with a broom.

Magrat thought that Ninja was a nice name for a girl.

She squared up to herself in the mirror again.

There was a knock at the door. Magrat went and opened it.

'Hai?' she said.

Hurker the poacher took a step backwards. He was already rather shaken. An angry wolf had trailed him part of the way through the forest.

'Um,' he said. He leaned forward, his shock changing to concern. 'Have you hurt your head, Miss?'

She looked at him in incomprehension. Then realization dawned. She reached up and took off the headband with the chrysanthemum pattern on it, without which it is almost impossible to properly seek cosmic wisdom by twisting an opponent's elbows through 360 degrees.

'No,' she said. 'What do you want?'

'Got a package for you,' said Hurker, presenting it.

It was about two feet long, and very thin.

'There's a note,' said Hurker helpfully. He shuffled around as she unfolded it, and tried to read it over her shoulder.

'It's private,' said Magrat.

'Is it?' said Hurker, agreeably.

'Yes!'

'I was tole you'd give me a penny for delivering it,' said the poacher. Magrat found one in her purse.

'Money forges the chains which bind the labouring classes,' she warned, handing it over. Hurker, who had never thought of himself as a labouring class in his life, but who was prepared to listen to almost any amount of gibberish in exchange for a penny, nodded innocently.

'And I hope your head gets better, Miss,' he said.

When Magrat was left alone in her kitchen-cum-dojo she unwrapped the parcel. It contained one slim white rod.

She looked at the note again. It said, 'I niver had time to Trane a replaysment so youll have to Do. You must goe to the city of Genua. I would of done thys myself only cannot by reason of bein dead. Ella Saturday muste NOTTE marry the prins. PS This is importent.'

She looked at her reflection in the mirror.

She looked down at the note again.

'PSPS Tell those 2 Olde Biddys they are Notte to come with Youe, they will onlie Ruine everythin.'

There was more.

'PSPSPS It has tendincy to resett to pumpkins but you will gett the hange of it in noe time.'

Magrat looked at the mirror again. And then down at the wand.

One minute life is simple, and then suddenly it stretches away full of complications.

'Oh, my,' she said. 'I'm a fairy godmother!'

Granny Weatherwax was still standing staring at the crazily-webbed fragments when Nanny Ogg ran in.

'Esme Weatherwax, what have you done? That's bad luck, that is . . . Esme?'

'Her? *Her?*'

'Are you all right?'

Granny Weatherwax screwed up her eyes for a moment, and then shook her head as if trying to dislodge an unthinkable thought.

'What?'

'You've gone all pale. Never seen you go all pale like that before.'

Granny slowly removed a fragment of glass from her hat.

'Well . . . bit of a turn, the glass breaking like that . . .' she mumbled.

Nanny looked at Granny Weatherwax's hand. It was bleeding. Then she looked at Granny Weatherwax's face, and decided that she'd never admit that she'd looked at Granny Weatherwax's hand.

'Could be a sign,' she said, randomly selecting a safe topic. 'Once someone dies, you get that sort of thing. Pictures fallin' off walls, clocks stopping . . . great big wardrobes falling down the stairs . . . that sort of thing.'

'I've never believed in that stuff, it's . . . what do you mean, *wardrobes* falling down the stairs?' said Granny. She was breathing deeply. If it wasn't well known that Granny Weatherwax was *tough*, anyone might have thought she had just had the shock of her life and was practically desperate to take part in a bit of ordinary everyday bickering.

'That's what happened after my Great-Aunt Sophie died,' said Nanny Ogg. 'Three days and four hours and six minutes *to the very minute* after she died, her wardrobe fell down the stairs. Our Darren and our Jason were trying to get it round the bend and it sort of slipped, just like that. Uncanny. Weeell, I wasn't going to leave it there for her Agatha, was I, only ever visited her mum on Hogswatchday, and it was me that nursed Sophie all the way through to the end—'

Granny let the familiar, soothing litany of Nanny Ogg's family feud wash over her as she groped for the teacups.

The Oggs were what is known as an extended family – in fact not only extended but elongated, protracted and persistent. No normal sheet of paper could possibly trace their family tree, which in any case was more like a mangrove thicket. And every single branch had a low-key, chronic vendetta against every other branch, based on such well-established *causes célèbres* as What Their Kevin Said About Our Stan At Cousin Di's Wedding and Who Got The Silver Cutlery That Auntie Em *Promised* Our Doreen Was To Have After She Died, I'd Like To Know, Thank You *Very* Much, *If* You Don't Mind.

Nanny Ogg, as undisputed matriarch, encouraged all sides indiscriminately. It was the nearest thing she had to a hobby.

The Oggs contained, in just one family, enough feuds to keep an entire Ozark of normal hillbillies going for a century.

And sometimes this encouraged a foolish outsider to join in and perhaps make an uncomplimentary remark about one Ogg to another Ogg. Whereupon *every single Ogg* would turn on him, every part of the family closing up together like the parts of a well-oiled, blue-steeled engine to deal instant merciless destruction to the interloper.

Ramtop people believed that the Ogg feud was a blessing. The thought of them turning their immense energy on the world in general was a terrible one. Fortunately, there was no one an Ogg would rather fight than another Ogg. It was *family*.

Odd things, families, when you came to think of it . . .

'Esme? You all right?'

'What?'

'You've got them cups rattling like nobody's business! *And* tea all over the tray.'

Granny looked down blankly at the mess, and rallied as best she could.

'Not my damn fault if the damn cups are too small,' she muttered.

The door opened.

'Morning, Magrat,' she added, without looking around. 'What're you doing here?'

It was something about the way the hinges creaked. Magrat could even open a door apologetically.

The younger witch sidled speechlessly into the room, face beetroot red, arms held behind her back.

'We'd just popped in to sort out Desiderata's things, as our duty to a sister witch,' said Granny loudly.

'And not to look for her magic wand,' said Nanny.

'Gytha Ogg!'

Nanny Ogg looked momentarily guilty, and then hung her head.

'Sorry, Esme.'

Magrat brought her arms around in front of her.

'Er,' she said, and blushed further.

'You found it!' said Nanny.

'Uh, no,' said Magrat, not daring to look Granny in the eyes. 'Desiderata gave it to . . . me.'

The silence crackled and hummed.

'*She* gave it to *you*?' said Granny Weatherwax.

'Uh. Yes.'

Nanny and Granny looked at one another.

'Well!' said Nanny.

'She does *know* you, doesn't she?' demanded Granny, turning back to Magrat.

'I used to come over here quite often to look at her books,' Magrat confessed. 'And . . . and she liked to cook foreign food and no-one else round here would eat it, so I'd come up to keep her company.'

'Ah-*ha*! Curryin' favour!' snapped Granny.

'But I never thought she'd leave me the wand,' said Magrat. 'Really I didn't!'

'There's probably some mistake,' said Nanny Ogg kindly. 'She probably wanted you to give it to one of us.'

'That'll be it, right enough,' said Granny. 'She knew you were good at running errands and so on. Let's have a look at it.'

She held out her hand.

Magrat's knuckles tightened on the wand.

'. . . she gave it me . . .' she said, in a tiny voice.

'Her mind was definitely wandering towards the end,' said Granny.

'. . . she gave it me . . .'

'Fairy godmotherin's a terrible responsibility,' said Nanny. 'You got to be resourceful and flexible and tactful and able to deal with complicated affairs of the heart and stuff. Desiderata would have known that.'

'. . . yes, but she gave it me . . .'

'Magrat Garlick, as senior witch I *command* you to give me the wand,' said Granny. 'They cause nothing but trouble!'

'Hold on, hold on,' said Nanny. 'That's going a bit far—'

'. . . no . . .' said Magrat.

'Anyway, you ain't senior witch,' said Nanny. 'Old Mother Dismass is older'n you.'

'Shut up. Anyway, she's non compost mental,' said Granny.

'. . . you can't order me. Witches are non-hierarchical . . .' said Magrat.

'That is wanton behaviour, Magrat Garlick!'

'No it's not,' said Nanny Ogg, trying to keep the peace. 'Wanton behaviour is where you go around without wearing any—'

She stopped. Both of the older witches watched a small piece of paper fall out of Magrat's sleeve and zigzag down to the floor. Granny darted forward and snatched it up.

'Aha!' she said triumphantly. 'Let's see what Desiderata *really* said . . .'

Her lips moved as she read the note. Magrat tried to wind herself up tighter.

A couple of muscles flickered on Granny's face. Then, calmly, she screwed up the note.

'Just as I thought,' she said, 'Desiderata says we are to give Magrat all the help we can, what with her being young and everything. Didn't she, Magrat?'

Magrat looked up into Granny's face.

You could call her out, she thought. The note was very clear. . . well, the bit about the older witches was, anyway . . . and you could make her read it aloud. It's as plain as day. Do you want to be third witch forever? And then the flame of rebellion, burning in a very unfamiliar hearth, died.

'Yes,' she muttered hopelessly, 'something like that.'

'It says it's very important we go to some place somewhere to help someone marry a prince,' said Granny.

'It's Genua,' said Magrat. 'I looked it up in Desiderata's books. And we've got to make sure she *doesn't* marry a prince.'

'A fairy godmother *stopping* a girl from marryin' a prince?' said Nanny. 'Sounds a bit . . . contrary.'

'Should be an easy enough wish to grant, anyway,' said Granny. 'Millions of girls don't marry a prince.'

Magrat made an effort.

'Genua really *is* a long way away,' she said.

'I should 'ope so,' said Granny Weatherwax. 'The last thing we want is foreign parts up close.'

'I mean, there'll be a lot of travelling,' said Magrat wretchedly. 'And you're . . . not as young as you were.'

There was a long, crowded silence.

'We start tomorrow,' said Granny Weatherwax firmly.

'Look,' said Magrat desperately, 'why don't I go by myself?'

''Cos you ain't experienced at fairy godmothering,' said Granny Weatherwax.

This was too much even for Magrat's generous soul.

'Well, nor are you,' she said.

'That's true,' Granny conceded. 'But the point is . . . the point is . . . the point is we've not been experienced for a lot longer than you.'

'We've got a lot of experience of not having any experience,' said Nanny Ogg happily.

'That's what counts every time,' said Granny.

There was only one small, speckled mirror in Granny's house. When she got home, she buried it at the bottom of the garden.

'There,' she said. '*Now* trying spyin' on me.'

It never seemed possible to people that Jason Ogg, master blacksmith and farrier, was Nanny Ogg's son. He didn't look as if he could possibly have been born, but as if he must have been constructed. In a shipyard. To his essentially slow and gentle nature genetics had seen fit to add muscles that should have gone to a couple of bullocks, arms like treetrunks, and legs like four beer barrels stacked in twos.

To his glowing forge were brought the stud stallions, the red-eyed and foam-flecked kings of the horse nation, the soup-plate-hoofed beasts that had kicked lesser men through walls. But Jason Ogg knew the secret of the mystic Horseman's Word, and he would go alone into the forge, politely shut the door, and lead the creature out again after half an hour, newly shod and strangely docile.*

Behind his huge brooding shape clustered the rest of Nanny Ogg's endless family and a lot of other townsfolk who, seeing some interesting activity involving witches, couldn't resist the opportunity for what was known in the Ramtops as a good oggle.

'We'm off then, our Jason,' said Nanny Ogg. 'They do say the streets in foreign parts are paved with gold. I could prob'ly make my fortune, eh?'

Jason's hairy brow creased in intense thought.

'Us could do with a new anvil down forge,' he volunteered.

'If I come back rich, you won't never have to go down the forge ever again,' said Nanny.

Jason frowned.

'But I *likes* t'forge,' he said, slowly.

Nanny looked momentarily taken aback. 'Well, then – then you shall have an anvil made of solid silver.'

'Wunt be no good, ma. It'd be too soft,' said Jason.

'If I brings you back an anvil made of solid silver

---

*Granny Weatherwax had once pressed him about this, and since there are no secrets from a witch, he'd shyly replied, 'Well, ma'am, what happens is, I gets hold of 'un and smacks 'un between the eyes with hammer before 'un knows what's 'appening, and then I whispers in his ear, I sez, "Cross me, you bugger, and I'll have thy goolies on t'anvil, thou knows I can."'

you shall have an anvil made of solid silver, my lad, whether you likes it or not!'

Jason hung his huge head. 'Yes, mum,' he said.

'You see to it that someone comes in to keep the house aired every day reg'lar,' said Nanny. 'I want a fire lit in that grate every morning.'

'Yes, mum.'

'And everyone's to go in through the back door, you hear? I've put a curse on the front porch. Where's those girls got to with my luggage?' She scurried off, a small grey bantam scolding a flock of hens.

Magrat listened to all this with interest. Her own preparations had consisted of a large sack containing several changes of clothes to accommodate whatever weather foreign parts might suffer from, and a rather smaller one containing a number of useful-looking books from Desiderata Hollow's cottage. Desiderata had been a great note-taker, and had filled dozens of little books with neat writing and chapter headings like 'With Wand and Broomstick Across the Great Nef Desert'.

What she had never bothered to do, it seemed, was write down any instructions for the wand. As far as Magrat knew, you waved it and wished.

Along the track to her cottage, several un-anticipated pumpkins bore witness to this as an unreliable strategy. One of them still thought it was a stoat.

Now Magrat was left alone with Jason, who shuffled his feet.

He touched his forelock. He'd been brought up

to be respectful to women, and Magrat fell broadly into this category.

'You will look after our mum, won't you, Mistress Garlick?' he said, a hint of worry in his voice. 'She'm acting awful strange.'

Magrat patted him gently on the shoulder.

'This sort of thing happens all the time,' she said. 'You know, after a woman's raised a family and so on, she wants to start living her own life.'

'Whose life she *bin* living, then?'

Magrat gave him a puzzled look. She hadn't questioned the wisdom of the thought when it had first arrived in her head.

'You see, what it is,' she said, making an explanation up as she went along, 'there comes a time in a woman's life when she wants to find herself.'

'Why dint she start looking here?' said Jason plaintively. 'I mean, I ain't wanting to talk out of turn, Miss Garlick, but we was looking to you to persuade her and Mistress Weatherwax not to go.'

'I tried,' said Magrat. 'I really did. I said, you don't want to go, I said. Anno domini, I said. Not as young as you used to be, I said. Silly to go hundreds of miles just for something like this, especially at your age.'

Jason put his head on one side. Jason Ogg wouldn't end up in the finals of the All-Discworld uptake speed trials, but he knew his own mother.

'You said all that to our mum?' he said.

'Look, don't worry,' said Magrat, 'I'm sure no harm can—'

There was a crash somewhere over their heads.

55

A few autumn leaves spiralled gently towards the ground.

'Bloody tree . . . who put that bloody tree there?' came a voice from on high.

'That'll be Granny,' said Magrat.

It was one of the weak spots of Granny Weatherwax's otherwise well-developed character that she'd never bothered to get the hang of steering things. It was alien to her nature. She took the view that it was her job to move and the rest of the world to arrange itself so that she arrived at her destination. This meant that she occasionally had to climb down trees she'd never climbed up. This she did now, dropping the last few feet and daring anyone to comment.

'Well, now we're all here,' said Magrat brightly.

It didn't work. Granny Weatherwax's eyes focused immediately somewhere around Magrat's knees.

'And what do you think you're wearing?' she said.

'Ah. Um. I thought . . . I mean, it gets cold up there . . . what with the wind and everything,' Magrat began. She had been dreading this, and hating herself for being so weak. After all, they *were* practical. The idea had come to her one night. Apart from anything else, it was almost impossible to do Mr Lobsang Dibbler's cosmic harmony death kicks when your legs kept getting tangled in a skirt.

'*Trousers?*'

'They're not exactly the same as ordinary—'

'And there's men 'ere lookin',' said Granny. 'I think it's shameful!'

'What is?' said Nanny Ogg, coming up behind her.

'Magrat Garlick, standin' there bifurcated,' said Granny, sticking her nose in the air.

'Just so long as she got the young man's name and address,' said Nanny Ogg amiably.

'Nanny!' said Magrat.

'I think they look quite comfy,' Nanny went on. 'A bit baggy, though.'

'I don't 'old with it,' said Granny. 'Everyone can see her legs.'

'No they can't,' said Nanny. 'The reason being, the material is in the way.'

'Yes, but they can see where her legs *are*,' said Granny Weatherwax.

'That's silly. That's like saying everyone's naked under their clothes,' said Magrat.

'Magrat Garlick, may you be forgiven,' said Granny Weatherwax.

'Well, it's true!'

'*I'm* not,' said Granny flatly, 'I got three vests on.'

She looked Nanny up and down. Gytha Ogg, too, had made sartorial preparations for foreign parts. Granny Weatherwax could find little to disapprove of, although she made an effort.

'And will you look at your hat,' she mumbled. Nanny, who had known Esme Weatherwax for seventy years, merely grinned.

'All the go, ain't it?' she said. 'Made by Mr Vernissage over in Slice. It's got willow reinforcing all the way up to the point and eighteen pockets inside. Can stop a blow with a hammer, this hat. And how about these?'

Nanny raised the hem of her skirt. She was wearing new boots. As boots, Granny Weatherwax could find nothing to complain of in them. They were of proper witch construction, which is to say that a loaded cart could have run over them without causing a dent in the dense leather. As boots, the only thing wrong with them was the colour.

'*Red?*' said Granny. 'That's no colour for a witch's boots!'

'I likes 'em,' said Nanny.

Granny sniffed. 'You can please yourself, I'm sure,' she said. 'I'm sure in foreign parts they goes in for all sorts of outlandish things. But you know what they say about women who wear red boots.'

'Just so long as they also say they've got dry feet,' said Nanny cheerfully. She put her door key into Jason's hand.

'I'll write you letters if you promise to find someone to read them to you,' she said.

'Yes, mum. What about the cat, mum?' said Jason.

'Oh, Greebo's coming with us,' said Nanny Ogg.

'What? But he's a cat!' snapped Granny Weatherwax. 'You can't take cats with you! I'm not going travellin' with no cat! It's bad enough travellin' with trousers and provocative boots!'

'He'll miss his mummy if he's left behind, won't he,' crooned Nanny Ogg, picking up Greebo. He hung limply, like a bag of water gripped around the middle.

To Nanny Ogg Greebo was still the cute little kitten that chased balls of wool around the floor.

To the rest of the world he was an enormous tomcat, a parcel of incredibly indestructible life forces in a skin that looked less like a fur than a piece of bread that had been left in a damp place for a fortnight. Strangers often took pity on him because his ears were non-existent and his face looked as though a bear had camped on it. They could not know that this was because Greebo, as a matter of feline pride, would attempt to fight or rape absolutely anything, up to and including a four-horse logging wagon. Ferocious dogs would whine and hide under the stairs when Greebo sauntered down the street. Foxes kept away from the village. Wolves made a detour.

'He's an old softy really,' said Nanny.

Greebo turned upon Granny Weatherwax a yellow-eyed stare of self-satisfied malevolence, such as cats always reserve for people who don't like them, and purred. Greebo was possibly the only cat who could snigger in purr.

'Anyway,' said Nanny, 'witches are supposed to *like* cats.'

'Not cats like him, they're not.'

'You're just not a cat person, Esme,' said Nanny, cuddling Greebo tightly.

Jason Ogg pulled Magrat aside.

'Our Sean read to me in the almanac where there's all these fearsome wild beasts in foreign parts,' he whispered. 'Huge hairy things that leap out on travellers, it said. I'd hate to think what'd happen if they leapt out on mum and Granny.'

Magrat looked up into his big red face.

'You will see no harm comes to them, won't you,' said Jason.

'Don't you worry,' she said, hoping that he needn't. 'I'll do my best.'

Jason nodded. 'Only it said in the almanac that some of them were nearly extinct anyway,' he said.

The sun was well up when the three witches spiralled into the sky. They had been delayed for a while because of the intractability of Granny Weatherwax's broomstick, the starting of which always required a great deal of galloping up and down. It never seemed to get the message until it was being shoved through the air at a frantic running speed. Dwarf engineers everywhere had confessed themselves totally mystified by it. They had replaced the stick and the bristles dozens of times.

When it rose, eventually, it was to a chorus of cheers.

The tiny kingdom of Lancre occupied little more than a wide ledge cut into the side of the Ramtop mountains. Behind it, knife-edge peaks and dark winding valleys climbed into the massive backbone of the central ranges.

In front, the land dropped abruptly to the Sto plains, a blue haze of woodlands, a broader expanse of ocean and, somewhere in the middle of it all, a brown smudge known as Ankh-Morpork.

A skylark sang, or at least started to sing. The

rising point of Granny Weatherwax's hat right underneath it completely put it off the rhythm.

'I ain't going any higher,' she said.

'If we go high enough we might be able to see where we're going,' said Magrat.

'You said you looked at Desiderata's maps,' said Granny.

'It looks different from up here, though,' said Magrat. 'More . . . sticking up. But I think we go . . . *that* way.'

'You sure?'

Which was the wrong question to ask a witch. Especially if the person doing the asking was Granny Weatherwax.

'Positive,' said Magrat.

Nanny Ogg looked up at the high peaks.

'There's a lot of *big* mountains that way,' she said.

They rose tier on tier, speckled with snow, trailing endless pennants of ice crystals high overhead. No one ski'd in the high Ramtops, at least for more than a few feet and a disappearing scream. No one ran up them wearing dirndls and singing. They were not nice mountains. They were the kind of mountains where winters went for their summer holidays.

'There's passes and things through them,' said Magrat uncertainly.

'Bound to be,' said Nanny.

You can use two mirrors like this, if you know the way of it: you set them so that they reflect each other. For if images *can* steal a bit of you, then images of images can amplify you, feeding you back on yourself, giving you power . . .

And your image extends forever, in reflections of reflections of reflections, and every image is the same, all the way around the curve of light.

Except that it isn't.

Mirrors contain infinity.

Infinity contains more things than you think.

Everything, for a start.

Including hunger.

Because there's a million billion images and only one soul to go around.

Mirrors give plenty, but they take away lots.

Mountains unfolded to reveal more mountains. Clouds gathered, heavy and grey.

'I'm sure we're going the right way,' said Magrat. Freezing rock stretched away. The witches flew along a maze of twisty little canyons, all alike.

'Yeah,' said Granny.

'Well, you won't let me fly high enough,' said Magrat.

'It's going to snow like blazes in a minute,' said Nanny Ogg.

It was early evening. Light was draining out of the high valleys like custard.

'I thought . . . there'd be villages and things,' said Magrat, 'where we could buy interesting native produce and seek shelter in rude huts.'

'You wouldn't even get trolls up here,' said Granny.

The three broomsticks glided down into a bare valley, a mere notch in the mountain side.

'And it's bloody cold,' said Nanny Ogg. She grinned. 'Why're they called rude huts, anyway?'

Granny Weatherwax climbed off her broomstick and looked at the rocks around her. She picked up a stone and sniffed it. She wandered over to a heap of scree that looked like any other heap of scree to Magrat, and prodded it.

'Hmm,' she said.

A few snow crystals landed on her hat.

'Well, well,' she said.

'What're you doing, Granny?' said Magrat.

'Cogitatin'.'

Granny walked to the valley's steep side and strolled along it, peering at the rock. Nanny Ogg joined her.

'Up here?' said Nanny.

'I reckon.'

''S a bit high for 'em, ain't it?'

'Little devils get everywhere. Had one come up in my kitchen once,' said Granny. '"Following a seam", he said.'

'They're buggers for that,' said Nanny.

'Would you mind telling me,' said Magrat, 'what you're doing? What's so interesting about heaps of stones?'

The snow was falling faster now.

'They ain't stones, they're spoil,' said Granny. She reached a flat wall of ice-covered rock, no different in Magrat's eyes from the rock available in a range of easy-to-die-on sizes everywhere in the mountains, and paused as if listening.

Then she stood back, hit the rock sharply with her broomstick, and spake thusly:

63

'Open up, you little sods!'

Nanny Ogg kicked the rock. It made a hollow boom.

'There's people catching their death of cold out here!' she added.

Nothing happened for a while. Then a section of rock swung in a few inches. Magrat saw the glint of a suspicious eye.

'Yes?'

'Dwarfs?' said Magrat.

Granny Weatherwax leaned down until her nose was level with the eye.

'My name,' she said, 'is Granny Weatherwax.'

She straightened up again, her face glowing with self-satisfaction.

'Who's that, then?' said a voice from somewhere below the eye. Granny's expression froze.

Nanny Ogg nudged her partner.

'We must be more'n fifty miles away from home,' she said. 'They might not have heard of you in these parts.'

Granny leaned down again. Accumulated snow-flakes cascaded off her hat.

'I ain't blaming you,' she said, 'but I know you'll have a King in there, so just you go and tell him Granny Weatherwax is here, will you?'

'He's very busy,' said the voice. 'We've just had a bit of trouble.'

'Then I'm sure he don't want any more,' said Granny.

The invisible speaker appeared to give this some consideration.

'We put writing on the door,' it said sulkily. 'In invisible runes. It's really expensive, getting proper invisible runes done.'

'I don't go around readin' doors,' said Granny.

The speaker hesitated.

'Weatherwax, did you say?'

'Yes. With a W. As in "witch".'

The door slammed. When it was shut, there was barely a visible crack in the rock.

The snow was falling fast now. Granny Weatherwax jiggled up and down a bit to keep warm.

'That's foreigners for you,' she said, to the frozen world in general.

'I don't think you can call dwarfs foreigners,' said Nanny Ogg.

'Don't see why not,' said Granny. 'A dwarf who lives a long way off has got to be foreign. That's what foreign means.'

'Yeah? Funny to think of it like that,' said Nanny.

They watched the door, their breath forming three little clouds in the darkening air. Magrat peered at the stone door.

'I didn't see any invisible runes,' she said.

''Corse not,' said Nanny. 'That's 'cos they're invisible.'

'Yeah,' said Granny Weatherwax. 'Don't be daft.'

The door swung open again.

'I spoke to the King,' said the voice.

'And what did he say?' said Granny expectantly.

'He said, "Oh, no! Not on top of everything else!"'

Granny beamed. 'I *knew* 'e would have heard of me,' she said.

In the same way that there are a thousand Kings of the Gypsies, so there are a thousand Kings of the Dwarfs. The term means something like 'senior engineer'. There aren't any Queens of the Dwarfs. Dwarfs are very reticent about revealing their sex, which most of them don't consider to be very important compared to things like metallurgy and hydraulics.

This king was standing in the middle of a crowd of shouting miners. He* looked up at the witches with the expression of a drowning man looking at a drink of water.

'Are you really any good?' he said.

Nanny Ogg and Granny Weatherwax looked at one another.

'I think 'e's talking to you, Magrat,' said Granny.

'Only we've had a big fall in gallery nine,' said the King. 'It looks bad. A very promising vein of gold-bearing quartz is irretrievably trapped.'

One of the dwarfs beside him muttered something.

'Oh, yeah. And some of the lads,' said the King vaguely. 'And then *you* turn up. So the way I look at it, it's probably fate.'

Granny Weatherwax shook the snow off her hat and looked around.

---

*Many of the more traditional dwarf tribes have no female pronouns, like 'she' or 'her'. It follows that the courtship of dwarfs is an incredibly tactful affair.

She was impressed, despite herself. You didn't often see proper dwarf halls these days. Most dwarfs were off earning big money in the cities down in the lowlands, where it was much easier to be a dwarf – for one thing, you didn't have to spend most of your time underground hitting your thumb with a hammer and worrying about fluctuations in the international metal markets. Lack of respect for tradition, that was the trouble these days. And take trolls. There were more trolls in Ankh-Morpork now than in the whole mountain range. Granny Weatherwax had nothing against trolls but she felt instinctively that if more trolls stopped wearing suits and walking upright, and went back to living under bridges and jumping out and eating people as nature intended, then the world would be a happier place.

'You'd better show us where the problem is,' she said. 'Lots of rocks fallen down, have they?'

'Pardon?' said the King.

It's often said that eskimos have fifty words for snow.*

This is not true.

It's also said that dwarfs have two hundred words for rock.

They don't. They have no words for rock, in the same way that fish have no words for water. They *do* have words for igneous rock, sedimentary rock, metamorphic rock, rock underfoot, rock dropping

---

*Well, not *often*. Not on a daily basis, anyway. At least, not everywhere. But probably in some cold countries people say, 'Hey, those eskimos! What a people! Fifty words for snow! Can you believe that? Amazing!' quite a lot.

on your helmet from above, and rock which looked interesting and which they could have sworn they left here yesterday. But what they don't have is a word meaning 'rock'. Show a dwarf a rock and he sees, for example, an inferior piece of crystalline sulphite of barytes.

Or, in this case, about two hundred tons of low-grade shale. When the witches arrived at the disaster site dozens of dwarfs were working feverishly to prop the cracked roof and cart away the debris. Some of them were in tears.

'It's terrible . . . terrible,' muttered one of them. 'A terrible thing.'

Magrat lent him her handkerchief. He blew his nose noisily.

'Could mean a big slippage on the fault line and then we've lost the whole seam,' he said, shaking his head. Another dwarf patted him on the back.

'Look on the bright side,' he said. 'We can always drive a horizontal shaft off gallery fifteen. We're bound to pick it up again, don't you worry.'

'Excuse me,' said Magrat, 'there *are* dwarfs behind all that stuff, are there?'

'Oh, yes,' said the King. His tone suggested that this was merely a regrettable side-effect of the disaster, because getting fresh dwarfs was only a matter of time whereas decent gold-bearing rock was a finite resource.

Granny Weatherwax inspected the rockfall critically.

'We shall have to have everyone out of here,' she said. 'This is goin' to have to be private.'

'I know how it is,' said the King. 'Craft secrets, I expect?'

'Something like that,' said Granny.

The King shooed the other dwarfs out of the tunnel, leaving the witches alone in the lantern light. A few bits of rock fell out of the ceiling.

'Hmm,' said Granny.

'You've gone and done it now,' said Nanny Ogg.

'Anything's possible if you set your mind to it,' said Granny vaguely.

'Then you'd better set yours good and hard, Esme. If the Creator had meant us to shift rocks by witchcraft, he wouldn't have invented shovels. Knowing when to use a shovel is what being a witch is all about. And put down that wheelbarrow, Magrat. You don't know nothing about machinery.'

'All right, then,' said Magrat. 'Why don't we try the wand?'

Granny Weatherwax snorted. 'Hah! Here? Whoever heard of a fairy godmother in a mine?'

'If I was stuck behind a load of rocks under a mountain *I'd* want to hear of one,' said Magrat hotly.

Nanny Ogg nodded. 'She's got a point there, Esme. There's no rule about where you fairy godmother.'

'I don't trust that wand,' said Granny. 'It looks wizardly to me.'

'Oh, come *on*,' said Magrat, 'generations of fairy godmothers have used it.'

Granny flung her hands in the air.

'All right, all right, all right,' she snapped. 'Go ahead! Make yourself look daft!'

Magrat took the wand out of her bag. She'd been dreading this moment.

It was made of some sort of bone or ivory; Magrat hoped it wasn't ivory. There had been markings on it once, but generations of plump fairy godmotherly hands had worn them almost smooth. Various gold and silver rings were set into the wand. Nowhere were there any instructions. Not so much as a rune or a sigil anywhere on its length indicated what you were supposed to do with it.

'I think you're supposed to wave it,' said Nanny Ogg. 'I'm pretty sure it's something like that.'

Granny Weatherwax folded her arms. 'That's not proper witching,' she said.

Magrat gave the wand an experimental wave. Nothing happened.

'Perhaps you have to say something?' said Nanny. Magrat looked panicky.

'What do fairy godmothers *say*?' she wailed.

'Er,' said Nanny, 'dunno.'

'Huh!' said Granny.

Nanny Ogg sighed. 'Didn't Desiderata tell you *anything*?'

'Nothing!'

Nanny shrugged.

'Just do your best, then,' she said.

Magrat stared at the pile of rocks. She shut her eyes. She took a deep breath. She tried to make her mind a serene picture of cosmic harmony. It was all very well for monks to go on about cosmic harmony, she reflected, when they were nicely tucked away on snowy mountains with only yetis to worry about. They never tried seeking inner peace with Granny Weatherwax glaring at them.

She waved the wand in a vague way and tried to put pumpkins out of her mind.

She felt the air move. She heard Nanny gasp.

She said, 'Has anything happened?'

After a while Nanny Ogg said, 'Yeah. Sort of. I hope they're hungry, that's all.'

And Granny Weatherwax said, 'That's fairy god-mothering, is it?'

Magrat opened her eyes.

There was still a heap, but it wasn't rock any more.

'There's a, wait for it, there's *a bit of a squash* in here,' said Nanny.

Magrat opened her eyes wider.

'*Still* pumpkins?'

'Bit of a squash. *Squash*,' said Nanny, in case anyone hadn't got it.

The top of the heap moved. A couple of small pumpkins rolled down almost to Magrat's feet, and a small dwarfish face appeared in the hole.

It stared down at the witches.

Eventually Nanny Ogg said, 'Everything all right?'

The dwarf nodded. Its attention kept turning to the pile of pumpkins that filled the tunnel from floor to ceiling.

'Er, yes,' it said. 'Is dad there?'

'Dad?'

'The King.'

'Oh.' Nanny Ogg cupped her hands around her mouth and turned to face up the tunnel. 'Hey, King!'

The dwarfs appeared. They looked at the pumpkins, too. The King stepped forward and stared up into the face of his son.

'Everything all right, son?'

'It's all right, dad. No faulting or anything.'

The King sagged with relief. Then, as an afterthought, he added, 'Everyone all right?'

'Fine, dad.'

'I was quite worried for a time there. Thought we might have hit a section of conglomerate or something.'

'Just a patch of loose shale, dad.'

'Good.' The King looked at the heap again. He scratched his beard. 'Can't help noticing you seem to have struck pumpkin.'

'I thought it was an odd kind of sandstone, dad.'

The King walked back to the witches.

'Can you turn anything into anything?' he said hopefully.

Nanny Ogg looked sideways at Magrat, who was still staring at the wand in a sort of shock.

'I think we only do pumpkins at the moment,' she said cautiously.

The King looked a little disappointed.

'Well, then,' he said, 'if there's anything I can do for you ladies . . . a cup of tea or something . . .'

Granny Weatherwax stepped forward. 'I was just thinking something like that myself,' she said.

The King beamed.

'Only more expensive,' said Granny.

The King stopped beaming.

Nanny Ogg sidled up to Magrat, who was shaking the wand and staring at it.

'Very clever,' she whispered. 'Why'd you think of pumpkins?'

'I didn't!'

'Don't you know how to work it?'

'No! I thought you just had to, you know, *want* something to happen!'

'There's probably more to it than just wishing,' said Nanny, as sympathetically as possible. 'There generally is.'

Some time around dawn, insofar as dawn happened in the mines, the witches were led to a river somewhere deep in the mountains, where a couple of barges were moored. A small boat was pulled up to a stone jetty.

'This'll take you right through the mountains,' said the King. 'I think it goes all the way to Genua, to tell the truth.' He took a large basket off an attendant dwarf. 'And we've packed you some lovely food,' he said.

'Are we going to go all the way in a boat?' said Magrat. She gave the wand a few surreptitious flourishes. 'I'm not good at boats.'

'Listen,' said Granny, climbing aboard, 'the river knows its way out of the mountains, which is more than we do. We can use the brooms later on, where the landscape's acting a bit more sensible.'

'And we can have a bit of a rest,' said Nanny, sitting back.

Magrat looked at the two older witches, who were

making themselves comfortable in the stern like a couple of hens settling down on a nest.

'Do you know how to row a boat?' she said.

'We don't have to,' said Granny.

Magrat nodded gloomily. Then a tiny bit of self-assertion flashed a fin.

'I don't think I do, too,' she ventured.

'That's all right,' said Nanny. 'If we sees you doing anything wrong, we'll be sure to tell you. Cheerio, your kingship.'

Magrat sighed, and picked up the oars.

'The flat bits go in the water,' said Granny helpfully.

The dwarfs waved. The boat drifted out into midstream, moving slowly in a circle of lantern light. Magrat found that all she really had to do was keep it pointing the right way in the current.

She heard Nanny say: 'Beats me why they're always putting invisible runes on their doors. I mean, you pays some wizard to put invisible runes on your door, and how do you know you've got value for money?'

She heard Granny say: 'No problem there. If you can't see 'em, you know you've got proper invisible runes.'

She heard Nanny say: 'Ah, that'd be it. Right, let's see what we've got for lunch.' There was a rustling noise.

'Well, well, well.'

'What is it, Gytha?'

'Pumpkin.'

'Pumpkin what?'

'Pumpkin nothing. Just pumpkin pumpkin.'

'Well, I suppose they've got a lot of pumpkin,' said Magrat. 'You know how it is at the end of the summer, there's always so much in the garden. I'm always at my wits' end to think of new types of chutney and pickles to use it all up—'

In the dim light she could see Granny's face which seemed to be suggesting that if Magrat was at her wits' end, it was a short stroll.

'*I*', said Granny, 'have never made a pickle in my life.'

'But you *like* pickles,' said Magrat. Witches and pickles went together like – she hesitated before the stomach-curdling addition of peaches and cream, and mentally substituted 'things that went together very well'. The sight of Nanny Ogg's single remaining tooth at work on a pickled onion could bring tears to the eyes.

'I likes 'em fine,' said Granny. 'I gets 'em *given* to me.'

'You know,' said Nanny, investigating the recesses of the basket, 'whenever I deals with dwarfs, the phrase "Duck's arse" swims across my mind.'

'Mean little devils. You should see the prices they tries to charge me when I takes my broom to be repaired,' said Granny.

'Yes, but you never pay,' said Magrat.

'That's not the point,' said Granny Weatherwax. 'They shouldn't be allowed to charge that sort of money. That's thievin', that is.'

'I don't see how it can be thieving if you don't pay anyway,' Magrat persisted.

'I never pay for anything,' said Granny. 'People never *let* me pay. I can't help it if people gives me things the whole time, can I? When I walks down the street people are always running out with cakes they've just baked, and fresh beer, and old clothes that've hardly been worn at all. "Oh, Mistress Weatherwax, pray take this basket of eggs", they say. People are always very kind. Treat people right an' they'll treat *you* right. That's respect. Not having to pay,' she finished, sternly, 'is what bein' a witch is all about.'

'Here, what's this?' said Nanny, pulling out a small packet. She unwrapped the paper and revealed several hard brown discs.

'My word,' said Granny Weatherwax, 'I take it all back. That's the famous dwarf bread, that is. They don't give that to just anyone.'

Nanny tapped it on the edge of the boat. It made a noise very similar to the kind of noise you get when a wooden ruler is held over the edge of a desk and plucked; a sort of hollow *boioioing* sound.

'They say it never goes stale even if you stores it for years,' said Granny.

'It'd keep you going for days and days,' said Nanny Ogg.

Magrat reached across, took one of the flat loaves, tried to break it, and gave up.

'You're supposed to *eat* it?' she said.

'Oh, I don't think it's for eating,' said Nanny. 'It's more for sort of—'

'—keeping you going,' said Granny. 'They say that—'

She stopped.

Above the noise of the river and the occasional drip of water from the ceiling they could all hear, now, the steady slosh-slosh of another craft heading towards them.

'Someone's following us!' hissed Magrat.

Two pale glows appeared at the edge of the lamplight. Eventually they turned out to be the eyes of a small grey creature, vaguely froglike, paddling towards them on a log.

It reached the boat. Long clammy fingers grabbed the side, and a lugubrious face rose level with Nanny Ogg's.

''ullo,' it said. 'It'sss my birthday.'

All three of them stared at it for a while. Then Granny Weatherwax picked up an oar and hit it firmly over the head. There was a splash, and a distant cursing.

'Horrible little bugger,' said Granny, as they rowed on. 'Looked like a troublemaker to me.'

'Yeah,' said Nanny Ogg. 'It's the slimy ones you have to watch out for.'

'I wonder what he wanted?' said Magrat.

After half an hour the boat drifted out through a cave mouth and into a narrow gorge between cliffs. Ice glistened on the walls, and there were drifts of snow on some of the outcrops.

Nanny Ogg looked around guilelessly, and then fumbled somewhere in the depths of her many skirts and produced a small bottle. There was a glugging noise.

'I bet there's a fine echo here,' she said, after a while.

'Oh no you don't,' said Granny firmly.

'Don't what?'

'Don't sing That Song.'

'Pardon, Esme?'

'I ain't going,' said Granny, 'if you insists on singing That Song.'

'What song would that be?' said Nanny innocently.

'You know the song to whom I am referring,' said Granny icily. 'You always get drunk and let me down and sing it.'

'Can't recall any song like that, Esme,' said Nanny Ogg meekly.

'The one,' said Granny, 'about the rodent that can't – that can't ever be persuaded to care about anything.'

'Oh,' said Nanny, beaming as light dawned, '*you* mean The Hedgehog Can Never Be Bugg—'

'That's the one!'

'But it's *traditional*,' said Nanny. 'Anyway, in foreign parts people won't know what the words mean.'

'They will the way you sings them,' said Granny. 'The way you sings them, creatures what lives on the bottoms of *ponds*'d know what they mean.'

Magrat looked over the side of the boat. Here and there the ripples were edged with white. The current was running a bit faster, and there were lumps of ice in it.

'It's only a folk song, Esme,' said Nanny Ogg.

'Hah!' said Granny Weatherwax. 'I should just say it *is* a folk song! I knows all about folk songs. Hah! You think you're listenin' to a nice song about . . . about cuckoos and fiddlers and nightingales and whatnot, and then it turns out to be about . . . about something else entirely,' she added darkly. 'You can't trust folk songs. They always sneak up on you.'

Magrat fended them off a rock. An eddy spun them around slowly.

'I know one about two little bluebirds,' said Nanny Ogg.

'Um,' said Magrat.

'They may start out by being bluebirds, but I bet they ends up some kind of mettyfor,' said Granny.

'Er, Granny,' said Magrat.

'It was bad enough Magrat telling me about may-poles and what's behind 'em,' said Granny. She added, wistfully, 'I used to enjoy looking at a may-pole of a spring morning.'

'I think the river's getting a bit sort of rough,' said Magrat.

'I don't see why people can't just let things be,' said Granny.

'I mean really quite rough, really . . .' said Magrat, pushing them away from a jagged rock.

'She's right, you know,' said Nanny Ogg. 'It's a bit on the choppy side.'

Granny looked over Magrat's shoulder at the river ahead. It had a cut-off look, such as might be associated with, for example, an imminent waterfall. The boat was now surging along. There was a muted roar.

'They never said anything about a waterfall,' she said.

'I 'spect they thought we'd find out for ourselves,' said Nanny Ogg, gathering up her possessions and hauling Greebo out of the bottom of the boat by the scruff of his neck. 'Very sparin' with information, your average dwarf. Thank goodness witches float. Anyway, they knew we'd got the brooms.'

'*You've* got brooms,' said Granny Weatherwax. 'How'm I supposed to get mine started in a *boat*? Can't run up and down, can I? And stop movin' about like that, you'll have us all over—'

'Get your foot out of the way, Esme—'

The boat rocked violently.

Magrat rose to the occasion. She pulled out the wand, just as a wavelet washed over the boat.

'Don't worry,' she said, 'I'll use the wand. I think I've got the hang of it now—'

'No!' screamed Granny Weatherwax and Nanny Ogg together.

There was a large, damp noise. The boat changed shape. It also changed colour. It became a cheery sort of orange.

'Pumpkins!' screamed Nanny Ogg, as she was gently tipped into the water. 'More bloody pump-kins!'

Lilith sat back. The ice around the river hadn't been that good as a mirror, but it had been good enough.

Well. A wishy-washy overgrown girl more suitable to the attentions of a fairy godmother than to being one, and a little old washerwoman-type who got drunk and sang songs. And a wand the stupid girl didn't know how to use.

It was annoying. More than that, it was demeaning. Surely Desiderata and Mrs Gogol could have achieved something better than this. You derived status by the strength of your enemies.

Of course, there was *her*. After all this time . . .

Of course. She approved of that. Because there would have to be three of them. Three was an important number for stories. Three wishes, three princes, three billy goats, three guesses . . . three witches. The maiden, the mother and the . . . other one. *That* was one of the oldest stories of all.

Esme Weatherwax had never understood stories. She'd never understood how *real* reflections were. If she had, she'd probably have been ruling the world by now.

'You're always looking in mirrors!' said a petulant voice. 'I hate it when you're always looking in mirrors!'

The Duc sprawled in a chair in one corner, all black silk and well-turned legs. Lilith would not normally allow anyone inside the nest of mirrors but it was, technically, his castle. Besides, he was too vain and stupid to know what was going on. She'd seen to that. At least, she'd thought she had. Lately, he seemed to be picking things up . . .

'I don't know why you have to do that,' he whined. 'I thought magic was just a matter of pointing and going whoosh.'

Lilith picked up her hat, and glanced at a mirror as she adjusted it.

'This way's safer,' she said. 'It's self-contained. When you use mirror magic, you don't have to rely on anyone except yourself. That's why no one's ever conquered the world with magic . . . yet. They try to take it from . . . other places. And there's always a price. But with mirrors, you're beholden to no one but your own soul.'

She lowered the veil from the hat brim. She preferred the privacy of a veil, outside the security of the mirrors.

'I hate mirrors,' muttered the Duc.

'That's because they tell you the truth, my lad.'

'It's cruel magic, then.'

Lilith tweaked the veil into a fetching shape.

'Oh, yes. With mirrors, all the power is your own. There's nowhere else it can come from,' she said.

'The swamp woman gets it from the swamp,' said the Duc.

'Ha! And it'll claim her one day. She doesn't understand what she's doing.'

'And you do?'

She felt a pang of pride. He was actually resenting her! She really had done a good job there.

'I understand stories,' she said. 'That's all I need.'

'But you haven't brought me the girl,' said the Duc. 'You promised me the girl. And then it'll be all over and I can sleep in a real bed and I won't need any more reflecting magic—'

But even a good job can go too far.

'You've had your fill of magic?' said Lilith sweetly. 'You'd like me to stop? It would be the easiest thing in the world. I found you in the gutter. Would you like me to send you back?'

His face became a mask of panic.

'I didn't mean that! I just meant . . . well, then everything will be real. Just one kiss, you said. I can't see why that's so hard to arrange.'

'The right kiss at the right time,' said Lilith. 'It has to be at the right time, otherwise it won't work.' She smiled. He was trembling, partly out of lust, mainly out of terror, and slightly out of heredity.

'Don't worry,' she said. 'It can't *not* happen.'

'And these witches you showed me?'

'They're just . . . part of the story. Don't worry about them. The story will just absorb them. And you'll get *her* because of stories. Won't that be nice? And now . . . shall we go? I expect you've got some ruling to do?'

He picked up the inflexion. It was an order. He stood up, extended an arm to take hers, and together they went down to the palace's audience chamber.

Lilith was proud of the Duc. Of course, there was his embarrassing little nocturnal problem, because his morphic field weakened when he slept, but that wasn't yet a major difficulty. And there was the trouble with mirrors, which showed him as he really was, but that was easily overcome by banning all mirrors save hers. And then there were his eyes. She couldn't do anything about the eyes. There was practically no magic that could do anything about someone's eyes. All she had been able to come up with there were the smoked glasses.

Even so, he was a triumph. And he was so grateful. She'd been good for him.

She'd made a man of him, for a start.

Some way downriver from the waterfall, which was the second highest anywhere on the Disc and had been discovered in the Year of the Revolving Crab by the noted explorer Guy de Yoyo,* Granny Weatherwax sat in front of a small fire with a towel around her shoulders and steamed.

'Still, look on the bright side,' said Nanny Ogg. 'At least I was holding my broom and you at the same time. And Magrat had hers. Otherwise we'd all be looking at the waterfall from underneath.'

'Oh, good. A silver lining,' said Granny, her eyes glinting evilly.

'Bit of an adventure, really,' said Nanny, grinning encouragingly. 'One day we'll look back on this and laugh.'

'Oh, good,' said Granny.

Nanny dabbed at the claw marks on her arm. Greebo, with a cat's true instinct for self-preservation, had clawed his way up his mistress and taken a flying leap to safety from the top of her head. Now he was curled up by the fire, dreaming cat dreams.

A shadow passed over them. It was Magrat, who had been combing the riverbanks.

'I think I've got nearly everything,' she said as she

---

*Of course, lots of dwarfs, trolls, native people, trappers, hunters and the merely badly lost had discovered it on an almost daily basis for thousands of years. But they weren't explorers and didn't count.

landed. 'Here's Granny's broomstick. And. . . oh, yes
. . . the wand.' She gave a brave little smile. 'Little
pumpkins were bobbing to the surface. That's how I
found it.'

'My word, that was lucky,' said Nanny Ogg
encouragingly. 'Hear that, Esme? We shan't be wanting
for food, at any rate.'

'And I've found the basket with the dwarf bread
in it,' said Magrat, 'although I'm afraid it might be
spoilt.'

'It won't be, take it from me,' said Nanny Ogg.
'You can't spoil dwarf bread. Well, well,' she said,
sitting down again. 'We've got quite a little picnic,
haven't we . . . and a nice bright fire and . . . and
a nice place to sit and . . . I'm sure there's lots of
poor people in places like Howondaland and suchlike who'd give anything to be here right now . . .'

'If you don't stop being so cheerful, Gytha Ogg, I
shall give you such a ding around the ear with the
flat of my hand,' said Granny Weatherwax.

'You sure you're not catching a chill?' said Nanny
Ogg.

'I'm dryin' out,' said Granny Weatherwax, 'from
the inside.'

'Look, I'm really sorry,' said Magrat. 'I *said* I was
sorry.'

Not that she was quite certain what for, she told
herself. The boat wasn't her idea. She hadn't put the
waterfall there. She hadn't even been in a position to
see it coming. She'd turned the boat into a pumpkin,
but she hadn't meant to. It could have happened
to anyone.

'I managed to save Desiderata's notebooks, too,' she said.

'Well, that's a blessing,' said Nanny Ogg. 'Now we know where we're lost.'

She looked around. They were through the worst of the mountains, but there were still peaks around and high meadows stretching to the snowline. From somewhere in the distance came the clonking of goat bells.

Magrat unfolded a map. It was creased, damp, and the pencil had run. She pointed cautiously to a smudged area.

'I think we're here,' she said.

'My word,' said Nanny Ogg, whose grasp of the principles of cartography was even shakier than Granny's. 'Amazing how we can all fit on that little bit of paper.'

'I think perhaps it would be a good idea at the moment if we just followed the river,' said Magrat. 'Without in any way going on it,' she added quickly.

'I suppose you didn't find *my* bag?' said Granny Weatherwax. 'It had pers'nal items in.'

'Probably sank like a stone,' said Nanny Ogg.

Granny Weatherwax stood up like a general who's just had news that his army has come second.

'Come on,' she said. 'Where to next, then?'

What was next was forest – dark and ferociously coniferous. The witches flew over it in silence. There were occasional, isolated cottages half-hidden in the trees. Here and there a crag loomed over the sylvanian gloom, shrouded in mist even in mid-afternoon. Once or twice they flew past castles, if that's what you could call them; they didn't look built, more extruded from the landscape.

It was the kind of landscape that had a particular type of story attached to it, featuring wolves and garlic and frightened women. A dark and thirsty story, a story that flapped wings against the moon . . .

'Der Flabberghast,' muttered Nanny.

'What's that?' said Magrat.

'It's foreign for bat.'

'I've always liked bats,' said Magrat. 'In general.'

The witches found that, by unspoken agreement, they were flying closer together.

'I'm getting hungry,' said Granny Weatherwax. 'And don't no one mention pumpkin.'

'There's dwarf bread,' said Nanny.

'There's always the dwarf bread,' said Granny. 'I fancy something cooked *this* year, thank you all the same.'

They flew past another castle, occupying the entire summit of a crag.

'What we need is a nice little town or something,' said Magrat.

'But the one down there will have to do,' said Granny.

They looked down at it. It wasn't so much a town as a huddle of houses, clustering together against the trees. It looked as cheerless as an empty hearth, but the shadows of the mountains were already speeding across the forest and something about the landscape tacitly discouraged night-time flying.

'Can't see many people about,' said Granny.

'Maybe they turn in early in these parts,' said Nanny Ogg.

'It's hardly even sunset,' said Magrat. 'Perhaps we ought to go up to that castle?'

They all looked at the castle.

'No-o-o,' said Granny slowly, speaking for all of them. 'We know our place.'

So they landed, instead, in what was presumably the town square. A dog barked, somewhere behind the buildings. A shutter banged closed.

'*Very* friendly,' said Granny. She walked over to a larger building that had a sign, unreadable under the grime, over the door. She gave the woodwork a couple of thumps.

'Open up!' she said.

'No, no, you don't say that,' said Magrat. She shouldered her way past, and tapped on the door. 'Excuse me! Bona fide travellers!'

'Bona what?' said Nanny.

'That's what you need to say,' said Magrat. 'Any inn has got to open up for bona fide travellers and give them succour.'

'Has it?' said Nanny, with interest. 'That sounds like a thing worth knowing.'

The door remained shut.

'Let me 'ave a go,' said Nanny. 'I know some foreign lingo.'

She hammered on the door.

'Openny vous, gunga din, chop-chop, pretty damn quick,' she said.

Granny Weatherwax listened carefully.

'That's speaking foreign, is it?'

'My grandson Shane is a sailor,' said Nanny Ogg. 'You'd be amazed, the words he learns about foreign parts.'

'I expects I would,' said Granny. 'And I 'opes they works better for him.'

She thumped on the door again. And this time it opened, very slowly. A pale face peered around it.

'Excuse me—' Magrat began.

Granny pushed the door open. The face's owner had been leaning on it; they could hear the scrape of his boots over the floor as he was shoved gently backwards.

'Blessings be on this house,' Granny said, perfunctorily. It was always a good opening remark for a witch. It concentrated people's minds on what *other* things might be on this house, and reminded them about any fresh cakes, newly-baked bread or bundles of useful old clothing that might have temporarily escaped their minds.

It looked like one of the other things had been on this house already.

It *was* an inn, of sorts. The three witches had never seen such a cheerless place in their lives. But it was quite crowded. A score or more pale-faced people watched them solemnly from benches around the walls.

Nanny Ogg sniffed.

'Cor,' she said. 'Talk about garlic!' And, indeed, bunches of it hung from every beam. 'You can't have too much garlic, I always say. I can see I'm going to like it here.'

She nodded to a white-faced man behind the bar.

'Gooden day, big-feller mine host! Trois beers pour favour avec us, silver plate.'

'What's a silver plate got to do with it?' demanded Granny.

'It's foreign for please,' said Nanny.

'I bet it isn't really,' said Granny. 'You're just making it up as you goes along.'

The innkeeper, who worked on the fairly simple principle that anyone walking through the door wanted something to drink, drew three beers.

'See?' said Nanny, triumphantly.

'I don't like the way everyone's looking at us,' said Magrat, as Nanny babbled on to the perplexed man in her very own esperanto. 'A man over there *grinned* at me.'

Granny Weatherwax sat down on a bench, endeavouring to position herself so that as small an amount of her body as possible was in contact with the wood, in case being foreign was something you could catch.

'There,' said Nanny, bustling up with a tray, 'nothing to it. I just cussed at him until he understood.'

'It looks horrible,' said Granny.

'Garlic sausage and garlic bread,' said Nanny. 'My favourite.'

'You ought to have got some fresh vegetables,' said Magrat the dietitian.

'I did. There's some garlic,' said Nanny happily, cutting a generous slice of eye-watering sausage. 'And I think I definitely saw something like pickled onions on one of the shelves.'

'Yes? Then we're going to need at least two rooms for tonight,' said Granny sternly.

'Three,' said Magrat, very quickly.

She risked another look around the room. The silent villagers were staring at them intently, with a look she could only describe to herself as a sort of hopeful sadness. Of course, anyone who spent much time in the company of Granny Weatherwax and Nanny Ogg got used to being stared at; they were the kind of people that filled every space from edge to edge. And probably people in these parts didn't often see strangers, what with the thick forests and all. And the sight of Nanny Ogg eating a sausage with extreme gusto would even outrank her pickled onion number as major entertainment anywhere.

Even so . . . the way people were staring . . .

Outside, deep in the trees, a wolf howled.

The assembled villagers shivered in unison, as though they had been practising. The landlord muttered something to them. They got up, reluctantly, and filed out of the door, trying to keep together. An old lady laid her hand on Magrat's shoulder for a moment, shook her head sadly, sighed, and then scuttled away. But Magrat was used to this, too. People often felt sorry for her when they saw her in Granny's company.

Eventually the landlord lurched across to them with a lighted torch, and motioned them to follow him.

'How did you make him understand about the beds?' said Magrat.

'I said, "Hey mister, jigajig toot sweet all same No. 3",' said Nanny Ogg.

Granny Weatherwax tried this under her breath, and nodded.

'Your lad Shane certainly gets around a bit, doesn't he,' she remarked.

'He says it works every time,' said Nanny Ogg.

In fact there *were* only two rooms, up a long, winding and creaky stairway. And Magrat got one to herself. Even the landlord seemed to want it that way. He'd been very attentive.

She wished he hadn't been so keen to bar the shutters, though. Magrat liked to sleep with a window open. As it was, it was too dark and stuffy.

Anyway, she thought, I *am* the fairy godmother. The others are just accompanying me.

She peered hopelessly at herself in the room's tiny cracked mirror and then lay and listened to them on the far side of the paper-thin wall.

'What're you turning the mirror to the wall for, Esme?'

'I just don't like 'em, staring like that.'

'They only stares if you're staring *at* 'em, Esme.'

Silence, and then: 'Eh, what's this round thing for, then?'

'I reckon it's supposed to be a pillow, Esme.'

'Hah! *I* don't call it a pillow. And there's no proper blankets, even. What'd you say this thing's called?'

'I think it's called a duvit, Esme.'

'*We* call them an eiderdown where I come from. Hah!'

There was a respite. Then:

'Have you brushed your tooth?'

And another pause. Then:

'Oo, you haven't half got cold feet, Esme.'

'No, they ain't. They're lovely and snug.'

And another silence. Then:

'Boots! Your boots! You've got your boots on!'

'I should just think I 'ave got my boots on, Gytha Ogg.'

'And your clothes! You haven't even undressed!'

'You can't be too careful in foreign parts. There could be all sorts out there, a-creepin' around.'

Magrat snuggled under the – what was it? – duvit, and turned over. Granny Weatherwax appeared to need one hour's sleep a night, whereas Nanny Ogg would snore on a fence rail.

'Gytha? *Gytha!* GYTHA!'

'Wha'?'

'Are you awake?'

''M now . . .'

'I keep 'earing a noise!'

'. . . so do I . . .'

Magrat dozed for a while.

'Gytha? GYTHA!'

'. . . wha' now? . . .'

'I'm sure someone rattled our shutters!'

'. . . not at our time of life . . . now g' back t' slee' . . .'

The air in the room was getting hotter and stuffier by the minute. Magrat got out of bed, unbolted the shutters and flung them back dramatically.

There was a grunt, and a distant thud of something hitting the ground.

The full moon streamed in. She felt a lot better for that, and got back into bed.

It seemed no time at all before the voice from next door woke her again.

'Gytha Ogg, what are you doing?'

'I'm 'aving a snack.'

'Can't you sleep?'

'Just can't seem to be able to get off, Esme,' said Nanny Ogg. 'Can't imagine why.'

'Here, that's garlic sausage you're eating! I'm actually sharing a bed with someone eating garlic sausage.'

'Hey, that's mine! Give it back—'

Magrat was aware of booted footsteps in the pit of the night, and the sound of a shutter being swung back in the next room.

She thought she heard a faint 'oof' and another muted thud.

'I thought you *liked* garlic, Esme,' said Nanny Ogg's resentful voice.

'Sausage is all right in its place, and its place ain't in bed. And don't you say a word. Now move over. You keep taking all the duvit.'

After a while the velvet silence was broken by Granny's deep and resonant snore. Shortly afterwards it was joined by the genteel snoring of Nanny, who had spent far more time sleeping in company than Granny and had evolved a more accommodating nasal orchestra. Granny's snore would have cut logs.

Magrat folded the horrible round hard pillow over her ears and burrowed under the bedclothes.

Somewhere on the chilly ground, a very large bat was trying to get airborne again. It had already been stunned twice, once by a carelessly opened shutter and once by a ballistic garlic sausage, and wasn't feeling very well at all. One more setback, it was thinking, and it's back off to the castle. Besides, it'd be sunrise soon.

Its red eyes glinted as it looked up at Magrat's open window. It tensed –

A paw landed on it.

The bat looked around.

Greebo had not had a very good night. He had investigated the whole place with regard to female cats, and found none. He had prowled among the middens, and drawn a blank. People in this town didn't throw the garbage away. They ate it.

He'd trotted into the woods and found some wolves and had sat and grinned at them until they got uncomfortable and went away.

Yes, it had been a very uneventful night. Until now.

The bat squirmed under his claw. It seemed to Greebo's small cat brain that it was trying to change its shape, and he wasn't having any of that from a mouse with wings on.

Especially now, when he had someone to play with.

*   *   *

Genua was a fairytale city. People smiled and were joyful the livelong day. Especially if they wanted to see *another* livelong day.

Lilith made certain of that. Of course, people had probably thought they were happy in the days before she'd seen to it that the Duc replaced the old Baron, but it was a random, untidy happiness, which was why it was so easy for her to move in.

But it wasn't a way of life. There was no pattern to it.

One day they'd thank her.

Of course, there were always a few difficult ones. Sometimes, people just didn't know how to act. You did your best for them, you ruled their city properly, you ensured that their lives were worthwhile and full of happiness every hour of the day and then, for no reason at all, they turned on you.

Guards lined the audience chamber. And there *was* an audience. Technically, of course, it was the ruler who gave the audience, but Lilith liked to see people watching. One pennyworth of example was worth a pound of punishment.

There wasn't a lot of crime in Genua these days. At least, not what would be considered crime elsewhere. Things like theft were easily dealt with and hardly required any kind of judicial process. Far more important, in Lilith's book, were crimes against narrative expectation. People didn't seem to know how they should behave.

Lilith held a mirror up to Life, and chopped all the bits off Life that didn't fit . . .

The Duc lounged bonelessly on his throne, one

leg dangling over the armrest. He'd never got the hang of chairs.

'And what has this one done?' he said, and yawned. Opening his mouth wide was something he *was* good at, at least.

A little old man cowered between two guards.

There's always someone willing to be a guard, even in places like Genua. Besides, you got a really smart uniform, with blue trousers and a red coat and a high black hat with a cockade in it.

'But I . . . I *can't* whistle,' quavered the old man. 'I . . . I didn't know it was compulsory . . .'

'But you are a toymaker,' said the Duc. 'Toymakers whistle and sing the whole day long.' He glanced at Lilith. She nodded.

'I don't know any . . . s-songs,' said the toymaker. 'I never got taught s-songs. Just how to make toys. I was 'prenticed at making toys. Seven years before the little hammer, man and boy . . .'

'It says here,' said the Duc, making a creditable impersonation of someone reading the charge sheet in front of him, 'that you don't tell the children stories.'

'No one ever told me about telling . . . s-stories,' said the toymaker. 'Look, I just make toys. Toys. That's all I'm good at. Toys. I make good t-toys. I'm just a t-toymaker.'

'You can't be a good toymaker if you don't tell stories to the children,' said Lilith, leaning forward.

The toymaker looked up at the veiled face.

'Don't know any,' he said.

'You don't know *any?*'

'I could t-tell 'em how to make toys,' the old man quavered.

Lilith sat back. It was impossible to see her expression under the veil.

'I think it would be a good idea if the People's Guards here took you away,' she said, 'to a place where you will certainly learn to sing. And possibly, after a while, you might even whistle. Won't that be nice?'

The old Baron's dungeons had been disgusting. Lilith had had them repainted and refurnished. With a lot of mirrors.

When the audience was over one member of the crowd slipped out through the palace kitchens. The guards on the side gate didn't try to stop her. She was a very important person in the small compass of their lives.

'Hello, Mrs Pleasant.'

She stopped, reached into her basket and produced a couple of roast chicken legs.

'Just tryin' a new peanut coating,' she said. 'Would value your opinions, boys.'

They took them gratefully. Everyone liked to see Mrs Pleasant. She could do things with a chicken that would almost make it glad it had been killed.

'And now I'm just going out to get some herbs,' she said.

They watched her as she went like a fat, determined arrow in the direction of the market place, which was right on the edge of the river. Then they ate the chicken legs.

Mrs Pleasant bustled among the market stalls; and she took great care to bustle. Even in Genua there were always people ready to tell a tale. *Especially* in Genua. She was a cook, so she bustled. And made sure she stayed fat and was, fortunately, naturally jolly. She made sure she had floury arms at all times. If she felt under suspicion, she'd say things like 'Lawks!' She seemed to be getting away with it so far.

She looked for the sign. And there it was. Perched up on the roof pole of a stall that was otherwise stacked with cages of hens, gazoots, Wheely cranes and other fowl, was a black cockerel. The voodoo doctor was In.

Even as her eye found it the cockerel's head turned to look at her.

Set a little way back from the rest of the stalls was a small tent, similar to many around the market. A cauldron bubbled in front of it on a charcoal fire. There were bowls beside it, and a ladle, and beside them a plate with coins on it. There were quite a lot of coins; people paid for Mrs Gogol's cooking whatever they thought it was worth, and the plate was hardly big enough.

The thick liquid in the cauldron was an unappetizing brown. Mrs Pleasant helped herself to a bowlful, and waited. Mrs Gogol had certain talents.

After a while a voice from the tent said, 'What's new, Mrs Pleasant?'

'She's shut up the toymaker,' said Mrs Pleasant, to the air in general. 'And yesterday it was old Devereaux the innkeeper for not being fat and not having a big red face. That's four times this month.'

'You come in, Mrs Pleasant.'

It was dark and hot inside the tent. There was another fire in there, and another pot. Mrs Gogol was hunched over it, stirring. She motioned the cook to a pair of bellows.

'Blow up the coals a tad, and we'll see what's what,' she said.

Mrs Pleasant obeyed. She didn't use magic herself, other than that necessary to get a roux to turn or bread to rise, but she respected it in others. Especially in the likes of Mrs Gogol.

The charcoal blazed white. The thick liquid in the pot began to churn. Mrs Gogol peered into the steam.

'What're you doing, Mrs Gogol?' said the cook anxiously.

'Trying to see what's goin' to happen,' said the voodoo woman. The voice dropped into the rolling growl of the psychically gifted.

Mrs Pleasant squinted into the roiling mass.

'Someone's going to be eatin' shrimp?' she said helpfully.

'Ye see that bit of okra?' said Mrs Gogol. 'Ye see the way the crab legs keep coming up just there?'

'You never were one to stint the crab meat,' said Mrs Pleasant.

'See the way the bubbles is so thick by the okuh leaves? See the way it all spirals around that purple onion?'

'I see it! I see it!' said Mrs Pleasant.

'And you know what that means?'

'Means it's going to taste real *fine*!'

'Sure,' said Mrs Gogol, kindly. 'And it means some people's coming.'

'Wow! How many?'

Mrs Gogol dipped a spoon into the seething mass and tasted it.

'Three people,' she said. She smacked her lips thoughtfully. 'Women.'

She dipped the spoon again.

'Have a taste,' she said. 'There's a cat, too. Ye can tell by the sassafras.' She smacked her lips. 'Grey. One eye.' She explored the cavity of a tooth with her tongue. 'The . . . left one.'

Mrs Pleasant's jaw dropped.

'They'll find you before they find me,' said Mrs Gogol. 'You lead 'em here.'

Mrs Pleasant stared at Mrs Gogol's grim smile and then back down at the mixture in the pot.

'They coming all this way for a taste?' she said.

'Sure.' Mrs Gogol sat back. 'You been to see the girl in the white house?'

Mrs Pleasant nodded. 'Young Embers,' she said. 'Yeah. When I can. When the Sisters are out at the palace. They got her real scared, Mrs Gogol.'

She looked down at the pot again, and back up to Mrs Gogol.

'Can you really see—?'

'I expect you've got things to marinate?' said Mrs Gogol.

'Yeah. Yeah.' Mrs Pleasant backed out, but with reluctance. Then she halted. Mrs Pleasant, at rest, was not easily moved again until she wanted to be.

'That Lilith woman says she can see the whole world in mirrors,' she said, in slightly accusing tones.

Mrs Gogol shook her head.

'All anyone gets in a mirror is themselves,' she said. 'But what you gets in a good gumbo is *everything.*'

Mrs Pleasant nodded. This was a well-known fact. She couldn't dispute it.

Mrs Gogol shook her head sadly when the cook had gone. A voodoo woman was reduced to all sorts of stratagems in order to appear knowing, but she felt slightly ashamed of letting an honest woman believe that she could see the future in a pot of gumbo. Because all you could see in a pot of Mrs Gogol's gumbo was that the future certainly contained a very good meal.

She'd really seen it in a bowl of jambalaya she'd prepared earlier.

Magrat lay with the wand under her pillow. She wobbled gently between sleep and wakefulness.

Certainly she was the best person for the wand. There was no doubt about that. Sometimes – and she hardly dared give the thought headroom, when she was under the same roof as Granny Weatherwax – she really wondered about the others' commitment to witchcraft. Half the time they didn't seem to *bother*.

Take medicine, for example. Magrat knew she was much better than them at herbs. She'd inherited several large books on the subject from Goodie

Whemper, her predecessor in the cottage, and had essayed a few tentative notes of her own as well. She could tell people things about the uses of Devil's Bit Scabious that would interest them so much they'd rush off, presumably to look for someone else to tell. She could fractionally distil, and double-distil, and do things that meant sitting up all night watching the colour of the flame under the retort. She *worked* at it.

Whereas Nanny just tended to put a hot poultice on everything and recommend a large glass of whatever the patient liked best on the basis that since you were going to be ill anyway you might as well get some enjoyment out of it. (Magrat forbade her patients alcohol, because of what it did to the liver; if they didn't know what it did to the liver, she spent some time telling them.)

And Granny . . . she just gave people a bottle of coloured water and told them they felt a lot better.

And what was so annoying was that they often did.

Where was the witchcraft in that?

With a wand, though, things could be different. You could help people a lot with a wand. Magic was there to make life better. Magrat knew this in the pink fluttering boudoir of her heart.

She dipped under the surface of sleep again.

And there was an odd dream. She never mentioned it to anyone afterwards because, well, you didn't. Not things like that.

But she thought she'd got up in the night, awakened by the silence, to get some more air. And as she passed the mirror she saw a movement in it.

It wasn't her face. It looked a lot like Granny Weatherwax. It smiled at her – a much nicer and friendlier smile than she'd ever got from Granny, Magrat recalled – and then vanished, the cloudy silver surface closing over it.

She hurried back to bed and awoke to the sound of a brass band, engaged in unrelenting oompah. People were shouting and laughing.

Magrat got dressed quickly, went out into the corridor, and knocked on the door of the older witches. There was no reply. She tried the handle.

After she'd rattled it a couple of times there was a thump as the chair wedged under the handle on the other side, the better to deter ravishers, burglars and other nocturnal intruders, fell over.

Granny Weatherwax's boots protruded from under the covers at one end of the bed. Nanny Ogg's bare feet, Nanny being something of a night-time revolver, were beside them. Faint snores rattled the jug on the washbasin; these were no longer the full-nosed roars of a quick forty-winks catnapper, but the well-paced growls of someone who intends to make a night of it.

Magrat knocked on the sole of Granny's boot.

'Hey, wake up! Something's going on.'

Granny Weatherwax waking up was quite an impressive sight, and one not seen by many people.

Most people, on waking up, accelerate through a quick panicky pre-consciousness check-up: who am I, where am I, who is he/she, good god, why am I cuddling a policeman's helmet, *what happened last night*?

And this is because people are riddled by Doubt. It is the engine that drives them through their lives. It is the elastic band in the little model aeroplane of their soul, and they spend their time winding it up until it knots. Early morning is the worst time – there's that little moment of panic in case You have drifted away in the night and something else has moved in. This never happened to Granny Weatherwax. She went straight from fast asleep to instant operation on all six cylinders. She never needed to find herself because she always knew who was doing the looking.

She sniffed. 'Something's burning,' she said.

'They've got a bonfire, too,' said Magrat.

Granny sniffed again.

'They're roasting *garlic*?' she said.

'I know. I can't imagine why. They're ripping all the shutters off the windows and burning them in the square and dancing around the fire.'

Granny Weatherwax gave Nanny Ogg a vicious jab with her elbow.

'Wake up, you.'

'Wstph?'

'I didn't get a wink of sleep all night,' said Granny reproachfully, 'what with her snoring.'

Nanny Ogg raised the covers cautiously.

'It's far too early in the morning for it to be early in the morning,' she said.

'Come on,' said Granny. 'We needs your skill with languages.'

*　　*　　*

105

The owner of the inn flapped his arms up and down and ran around in circles. Then he pointed at the castle that towered over the forest. Then he sucked vigorously at his wrist. Then he fell over on his back. And then he looked expectantly at Nanny Ogg, while behind him the bonfire of garlic and wooden stakes and heavy window shutters burned merrily.

'No,' said Nanny, after a while. 'Still non conprendy, mine hair.'

The man got up, and brushed some dust off his leather breeches.

'I think he's saying that someone's dead,' said Magrat. 'Someone in the castle.'

'Well, I must say, everyone seems very cheerful about it,' said Granny Weatherwax severely.

In the sunlight of the new day the village looked far more cheerful. Everyone kept nodding happily at the witches.

'That's because it was probably the landlord,' said Nanny Ogg. 'Bit of a bloodsucker, I think he's sayin'.'

'Ah. That'd be it, then.' Granny rubbed her hands together and looked approvingly at the breakfast table, which had been dragged out into the sunshine. 'Anyway, the food has certainly improved. Pass the bread, Magrat.'

'Everyone keeps smiling and waving at us,' said Magrat. 'And look at all this food!'

'That's only to be expected,' said Granny, with her mouth full. 'They've only had us here one night and already they're learnin' it's *lucky* to be kind to witches. Now help me get the lid off this honey.'

Under the table, Greebo sat and washed himself. Occasionally he burped.

Vampires have risen from the dead, the grave and the crypt, but have never managed it from the cat.

Dear Jason and all at No. 21, No. 34, No. 15, No. 87 and No. 61 but not at No. 18 until she gives back the bowl she definitly borrowed whatever she says,

Well here we are, cor what a lark so far, dont arsk ME about pumkins, still, no harm done. Im drawin a picture of where we stayed larst night I have put an X on our room where our room is. The weather—

'What are you doing, Gytha? We're ready to leave.'

Nanny Ogg looked up, her face still creased with the effort of composition.

'I thought it would be nice to send something to our Jason. You know, to stop him worryin'. So I done a drawing of this place on a piece of card and Mine Hair here will give it to someone going our way. You never know, it might get there.'

—continues Fine.

Nanny Ogg sucked the end of her pencil. Not for the first time in the history of the universe, someone for whom communication normally came as effortlessly as a dream was stuck for inspiration when faced with a few lines on the back of a card.

Well that about wraps it up for now, will ~~fight~~ *wright again soone MUM. P.S. the Cat is looking very Peeky I think he misses his Home.*

'Will you come *on*, Gytha? Magrat's getting my broom started for me.'

P.P.S. Granny sends her Love.

Nanny Ogg sat back, content in the knowledge of a job well done.*

Magrat reached the end of the town square and stopped to rest.

Quite an audience had gathered to see a woman with legs. They were very polite about it. Somehow, that made it worse.

'It doesn't fly unless you run really fast,' she explained, aware even as she spoke how stupid this sounded, especially if you were listening in a foreign language. 'I think it's called hump starting.'

She took a deep breath, scowled in concentration, and ran forward again.

This time it started. It jolted in her hands. The bristles rustled. She managed to slip it into neutral before it could drag her along the ground. One thing about Granny Weatherwax's broomstick – it was one of the very old-fashioned ones, built in the days when broomsticks were built to last and not fall apart with woodworm after ten years – was that while it might take some starting, when it went it didn't hang about.

Magrat had once considered explaining the symbolism of the witches' broomstick to Granny Weatherwax, and decided not to. It would have been worse than the row about the significance of the maypole.

---

*Nanny Ogg sent a number of cards home to her family, not a single one of which got back before she did. This is traditional, and happens everywhere in the universe.

Departure took some time. The villagers insisted on giving them little gifts of food. Nanny Ogg made a speech which no one understood but which was generally cheered. Greebo, hiccuping occasionally, oozed into his accustomed place among the bristles of Nanny's broomstick.

As they rose above the forest a thin plume of smoke also rose from the castle. And then there were flames.

'I see people dancing in front of it,' said Magrat.

'Always a dangerous business, rentin' property,' said Granny Weatherwax. 'I expect he was a bit lax when it came to redecoratin' and repairin' the roof and suchlike. People take against that kind of thing. My landlord hasn't done a hand's turn on my cottage the whole time I've been there,' she added. 'It's shameful. And me an old woman, too.'

'I thought you owned your place,' said Magrat, as the broomsticks set off over the forest.

'She just ain't paid no rent for sixty years,' said Nanny Ogg.

'Is that my fault?' said Granny Weatherwax. 'It's not *my* fault. I'd be quite willin' to pay.' She smiled a slow, self-confident smile. 'All he has to do is *ask*,' she added.

This is the Discworld, seen from above, its cloud formations circling in long curved patterns.

Three dots emerged from the cloud layer.

'I can see why travellin' doesn't catch on. I call this boring. Nothing but forest for hours and hours.'

'Yes, but flying gets you to places quickly, Granny.'

'How long've we been flying, anyway?'

'About ten minutes since you last asked, Esme.'

'You see? *Boring*.'

'It's sitting on the sticks I don't like. I reckon there ought to be a special broomstick for going long distances, right? One you could stretch out on and have a snooze.'

They all considered this.

'And have your meals on,' added Nanny. 'Proper meals, I mean. With gravy. Not just sandwiches and stuff.' An experiment in aerial cookery on a small oil burner had been hastily curtailed after it threatened to set fire to Nanny's broomstick.

'I suppose you could do it if you had a really *big* broomstick,' said Magrat. 'About the size of a tree, perhaps. Then one of us could do the steering and another one could do the cooking.'

'It'd never happen,' said Nanny Ogg. 'The reason being, the dwarfs would make you pay a fortune for a stick that big.'

'Yes, but what you could do,' said Magrat, warming to her subject, 'is get people to pay you to give them rides. There must be lots of people fed up with highwaymen and . . . and being seasick and that sort of thing.'

'How about it, Esme?' said Nanny Ogg. 'I'll do the steering and Magrat'll do the cooking.'

'What shall *I* do, then?' said Granny Weatherwax suspiciously.

'Oh . . . well . . . there ought to be someone to,

you know, welcome people onto the stick and give them their meals,' said Magrat. 'And tell them what to do if the magic fails, for example.'

'If the magic fails everyone'll crash into the ground and die,' Granny pointed out.

'Yes, but someone will have to tell them how to do that,' said Nanny Ogg, winking at Magrat. 'They won't know how to, not being experienced in flying.'

'And we could call ourselves . . .' she paused. As always on the Discworld, which was right on the very edge of unreality, little bits of realness crept in whenever someone's mind was resonating properly. This happened now.

'. . . Three Witches Airborne,' she said. 'How about that?'

'*Broomsticks* Airborne,' said Magrat. 'Or Pan . . . air . . .'

'There's no need to bring religion into it,' sniffed Granny.

Nanny Ogg looked slyly from Granny to Magrat.

'We *could* call it Vir—' she began.

A gust of wind caught all three sticks and whirled them up. There was a brief panic as the witches brought them under control.

'Load of nonsense,' muttered Granny.

'Well, it passes the time,' said Nanny Ogg.

Granny looked morosely at the greenery below.

'You'd never get people to do it,' she said. 'Load of nonsense.'

Dear Jason en famile,
Overleaf on the other side please find enclosed a

sketch of somewhere some king died and was buried,
search me why. It's in some village wear we stopped
last night. We had some stuff it was chewy you'll
never guess it was snails, and not bad and Esme had
three helpins before she found out and then had a
Row with the cook and Magrat was sick all night just
at the thought of it and had the dire rear. Thinking
of you your loving MUM. PS the privies here are
DESGUSTING, they have them INDORES, so much
for HIGEINE.

Several days passed.

In a quiet little inn in a tiny country Granny
Weatherwax sat and regarded the food with deep
suspicion. The owner hovered with the frantic expression of one who knows, even before he starts,
that he's not going to come out of this ahead of the
game.

'Good simple home cooking,' said Granny.
'That's all I require. You know me. I'm not the
demanding sort. No one could say I'm the demanding sort. I just want simple food. Not all grease and
stuff. It comes to something when you complain
about something in your lettuce and it turns out to
be what you ordered.'

Nanny Ogg tucked her napkin into the top of her
dress and said nothing.

'Like that place last night,' said Granny. 'You'd
think you'd be all right with sandwiches, wouldn't
you? I mean . . . sandwiches? Simplest food there is
in the whole world. You'd think even foreigners
couldn't get sandwiches wrong. Hah!'

'They didn't call them sandwiches, Granny,' said Magrat, her eyes dwelling on the owner's frying pan. 'They called them . . . I think they called them smorgy's board.'

'They was nice,' said Nanny Ogg. 'I'm very partial to a pickled herring.'

'But they must think we're daft, not noticing they'd left off the top slice,' said Granny triumphantly. 'Well, I told them a thing or two! Another time they'll think twice before trying to swindle people out of a slice of bread that's theirs by rights!'

'I expect they will,' said Magrat darkly.

'And I don't hold with all this giving things funny names so people don't know what they're eating,' said Granny, determined to explore the drawbacks of international cookery to the full. 'I like stuff that tells you plain what it is, like . . . well . . . Bubble and Squeak, or . . . or . . .'

'Spotted Dick,' said Nanny absently. She was watching the progress of the pancakes with some anticipation.

'That's right. Decent honest food. I mean, take that stuff we had for lunch. I'm not saying it wasn't nice,' said Granny graciously. 'In a foreign sort of way, of course. But they called it Cwuissses dee Grenolly, and who knows what that means?'

'Frogs' legs,' translated Nanny, without thinking.

The silence was filled with Granny Weatherwax taking a deep breath and a pale green colour creeping across Magrat's face. Nanny Ogg now thought quicker than she had done for a very long time.

'Not *actual* frogs' legs,' she said hurriedly. 'It's

like Toad-in-the-Hole is really only sausage and batter puddin'. It's just a joke name.'

'It doesn't sound very funny to me,' said Granny. She turned to glare at the pancakes.

'At least they can't muck up a decent pancake,' she said. 'What'd they call them here?'

'Crap suzette, I think,' said Nanny.

Granny forbore to comment. But she watched with grim satisfaction as the owner finished the dish and gave her a hopeful smile.

'Oh, now he expects us to eat them,' she said. 'He only goes and sets fire to them, and then he still expects us to eat them!'

It might later have been possible to chart the progress of the witches across the continent by some sort of demographic survey. Long afterwards, in some quiet, onion-hung kitchens, in sleepy villages nestling among hot hills, you might have found cooks who *wouldn't* twitch and try to hide behind the door when a stranger came into the kitchen.

Dear Jason,

It is defnity more warmer here, Magrat says it is because we are getting further from the Hub and, a funny thing, all the money is different. You have to change it for other money which is all different shapes and is not proper money at all in my opnion. We generally let Esme sort that out, she gets a very good rate of exchange, it is amazing, Magrat says she will write a book called Travelling on One Dollar a Day, and it's always the same dollar. Esme is getting to act just like a foreigner, yesterday she took her shawl off, next thing it will be dancing on tables. This is a picture of some famous bridge or other. Lots of love, MUM.

The sun beat down on the cobbled street, and particularly on the courtyard of a little inn.

'It's hard to imagine,' said Magrat, 'that it's autumn back home.'

'Garkon? Mucho vino aveck zei, grassy ass.'

The innkeeper, who did not understand one word and was a good-natured man who certainly did not deserve to be called a garkon, smiled at Nanny. He'd smile at anyone with such an unlimited capacity for drink.

'I don't hold with putting all these tables out in the street, though,' said Granny Weatherwax, although without much severity. It was pleasantly warm. It wasn't that she didn't like autumn, it was a season she always looked forward to, but at her time of life it was nice to know that it was happening hundreds of miles away while she wasn't there.

Underneath the table Greebo dozed on his back with his legs in the air. Occasionally he twitched as he fought wolves in his sleep.

'It says in Desiderata's notes,' said Magrat, turning the stiff pages carefully, 'that in the late summer here they have this special traditional ceremony where they let a lot of bulls run through the street.'

'That'd be something worth seeing,' said Granny Weatherwax. 'Why do they do it?'

'So all the young men can chase them to show

how brave they are,' said Magrat. 'Apparently they pull their rosettes off.'

A variety of expressions passed across Nanny Ogg's wrinkled face, like weather over a stretch of volcanic badlands.

'Sounds a bit strange,' she said at last. 'What do they do that for?'

'She doesn't explain it very clearly,' said Magrat. She turned another page. Her lips moved as she read on. 'What does cojones mean?'

They shrugged.

'Here, you want to slow down on that drink,' said Granny, as a waiter put down another bottle in front of Nanny Ogg. 'I wouldn't trust any drink that's green.'

'It's not like proper drink,' said Nanny. 'It says on the label it's made from herbs. You can't make a serious drink out of just herbs. Try a drop.'

Granny sniffed the opened bottle.

'Smells like aniseed,' she said.

'It says "Absinthe" on the bottle,' said Nanny.

'Oh, that's just a name for wormwood,' said Magrat, who was good at herbs. 'My herbal says it's good for stomach diforders and prevents sicknefs after meals.'

'There you are, then,' said Nanny. 'Herbs. It's practic'ly medicine.' She poured a generous measure for the other two. 'Give it a go, Magrat. It'll put a cheft on your cheft.'

Granny Weatherwax surreptitiously loosened her boots. She was also debating whether to remove her vest. She probably didn't need all three.

'We ought to be getting on,' she said.

'Oh, I'm fed up with the broomsticks,' said Nanny. 'More than a couple of hours on a stick and I've gone rigid in the dairy air.'

She looked expectantly at the other two. 'That's foreign for bum,' she added. 'Although, it's a funny thing, in some foreign parts "bum" means "tramp" and "tramp" means "hobo". Funny things, words.'

'A laugh a minute,' said Granny.

'The river's quite wide here,' said Magrat. 'There's big boats. I've never been on a proper boat. You know? The kind that doesn't sink easily?'

'Broomsticks is more witchy,' said Granny, but not with much conviction. She did not have Nanny Ogg's international anatomical vocabulary, but bits of her she wouldn't even admit to knowing the names of were definitely complaining.

'I saw them boats,' said Nanny. 'They looked like great big rafts with houses on. You wouldn't hardly know you're *on* a boat, Esme. 'Ere, what's he doing?'

The innkeeper had hurried out and was taking the jolly little tables back inside. He nodded at Nanny and spoke with a certain amount of urgency.

'I think he wants us to go inside,' said Magrat.

'I likes it out here,' said Granny. 'I LIKES IT OUT HERE, THANK YOU,' she repeated. Granny Weatherwax's approach to foreign tongues was to repeat herself loudly and slowly.

''Ere, you stop trying to take our table away!' snapped Nanny, thumping his hands.

The innkeeper spoke hurriedly and pointed up the street.

Granny and Magrat glanced inquiringly at Nanny Ogg. She shrugged.

'Didn't understand any of that,' she admitted.

'WE'RE STOPPIN' WHERE WE ARE, THANK YOU,' said Granny. The innkeeper's eyes met hers. He gave in, waved his hands in the air in exasperation, and went inside.

'They think they can take advantage of you when you're a woman,' said Magrat. She stifled a burp, discreetly, and picked up the green bottle again. Her stomach was feeling a lot better already.

'That's very true. D'you know what?' said Nanny Ogg, 'I barricaded meself in my room last night and a man didn't even *try* to break in.'

'Gytha Ogg, sometimes you—' Granny stopped as she caught sight of something over Nanny's shoulder.

'There's a load of *cows* coming down the street,' she said.

Nanny turned her chair around.

'It must be that bull thing Magrat mentioned,' she said. 'Should be worth seein'.'

Magrat glanced up. All along the street people were craning out of every second-storey window. A jostle of horns and hooves and steaming bodies was approaching rapidly.

'There's people up there *laughing* at us,' she said accusingly.

Under the table Greebo stirred and rolled over. He opened his good eye, focused on the approaching bulls, and sat up. This looked like being fun.

'Laughin'?' said Granny. She looked up. The people aloft did indeed appear to be enjoying a joke.

Her eyes narrowed.

'We're just goin' to carry on as if nothin' is happening,' she declared.

'But they're quite big bulls,' said Magrat nervously.

'They're *nothing* to do with *us*,' said Granny. 'It's nothin' to do with *us* if a lot of foreigners want to get excited about things. Now pass me the herbal wine.'

As far as Lagro te Kabona, innkeeper, could remember the events of that day, they seemed to happen like this:

It was the time of the Thing with the Bulls. And the mad women just sat there, drinking absinthe as if it was water! He tried to get them to come indoors, but the old one, the skinny one, just shouted at him. So he let them bide, but left the door open – people soon got the message when the bulls came down the street with the young men of the village after them. Whoever snatched the big red rosette from between the horns of the biggest bull got the seat of honour at that night's feast plus – Lagro smiled a smile of forty years' remembrance – a certain informal but highly enjoyable relationship with the young women of the town for quite some time after . . .

And the mad women just sat there.

The leading bull had been a bit uncertain about this. Its normal course of action would be to roar and paw the ground a bit to get the targets running in an interesting way and its mind wasn't able to cope with this lack of attention, but that hadn't been its major problem, because its major problem had been twenty other bulls right behind it.

And even that ceased to be its major problem, because the terrible old woman, the one all in black, had stood up, muttered something at it and smacked it between the eyes. Then the horrible dumpy one whose stomach had the resilience and capacity of a galvanized water tank fell backwards off her chair, laughing, and the young one – that is, the one who was younger than the other two – started flapping at the bulls as if they were ducks.

And then the street was full of angry, bewildered bulls, and a lot of shouting, terrified young men. It's one thing to chase a lot of panicking bulls, and quite another to find that they're suddenly trying to run the other way.

The innkeeper, from the safety of his bedroom window, could hear the horrible women shouting things to one another. The dumpy one kept laughing and shouting some sort of battle cry— 'Trythe-HorsemanswordEsme!' and then the younger one, who was pushing her way through the animals as if being gored to death was something that only happened to other people, found the lead bull and took *the* rosette off it, with the same air of concern as an old woman may take a thorn out of her cat's paw. She held it as if she didn't know what it was or what she should do with it . . .

The sudden silence affected even the bulls. Their tiny little bloodshot brains sensed something wrong. The bulls were embarrassed.

Fortunately, the horrible women left on a river-boat that afternoon, after one of them rescued her cat which had cornered twenty-five stone of confused bull and was trying to toss it in the air and play with it.

That evening Lagro te Kabona made a point of being very, very kind to his old mother.

And the village held a flower festival next year, and no one ever talked about the Thing with the Bulls ever, ever again.

At least, not in front of the men.

The big paddlewheel sloshed through the thick brown soup of the river. The motive power was several dozen trolls under a sun-shade, trudging along an endless belt. Birds sang in the trees on the distant banks. The scent of hibiscus wafted across the water, almost but unfortunately not quite over-powering the scent of the river itself.

'Now *this,*' said Nanny Ogg, 'is more like it.'

She stretched out on the deckchair and turned to look at Granny Weatherwax, whose brows were knitted in the intense concentration of reading.

Nanny's mouth spread in an evil grin.

'You know what this river's called?' she said.

'No.'

''S called the Vieux River.'

'Yes?'

'Know what that means?'

'No.'

'The Old (Masculine) River,' said Nanny.

'Yes?'

'Words have sex in foreign parts,' said Nanny, hopefully.

Granny didn't budge.

'Wouldn't be at all surprised,' she murmured. Nanny sagged.

'That's one of Desiderata's books, isn't it?'

'Yes,' said Granny. She licked her thumb decorously and turned the page.

'Where's Magrat gone?'

'She's having a lie-down in the cabin,' said Granny, without looking up.

'Tummy upset?'

'It's her head this time. Now be quiet, Gytha. I'm having a read.'

'What about?' said Nanny cheerfully.

Granny Weatherwax sighed, and put her finger on the page to mark her place.

'This place we're going to,' she said. 'Genua. Desiderata says it's decadent.'

Nanny Ogg's smile remained fixed.

'Yes?' she said. 'That's good, is it? I've never been to a city before.'

Granny Weatherwax paused. She'd been pondering for some while. She wasn't at all certain about the meaning of the word 'decadent'. She'd dismissed the possibility that it meant 'having ten teeth' in the same sense that Nanny Ogg, for example, was unident. Whatever it meant, it was something Desiderata had felt necessary to write down. Granny Weatherwax did not generally trust books as a means of information, but now she had no choice.

She had a vague idea that 'decadent' had something to do with not opening the curtains all day.

'She says it's also a city of art, wit and culture,' said Granny.

'We shall be all right there, then,' said Nanny confidently.

'Particularly noted for the beauty of its women, she says here.'

'We shall fade right in, no trouble.'

Granny turned the pages carefully. Desiderata had paid close attention to affairs all over the Disc. On the other hand, she hadn't been writing for readers other than herself, so her notes tended to the cryptic and were *aides mémoire* rather than coherent accounts.

Granny read: 'Now L. rules the citie as the power behint the throne, and Baron S. they say has been killd, drowned in the river. He was a wicked man tho not I think as wicked as L, for she says she wants to make it a Magic Kingdom, a Happy and Peaseful place, and wen people do that look out for Spies on every corner and no manne dare speak out, for who dare speke out against Evile done in the name of Happyness and Pease? All the Streetes are clean and Axes are sharp. But E. is safe at least, for now. L. has plans for her. And Mrs G who was the Baron's *amour* hides in the swamp and fites back with swamp magic, but you cannot fite mirror magic which is all Reflection.'

Fairy godmothers came in twos, Granny knew. So that was Desiderata and . . . and L . . . but who was this person in the swamp?

'Gytha?' said Granny.

'Wazzat?' said Nanny Ogg, who was dozing off.

'Desiderata says some woman here is someone's armour.'

'Prob'ly a mettyfor,' said Nanny Ogg.

'Oh,' said Granny darkly, 'one of *them* things.'

'But no one can stop Mardi Gras,' she read. 'If anything canne be done it be on Samedi Nuit Morte, the last night of carnivale, the night halfway between the Living and the Dead, when magic flows in the streets. If L. is vooneruble it is then, for carnivale is everythinge she hates . . .'

Granny Weatherwax pulled her hat down over her eyes to shield them from the sun.

'It says here they have a great big carnival every year,' she said. 'Mardi Gras, it's called.'

'That means Fat Lunchtime,' said Nanny Ogg, international linguist. 'Garkon! Etcetra gross Mint Tulip avec petit bowl de peanuts, pour favour!'

Granny Weatherwax shut the book.

She would not of course admit it to a third party, least of all another witch, but as Genua drew nearer Granny was becoming less and less confident.

She was waiting in Genua. After all this time! Staring at her out of the mirror! Smiling!

The sun beat down. She tried defying it. Sooner or later she was going to have to give in, though. It was going to be time to remove another vest.

Nanny Ogg sat and drew cards for her relatives for a while, and then yawned. She was a witch who liked noise and people around her. Nanny Ogg was getting bored. It was a big boat, more like a floating inn, and she felt certain there was some excitement somewhere.

She laid her bag on her seat and wandered away to look for it.

The trolls plodded on.

The sun was red, fat and low when Granny Weatherwax awoke. She looked around guiltily from the shelter of her hatbrim in case anyone had noticed her asleep. Falling asleep during the day was something only old women did, and Granny Weatherwax was an old woman only when it suited her purposes.

The only spectator was Greebo, curled up on Nanny's chair. His one good eye was fixed on her, but it wasn't so terrifying as the milky white stare of his blind one.

'Just considerin' our strategy,' she muttered, just in case.

She closed the book and strode off to their cabin. It wasn't a big one. Some of the staterooms looked huge, but what with the herbal wine and everything Granny hadn't felt up to using any Influence to get one.

Magrat and Nanny Ogg were sitting on a bunk, in gloomy silence.

'I feels a bit peckish,' said Granny. 'I smelled stew on the way here, so let's go and have a look, eh? What about that?'

The other two continued to stare at the floor.

'I suppose there's always pumpkin,' said Magrat. 'And there's always the dwarf bread.'

'There's always dwarf bread,' said Nanny automatically. She looked up, her face a mask of shame.

'Er, Esme . . . er . . . you know the money . . .'

'The money what we all gave you to keep in your knickers for safety?' said Granny. Something about the way the conversation was going suggested the first few pebbles slipping before a major landslide.

'That's the money I'm referrin' to . . . er . . .'

'The money in the big leather bag that we were goin' to be very careful about spendin'?' said Granny.

'You see . . . the money . . .'

'Oh, that money,' said Granny.

'. . . is gone . . .' said Nanny.

'*Stolen?*'

'She's been *gambling*,' said Magrat, in tones of smug horror. 'With *men*.'

'It wasn't gambling!' snapped Nanny. 'I never gamble! They were no good at cards! I won no end of games!'

'But you *lost* money,' said Granny.

Nanny Ogg looked down again, and muttered something.

'What?' said Granny.

'I said I won nearly all of them,' said Nanny. 'And then I thought, here, we could really have a bit of money to, you know, spend in the city, and I've always been very good at Cripple Mr Onion . . .'

'So you decided to bet heavily,' said Granny.

'How did you know that?'

'Got a feelin' about it,' said Granny wearily. 'And suddenly everyone else was lucky, am I right?'

'It was weird,' said Nanny.

'Hmm.'

'Well, it's not *gambling*,' said Nanny. 'I didn't see it was gambling. They were no good when I started playing. It's not gambling to play against someone who's no good. It's common sense.'

'There was nearly fourteen dollars in that bag,' said Magrat, 'not counting the foreign money.'

'Hmm.'

Granny Weatherwax sat down on the bunk and drummed her fingers on the woodwork. There was a faraway look in her eyes. The phrase 'card sharp' had never reached her side of the Ramtops, where people were friendly and direct and, should they encounter a professional cheat, tended to nail his hand to the table in an easy and outgoing manner without asking him what he called himself. But human nature was the same everywhere.

'You're not upset, are you, Esme?' said Nanny anxiously.

'Hmm.'

'I expect I can soon pick up a new broom when we get home.'

'Hm . . . *what*?'

'After she lost all her money she bet her broom,' said Magrat triumphantly.

'Have we got any money at all?' said Granny.

A trawl of various pockets and knicker legs produced forty-seven pence.

'Right,' said Granny. She scooped it up. 'That ought to be enough. To start with, anyway. Where are these men?'

'What are you going to do?' said Magrat.

'I'm going to play cards,' said Granny.

'You can't do that!' said Magrat, who had recognized the gleam in Granny's eye. 'You're going to use magic to win! You mustn't use magic to win! Not to affect the laws of chance! That's *wicked*!'

*   *   *

The boat was practically a floating town, and in the balmy night air no-one bothered much about going indoors. The riverboat's flat deck was dotted with groups of dwarfs, trolls and humans, lounging among the cargo. Granny threaded her way between them and headed for the long saloon that ran almost the entire length of the boat. There was the sound of revelry within.

The riverboats were the quickest and easiest transport for hundreds of miles. On them you got, as Granny would put it, all sorts, and the riverboats going downstream were always crowded with a certain type of opportunist as Fat Lunchtime approached.

She walked into the saloon. An onlooker might have thought it had a magic doorway. Granny Weatherwax, as she walked towards it, strode as she usually strode. As soon as she passed through, though, she was suddenly a bent old woman, hobbling along, and a sight to touch all but the wickedest heart.

She approached the bar, and then stopped. Behind it was the biggest mirror Granny had ever seen. She stared fixedly at it, but it seemed safe enough. Well, she'd have to risk it.

She hunched her back a little more and addressed the barman.

'Excuzee moir, young homme,' she began.*

The barman gave her a disinterested look and went on polishing a glass.

---

*Something about Nanny Ogg rubbed off on people.

'What can I do for you, old crone?' he said.

There was only the faintest suggestion of a flicker in Granny's expression of elderly imbecility.

'Oh . . . you can understand me?' she said.

'We get all sorts on the river,' said the barman.

'Then I was wondering if you could be so kind as to loan me a deck, I thinks it's called, of cards,' quavered Granny.

'Going to play a game of Old Maid, are you?' said the barman.

There was a chilly flicker across Granny's eyes again as she said, 'No. Just Patience. I'd like to try and get the hang of it.'

He reached under the counter and tossed a greasy pack towards her.

She thanked him effusively and tottered off to a small table in the shadows, where she dealt a few cards randomly on the drink-ringed surface and stared at them.

It was only a few minutes later that a gentle hand was laid on her shoulder. She looked up into a friendly, open face that anyone would lend money to. A gold tooth glittered as the man spoke.

'Excuse me, good mother,' he said, 'but my friends and I' – he gestured to some more welcoming faces at a nearby table – 'would feel much more comfortable in ourselves if you were to join us. It can be very dangerous for a woman travelling by herself.'

Granny Weatherwax smiled nicely at him, and then waved vaguely at her cards.

'I can never remember whether the ones are worth

more or less than the pictures,' she said. 'Forget my own head next, I expect!'

They all laughed. Granny hobbled to the other table. She took the vacant seat, which put the mirror right behind her shoulder.

She smiled to herself and then leaned forward, all eagerness.

'So tell me,' she said, 'how do you play this game, then?'

All witches are very conscious of stories. They can *feel* stories, in the same way that a bather in a little pool can feel the unexpected trout.

Knowing how stories work is almost all the battle.

For example, when an obvious innocent sits down with three experienced card sharpers and says 'How do you play this game, then?', someone is about to be shaken down until their teeth fall out.

Magrat and Nanny Ogg sat side by side on the narrow bunk. Nanny was distractedly tickling Greebo's stomach, while he purred.

'She'll get into terrible trouble if she uses magic to win,' said Magrat. 'And you know how she hates losing,' she added.

Granny Weatherwax was not a good loser. From her point of view, losing was something that happened to other people.

'It's her eggo,' said Nanny Ogg. 'Everyone's got one o' them. A eggo. And she's got a great big one. Of course, that's all part of bein' a witch, having a big eggo.'

'She's *bound* to use magic,' said Magrat. 'It's tempting Fate, using magic in a game of chance,' said Nanny Ogg. 'Cheatin's all right. That's practic'ly *fair*. I mean, anyone can cheat. But using magic – well, it's tempting Fate.'

'No. Not Fate,' said Magrat darkly.

Nanny Ogg shivered.

'Come on,' said Magrat. 'We can't let her do it.'

'It's her eggo,' said Nanny Ogg weakly. 'Terrible thing, a big eggo.'

'I got', said Granny, 'three little pictures of kings and suchlike and three of them funny number one cards.'

The three men beamed and winked at one another.

'That's Triple Onion!' said the one who had introduced Granny to the table, and who had turned out to be called Mister Frank.

'And that's good, is it?' said Granny.

'It means you win yet again, dear lady!' He pushed a pile of pennies towards her.

'Gosh,' said Granny. 'That means I've got . . . what would it be . . . almost five dollars now?'

'Can't understand it,' said Mister Frank. 'It must be the famous beginner's luck, eh?'

'Soon be poor men if it goes on like this,' said one of his companions.

'She'll have the coats off our backs, right enough,' said the third man. 'Haha.'

'Think we should give up right now,' said Mister Frank. 'Haha.'

'Haha.'

'Haha.'

'Oh, I want to go on,' said Granny, grinning anxiously. 'I'm just getting the hang of it.'

'Well, you'd better give us a sporting chance to win a little bit back, haha,' said Mister Frank. 'Haha.'

'Haha.'

'Haha.'

'Haha. What about half a dollar a stake? Haha?'

'Oh, I reckon she'll want a dollar a stake, a sporting lady like her,' said the third man.

'Haha!'

Granny looked down at her pile of pennies. For a moment she looked uncertain and then, they could see, she realized: how much could she lose, the way the cards were going?

'Yes!' she said. 'A dollar a stake!' She blushed. 'This is *exciting*, isn't it!'

'Yeah,' said Mister Frank. He drew the pack towards him.

There was a horrible noise. All three men stared at the bar, where shards of mirror were cascading to the floor.

'What happened?'

Granny gave him a sweet old smile. She hadn't appeared to look around.

'I reckon the glass he was polishing must of slipped out of his hand and smashed right into the mirror,' she said. 'I do hope he don't have to pay for it out of his wages, the poor boy.'

The men exchanged glances.

'Come on,' said Granny, 'I've got my dollar all ready.'

Mister Frank looked nervously at the ravaged frame. Then he shrugged.

The movement dislodged something somewhere. There was a muffled snapping noise, like a mouse-trap carrying out the last rites. Mister Frank went white and gripped his sleeve. A small metal contraption, all springs and twisted metal, fell out. A crumpled-up Ace of Cups was tangled up in it.

'Whoops,' said Granny.

Magrat peered through the window into the saloon. 'What's she doin' now?' hissed Nanny Ogg.

'She's grinning again,' said Magrat.

Nanny Ogg shook her head. 'Eggo,' she said.

Granny Weatherwax had that method of play that has reduced professional gamblers to incoherent rage throughout the multiverse.

She held her cards tightly cupped in her hands a few inches from her face, allowing the merest fraction of each one to protrude. She glared at them as if daring them to offend her. And she never seemed to take her eyes off them, except to watch the dealing.

And she took far too long. And she never, ever, took risks.

After twenty-five minutes she was down one dollar and Mister Frank was sweating. Granny had already helpfully pointed out three times that he'd accidentally dealt cards off the bottom of the deck, and she'd asked for another pack 'because, look, this one's got all little marks on the back.'

It was her eyes, that was what it was. Twice he'd folded on a perfectly good three-card Onion only to find that she'd been holding a lousy double Bagel. Then the third time, thinking he'd worked out her play, he'd called her out and run a decent flush right into the maw of a five-card Onion that the old bag must have been patiently constructing for ages. And then – his knuckles went white – and then the dreadful, terrible hag had said, 'Have I won? With all these little cards? Gorsh – aren't I the lucky one!'

And then she started humming when she looked at her cards. Normally, the three of them would have welcomed this sort of thing. The teeth tappers, the eyebrow raisers, the ear rubbers – they were as good as money in the sock under the mattress, to a man who knew how to read such things. But the appalling old crone was as transparent as a lump of coal. And the humming was . . . insistent. You found yourself trying to follow the tune. It made your teeth tingle. Next thing you were glumly watching while she laid down a measly Broken Flush in front of your even more measly two-card Onion and said, 'What, is it me again?'

Mister Frank was desperately trying to remember how to play cards without his sleeve device, a handy mirror and a marked deck. In the teeth of a hum like a fingernail down a blackboard.

It wasn't as if the ghastly old creature even knew how to play properly.

After an hour she was four dollars ahead and

when she said, 'I *am* a lucky girl!' Mister Frank bit through his tongue.

And then he got a natural Great Onion. There was no realistic way to beat a Great Onion. It was something that happened to you once or twice in a lifetime.

She folded! The old bitch folded! She abandoned one blasted dollar and she folded!

Magrat peered through the window again.

'What's happening?' said Nanny.

'They all look very angry.'

Nanny took off her hat and removed her pipe. She lit it and tossed the match overboard. 'Ah. She'll be humming, you mark my words. She's got a very annoying hum, has Esme.' Nanny looked satisfied. 'Has she started cleaning out her ear yet?'

'Don't think so.'

'No one cleans out her ear like Esme.'

She was cleaning out her ear!

It was done in a very ladylike way, and the daft old baggage probably wasn't even aware she was doing it. She just kept inserting her little finger in her ear and swivelling it around. It made a noise like a small pool cue being chalked.

It was displacement activity, that's what it was. They all cracked in the end . . .

She folded again! And it had taken him bloody five bloody minutes to put together a bloody double Onion!

*   *   *

'I remember,' said Nanny Ogg, 'when she come over our house for the party when King Verence got crowned and we played Chase My Neighbour Up the Passage with the kiddies for ha'pennies. She accused Jason's youngest of cheating and sulked for a week afterwards.'

'Was he cheating?'

'I expect so,' said Nanny proudly. 'The trouble with Esme is that she don't know how to lose. She's never had much practice.'

'Lobsang Dibbler says sometimes you have to lose in order to win,' said Magrat.

'Sounds daft to me,' said Nanny. 'That's Yen Buddhism, is it?'

'No. They're the ones who say you have to have lots of money to win,' said Magrat.* 'In the Path of the Scorpion, the way to win is to lose every fight except the last one. You use the enemy's strength against himself.'

'What, you get him to hit himself, sort of thing?' said Nanny. 'Sounds daft.'

Magrat glowered.

'What do you know about it?' she said, with uncharacteristic sharpness.

'What?'

'Well, I'm fed up!' said Magrat. 'At least I'm making an effort to learn things! I don't go around

---

*The Yen Buddhists are the richest religious sect in the universe. They hold that the accumulation of money is a great evil and burden to the soul. They therefore, regardless of personal hazard, see it as their unpleasant duty to acquire as much as possible in order to reduce the risk to innocent people.

just bullying people and acting bad-tempered all the time!'

Nanny took her pipe out of her mouth.

'I'm not bad-tempered,' she said mildly.

'I wasn't talking about you!'

'Well, Esme's always been bad-tempered,' said Nanny. 'It comes natural to her.'

'And she hardly ever does real magic. What good is being a witch if you don't do magic? Why doesn't she use it to help people?'

Nanny peered at her through the pipe smoke.

''Cos she knows how good she'd be at it, I suppose,' she said. 'Anyway, I've known her a long time. Known the whole family. All the Weatherwaxes is good at magic, even the men. They've got this magical streak in 'em. Kind of a curse. Anyway . . . she thinks you can't help people with magic. Not *properly*. It's true, too.'

'Then what good—?'

Nanny prodded at the pipe with a match.

'I seem to recall she come over and helped you out when you had that spot of plague in your village,' she said. 'Worked the clock around, I recall. Never known her not treat someone ill who needed it, even when they, you know, were pretty oozy. And when the big ole troll that lives under Broken Mountain came down for help because his wife was sick and everyone threw rocks at him, I remember it was Esme that went back with him and delivered the baby. Hah . . . then when old Chickenwire Hopkins threw a rock at *Esme* a little while afterwards all his barns was mysteriously trampled flat in the night.

She always said you can't help people with magic, but you can help them with skin. By doin' real things, she meant.'

'I'm not saying she's not basically a nice person—' Magrat began.

'Hah! *I* am. You'd have to go a long day's journey to find someone basically nastier than Esme,' said Nanny Ogg, 'and this is *me* sayin' it. She knows exactly what she is. She was born to be good and she don't like it.'

Nanny tapped her pipe out on the rail and turned back to the saloon.

'What you got to understand about Esme, my girl,' she said, 'is that she's got a psycholology as well as a big eggo. I'm damn glad I ain't.'

Granny was twelve dollars ahead. Everything else in the saloon had stopped. You could hear the distant splash of the paddles and the cry of the leadman.

Granny won another five dollars with a three-card Onion.

'What do you mean, a psycholology?' said Magrat. 'Have you been reading books?'

Nanny ignored her.

'The thing to watch out for now,' she said, 'is when she goes "tch, tch, tch" under her breath. That comes after the ear-cleanin'. It gen'rally means she's plannin' somethin'.'

Mister Frank drummed his fingers on the table, realized to his horror that he was doing it, and bought three new cards to cover his confusion. The old baggage didn't appear to notice.

He stared at the new hand.

He ventured two dollars and bought one more card.

He stared again.

What were the odds, he thought, against getting a Great Onion twice in one day?

The important thing was not to panic.

'I think,' he heard himself say, 'that I may hazard another two dollars.'

He glanced at his companions. They obediently folded, one after another.

'Well, I don't know,' said Granny, apparently talking to her cards. She cleaned her ear again. 'Tch, tch, tch. What d'you call it when, you know, you want to put more money in, sort of thing?'

'It's called raising,' said Mister Frank, his knuckles going white.

'I'll do one of them raisins, then. Five dollars, I think.'

Mister Frank's knees ground together.

'I'll see you and raise you ten dollars,' he snapped.

'I'll do that too,' said Granny.

'I can go another twenty dollars.'

'I—' Granny looked down, suddenly crestfallen. 'I've . . . got a broomstick.'

A tiny alarm bell rang somewhere at the back of Mister Frank's mind, but now he was galloping headlong to victory.

'Right!'

He spread the cards on the table.

The crowd sighed.

He began to pull the pot towards him.

Granny's hand closed over his wrist.

'I ain't put *my* cards down yet,' she said archly.

'You don't need to,' snapped Mister Frank. 'There's no chance you could beat that, madam.'

'I can if I can Cripple it,' said Granny. 'That's why it's called Cripple Mister Onion, ain't it?'

He hesitated.

'But – but – you could only do that if you had a perfect nine-card run,' he burbled, staring into the depths of her eyes.

Granny sat back.

'You know,' she said calmly, 'I *thought* I had rather a lot of these black pointy ones. That's good, is it?'

She spread the hand. The collective audience made a sort of little gasping noise, in unison.

Mister Frank looked around wildly.

'Oh, very well done, madam,' said an elderly gentleman. There was a round of polite applause from the crowd. The big, inconvenient crowd.

'Er . . . yes,' said Mister Frank. 'Yes. Well done. You're a very quick learner, aren't you.'

'Quicker'n you. You owe me fifty-five dollars and a broomstick,' said Granny.

Magrat and Nanny Ogg were waiting for her as she swept out.

'Here's your broom,' she snapped. 'And I hopes you've got all your stuff together, 'cos we're leaving.'

'Why?' said Magrat.

'Because as soon as it gets quiet, some men are going to come looking for us.'

They scurried after her towards their tiny cabin.

'You weren't using magic?' said Magrat.

'No.'

'And not cheating?' said Nanny Ogg.

'No. Just headology,' said Granny.

'Where did you learn to play like that?' Nanny demanded.

Granny stopped. They cannoned into her.

'Remember last winter, when Old Mother Dismass was taken really bad and I went and sat up with her every night for almost a month?'

'Yes?'

'You sit up every night dealing Cripple Mister Onion with someone who's got a detached retina in her second sight and you soon learn how to play,' said Granny.

Dear Jason and everyone,

What you get more of in foreign parts is smells, I am getting good at them. Esme is shouting at everyone, I think she thinks they're bein forein just to Spite her, don't know when I last saw her enjoi herselfe so much. Mind you they need a good Shakin up if you ask me, for lunch we stopped somehwere and they did Steak Tartere and they acted VERY snooty just becos I wanted myne well done. All the best, MUM

The moon was closer here.

The orbit of the Discworld's moon meant that

it was quite high when it passed over the high Ramtops. Here, nearer to the Rim, it was bigger And more orange.

'Like a pumpkin,' said Nanny Ogg.

'I thought we said we weren't going to mention pumpkins,' said Magrat,

'Well, we didn't have any supper,' said Nanny.

And there was another thing. Except during the height of summer the witches weren't used to warm nights. It didn't seem right, gliding along under a big orange moon over dark foliage that clicked and buzzed and whirred with insects.

'We must be far enough from the river now,' said Magrat. 'Can't we land, Granny? No one could have followed us!'

Granny Weatherwax looked down. The river in this countryside meandered in huge glistening curves, taking twenty miles to cover five. The land between the snaking water was a patchwork of hillsides and woodlands. A distant glow might have been Genua itself.

'Riding a broomstick all night is a right pain in the itinerant,' said Nanny.

'Oh, all *right*.'

'There's a town over there,' said Magrat. 'And a castle.'

'Oh, not another one . . .'

'It's a nice little castle,' said Magrat. 'Can't we just call in? I'm fed up with inns.'

Granny looked down. She had very good night vision.

'Are you sure that's a castle?' she said.

'I can see the turrets and everything,' said Magrat. 'Of course it's a castle.'

'Hmm. I can see more than turrets,' said Granny. 'I think we'd better have a look at this, Gytha.'

There was never any noise in the sleeping castle, except in the late summer when ripe berries fell off the bramble vines and burst softly on the floor. And sometimes birds would try to nest in the thorn thickets that now filled the throne room from floor to ceiling, but they never got very far before they, too, fell asleep. Apart from that, you'd need very keen hearing indeed to hear the growth of shoots and the opening of buds.

It had been like this for ten years. There was no sound in the—

'Open up there!'

'Bony fidy travellers seeking sucker!'

—no sound in the—

'Here, give us a leg up, Magrat. Right. Now . . .' There was a tinkle of broken glass. 'You've broken their window!'

—*not a sound* in the—

'You'll have to offer to pay for it, you know.'

The castle gate swung open slowly. Nanny Ogg peered around it at the other two witches, while pulling thorns and burrs from her hair.

'It's bloody disgusting in here,' she said. 'There's people asleep all over the place with spiders' webs all over 'em. You were right, Esme. There's been magic going on.'

The witches pushed their way through the

overgrown castle. Dust and leaves had covered the carpets. Young sycamores were making a spirited attempt to take over the courtyard. Vines festooned every wall.

Granny Weatherwax pulled a slumbering soldier to his feet. Dust billowed off his clothes.

'Wake up,' she demanded.

'Fzhtft,' said the soldier, and slumped back.

'It's like that everywhere,' said Magrat, fighting her way through a thicket of bracken that was growing up from the kitchen regions. 'There's the cooks all snoring and nothing but mould in the pots! There's even mice asleep in the pantry!'

'Hmm,' said Granny. 'There'll be a spinning wheel at the bottom of all this, you mark my words.'

'A Black Aliss job?' said Nanny Ogg.

'Looks like it,' said Granny. Then she added, quietly, 'Or someone like her.'

'Now *there* was a witch who knew how stories worked,' said Nanny. 'She used to be in as many as three of 'em at once.'

Even Magrat knew about Black Aliss. She was said to have been the greatest witch who ever lived – not exactly *bad*, but so powerful it was sometimes hard to tell the difference. When it came to sending palaces to sleep for a hundred years or getting princesses to spin straw into Glod,* no one did it better than Black Aliss.

'I met her once,' said Nanny, as they climbed the

---

*Black Aliss wasn't very good with words either. They had to give her quite a lot of money to go away and not make a scene.

castle's main staircase, which was a cascade of Old Man's Trousers. 'Old Deliria Skibbly took me to see her once, when I was a girl. Of course, she was getting pretty . . . eccentric by then. Gingerbread houses, that kind of thing.' She spoke sadly, as one might talk about an elderly relative who'd taken to wearing her underwear outside her clothes.

'That must have been before those two children shut her up in her own oven?' said Magrat, untangling her sleeve from a briar.

'Yeah. Sad, that. I mean, she didn't really ever *eat* anyone,' said Nanny. 'Well. Not often. I mean, there was talk, but . . .'

'That's what happens,' said Granny. 'You get too involved with stories, you get confused. You don't know what's really real and what isn't. And they get you in the end. They send you weird in the head. I don't like stories. They're not real. I don't like things that ain't real.'

She pushed open a door.

'Ah. A chamber,' she said sourly. 'Could even be a bower.'

'Doesn't the stuff grow quickly!' said Magrat.

'Part of the time spell,' said Granny. 'Ah. There she is. Knew there'd be someone somewhere.'

There was a figure lying on a bed, in a thicket of rose bushes.

'And there's the spinning wheel,' said Nanny, pointing to a shape just visible in a clump of ivy.

'Don't touch it!' said Granny.

'Don't worry, I'll pick it up by the treadle and pitch it out of the window.'

'How do you know all this?' said Magrat.

''Cos it's a rural myth,' said Nanny. 'It's happened lots of times.'

Granny Weatherwax and Magrat looked down at the sleeping figure of a girl of about thirteen, almost silvery under the dust and pollen.

'Isn't she pretty,' sighed Magrat, the generous-hearted.

From behind them came the crash of a spinning wheel on some distant cobbles, and then Nanny Ogg appeared, brushing her hands.

'Seen it happen a dozen times,' she said.

'No you ain't,' said Granny.

'Once, anyway,' said Nanny, unabashed. 'And I *heard* about it dozens of times. Everyone has. Rural myth, like I said. Everyone's heard about it happening in their cousin's friend's neighbour's village—'

'That's because it does,' said Granny.

Granny picked up the girl's wrist.

'She's asleep because she'll have got a—' Nanny said.

Granny turned.

'I know, I know. I know, right? I know as well as you. You think I don't know?' She bent over the limp hand. 'That's fairy godmothering, this is,' she added, half to herself. 'Always do it *impressively*. Always meddling, always trying to be in control! Hah! Someone got a bit of poison? Send everyone to sleep for a hundred years! Do it the *easy* way. All this for one prick. As if that was the end of the world.' She paused. Nanny Ogg was standing behind her. There was no possible way she could have detected her expression. 'Gytha?'

'Yes, Esme?' said Nanny Ogg innocently.

'I can *feel* you grinnin'. You can save the tu'penny-ha'penny psycholology for them as wants it.'

Granny shut her eyes and muttered a few words.

'Shall I use my wand?' said Magrat hesitantly.

'Don't you dare,' said Granny, and went back to her muttering.

Nanny nodded. 'She's definitely getting a bit of colour back,' she said.

A few minutes later the girl opened her eyes and stared up blearily at Granny Weatherwax.

'Time to get up,' said Granny, in an unusually cheerful voice, 'you're missing the best part of the decade.'

The girl tried to focus on Nanny, then on Magrat, and then looked back at Granny Weatherwax.

'You?' she said.

Granny raised her eyebrows and looked at the other two.

'Me?'

'You are – still here?'

'Still?' said Granny. 'Never been here before in my life, Miss.'

'But—' the girl looked bewildered. And frightened, Magrat noticed.

'I'm like that myself in the mornings, dear,' said Nanny Ogg, taking the girl's other hand and patting it. 'Never at my best till I've had a cup of tea. I expect everyone else'll be waking up any minute. Of course, it'll take 'em a while to clean the rats' nests out of the kettles – Esme?'

Granny was staring at a dust-covered shape on the wall.

'Meddling . . .' she whispered.

'What's up, Esme?'

Granny Weatherwax strode across the room and wiped the dust off a huge ornate mirror.

'Hah!' she said, and spun around. 'We'll be going now,' she said.

'But I thought we were going to have a rest. I mean, it's nearly dawn,' said Magrat.

'No sense in outstaying our welcome,' said Granny, as she left the room.

'But we haven't even *had* a . . .' Magrat began. She glanced at the mirror. It was a big oval one, in a gilt frame. It looked perfectly normal. It wasn't like Granny Weatherwax to be frightened of her own reflection.

'She's in one of her moods again,' said Nanny Ogg. 'Come on. No sense in staying here.' She patted the bewildered princess on the head. 'Cheerio, Miss. A couple of weeks with a broom and an axe and you'll soon have the old place looking like new.'

'She looked as if she recognized Granny,' said Magrat, as they followed the stiff hurrying figure of Esme Weatherwax down the stairs.

'Well, we know she doesn't, don't we,' said Nanny Ogg. 'Esme has never been in these parts in her life.'

'But I still don't see why we have to rush off,'

Magrat persisted. 'I expect people will be jolly grateful that we've broken the spell and everything.'

The rest of the palace was waking up. They jogged past guards staring in amazement at their cobwebbed uniforms and the bushes that were growing everywhere. As they crossed the forested courtyard an older man in faded robes staggered out of a doorway and leaned against the wall, trying to get his bearings. Then he saw the accelerating figure of Granny Weatherwax.

'You?' he shouted, and, 'Guards!'

Nanny Ogg didn't hesitate. She snatched Magrat's elbow and broke into a run, catching up with Granny Weatherwax at the castle gates. A guard who was better at mornings than his colleague staggered forward and made an attempt to bar their way with his pike, but Granny just pushed at it and swivelled him around gently.

Then they were outside and running for the broomsticks leaning against a convenient tree. Granny snatched at hers without stopping and, for once, it fired up on almost the first attempt.

An arrow whiffled past her hat and stuck in a branch.

'I don't call *that* gratitude,' said Magrat, as the brooms glided up and over the trees.

'A lot of people are never at their best just after waking up,' said Nanny.

'Everyone seemed to think they knew you, Granny,' said Magrat.

Granny's broomstick jerked in the wind.

'They didn't!' she shouted. 'They never saw me before, all right?'

They flew on in troubled silence for a while.

Then Magrat, who in Nanny Ogg's opinion had an innocent talent for treading on dangerous ground, said: 'I wonder if we did the right thing? I'm sure it was a job for a handsome prince.'

'Hah!' said Granny, who was riding ahead. 'And what good would that be? Cutting your way through a bit of bramble is how you can tell he's going to be a good husband, is it? That's fairy godmotherly thinking, that is! Goin' around inflicting happy endings on people whether they wants them or not, eh?'

'There's nothing wrong with happy endings,' said Magrat hotly.

'Listen, happy endings is fine if they *turn out* happy,' said Granny, glaring at the sky. 'But you can't make 'em for other people. Like the only way you could make a happy marriage is by cuttin' their heads off as soon as they say "I do", yes? You can't make happiness . . .'

Granny Weatherwax stared at the distant city.

'All you can do,' she said, 'is make an ending.'

They had breakfast in a forest clearing. It was grilled pumpkin. The dwarf bread was brought out for inspection. But it was miraculous, the dwarf bread. No one ever went hungry when they had some dwarf bread to avoid. You only had to look at it for a moment, and instantly you could think of dozens of things you'd rather eat. Your boots, for example. Mountains. Raw sheep. Your own foot.

Then they tried to get some sleep. At least, Nanny and Magrat did. But all it meant was that they lay awake and listened to Granny Weatherwax muttering under her breath. They'd never seen her so upset.

Afterwards, Nanny suggested that they walk for a while. It was a nice day, she said. This was an interesting kind of forest, she said, with lots of new herbs which could do with bein' looked at. Everyone'd feel better for a stroll in the sunshine, she said. It'd improve their tempers.

And it was, indeed, a nice forest. After half an hour or so, even Granny Weatherwax was prepared to admit that in certain respects it wasn't totally foreign and shoddy. Magrat wandered off the path occasionally, picking flowers. Nanny even sang a few verses of 'A Wizard's Staff Has A Knob On The End' with no more than a couple of token protests from the other two.

But there was still something wrong. Nanny Ogg and Magrat could feel something between them and Granny Weatherwax, some sort of mental wall, something important deliberately hidden and unsaid. Witches usually had few secrets from one another, if only because they were all so nosy that there was never any chance to *have* secrets. It was worrying.

And then they turned a corner by a stand of huge oak trees and met the little girl in the red cloak.

She was skipping along in the middle of the path, singing a song that was simpler and a good deal cleaner than any in Nanny Ogg's repertoire. She didn't see the witches until she was almost on top of them. She stopped, and then smiled innocently.

'Hello, old women,' she said.

'Ahem,' said Magrat.

Granny Weatherwax bent down.

'What're you doing out in the forest all by yourself, young lady?'

'I'm taking this basket of goodies to my granny,' said the girl.

Granny straightened up, a faraway look in her eyes.

'Esme,' said Nanny Ogg urgently.

'I know. I know,' said Granny.

Magrat leaned down and set her face in the idiot grimace generally used by adults who'd love to be good with children and don't stand a dog's chance of ever achieving it. 'Er. Tell me, Miss . . . did your mother tell you to watch out for any bad wolves that might happen to be in the vicinity?'

'That's right.'

'And your granny . . .' said Nanny Ogg. 'I guess she's a bit bed-bound at the moment, right?'

'That's why I'm taking her this basket of goodies—' the child began.

'Thought so.'

'Do you know my granny?' said the child.

'Ye-ess,' said Granny Weatherwax. 'In a way.'

'It happened over Skund way when I was a girl,' said Nanny Ogg quietly. 'They never even found the gran—'

'And where is your granny's cottage, little girl?' said Granny Weatherwax loudly, nudging Nanny sharply in the ribs.

The girl pointed up a side track.

'You're not the wicked witch, are you?' she said.

Nanny Ogg coughed.

'Me? No. We're – we're—' Granny began.

'Fairies,' said Magrat.

Granny Weatherwax's mouth dropped open. Such an explanation would never have occurred to her.

'Only my mummy warned me about the wicked witch too,' said the girl. She gave Magrat a sharp look. 'What kind of fairies?'

'Er. Flower fairies?' said Magrat. 'Look, I've got a wand—'

'Which ones?'

'What?'

'Which flowers?'

'Er,' said Magrat. 'Well. I'm . . . Fairy Tulip and that's . . .' she avoided looking directly at Granny, '. . . Fairy . . . Daisy . . . and this is . . .'

'Fairy Hedgehog,' said Nanny Ogg.

This addition to the supernatural pantheon was given due consideration.

'You can't be Fairy Hedgehog,' said the child, after some thought. 'A hedgehog's not a flower.'

'How do you know?'

''Cos it's got spikes.'

'So's holly. *And* thistles.'

'Oh.'

'And I've got a wand,' said Magrat. Only now did she risk a look at Fairy Daisy.

'We ought to be getting along,' said Granny Weatherwax. 'You just stay here with Fairy Tulip, I think it was, and we'll just go and make sure your granny's all right. All right?'

'I bet it's not a real wand,' said the child, ignoring her and facing Magrat with a child's unerring ability to find a weak link in any chain. 'I bet it can't turn things into things.'

'Well—' Magrat began.

'I *bet*,' said the girl, '*I* bet you can't turn that tree stump over there into . . . into . . . into a *pumpkin*. Haha, bet you anything you can't. Bet you a trillion dollars you can't turn that stump into a pumpkin.'

'I can see the two of you are going to get along fine,' said Fairy Hedgehog. 'We won't be long.'

Two broomsticks skimmed low above the forest path.

'Could just be coincidence,' said Nanny Ogg.

''T'aint,' said Granny. 'The child even has a red cloak on!'

'I had a red cloak when I was fifteen,' said Nanny.

'Yes, but your granny lived next door. You didn't have to worry about wolves when you visited her,' said Granny.

'Except old Sumpkins the lodger.'

'Yes, but that was just coincidence.'

A trail of blue smoke drifted among the trees ahead of them. Somewhere away to one side there was the sound of a falling tree.

'Woodcutters!' said Nanny. 'It's all right if there's woodcutters! One of them rushes in—'

'That's only what children get told,' said Granny,

as they sped onwards. 'Anyway, that's no good to the grandmother, is it? She's already *been* et!'

'I always hated that story,' said Nanny. 'No one ever cares what happens to poor defenceless old women.'

The path vanished abruptly on the edge of a glade. Hemmed in by the trees was a straggly kitchen garden, in which a few pathetic stalks fought for what little sun there was. In the middle of the garden was what had to be a thatched cottage because no one would build a haystack that badly.

They leapt off the broomsticks, leaving them to drift to a halt in the bushes, and hammered on the cottage door.

'We could be too late,' said Nanny. 'The wolf might—'

After a while there was the muffled sound of someone shuffling across the floor within, and then the door opened a crack. A suspicious eye was visible in the gloom.

'Yes?' said a small and quavering voice from somewhere beneath the eye.

'Are you grandmother?' Granny Weatherwax demanded.

'Are you the taxgatherers, dear?'

'No, ma'am, we're—'

'—fairies,' said Fairy Hedgehog quickly.

'I don't open the door to people I don't know, dear,' said the voice, and then it took on a slightly petulant tone. "Specially people who never does the washing up even after I leaves out a bowl of nearly fresh milk for 'em.'

'We'd like to talk to you for a few minutes,' said Fairy Daisy.

'Yes? Have you got any identification, dear?'

'I *know* we've got the right grandmother,' said Fairy Hedgehog. 'There's a family likeness. She's got big ears.'

'Look, it's not *her* that's got the big ears,' snapped Fairy Daisy. 'It'll be the wolf that's got big ears. That's the whole point. Don't you ever pay attention?'

The grandmother watched them with interest. After a lifetime of believing in them she was seeing fairies for the first time, and it was an experience. Granny Weatherwax caught her perplexed expression.

'Put it like this, ma'am,' she said, in a despotically reasonable tone of voice, 'how would you like to be eaten alive by a wolf?'

'I don't think I would like that, dear, no,' said the hidden grandmother.

'The alternative's us,' said Granny.

'Lawks. Are you sure?'

'On our word as fairies,' said Fairy Hedgehog.

'Well. Really? All right. You can come in. But none of your tricks. And mind you do the washing up. You haven't got a pot of gold about you, have you?'

'That's pixies, isn't it?'

'No, they're the ones in wells. It's goblins she means.'

'Don't be daft. They're the ones you get under bridges.'

'That's trolls. Everyone knows that's trolls.'

'Not us, anyway.'

'Oh,' said the grandmother. 'I might have known.'

Magrat liked to think she was good with children, and worried that she wasn't. She didn't like them very much, and worried about this too. Nanny Ogg seemed to be effortlessly good with children by alternately and randomly giving them either a sweet or a thick ear, while Granny Weatherwax ignored them for most of the time and that seemed to work just as well. Whereas Magrat *cared*. It didn't seem fair.

'Bet you a million trillion zillion dollars you can't turn *that* bush into a pumpkin,' said the child.

'But, look, all the others got turned into pumpkins,' Magrat pointed out.

'It's bound not to work sooner or later,' said the child placidly.

Magrat looked helplessly at the wand. She'd tried everything – wishing, sub-vocalizing and even, when she'd thought the other witches were out of earshot, banging it against things and shouting, 'Anything but pumpkins!'

'You don't know how to do it really, do you,' stated the child.

'Tell me,' said Magrat, 'you said your mummy knows about the big bad wolf in the woods, didn't you?'

'That's right.'

'But *nevertheless* she sent you out by yourself to take those goodies to your granny?'

'That's right. Why?'

'Nothing. Just thinking. And you owe me a million trillion zillion squillion dollars.'

There's a certain freemasonry about grandmothers, with the added benefit that no one has to stand on one leg or recite any oaths in order to join. Once inside the cottage, and with a kettle on the boil, Nanny Ogg was quite at home. Greebo stretched out in front of the meagre fire and dozed off as the witches tried to explain.

'I don't see how a wolf can get in here, dear,' said the grandmother kindly. 'I mean, they're *wolves*. They can't open doors.'

Granny Weatherwax twitched aside a rag of curtain and glared out at the clearing.

'We know,' she said.

Nanny Ogg nodded towards the little bed in an alcove by the fireplace.

'Is that where you always sleep?' she said.

'When I'm feeling poorly, dear. Other times I sleeps in the attic.'

'I should get along up there now, if I was you. And take my cat up with you, will you? We don't want him getting in the way.'

'Is this the bit where you clean the house and do all the washing for a saucer of milk?' said the grandmother hopefully.

'Could be. You never know.'

'Funny, dear. I was expecting you to be shorter—'

'We get out in the fresh air a lot,' said Nanny. 'Off you go now.'

That left the two of them. Granny Weatherwax looked around the cave-like room. The rushes on the floor were well on the way to composthood. Soot encrusted the cobwebs on the ceiling.

The only way housework could be done in this place was with a shovel or, for preference, a match.

'Funny, really,' said Nanny, when the old woman had climbed the rickety stairs. 'She's younger'n me. Mind you, I take exercise.'

'You never took exercise in your life,' said Granny Weatherwax, still watching the bushes. 'You never did anything you didn't want to do.'

'That's what I mean,' said Nanny happily. 'Look, Esme, I still say this could all be just—'

'It ain't! I can *feel* the story. Someone's been making stories happen in these parts, I know it.'

'And you know who, too. Don't you, Esme?' said Nanny slyly.

She saw Granny look around wildly at the grubby walls.

'I reckon she's too poor to afford a mirror,' said Nanny. 'I ain't blind, Esme. And I know mirrors and fairy godmothers go together. So what's going on?'

'I ain't saying. I don't want to look a fool if I'm wrong. I'm not going to – there's something coming!'

Nanny Ogg pressed her nose against the dirty window.

'Can't see anything.'

'The bushes moved. Get into the bed!'

'Me? I thought it was you who was going into the bed!'

'Can't imagine why you'd think that.'

'No. Come to think of it, neither can I,' said Nanny wearily. She picked up the floppy mob-cap from the bedpost, put it on, and slid under the patchwork quilt.

''Ere, this mattress is stuffed with straw!'

'You won't have to lie on it for long.'

'It prickles! And I think there's *things* in it.'

Something bumped against the wall of the house. The witches fell silent.

There was a snuffling noise under the back door.

'You know,' whispered Nanny, as they waited, 'the scullery's terrible. There's no firewood. And there's hardly any food. And there's a jug of milk that's practically on the march—'

Granny sidled quickly across the room to the fireplace, and then back to her station by the front door.

After a moment there was a scrabbling at the latch, as if it was being operated by someone who was unfamiliar either with doors or with fingers.

The door creaked open slowly.

There was an overwhelming smell of musk and wet fur.

Uncertain footsteps tottered across the floor and towards the figure huddling under the bed-clothes.

Nanny raised the mob-cap's floppy frill just enough to see out.

'Wotcha,' she said, and then, 'Oh, blimey, I never realized you had teeth *that* big – '

Granny Weatherwax pushed the door shut and

stepped forward briskly. The wolf spun around, a paw raised protectively.

'Nooaaaaaw!'

Granny hesitated for a second, and then hit it very hard on the head with a cast-iron frying pan.

The wolf crumpled.

Nanny Ogg swung her legs out of the bed.

'When it happened over Skund way they said it was a werewolf or something, and I thought, no, werewolves aren't like that,' she said. 'I never thought it was a *real* wolf. Gave me quite a turn, that.'

'Real wolves don't walk on their hind legs and open doors,' said Granny Weatherwax. 'Come on, help me get it outside.'

'Took me right back, seeing a great big hairy slathering thing heading towards me,' said Nanny, picking up one end of the stunned creature. 'Did you ever meet old Sumpkins?'

It was, indeed, a normal-looking wolf, except that it was a lot thinner than most. Ribs showed plainly under the skin and the fur was matted. Granny hauled a bucket of cloudy water from the well next to the privy and poured it over its head.

Then she sat down on a tree stump and watched it carefully. A few birds sang, high in the branches.

'It spoke,' she said. 'It tried to say "no".'

'I wondered about that,' said Nanny. 'Then I thought maybe I was imagining things.'

'No point in imagining anything,' said Granny. 'Things are bad enough as they are.'

The wolf groaned. Granny handed the frying pan to Nanny Ogg.

After a while she said, 'I think I'm going to have a look inside its head.'

Nanny Ogg shook her head. 'I wouldn't do that, if I was you.'

'I'm the one who's me, and I've got to know. Just you stand by with the frying pan.'

Nanny shrugged.

Granny concentrated.

It is very difficult to read a human mind. Most humans are thinking about so many things at any given moment that it is almost impossible to pick out one stream in the flood.

Animal minds are different. Far less cluttered. Carnivore minds are easiest of all, especially before meals. Colours don't exist in the mental world, but, if they did, a hungry carnivore mind would be hot and purple and sharp as an arrow. And herbivore minds are simple, too – coiled silver springs, poised for flight.

But this wasn't any kind of normal mind. It was two minds.

Granny had sometimes picked up the mind of hunters in the forest, when she was sitting quietly of an evening and letting her mind wander. Just occasionally they felt like this, or at least like a faint shadow of this. Just occasionally, when the hunter was about to make a kill, the random streams of thought came together. But this was different. This was the opposite – this was cracked and crippled attempts at cogitation peeling away from the sleek arrowhead of predatory intent. This was a predatory mind trying to *think*.

No wonder it was going mad.

She opened her eyes.

Nanny Ogg held the frying pan over her head. Her arm trembled.

'Well,' she said, 'who's there?'

'I could do with a glass of water,' said Granny. Natural caution surfaced through the turmoil of her mind. 'Only not out of that well, mind you.'

Nanny relaxed a little. When a witch started rummaging in someone else's mind, you could never be sure who was coming back. But Granny Weatherwax was the best. Magrat might always be trying to find herself, but Granny didn't even understand the idea of the search. If she couldn't find the way back to her own head, there wasn't a path.

'There's that milk in the cottage,' Nanny volunteered.

'What colour was it again?'

'Well . . . still fairly white.'

'Okay.'

When Nanny Ogg's back was safely turned Granny permitted herself a small shudder.

She stared at the wolf, wondering what she could do for it. A normal wolf wouldn't enter a cottage, even if it could open the door. Wolves didn't come near humans at all, except if there were a lot of them and it was the end of a very hard winter. And they

163

didn't do that because they were big and bad and wicked, but because they were wolves.

This wolf was trying to be human.

There was probably no cure.

'Here's your milk,' said Nanny Ogg.

Granny reached up and took it without looking.

'Someone made this wolf think it was a person,' she said. 'They made it think it was a person and then they didn't think any more about it. It happened a few years ago.'

'How do you know?'

'I've . . . got its memories,' said Granny. And instincts, too, she thought. She knew it'd be some days before she'd stop wanting to chase sledges over the snow.

'Oh.'

'It's stuck between species. In its head.'

'Can we help it?' said Nanny.

Granny shook her head.

'It's gone on for too long. It's habit now. And it's starving. It can't go one way, it can't go t'other. It can't act like a wolf, and it can't manage being a human. And it can't go on like it is.'

She turned to face Nanny for the first time. Nanny took a step back.

'You can't imagine how it feels,' she said. 'Wandering around for years. Not capable of acting human, and not able to be a wolf. You can't imagine how that feels.'

'I reckon maybe I can,' said Nanny. 'In your face. Maybe I can. Who'd do that to a creature?'

'I've got my suspicions.'

They looked around.

Magrat was approaching, with the child. Beside them walked one of the woodcutters.

'Hah,' said Granny. 'Yes. Of course. There's always got to be' – she spat the words – 'a *happy ending*.'

A paw tried to grip her ankle.

Granny Weatherwax looked down into the wolf's face.

'Preeees,' it growled. 'Annn enndinggg? Noaaaow?'

She knelt down, and took the paw.

'Yes?' she said.

'Yessss!'

She stood up again, all authority, and beckoned to the approaching trio.

'Mr Woodcutter?' she said. 'A job for you . . .'

The woodcutter never understood why the wolf laid its head on the stump so readily.

Or why the old woman, the one in whom anger roiled like pearl barley in a bubbling stew, insisted afterwards that it be buried properly instead of skinned and thrown in the bushes. She had been very insistent about that.

And that was the end of the big bad wolf.

It was an hour later. Quite a few of the woodcutters had wandered up to the cottage, where there seemed to be a lot of interesting activity going on. Wood-cutting is not a job that normally offers much in the way of diversion.

Magrat was washing the floor with as much magical

165

assistance as could be afforded by a bucket of soapy water and a scrubbing brush. Even Nanny Ogg, whose desultory interest in the proud role of housewife had faded completely just as soon as her eldest daughter was old enough to hold a duster, was cleaning the walls. The old grandmother, who wasn't entirely in touch with events, was anxiously following both of them around with a saucer of milk. Spiders who had inherited the ceiling for generations were urged gently but firmly out of the door.

And Granny Weatherwax was walking around the clearing with the head woodcutter, a barrel-chested young man who clearly thought he looked better in his studded leather wristlets than was, in fact, the case.

'It's been around for years, right?' he said. 'Always lurking around the edges of villages and that.'

'And you never tried talking to it?' said Granny.

'Talk to it? It's a *wolf*, right? You don't talk to *wolves*. Animals can't talk.'

'Hmm. I see. And what about the old woman? There's a lot of you woodcutters. Did you ever, you know, drop in to see her?'

'Huh? No fear!'

'Why?'

The head woodcutter leaned forward conspiratorially.

'Well, they say she's a witch, right?'

'Really?' said Granny. 'How do you know?'

'She's got all the signs, right?'

'What signs are those?'

The woodcutter was pricked by a slight un-easiness.

'Well . . . she's . . . she lives all by herself in the wood, right?'

'Yes . . . ?'

'And . . . and . . . she's got a hook nose and she's always muttering to herself . . .'

'Yes . . . ?'

'And she's got no teeth, right?'

'Lawks,' said Granny. 'I can see where you wouldn't want to be having with the likes of her, right?'

'Right!' said the woodcutter, relieved.

'Quite likely turn you into just about anything as soon as look at you, right?' Granny stuck her finger in her ear and twiddled it reflectively.

'They can do that, you know.'

'I bet they can. I bet they can,' said Granny. 'Makes me glad there's all you big strong lads around. Tch, tch. Hmm. Can I have a look at your chopper, young man?'

He handed over his axe. Granny sagged dramatically as she grasped it. There were still traces of wolf blood on the blade.

'Deary me, it's a big one,' she said. 'And you're good with this, I expect.'

'Won the silver belt two years running at the forest revels,' said the woodcutter proudly.

'Two years running? Two years running? Lawks. That *is* good. That's *very* good. And here's me hardly able to lift it.' Granny grasped the axe in one hand and swung it inexpertly. The woodcutter jumped backwards as the blade whirred past his face and then buried itself a quarter of an inch deep in a tree.

'Sorry about that,' said Granny Weatherwax. 'Aren't I a daft old woman! Never was any good with anything technical!'

He grinned at her, and tried to pull the axe free.

He sank to his knees, his face suddenly white.

Granny leaned down until she was level with his ear.

'You could have seen to the old woman,' she said quietly. 'You could have talked to the wolf. But you didn't, right?'

He tried to speak, but his teeth didn't seem to want to part.

'I can see you're very sorry about all that,' she said. 'I can see you're seein' the error of your ways. I bet you can't wait to be up and repairing her cottage for her, and getting the garden back in good order, and seeing she has fresh milk every day and a good supply of wood, right? In fact I wouldn't be surprised if you wasn't generous enough to build her a *new* cottage, with a proper well an' all. Somewhere near the village so she don't have to live alone, right? You know, I can see the future sometimes and I just *know* that's what's goin' to happen, *right*?'

Sweat ran off his face. Now his lungs didn't seem to be operating, either.

'An' I knows you're goin' to keep your word, and I'm so pleased about it that I'm going to make sure you're especially lucky,' said Granny, her voice still in the same pleasant monotone. 'I knows it can be a dangerous job, woodchoppin'. People can get hurt. Trees can accidentally fall on 'em, or the top of their chopper can suddenly come off and cut their head open.' The woodcutter shuddered as Granny went on: 'So what I'm goin' to do is a little spell to make sure that none of this 'appens to you. On account of me bein' so grateful. Because of you helpin' the old lady. Right? Just nod.'

He managed to move his head a fraction. Granny Weatherwax smiled.

'There!' she said, standing up and brushing a speck of leafmould off her dress. 'You see how sweet life can be, if we all helps one another?'

The witches left around lunchtime. By then the old woman's garden was full of people, and the air with the sound of sawing and hammering. News like Granny Weatherwax travels fast. Three woodcutters were digging over the vegetable plot, two more were fighting to clean the chimney, and four of them were halfway down a new well that was being dug with impressive speed.

The old grandmother, who was still the kind of person who hangs on to one idea until another one dislodges it by force, was running out of saucers to put the milk in.

The witches sneaked away in all the busyness.

'There,' said Magrat, as they strolled down the path, 'it just goes to show how people will pitch in and help, if only someone sets an example. You don't have to bully people all the time, you know.'

Nanny Ogg glanced at Granny.

'I saw you talking to the head woodcutter,' she said. 'What was you talking about?'

'Sawdust,' said Granny.

'Oh, yes?'

'One of the woodcutters told *me*,' said Magrat, 'that there's been other odd things happening in this forest. Animals acting human, he said. There used to be a family of bears living not far away.'

'Nothing unusual about a family of bears living together,' said Nanny. 'They're very convivial animals.'

'In a cottage?'

'*That's* unusual.'

'That's what I mean,' said Magrat.

'You'd definitely feel a bit awkward about going round to borrow a cup of sugar,' said Nanny. 'I expect the neighbours had something to say about it.'

'Yes,' said Magrat. 'They said "oink".'

'What'd they say "oink" for?'

'Because they couldn't say anything else. They were pigs.'

'We had people like that next door when we lived at—' Nanny began.

'I mean *pigs*. You know. Four legs? Curly tail? What pork is before it's pork? Pigs.'

'Can't see anyone letting pigs live in a cottage,' said Granny.

'He said they didn't. The pigs built their own. There were three of them. Little pigs.'

'What happened to them?' said Nanny.

'The wolf ate them. They were the only animals stupid enough to let him get near them, apparently.

Nothing was found of them except their spirit level.'

'That's a shame.'

'The woodcutter says they didn't build very good houses, mind you.'

'Well, it's only to be expected. What with the trotters and all,' said Nanny.

'He says the roof leaks something dreadful, right over his bed.'

The witches walked on in silence.

'I remember hearing once,' said Nanny, with the occasional glance at Granny Weatherwax, 'about some ole enchantress in history who lived on an island and turned shipwrecked sailors into pigs.'

'That's a terrible thing to do,' said Magrat, on cue.

'I suppose it's all according to what you really *are*, inside,' said Nanny. 'I mean, look at Greebo here.' Greebo, curled around her shoulders like a smelly fur, purred. 'He's practically a human.'

'You do talk a lot of tosh, Gytha,' said Granny Weatherwax.

'That's 'cos people won't tell me what they *really* think is going on,' said Nanny Ogg, grimly.

'I said I'm not sure,' said Granny.

'You looked into the wolf's mind.'

'Yes. I did.'

'Well, then . . .'

Granny sighed. 'Someone's been here before us. Passing through. Someone who knows about the power of stories, and uses 'em. And the stories have . . . kind of hung around. They do that, when they get fed . . .'

'What'd anyone want to do that for?' said Nanny.

'*Practice*,' said Granny.

'Practice? What for?' said Magrat.

'I expect we'll find out presently,' said Granny gnomically.

'You ought to tell me what you think,' said Magrat. 'I am the official godmother around here, you know. I ought to be told things. You've got to tell me things.'

Nanny Ogg went chilly. This was the kind of emotional countryside with which she was, as head Ogg, extremely familiar. That sort of comment at this sort of time was like the tiny sliding of snow off the top branch of a tall tree high in the mountains during the thaw season. It was one end of a process that, without a doubt, would end with a dozen villages being engulfed. Whole branches of the Ogg family had stopped talking to other branches of the Ogg family because of a 'Thank you very much' in the wrong tones and the wrong place, and this was far worse.

'Now,' she said hurriedly, 'why don't we—'

'I don't have to explain anything,' said Granny Weatherwax.

'But we're supposed to be *three* witches,' said Magrat. 'If you can call us witches,' she added.

'What do you mean by that, pray?' said Granny.

'Pray?' thought Nanny. Someone has ended a sentence with 'pray?' That's like that bit when someone hits someone else with a glove and then throws it on the floor. There's no going back when someone's ended a sentence with 'pray?' But she tried, anyway.

'How about a nice—'

Magrat plunged on with the brave desperation of someone dancing in the light of their burning bridges.

'Well,' she said, 'it seems to *me*—'

'Yes?' said Granny.

'It seems to *me*,' Magrat tried again, 'that the only *magic* we do is all – well, headology. Not what anyone else would call magic. It's just glaring at people and tricking them. Taking advantage of their gullibility. It wasn't what I expected when *I* set out to become a witch—'

'And who says,' said Granny Weatherwax, slowly and deliberately, 'that you've become a witch now?'

'My word, the wind is getting up, perhaps we should – ' said Nanny Ogg.

'*What* did you say?' said Magrat.

Nanny Ogg put her hand over her eyes. Asking someone to repeat a phrase you'd not only heard very clearly but were also exceedingly angry about was around Defcon II in the lexicon of squabble.

'I should have thought my voice was clear enough,' said Granny. 'I'm very amazed my voice wasn't clear enough. It sounded clear enough to *me*.'

'Looks a bit gusty, why don't we—?'

'Well, I should just think I can be smug and bad-tempered and ill-considerate enough to be a witch,' said Magrat. 'That's all that's required, isn't it?'

'Ill-considerate? *Me*?'

'You like people who need help, because when

they need help they're weak, and helping them makes you feel *strong*! What harm would a bit of magic do?'

'Because it'd never stop at just a bit, you stupid girl!'

Magrat backed off, her face flushed. She reached into her bag and pulled out a slim volume, which she flourished like a weapon.

'Stupid I may be,' she panted, 'but at least I'm trying to learn things! Do you know the kind of things people can use magic for? Not just illusion and bullying! There's people in this book that can . . . can . . . walk on hot coals, and stick their hands in a fire and not get hurt!'

'Cheap trickery!' said Granny.

'They really can!'

'Impossible. No one can do that!'

'It shows they can control things! Magic's got to be more than just knowing things and manipulating people!'

'Oh? It's all wishing on stars and fairy dust, is it? *Making* people happier?'

'There's got to be some of that! Otherwise what's the good of *anything*? Anyway . . . when I went to Desiderata's cottage you were looking for the wand, weren't you?'

'I just didn't want it falling into the wrong hands!'

'Like any hands but yours, I expect!'

They glared at each other.

'Haven't you got any romance in your soul?' said Magrat plaintively.

'No,' said Granny. 'I ain't. And stars don't care what you wish, and magic don't make things better, and no one doesn't get burned who sticks their hand in a fire. If you want to amount to anything as a witch, Magrat Garlick, you got to learn three things. What's real, what's not real, and what's the difference—'

'And always get the young man's name and address,' said Nanny. 'It worked for me every time. Only joking,' she said, as they both glared at her.

The wind was rising, here on the edge of the forest. Bits of grass and leaves whirled through the air.

'We're going the right way, anyway,' said Nanny madly, seeking anything that would be a distraction. 'Look. It says "Genua" on the signpost.'

It did indeed. It was an old, worm-eaten signpost right on the edge of the forest. The end of the arm had been carved into the likeness of a pointing finger.

'A proper road, too,' Nanny burbled on. The row cooled a bit, simply because both sides were not talking to each other. Not simply not exchanging vocal communication – that's just an absence of speaking. This went right through that and out the other side, into the horrible glowering worlds of Not Talking to One Another.

'Yellow bricks,' said Nanny. 'Whoever heard of anyone making a road out of yellow bricks?'

Magrat and Granny Weatherwax stood looking in opposite directions with their arms folded.

'Brightens the place up, I suppose,' said Nanny.

On the horizon, Genua sparkled in the middle of some more greenery. In between, the road dipped into a wide valley dotted with little villages. A river snaked through them on the way to the city.

The wind whipped at their skirts.

'We'll never fly in this,' said Nanny, still womanfully trying to make enough conversation for three people.

'So we'll walk, then, eh?' she said, and added, because there's a spark of spitefulness even in innocent souls like Nanny Ogg's, 'Singing as we go, how about it?'

'I'm sure it's not my place to mind what anyone chooses to do,' said Granny. 'It's nothing to do with me. I expect *some* people with wands and big ideas might have something to say.'

'Huh!' said Magrat.

They set off along the brick road towards the distant city, in single file with Nanny Ogg as a kind of mobile buffer state in the middle.

'What some people need,' said Magrat, to the world in general, 'is a bit more heart.'

'What some people need,' said Granny Weatherwax, to the stormy sky, 'is a lot more brain.'

Then she clutched at her hat to stop the wind from blowing it off.

What *I* need, thought Nanny Ogg fervently, is a drink.

Three minutes later a farmhouse dropped on her head.

*   *   *

By this time the witches were well spaced out. Granny Weatherwax was striding along in front, Magrat was sulking along at the rear, and Nanny was in the middle.

As she said afterwards, it wasn't even as if she was singing. It was just that one moment there was a small, plump witch, and the next there was the collapsing remains of a wooden farmhouse.

Granny Weatherwax turned and found herself looking at a crumbling, unpainted front door. Magrat nearly walked into a back door of the same grey, bleached wood.

There was no sound but the crackle of settling timber.

'Gytha?' said Granny.

'Nanny?' said Magrat.

They both opened their doors.

It was a very simple design of house, with two downstairs rooms separated by a front-to-back passageway. In the middle of the passageway, surrounded by shattered and termite-ridden floorboards, under the pointy hat that had been rammed down to her chin, was Nanny Ogg. There was no sign of Greebo.

'Wha' happened?' she said. 'Wha' happened?'

'A farmhouse dropped on your head,' said Magrat.

'Oh. One o' them things,' said Nanny vaguely.

Granny gripped her by the shoulders.

'Gytha? How many fingers am I holding up?' she said urgently.

'Wha' fingers? 'S'all gone dark.'

177

Magrat and Granny gripped the brim of Nanny's hat and half lifted, half unscrewed it from her head. She blinked at them.

'That's the willow reinforcement,' she said, as the pointy hat creaked back into shape like a resurrecting umbrella. She was swaying gently. 'Stop a hammer blow, a hat with willow reinforcement. All them struts, see. Distributes the force. I shall write to Mr Vernissage.'

Magrat, bemused, looked around the little house. 'It just dropped out of the sky!' she said.

'Could have been a big tornado or something somewhere,' said Nanny Ogg. 'Picked it up, see, then the wind drops and down it comes. You get funny things happening in high winds. Remember that big gale we had last year? One of my hens laid the same egg four times.'

'She's rambling,' said Magrat.

'No I ain't, that's just my normal talking,' said Nanny.

Granny Weatherwax peered into one of the rooms. 'I suppose there wouldn't be any food and drink about the place?' she said.

'I think I could force myself to drink some brandy,' said Nanny quickly.

Magrat peered up the stairs.

'Coo-ee,' she called, in the strangled voice of someone who wants to be heard without doing anything so bad-mannered as raise their voice. 'Is there anyone here?'

Nanny, on the other hand, looked under the stairs. Greebo was a cowering ball of fur in a corner. She hauled him out by the scruff of his neck and gave him a slightly bewildered pat. Despite Mr Vernissage's millinery masterpiece, despite the worm-eaten floor, and despite even the legendary thick skull of the Oggs, she was definitely feeling several twinkles short of a glitter and suffering a slight homesick-tinged dip in her usual sunny nature. People didn't hit you over the head with farmhouses back home.

'You know, Greebo,' she said, 'I don't think we're in Lancre.'

'I've found some jam,' said Granny Weatherwax, from the kitchen.

It didn't take a lot to cheer up Nanny Ogg. 'That's fine,' she called out. 'It'll go nicely on the dwarf bread.'

Magrat came into the room.

'I'm not sure we should be taking other people's provisions,' she said. 'I mean, this place must belong to someone.'

'Oh. Did someone speak, Gytha?' said Granny Weatherwax archly.

Nanny rolled her eyes.

'I was merely saying, Nanny,' said Magrat, 'that this isn't our property.'

'She says it don't belong to us, Esme,' said Nanny.

'Tell anyone who wants to know, Gytha, that it's like salvage from a shipwreck,' said Granny.

'She says finders keepers, Magrat,' said Nanny.

Something flickered past the window. Magrat went and peered out through the grimy pane.

'That's funny. There's a lot of dwarfs dancing round the house,' she said.

'Oh, yes?' said Nanny, opening a cupboard.

Granny stiffened. 'Are they – I means, ask her if they're singing,' she said.

'They singing, Magrat?'

'I can hear something,' said Magrat. 'Sounds like "Dingdong, dingdong".'

'That's a dwarf song all right,' said Nanny. 'They're the only people who can make a hiho last all day.'

'They seem very happy about it,' said Magrat doubtfully.

'Probably it was their farmhouse and they're glad to get it back.'

There was a hammering on the back door. Magrat opened it. A crowd of brightly dressed and embarrassed dwarfs stepped back hurriedly and then peered up at her.

'Er,' said the one who was apparently the leader, 'is . . . is the old witch dead?'

'Which old witch?' said Magrat.

The dwarf looked at her for a while with his mouth open. He turned and had a whispered consultation with his colleagues. Then he turned back.

'How many have you got?'

'There's a choice of two,' said Magrat. She wasn't feeling in a very good mood and wasn't prompted to aid the conversation more than necessary. Uncharacteristic nastiness made her add, 'Free for the asking.'

'Oh.' The dwarf considered this. 'Well, which old witch did the house land on?'

'Nanny? No, she's not dead. She's just a bit stunned. But thanks all the same for asking,' said Magrat. 'That's very kind of you.'

This seemed to puzzle the dwarfs. They went into a huddle. There was a lot of *sotto voce* arguing.

Then the head dwarf turned back to Magrat. He removed his helmet and turned it around and around nervously in his hands.

'Er,' he said, 'can we have her boots?'

'What?'

'Her boots?' said the dwarf, blushing. 'Can we have them, please?'

'What do you want her boots for?'

The dwarf looked at her. Then he turned and went into a huddle with his colleagues again. He turned back to Magrat.

'We've just got this . . . feeling . . . that we ought to have her boots,' he said.

He stood there blinking.

'Well, I'll go and ask,' said Magrat. 'But I don't think she'll say yes.'

As she went to close the door the dwarf twiddled his hat some more.

'They *are* ruby-coloured, aren't they?' he said.

'Well, they're red,' said Magrat. 'Is red all right?'

'They've got to be red.' All the other dwarfs nodded. 'It's no good if they're not red.'

Magrat gave him a blank look and shut the door.

'Nanny,' she said slowly, when she was back in the kitchen, 'there's some dwarfs outside who want your boots.'

Nanny looked up. She'd found a stale loaf in a

cupboard and was industriously chewing. It was amazing what you'd eat if the alternative was dwarf bread.

'What d'they want 'em for?' she said.

'Didn't say. They just said they had a feeling they want your boots.'

'That sounds highly suspicious to me,' said Granny.

'Old Shaker Wistley over Creel Springs way was a devil for boots,' said Nanny, putting down the breadknife. 'Especially black button boots. He used to collect 'em. If he saw you going past in a new pair he had to go and have a lie-down.'

'I reckon that's a bit *sophisticated* for dwarfs,' said Granny.

'Maybe they want to drink out of 'em,' said Nanny.

'What do you mean, drink out of them?' said Magrat.

'Ah, well, that's what they do in foreign parts,' said Nanny. 'They drink fizzy wine out of ladies' boots.'

They all looked down at Nanny's boots.

Not even Nanny could imagine what anyone would want to drink out of them, or what they would do afterwards.

'My word. That's even more sophisticated than old Shaker Wistley,' said Nanny reflectively.

'They seemed a bit puzzled about it,' said Magrat.

'I expect they would be. It ain't often people get a feeling they ought to go around pulling a decent witch's boots off. This sounds like another story flapping around. I think,' said Granny Weatherwax, 'that we ought to go and talk to these dwarfs.'

She strode out into the passageway and opened the door.

'Yes?' she demanded.

The dwarfs backed away at the sight of her. There was a lot of whispering and elbowing and muttered comments in the nature of 'No, *you*', and 'I asked *last* time'. Finally a dwarf was pushed forward. It might have been the original dwarf. It was hard to tell, with dwarfs.

'Er,' he said. 'Er. Boots?'

'What *for*?' said Granny.

The dwarf scratched its head. 'Damned if I know,' he said. 'We were just wondering about it ourselves, 's'matterofact. We were just coming off shift in the coal mine half an hour ago, we saw the farmhouse land on . . . on the witch, an' . . . well . . .'

'You just *knew* you had to run up and steal her boots?' said Granny.

The dwarf's face widened into a relieved grin.

'That's right!' he said. 'And sing the Ding-dong song. Only she was supposed to be squashed. No offence meant,' he added quickly.

'It's the willow reinforcement,' said a voice behind Granny. 'Worth its weight in glod.'

Granny stared for a while, and then smiled.

'I think you lads ought to come inside,' she said. 'I've got some questions to ask you.'

The dwarfs looked very uncertain.

'Um,' said the spokesdwarf.

'Nervous of going into a house with witches in it?' said Granny Weatherwax.

The spokesdwarf nodded, and then went red. Magrat and Nanny Ogg exchanged glances behind Granny's back. Something had definitely gone wrong somewhere. In the mountains dwarfs certainly weren't afraid of witches. The problem was to stop them digging up your floor.

'You've been down from the mountains for some time, I expect,' said Granny.

'Very promising seam of coal down here,' mumbled the spokesdwarf, twiddling his hat.

'Bet it's a long time since you've had proper dwarf bread, then,' said Granny.

The spokesdwarf's eyes misted over.

'Baked from the finest stone-ground grit, just like mother used to jump up and down on it,' Granny went on.

A sort of collective sigh went up from the dwarfs.

'You just can't get it down here,' said the spokesdwarf, to the ground. 'It's the water, or something. It falls to bits after hardly any years at all.'

'They puts *flour* in it,' said someone behind him, sourly.

'It's worse'n that. The baker over in Genua puts dried fruit in it,' said another dwarf.

'Well, now,' said Granny, rubbing her hands together, 'I may be able to help you here. Could be I've got some dwarf bread to spare.'

'Nah. Not proper dwarf bread,' said the spokesdwarf moodily. 'Proper dwarf bread's got to be dropped in rivers and dried out and sat on and left and looked at every day and put away again. You just can't get it down here.'

'This could be,' said Granny Weatherwax, 'your lucky day.'

'To be frank,' said Nanny Ogg, 'I think the cat pissed on some of it.'

The spokesdwarf looked up, his eyes aglow.

'Hot damn!'

Dear Jason et everybody,

Whot a life, all kinds of thing goin on, what with talkin wolves and women asleep in castles, I shall have a story or two to tell you when I gets back and no mistake. Also, dont tawk to me about farmhouses, which reminds me, please send somone to Mr Vernissage over in Slice and present Mrs Ogg's compluments and what a good hat he makes, he can say 'As Approved by Nanny Ogg', it stops 100% of all known farmhouses, also, if you writes to people saying how good their stuff is sometimes you get free stuff, there could be a new hat in this for me so see to it.

Lilith stepped out from her room of mirrors. Shadowy images of herself trailed after her, fading.

Witches ought to be squashed when a farmhouse lands on them. Lilith knew that. All squashed, except for their boots sticking out.

Sometimes she despaired. People just didn't seem able to play their parts properly.

She wondered whether there was such a thing as the *opposite* of a fairy godmother. Most things had their opposite, after all. If so, she wouldn't be a *bad* fairy godmother, because that's just a good fairy godmother seen from a different viewpoint.

The opposite would be someone who was poison to stories and, thought Lilith, quite the most evil creature in the world.

Well, here in Genua was one story no one could stop. It had momentum, this one. Try to stop it and it'd absorb you, make you part of its plot. She didn't have to do a thing. The story would do it for her. And she had the comfort of knowing that she couldn't lose. After all, she was the good one.

She strolled along the battlements and down the stairs to her own room, where the two sisters were waiting. They were good at waiting. They could sit for hours without blinking.

The Duc refused even to be in the same room as them.

Their heads turned as she came in.

She'd never given them voices. It wasn't necessary. It was enough that they were beautiful and could be made to understand.

'Now you must go to the house,' she said. 'And this is very important. Listen to me. Some people will be coming to see Ella tomorrow. You must let them do so, do you understand?'

They were watching her lips. They watched anything that moved.

'We shall need them for the story. It won't work properly unless they try to stop it. And afterwards . . . perhaps I will give you voices. You'll like that, won't you?'

They looked at one another, and then at her. And then at the cage in the corner of the room.

Lilith smiled, and reached in, and took out two white mice.

'The youngest witch might be just your type,' she said. 'I shall have to see what I can do with her. And now . . . open . . .'

The broomsticks drifted through the afternoon air.

For once, the witches weren't arguing.

The dwarfs had been a taste of home. It would have done anyone's heart good to see the way they just sat and stared at the dwarf bread, as if consuming it with their eyes, which was the best way to consume dwarf bread. Whatever it was that had driven them to seek ruby-coloured boots seemed to wear off under its down-to-earth influence. As Granny said, you could look a long way before you found anything realer than dwarf bread.

Then she'd gone off alone to talk to the head dwarf.

She wouldn't tell the others what he'd told her, and they didn't feel bold enough to ask. Now she flew a little ahead of them.

Occasionally she'd mutter something like 'God-mothers!' or 'Practising!'

But even Magrat, who hadn't had as much experience, could *feel* Genua now, as a barometer feels the air pressure. In Genua, stories came to life. In Genua, someone set out to make dreams come true.

Remember some of your dreams?

*   *   *

Genua nestled on the delta of the Vieux river, which was the source of its wealth. And Genua was wealthy. Genua had once controlled the river mouth and taxed its traffic in a way that couldn't be called piracy because it was done by the city government, and therefore sound economics and perfectly all right. And the swamps and lakes back in the delta provided the crawling, swimming and flying ingredients of a cuisine that would have been world famous if, as has already been indicated, people travelled very much.

Genua was rich, lazy and unthreatened, and had once spent quite a lot of time involved in that special kind of civic politics that comes naturally to some city states. For example, once it had been able to afford the largest branch of the Assassins' Guild outside Ankh-Morpork, and its members were so busy that you sometimes had to wait for months.*

But the Assassins had all left years ago. Some things sicken even jackals.

The city came as a shock. From a distance, it looked like a complicated white crystal growing out of the greens and browns of the swamp.

Closer to, it resolved into, firstly, an outer ring of smaller buildings, then an inner ring of large, impressive white houses and, finally, at the very centre, a palace. It was tall and pretty and multi-turreted,

---

*Whereas in Ankh-Morpork, business was often so slow that some of the more go-ahead Guild members put adverts in shop windows offering deals like 'Stab two, poison one free'.

like a toy castle or some kind of confectionery extravaganza. Every slim tower looked designed to hold a captive princess.

Magrat shivered. But then she thought of the wand. A godmother had responsibilities.

'Reminds me of another one of them Black Aliss stories,' said Granny Weatherwax. 'I remember when she locked up that girl with the long pigtails in a tower just like one of them. Rumple-stiltzel or someone.'

'But she got out,' said Magrat.

'Yes, it does you good to let your hair down,' said Nanny.

'Huh. Rural myths,' said Granny.

They drew nearer to the city walls. Then Magrat said, 'There's guards on the gate. Are we going to fly over?'

Granny stared at the highest tower through narrowed eyes. 'No,' she said. 'We'll land and walk in. So's not to worry people.'

'There's a nice flat green bit just behind those trees,' said Magrat.

Granny walked up and down experimentally. Her boots squeaked and gurgled in watery accusation.

'Look, I *said* I'm sorry,' said Magrat. 'It just looked so flat!'

'Water gen'rally does,' said Nanny, sitting on a tree stump and wringing out her dress.

'But even you couldn't tell it was water,' said Magrat. 'It looks so . . . so *grassy* with all that weed and stuff floating on it.'

'Seems to me the land and the water round here can't decide who is which,' said Nanny. She looked around at the miasmic landscape.

Trees grew out of the swamp. They had a jagged, foreign look and seemed to be rotting as they grew. Where the water was visible, it was black like ink. Occasionally a few bubbles would eructate to the surface like the ghosts of beans on bath night. And somewhere over in the distance was the river, if it was possible to be that sure in this land of thick water and ground that wobbled when you set foot on it.

She blinked.

'That's odd,' she said.

'What?' said Granny.

'Thought I saw . . . something running . . .' muttered Nanny. 'Over there. Between the trees.'

'Must be a duck then, in this place.'

'It was bigger'n a duck,' said Nanny. 'Funny thing is, it looked a bit like a little house.'

'Oh yes, running along with smoke coming out of the chimney, I expect,' said Granny witheringly.

Nanny brightened. 'You saw it too?'

Granny rolled her eyes.

'Come on,' she said, 'let's get to the road.'

'Er,' said Magrat, 'how?'

They looked at the nominal ground between their reasonably dry refuge and the road. It had a yellowish appearance. There were floating branches and tufts of suspiciously green grass. Nanny pulled a branch off the fallen tree she was sitting on and tossed it a few yards. It struck damply, and sank with the noise of someone trying to get the last bit out of the milkshake.

'We fly over to it, of course,' Nanny said.

'You two can,' said Granny. 'There's nowhere for me to run and get mine started.'

In the end Magrat ferried her across on her broom, Nanny bringing up the rear with Granny's erratic stick in tow.

'I just 'ope no-one saw us, that's all,' said Granny, when they'd reached the comparative safety of the road.

Other roads joined the swamp causeway as they got nearer to the city. They were crowded, and there was a long line at the gate.

From ground level, the city was even more impressive. Against the steam of the swamps it shone like a polished stone. Coloured flags flew over the walls.

'Looks very jolly,' said Nanny.

'Very *clean*,' said Magrat.

'It just looks like that from outside,' said Granny, who had seen a city before. 'When you get inside it'll be all beggars and noise and gutters full of I don't know what, you mark my words.'

'They're turning quite a lot of people away,' said Nanny.

'They said on the boat that lots of people come here for Fat Lunchtime,' said Granny. 'Probably you get lots of people who ain't the right sort.'

Half a dozen guards watched them approach.

'Very smartly turned out,' said Granny. 'That's what I like to see. Not like at home.'

There were only six suits of chain mail in the whole of Lancre, made on the basis of one-size-doesn't-quite-fit-all. Bits of string and wire had to be employed to take in the slack, since in Lancre the role of palace guard was generally taken by any citizen who hadn't got much to do at the moment.

These guards were all six-footers and, even Granny had to admit, quite impressive in their jolly red-and-blue uniforms. The only other *real* city guards she'd ever seen were those in Ankh-Morpork. The sight of Ankh-Morpork's city guard made thoughtful people wonder who could possibly attack that was worse. They certainly weren't anything to look at.

To her amazement, two pikes barred her way as she stepped under the arched gateway.

'We're not attacking, you know,' she said.

A corporal gave her a salute.

'No ma'am,' he said. 'But we have orders to stop borderline cases.'

'Borderline?' said Nanny. 'What's borderline about us?'

The corporal swallowed. Granny Weatherwax's gaze was a hard one to meet.

'Well,' he said, 'you're a bit . . . grubby.'

There was a ringing silence. Granny took a deep breath.

'We had a bit of an accident in the swamp,' said Magrat quickly.

'I'm sure it'll be all right,' said the corporal wretchedly. 'The captain'll be here directly. Only there's all kinds of trouble if we let the wrong sort in. You'd be amazed at some of the people we get here.'

'Can't go letting the wrong sort in,' said Nanny Ogg. 'We wouldn't want you to let the wrong sort in. I daresay we wouldn't want to come into the kind of city that'd let the wrong sort in, would we, Esme?'

Magrat kicked her on the ankle.

'Good thing we're the right sort,' said Nanny.

'What's happening, corporal?'

The captain of the guard strolled out of a door in the archway and walked over to the witches.

'These . . . ladies want to come in, sir,' said the corporal.

'Well?'

'They're a bit . . . you know, not one hundred per cent clean,' said the corporal, wilting under Granny's stare. 'And one of them's got messy hair—'

'Well!' snapped Magrat.

'—and one of them looks like she uses bad language.'

'What?' said Nanny, her grin evaporating. 'I'll tan your hide, you little bugger!'

'But, corporal, they have got brooms,' said the captain. 'It's very hard for cleaning staff to look tidy all the time.'

'Cleaning staff?' said Granny.

'I'm sure they're as anxious as you are to get tidied up,' said the captain.

'Excuse me,' said Granny, empowering the words with much the same undertones as are carried by words like 'Charge!' and 'Kill!', 'Excuse me, but does this pointy hat I'm wearing mean anything to you?'

The soldiers looked at it politely.

'Can you give me a clue?' said the captain, eventually.

'It means—'

'We'll just trot along in, if it's all the same to you,' said Nanny Ogg. 'Got a lot of cleaning up to do.' She flourished her broomstick. 'Come, ladies.'

She and Magrat grasped Granny's elbows firmly and propelled her under the archway before her fuse burned out. Granny Weatherwax always held that you ought to count up to ten before losing your temper. No one knew why, because the only effect of this was to build up the pressure and make the ensuing explosion a whole lot worse.

The witches didn't stop until they were out of sight of the gate.

'Now, Esme,' said Nanny soothingly, 'you shouldn't take it personal. And we are a bit mucky, you must admit. They were just doing their job, all right? How about that?'

'They treated us as if we was *ordinary people*,' said Granny, in a shocked voice.

'This *is* foreign parts, Granny,' said Magrat. 'Anyway, you said the men on the boat didn't recognize the hat, either.'

'But then I dint want 'em to,' said Granny. 'That's different.'

'It's just an . . . an incident, Granny,' said Magrat. 'They were just stupid soldiers. They don't even know a proper free-form hairstyle when they see it.'

Nanny looked around. Crowds milled past them, almost in silence.

'And you must admit it's a nice clean city,' she said.

They took stock of their surroundings.

It was certainly the cleanest place they'd ever seen. Even the cobblestones had a polished look.

'You could eat your tea off the street,' said Nanny, as they strolled along.

'Yes, but you'd eat your tea off the street anyway,' said Granny.

'I wouldn't eat all of it. Even the gutters are scrubbed. Not a Ronald* in sight, look.'

'Gytha!'

'Well, *you* said that in Ankh-Morpork—'

'This is somewhere else!'

'It's so spotless,' said Magrat. 'Makes you wish you'd cleaned your sandals.'

'Yeah.' Nanny Ogg squinted along the street. 'Makes you wish you were a better person, really.'

'Why are you two whispering?' said Granny.

She followed their gaze. There was a guard standing on the street corner. When he saw them looking at him he touched his helmet and gave them a brief smile.

'Even the guards are polite,' said Magrat.

'And there's so many of them, too,' said Granny.

'Amazing, really, needing all these guards in a city where people are so clean and quiet,' said Magrat.

'Perhaps there's so much niceness to be spread

---

*Ronald the Third of Lancre, believed to be an extremely unpleasant monarch, was remembered by posterity only in this obscure bit of rhyming slang.

around they need a lot of people to do it,' said Nanny Ogg.

The witches wandered through the packed streets.

'Nice houses, though,' said Magrat. 'Very decorative and olde-worlde.'

Granny Weatherwax, who lived in a cottage that was as olde-worlde as it was possible to be without being a lump of metamorphic rock, made no comment.

Nanny Ogg's feet started to complain.

'We ought to find somewhere to stop the night,' she said. 'We can look for this girl in the morning. We'll all do a lot better for a good night's sleep.'

'And a bath,' said Magrat. 'With soothing herbs.'

'Good idea. I could just do with a bath too,' said Nanny.

'My word, doesn't autumn roll around quickly,' said Granny sourly.

'Yeah? When did *you* last have a bath, Esme?'

'What do you mean, *last*?'

'See? Then there's no call to make comments about my ablutions.'

'Baths is unhygienic,' Granny declared. 'You know I've never agreed with baths. Sittin' around in your own dirt like that.'

'What do *you* do, then?' said Magrat.

'I just washes,' said Granny. 'All the bits. You know. As and when they becomes available.'

*   *   *

However available they were, and no further information was vouchsafed on this point, they were
certainly more available than accommodation in
Genua in Fat Lunchtime.

All the taverns and inns were more than full.
Gradually the press of crowds pushed them out
of the main streets and into the less fashionable
quarters of the city, but still there was no room for
the three of them.

Granny Weatherwax had had enough.

'The very next place we see,' she said, setting her
jaw firmly, 'we're goin' in. What's that inn over
there?'

Nanny Ogg peered at the sign.

'Hotel . . . No . . . Va . . . cancies,' she muttered,
and then brightened up. 'Hotel Nova Cancies,' she
repeated. 'That means "new, er, Cancies" in foreign,'
she added helpfully.

'It'll do,' said Granny.

She pushed open the door. A round, red-faced
man looked up from the desk. He was new to the
job and very nervous; the last incumbent had disappeared for not being round and red-faced enough.

Granny didn't waste time.

'You see this hat?' she demanded. 'You see this
broom?'

The man looked from her to the broom, and
back again.

'Yes?' he said. 'What's that mean?'

'Means we want three rooms for the night,' said
Granny, looking smugly at the other two.

'With sausage,' said Nanny.

'And one vegetarian meal,' said Magrat.

The man looked at all three of them. Then he went over to the door.

'You see this door? You see this sign?' he said.

'We don't bother about signs,' said Granny.

'Well, then,' said the man, 'I give up. What's a pointy hat and a broom really mean?'

'That means I'm a witch,' said Granny.

The man put his head on one side.

'Yeah?' he said. 'Is that another word for daft old woman?'

Dear Jason and everyone, wrote Nanny Ogg, *Dyou know, they dont know about witches here, thats how bakcward they are in foreign parts. A man gave Esme some Cheek and she would of lost her Temper so me and Magrat and I got hold of her and rushed her out because if you make someone think they've been turned into something there's always trouble, you remember what happened larst time when afterwards you had to go and dig a pond for Mr Wilkins to live in . . .*

They had managed to find a table to themselves in a tavern. It was packed with people of all species. The noise was at shouting level and smoke wreathed the air.

'Will you stop that scribbling, Gytha Ogg. It gets on my nerves,' snapped Granny.

'They *must* have witches here,' said Magrat. 'Everywhere has witches. You've got to have witches abroad. You find witches everywhere.'

'Like cockroaches,' said Nanny Ogg cheerfully.

'You should've let me make him believe he was a frog,' muttered Granny.

'You can't do that, Esme. You can't go around making people believe they're things just because they've been cheeky and don't know who you are,' said Gytha. 'Otherwise we'd be up to here in people hopping about.'

Despite many threats, Granny Weatherwax had never turned anyone into a frog. The way she saw it, there was a technically less cruel but cheaper and much more satisfying thing you could do. You could leave them human and make them *think* they were a frog, which also provided much innocent entertainment for passers-by.

'I always felt sorry for Mr Wilkins,' said Magrat, staring moodily at the table top. 'It was so sad watching him try to catch flies on his tongue.'

'He shouldn't have said what he said,' said Granny.

'What, that you were a domineering old busybody?' said Nanny innocently.

'I don't mind criticism,' said Granny. 'You know me. I've never been one to take offence at criticism. No one could say I'm the sort to take offence at criticism—'

'Not twice, anyway,' said Nanny. 'Not without blowing bubbles.'

'It's just that I can't stand unfairness,' said Granny. 'And you stop that grinning! Anyway, I don't see why you're making a fuss about it. It wore off after a couple of days.'

'Mrs Wilkins says he still goes out swimming

a lot,' said Nanny. 'It's given him a whole new interest, she said.'

'Perhaps they have a different kind of witch in the city,' said Magrat hopelessly. 'Perhaps they wear different sorts of clothes.'

'There's only one kind of witch,' said Granny. 'And we're it.'

She looked around the room. Of course, she thought, if someone was keeping witches out, people *wouldn't* know about them. Someone who didn't want anyone else meddling here. But she let us in . . .

'Oh, well, at least we're in the dry,' said Nanny. A drinker standing in a crowd behind her threw back his head to laugh and spilled beer down her back.

She muttered something under her breath.

Magrat saw the man look down to take another swig and stare, wide-eyed, into the mug. Then he dropped it and fought his way out of the room, clutching at his throat.

'What did you do to his drink?' she said.

'You ain't old enough to be told,' said Nanny.

At home, if a witch wanted a table to herself it . . . just happened. The sight of the pointy hat was enough. People kept a polite distance, occasionally sending free drinks to her. Even Magrat got respect, not particularly because anyone was in awe of her, but because a slight to one witch was a slight to all witches and no one wanted Granny Weatherwax coming around to explain this to them. Here they were being *jostled*, as if they were *ordinary*. Only Nanny Ogg's warning hand on Granny Weatherwax's arm was keeping a dozen jovial drinkers from

unnatural amphibianhood, and even Nanny's usually very elastic temper was beginning to twang. She
always prided herself on being as ordinary as muck,
but there was ordinary and there was ordinary. It was
like being that Prince Whatsisname, in the nursery
story, who liked to wander around his kingdom
dressed up as a commoner; she'd always had a
shrewd suspicion that the little pervert made sure
people knew who he was beforehand, just in case
anyone tried to get too common. It was like getting
muddy. Getting muddy when you had a nice hot tub
to look forward to was fun; getting muddy when all
you had to look forward to was more mud was no
fun at all. She reached a conclusion.

'Hey, why don't we have a drink?' said Nanny
Ogg brightly. 'We'd all feel better for a drink.'

'Oh no,' said Granny. 'You caught me with that
herbal drink last time. I'm sure there was alcohol in
that. I definitely felt a bit woozy after the sixth glass.
I ain't drinking any more foreign muck.'

'You've got to drink something,' said Magrat
soothingly. 'I'm thirsty, anyway.' She looked vaguely
at the crowded bar. 'Perhaps they do some kind of
fruit cup, or something.'

'Bound to,' said Nanny Ogg. She stood up,
glanced at the bar, and surreptitiously removed a
hatpin from her hat. 'Shan't be a moment.'

The two of them were left in their own private
gloom. Granny sat staring fixedly in front of her.

'You really shouldn't take it so bad, just because
people aren't showing you any respect,' said Magrat,
pouring soothing oil on the internal fires. 'They've

hardly ever shown me any respect at all. It's not a problem.'

'If you ain't got respect, you ain't got a thing,' said Granny distantly.

'Oh, I don't know. I've always managed to get along,' said Magrat.

'That's 'cos you're a wet hen, Magrat Garlick,' said Granny.

There was a short, hot silence, ringing with the words that shouldn't have escaped and a few grunts of pained surprise from the direction of the bar.

I know she's always thought that, Magrat told herself within the glowing walls of her embarrassment. I just never thought she'd ever say it. And she'll never say sorry, because that's not the kind of thing she does. She just expects people to forget things like that. I was just trying to be friends again. If she ever really has any friends.

'Here we are then,' said Nanny Ogg, emerging from the crush with a tray. 'Fruit drinks.'

She sat down and looked from one to the other.

'Made from bananas,' she said, in the hope of striking a spark of interest from either woman. 'I remember our Shane brought a banana home once. My, we had a good laugh about that. I said to the man, "What kind of fruit drinks do people drink around here?" and this is what he gave me. Made from bananas. A banana drink. You'll like it. It's what everyone drinks here. It's got bananas in it.'

'It's certainly very . . . strongly flavoured,' said Magrat, sipping hers cautiously. 'Has it got sugar in it too?'

'Very likely,' said Nanny. She looked at Granny's middle-distance frown for a moment, and then picked up her pencil and licked the end professionally.

Anywey one good thing is the drink here is v. cheap theres this one called a Bananana dakry which is basicly Rum with a banananana* in it. I can feel it doin me good. It is v. damp here. I hope we find somewhere to stay tonigt I expect we shal becaus Esme alweys falls on her feet or at any rate on someones feet. I have drawern a picture of a banananana dakry you can see it is empty right down to the bottom. Love, MUM XXXX

In the end they found a stable. It was, as Nanny Ogg cheerfully commented, probably warmer and more hygienic than any of the inns and there were millions of people in foreign parts who'd give their right arms for such a comfy, dry place to sleep.

This cut about as much ice as a soap hacksaw.

It doesn't take much to make witches fall out.

Magrat lay awake, using her sack of clothes as a pillow and listening to the warm soft rain on the roof.

It's all gone wrong before we've even started, she thought. I don't know why I let them come with me. I'm perfectly capable of doing something by myself for once, but they always treat me as if I was a . . . a wet hen. I don't see why I should have to put up with

---

*Nanny Ogg knew how to start spelling 'banana', but didn't know how you stopped.

her sulking and snapping at me the whole time. What's so special about her, anyway? She hardly ever *does* anything really magical, whatever Nanny says. She really *does* just shout a lot and bully people. And as for Nanny, she means well but she has no sense of responsibility, I thought I'd *die* when she started singing the Hedgehog Song in the inn, I just hope to goodness the people didn't know what the words meant.

I'm the fairy godmother around here. We're not at home now. There's got to be different ways of doing things, in foreign parts.

She got up at first light. The other two were asleep, although 'asleep' was too moderate a word for the sounds Granny Weatherwax was making.

Magrat put on her best dress, the green silk one that was unfortunately now a mass of creases. She took out a bundle of tissue paper and slowly un-wrapped her occult jewellery; Magrat bought occult jewellery as a sort of distraction from being Magrat. She had three large boxes of the stuff and was still exactly the same person.

She did her best to remove the straw from her hair. Then she unpacked the magic wand.

She wished she had a mirror to inspect herself in.

'I've got the wand,' she said quietly. 'I don't see why I need any help. Desiderata *said* I was to tell them not to help.'

It crossed her mind to reflect that Desiderata had been very lax on that point. The one thing you could be sure of, if you told Granny Weatherwax and Nanny Ogg not to help, was that they would rush to help if only out of spite. It was quite surprising to Magrat that anyone as clever as Desiderata should have slipped up on that minor point. She'd probably got a psycholology too – whatever *that* was.

Moving quietly, so as not to wake the other two, she opened the door and stepped lightly into the damp air. Wand at the ready, she was prepared to give the world whatever it wished for.

It would help if this included pumpkins.

Nanny Ogg opened one eye as the door creaked shut.

She sat up and yawned and scratched herself. She fumbled in her hat and retrieved her pipe. She nudged Granny Weatherwax in the ribs.

'I ain't asleep,' said Granny.

'Magrat's gone off somewhere.'

'Hah!'

'And I'm going out to get something to eat,' muttered Nanny. There was no talking to Esme when she was in that kind of mood.

As she stepped out Greebo dropped lightly off a beam and landed on her shoulder.

Nanny Ogg, one of life's great optimists, stepped out to take whatever the future had to offer.

Preferably with rum and bananas in it.

The house wasn't hard to find. Desiderata had made very exact notes.

Magrat's gaze took in the high white walls and

ornate metal balconies. She tried to straighten a few wrinkles in her dress, tugged some recalcitrant bits of hay from her hair, and then marched up the driveway and knocked on the door.

The knocker broke off in her hand.

Looking around anxiously lest someone should have noted this vandalism, Magrat tried to wedge it back. It fell off, knocking a lump out of the marble step.

Finally she knocked gently with her knuckle. A fine cloud of paint dust lifted off the door and floated down to the ground. That was the only effect.

Magrat considered her next move. She was pretty sure that fairy godmothers weren't supposed to leave a little card pushed under the door saying something like 'Called today but you were out, please contact the depot for a further appointment.' Anyway, this wasn't the kind of house that got left empty; there would be a score of servants infesting a place like this.

She crunched over the gravel and peered around the side of the house. Maybe the back door . . . witches were generally more at home around back doors . . .

Nanny Ogg always was. She was heading for the one belonging to the palace. It was easy enough to get into; this wasn't a castle like the ones back home, which expressed very clear ideas about inside and outside and were built to keep the two separate. This was, well, a fairytale castle, all icing-sugar battlements and tiny, towering turrets. Anyway, no one took much notice of little old ladies. Little old ladies were by definition harmless, although in a string of villages across several thousand miles of continent this definition was currently being updated.

Castles, in Nanny Ogg's experience, were like swans. They looked as if they were drifting regally through the waters of Time, but in fact there was a hell of a lot of activity going on underneath. There'd be a maze of pantries and kitchens and laundries and stables and breweries – she liked the idea of breweries – and people never noticed another old biddy around the place, eating any spare grub that was lying around.

Besides, you got gossip. Nanny Ogg liked gossip, too.

Granny Weatherwax wandered disconsolately along the clean streets. She wasn't looking for the other two. She was quite certain of that. Of course, she might just happen to bump into them, sort of accidentally, and give them a meaningful look. But she certainly wasn't looking for them.

There was a crowd at the end of the street. Working on the reasonable assumption that Nanny Ogg might be in the middle of it, Granny Weatherwax drifted over.

Nanny wasn't there. But there was a raised platform. And a small man in chains. And some bright-uniformed guards. One of them was holding an axe.

You did not have to be a great world traveller to understand that the purpose of this tableau was not to give the chained man a signed testimonial and a collection from everyone at the office.

Granny nudged a bystander.

'What's happening?'

The man looked sideways at her.

'The guards caught him thieving,' he said.

'Ah. Well, he looks guilty enough,' said Granny. People in chains had a tendency to look guilty. 'So what're they going to do to him?'

'Teach him a lesson.'

'How d'they do that, then?'

'See the axe?'

Granny's eyes hadn't left it the whole time. But now she let her attention rove over the crowd, picking up scraps of thought.

An ant has an easy mind to read. There's just one stream of big simple thoughts: Carry, Carry, Bite, Get Into The Sandwiches, Carry, Eat. Something like a dog is more complicated – a dog can be thinking several thoughts at the same time. But a human mind is a great sullen lightning-filled cloud of thoughts, all of them occupying a finite amount of brain processing time. Finding whatever the owner *thinks* they're thinking in the middle of the smog of prejudices, memories, worries, hopes and fears is almost impossible.

But enough people thinking much the same thing can be heard, and Granny Weatherwax was aware of the fear.

'Looks like it'll be a lesson he won't forget in a hurry,' she murmured.

'I reckon he'll forget it quite quickly,' said the

watcher, and then shuffled away from Granny, in the same way that people move away from lightning rods during a thunderstorm.

And at this point Granny picked up the discordant note in the orchestra of thought. In the middle of it were two minds that were not human.

Their shape was as simple, clean and purposeful as a naked blade. She'd felt minds like that before, and had never cherished the experience.

She scanned the crowd and found the minds' owners. They were staring unblinkingly at the figures on the platform.

The watchers were women, or at least currently the same shape as women; taller than she was, slender as sticks, and wearing broad hats with veils that covered their faces. Their dresses shimmered in the sunlight – possibly blue, possibly yellow, possibly green. Possibly patterned. It was impossible to tell. The merest movement changed the colours.

She couldn't make out their faces.

There were witches in Genua all right. One witch, anyway.

A sound from the platform made her turn.

And she knew why people in Genua were quiet and nice.

There were countries in foreign parts, Granny had heard, where they chopped off the hands of thieves so that they wouldn't steal again. And she'd never been happy with that idea.

They didn't do that in Genua. They cut their heads off so they wouldn't *think* of stealing again.

Granny knew exactly where the witches were in Genua now.

They were in charge.

Magrat reached the house's back door. It was ajar.

She pulled herself together again.

She knocked, in a polite, diffident sort of way.

'Er—' she said.

A bowlful of dirty water hit her full in the face. Through the tidal roaring of a pair of ears full of suds, she heard a voice say, 'Gosh, I'm sorry. I didn't know anyone was standing there.'

Magrat wiped the water out of her eyes, and tried to focus on the dim figure in front of her. A kind of narrative certainty rose in her mind.

'Is your name Ella?' she said.

'That's right. Who're you?'

Magrat looked her new-found god-daughter up and down. She was the most attractive young woman Magrat had ever seen – skin as brown as a nut, hair so blonde as to be almost white, a combination not totally unusual in such an easygoing city as Genua had once been.

What were you supposed to say at a time like this?

She removed a piece of potato peel from her nose.

'I'm your fairy godmother,' she said. 'Funny thing, it sounds silly now I come to tell someone—'

Ella peered at her.

'*You*?'

'Um. Yes. I've got the wand, and everything.'

Magrat waggled the wand, in case this helped. It didn't.

Ella put her head on one side.

'I thought you people were supposed to appear in a shower of glittering little lights and a twinkly noise,' she said suspiciously.

'Look, you just get the wand,' said Magrat desperately. 'You don't get a whole book of instructions.'

Ella gave her another searching look. Then she said, 'I suppose you'd better come in, then. You're just in time. I was making a cup of tea, anyway.'

The iridescent women got into an open-topped carriage. Beautiful as they were, Granny noted, they walked awkwardly.

Well, they would. They wouldn't be used to legs.

She also noticed the way people didn't look at the carriage. It wasn't that they didn't see it. It was simply that they wouldn't let their gaze dwell on it, as if merely recognizing it would lead them into trouble.

And she noticed the coach horses. They had better senses than the humans did. They knew what was behind them, and they didn't like it at all.

She followed them as they trotted, flat-eared and wild-eyed, through the streets. Eventually they were driven into the driveway of a big and dilapidated house near the palace.

Granny lurked by the wall and noted the details. Plaster was dropping off the house walls, and even the knocker had fallen off the door.

Granny Weatherwax did not believe in atmospheres. She did not believe in psychic auras. Being a witch, she'd always thought, depended more on what you *didn't* believe. But she was prepared to believe that there was something very unpleasant in that house. Not *evil*. The two not-exactly-women weren't evil, in the same way that a dagger or a sheer cliff isn't evil. Being evil means being able to make choices. But the hand wielding a dagger or pushing a body over a cliff could be evil, and something like that was going on.

She really wished that she didn't know who was behind it.

People like Nanny Ogg turn up everywhere. It's as if there's some special morphic generator dedicated to the production of old women who like a laugh and aren't averse to the odd pint, especially of some drink normally sold in very small glasses. You find them all over the place, often in pairs.*

They tend to attract one another. Possibly they broadcast inaudible signals indicating that here is someone who could be persuaded to go 'Ooo' at pictures of other people's grandchildren.

Nanny Ogg had found a friend. Her name was Mrs Pleasant, she was a cook, and she was the first black person Nanny had ever spoken to.‡ She was also a cook of that very superior type who spends

---

*Always in front of you in any queue, for a start.
‡Racism was not a problem on the Discworld, because – what with trolls and dwarfs and so on – speciesism was more interesting. Black and white lived in perfect harmony and ganged up on green.

most of the time holding court in a chair in the centre of the kitchen, apparently taking very little heed of the activity going on around her.

Occasionally she'd give an order. And they'd only need to be occasionally, because she'd seen to it over the years that people either did things her way or not at all. Once or twice, with some ceremony, she'd get up, taste something, and maybe add a pinch of salt.

Such people are always ready to chat to any wandering pedlars, herbalists, or little old women with cats on their shoulders. Greebo rode on Nanny's shoulder as though he'd just eaten the parrot.

'You be a-comin' here for Fat Lunchtime, then?' said Mrs Pleasant.

'Helping a friend with a bit of business,' said Nanny. 'My, these biscuits are tasty.'

'I means, I see by your eye,' said Mrs Pleasant, pushing the plate nearer to her, 'that you are of a magical persuasion.'

'Then you sees a lot further than most people in these parts,' said Nanny. 'Y'know, what'd improve these biscuits no end'd be something to dip 'em in, what d'you think?'

'How 'bout something with bananas in it?'

'Bananas would be just the thing,' said Nanny happily. Mrs Pleasant waved imperiously at one of the maids, who set to work.

Nanny sat on her chair, swinging her stumpy legs and looking around the kitchen with interest. A score of cooks were working with the single-mindedness of an artillery platoon laying down a barrage. Huge cakes were being constructed. In the fireplaces whole carcasses of animals were being roasted; turnspit dogs galloped in their treadmills. A huge man with a bald head and a scar right across his face was patiently inserting little sticks into sausages.

Nanny hadn't had any breakfast. Greebo *had* had some breakfast, but this didn't make any difference. They were both undergoing a sort of exquisite culinary torture.

They both turned, as if hypnotized, to watch two maids stagger by under a tray of canapés.

'I can see you is a very observant woman, Mrs Ogg,' said Mrs Pleasant.

'Just a slice,' said Nanny, without thinking.

'I also determines,' Mrs Pleasant said, after a while, 'that you have a cat of no usual breed upon your shoulder there.'

'You're right there.'

'I knows I'm right.'

A brimming glass of yellow foam was slid in front of Nanny. She looked at it reflectively and tried to get back to the matter in hand.

'So,' she said, 'where would I go, do you think, to find out about how you do magic in –'

'Would you like somethin' to eat?' said Mrs Pleasant.

'What? My word!'

Mrs Pleasant rolled her eyes.

'Not this stuff. I wouldn't eat this stuff,' she said bitterly.

Nanny's face fell.

'But you cook it,' she pointed out.

'Only 'cos I'm *told* to. The old Baron knew what good food was. This stuff? It's nothing but pork and beef and lamb and rubbish for them that never tasted anything better. The only thing on four legs that's worth eating is alligator. I mean *real* food.'

Mrs Pleasant looked around at the kitchen.

'Sara!' she shouted.

One of the sub-cooks turned around.

'Yes, 'm?'

'Me and this lady is just going out. Just you see to everything, okay?'

'Yes, 'm.'

Mrs Pleasant stood up and nodded meaningfully at Nanny Ogg.

'Walls have ears,' she said.

'Coo! Do they?'

'We goin' to go for a little stroll.'

There were, it now seemed to Nanny Ogg, two cities in Genua. There was the white one, all new houses and blue-roofed palaces, and around it and even under it was the old one. The new one might not like the presence of the old one, but it couldn't quite ever do without it. Someone, somewhere, has to do the cooking.

Nanny Ogg quite liked cooking, provided there were other people around to do things like chop up the vegetables and wash the dishes afterwards. She'd always reckoned that she could do things to a bit of beef that the bullock had never thought of. But now she realized that wasn't cooking. Not compared to cooking in Genua. It was just staying alive as pleasantly as possible. Cooking anywhere outside Genua was just heating up things like bits of animals and birds and fish and vegetables until they went brown.

And yet the weird thing was that the cooks in Genua had nothing edible to cook; at least, not what Nanny would have thought of as food. To her mind, food went around on four legs, or possibly one pair of legs and one pair of wings. Or at least it had fins on. The idea of food with more than four legs was an entirely new kettle of fi— of miscellaneous swimming things.

They didn't have much to cook in Genua. So they cooked *everything*. Nanny had never heard of prawns or crawfish or lobsters; it just looked to her as though the citizens of Genua dredged the river bottom and boiled whatever came up.

The point was that a good Genuan cook could more or less take the squeezings of a handful of mud, a few dead leaves and a pinch or two of some unpronounceable herbs and produce a meal to make a gourmet burst into tears of gratitude and swear to be a better person for the rest of their entire life if they could just have one more plateful.

Nanny Ogg ambled along as Mrs Pleasant led her through the market. She peered at cages of snakes, and racks of mysteriously tendrilled herbs. She prodded trays of bivalves. She stopped for a chat to the Nanny Ogg-shaped ladies who ran the little stalls that, for a couple of pennies, dispensed strange chowders and shellfish in a bun. She sampled everything. She was enjoying herself immensely. Genua, city of cooks, had found the appetite it deserved.

She finished a plate of fish and exchanged a nod and a grin with the little old woman who ran the fish stall.

'Well, all this is—' she began, turning to Mrs Pleasant.

Mrs Pleasant had gone.

Some people would have bustled off to look for her in the crowds, but Nanny Ogg just stood and thought.

I asked about magic, she thought, and she brought me here and left me. Because of them walls with ears in, I expect. So maybe I got to do the rest myself.

She looked around her. There was a very rough tent a little way from the stalls, right by the river. There was no sign outside it, but there was a pot bubbling gently over a fire. Rough clay bowls were stacked beside the pot. Occasionally someone would step out of the crowd, help themselves to a bowlful of whatever was in the pot, and then throw a handful of coins into the plate in front of the tent.

Nanny wandered over and looked into the pot. Things came to the surface and sank again. The general colour was brown. Bubbles formed, grew, and burst stickily with an organic 'blop'. Anything could be happening in that pot. Life could be spontaneously creating.

Nanny Ogg would try anything once. Some things she'd try several thousand times.

She unhooked the ladle, picked up a bowl, and helped herself.

A moment later she pushed aside the tent flap and looked into the blackness of the interior.

A figure was seated cross-legged in the gloom, smoking a pipe.

'Mind if I step inside?' said Nanny.

The figure nodded.

Nanny sat down. After a decent interval she pulled out her own pipe.

'Mrs Pleasant's a friend of yours, I expect.'

'She knows me.'

'Ah.'

From outside, there was the occasional clink as customers helped themselves.

Blue smoke coiled from Nanny Ogg's pipe.

'I don't reckon,' she said, 'that many people goes away without paying.'

'No.'

After another pause Nanny Ogg said: 'I 'spects some of 'em tries to pay with gold and jewels and scented ungulants and stuff like that?'

'No.'

'Amazin'.'

Nanny Ogg sat in silence for a while, listening to the distant noises of the market and summoning her powers.

'What's it called?'

'Gumbo.'

'It's good.'

'I know.'

'I reckon anyone who could cook like that could

do anything' – Nanny Ogg concentrated – 'Mrs . . . Gogol.'

She waited.

'Pretty near, Mrs Ogg.'

The two women stared at one another's shadowy outline, like plotters who had given the sign and countersign and were waiting to see what would happen next.

'Where I come from, we call it witchcraft,' said Nanny, under her breath.

'Where I come from, we call it voodoo,' said Mrs Gogol.

Nanny's wrinkled forehead wrinkled still further.

'Ain't that all messin' with dolls and dead people and stuff?' she said.

'Ain't witchcraft all runnin' around with no clothes on and stickin' pins in people?' said Mrs Gogol levelly.

'Ah,' said Nanny. 'I sees what you mean.'

She shifted uneasily. She was a fundamentally honest woman.

'I got to admit, though . . .' she added, 'some-times . . . maybe just one pin . . .'

Mrs Gogol nodded gravely. 'Okay. Sometimes . . . maybe just one zombie,' she said.

'But only when there ain't no alternative.'

'Sure. When there ain't no alternative.'

'When . . . you know . . . people ain't showing respect, like.'

'When the house needs paintin'.'

Nanny grinned, toothily. Mrs Gogol grinned, outnumbering her in teeth by a factor of thirty.

'My full name's Gytha Ogg,' she said. 'People calls me Nanny.'

'My full name's Erzulie Gogol,' said Mrs Gogol. 'People call me Mrs Gogol.'

'The way I saw it,' said Nanny, 'this is foreign parts, so maybe there's a *different* kind of magic. Stands to reason. The trees is different, the people is different, the drinks is different and has got banana in 'em, so the magic'd be different too. Then I thought . . . Gytha, my girl, you're never too old to learn.'

'Sure thing.'

'There's something wrong with this city. Felt it as soon as we set foot here.'

Mrs Gogol nodded.

There was no sound for a while but the occasional puffing of a pipe.

Then there was a clink from outside, followed by a thoughtful pause.

A voice said, 'Gytha Ogg? I know you're in there.'

The outline of Mrs Gogol took its pipe out of its mouth.

'That's good,' she said. 'Good sense of taste there.'

The tent flap opened.

'Hallo, Esme,' said Nanny Ogg.

'Blessings be on this . . . tent,' said Granny Weatherwax, peering into the gloom.

'This here's Mrs Gogol,' said Nanny. 'She's by way of bein' a voodoo lady. That's what witches are in these parts.'

'They ain't the only witches in *these* parts,' said Granny.

'Mrs Gogol was very impressed at you detecting me in here,' said Nanny.

'It wasn't hard,' said Granny. 'Once I'd spotted that Greebo washing himself outside, the rest was all deduction.'

In the gloom of the tent Nanny had formed a mental picture of Mrs Gogol as being old. What she hadn't expected, when the voodoo lady stepped out into the open air, was a handsome middle-aged woman taller than Granny. Mrs Gogol wore heavy gold earrings, a white blouse and a full red skirt with flounces. Nanny could feel Granny Weatherwax's disapproval. What they said about women with red skirts was even worse than whatever they said about women with red shoes, whatever *that* was.

Mrs Gogol stopped and raised an arm. There was a flurry of wings.

Greebo, who had been rubbing obsequiously against Nanny's leg, looked up and hissed. The largest and blackest cockerel Nanny had ever seen had settled on Mrs Gogol's shoulder. It turned on her the most intelligent stare she had ever seen on a bird.

'My word,' she said, taken aback. 'That's the biggest cock I've ever seen, and I've seen a few in my time.'

Mrs Gogol raised one disapproving eyebrow.

'She never had no proper upbringing,' said Granny.

'What with living next to a chicken farm and all, *is what I was going to say next*,' said Nanny.

'This is Legba, a dark and dangerous spirit,' said Mrs Gogol. She leaned closer and spoke out of the corner of her mouth. 'Between you and me, he just a big black cockerel. But you know how it is.'

'It pays to advertise,' Nanny agreed. 'This is Greebo. Between you and me, he's a fiend from hell.'

'Well, he's a cat,' said Mrs Gogol, generously. 'It's only to be expected.'

Dear Jason and everyone,

Isn't it amazing the things what happen when you dont expect it, for example we met Mrs Gogol who works as a coke by day but is a Voodoo witch, you mustnt beleive all the stuff about black magic, exetra, this is a Blind, shes just like us only different. Its true about the zombies though but its not what you think . . .

Genua was a strange city, Nanny decided. You got off the main streets, walked along a side road, went through a little gate and suddenly there were trees everywhere, with moss and them llamas hanging from them, and the ground began to wobble underfoot and become swamp. On either side of the track there were dark pools in which, here and there, among the lilies, were the kind of logs the witches had never seen before.

'Them's bloody big newts,' she said.

'They're alligators.'

'By gods. They must get good grub.'

'Yeah!'

Mrs Gogol's house itself looked a simple affair of driftwood from the river, roofed with moss and built out over the swamp itself on four stout poles. It was close enough to the centre of the city that Nanny could hear street cries and the clip-clop of hooves, but the shack in its little swamp was wreathed in silence.

'Don't people bother you here?' said Nanny.

'Not them as I don't want to meet.' The lily pads moved. A v-shaped ripple drifted across the nearest pool.

'Self-reliance,' said Granny approvingly. 'That's always very important.'

Nanny regarded the reptiles with a calculating stare. They tried to match it, and gave up when their eyes started watering.

'I reckon I could just do with a couple of them at home,' she said thoughtfully, as they slid away again. 'Our Jason could dig another pond, no problem. What was it you said they et?'

'Anything they want to.'

'I knows a joke about alligators,' said Granny, in the tones of one announcing a great and solemn truth.

'You never!' said Nanny Ogg. 'I never heard you tell a joke in your whole life!'

'Just because I don't *tell* 'em don't mean I don't *know* 'em,' said Granny haughtily. 'It's about this man—'

'What man?' said Nanny.

'*This man* went into an inn. Yes. It was an inn. And he saw a sign. The sign said "We serve every kind of sandwich." So he said "Get me an alligator sandwich – and make it quick!"'

They looked at her.

Nanny Ogg turned to Mrs Gogol.

'So . . . you live alone here, then?' she said brightly. 'Not a living soul around?'

'In a manner of speakin',' said Mrs Gogol.

'You see, the point is, alligators are—' Granny began, in a loud voice, and then stopped.

The shack's door had opened.

This was another big kitchen.* Once upon a time it had provided employment for half a dozen cooks. Now it was a cave, its far corners shadowy, its hanging saucepans and tureens dulled by dust. The big tables had been pushed to one side and stacked almost ceiling high with ancient crockery; the stoves, which looked big enough to take whole cows and cook for an army, stood cold.

In the middle of the grey desolation someone had set up a small table by the fireplace. It was on a square of bright carpet. A jam-jar contained flowers that had been arranged by the simple method of grabbing a handful of them and ramming them in. The effect was a little area of slightly soppy brightness in the general gloom.

Ella shuffled a few things around desperately

---

*As Desiderata said, fairy godmothers tend to get heavily involved with kitchens.

and then stood looking at Magrat with a sort of defensively shy smile.

'Silly of me, really. I expect you're used to this sort of thing,' she said.

'Um. Yes. Oh, yes. All the time,' said Magrat.

'It was just that I expected you to be a bit . . . older? Apparently you were at my christening?'

'Ah. Yes?' said Magrat. 'Well, you see, the thing is – '

'Still, I expect you can look like whatever you want,' said Ella helpfully.

'Ah. Yes. Er.'

Ella looked slightly puzzled for a moment, as if trying to work out why – if Magrat could look like whatever she wanted – she'd chosen to look like Magrat.

'Well, now,' she said. 'What do we do next?'

'You mentioned tea,' said Magrat, buying time.

'Oh, sure.' Ella turned to the fireplace, where a blackened kettle hung over what Granny Weatherwax always called an optimist's fire.*

'What's your name?' she said over her shoulder.

'Magrat,' said Magrat, sitting.

'That's a . . . nice name,' said Ella, politely. 'Of course, you know mine. Mind you, I spend so much time cooking over this wretched thing now that Mrs Pleasant calls me Embers. Silly, isn't it.'

Emberella, thought Magrat. I'm fairy godmothering a girl who sounds like something you put up in the rain.

---

*Two logs and hope.

'It could use a little work,' she conceded.

'I haven't the heart to tell her off, she thinks it sounds jolly,' she said. '*I* think it sounds like something you put up in the rain.'

'Oh, I wouldn't say that,' said Magrat. 'Uh. Who's Mrs Pleasant?'

'She's the cook at the palace. She comes around to cheer me up when they're out . . .'

Ella spun around, holding the blackened kettle like a weapon.

'I'm *not* going to that ball!' she snapped. 'I'm *not* going to marry the prince! Do you understand?'

The words came out like steel ingots.

'Right! Right!' said Magrat, taken aback by their force.

'He looks slimy. He makes my flesh crawl,' said Embers darkly. 'They say he's got funny eyes. And everyone knows what he does at night!'

Everyone bar one, Magrat thought. No one ever tells me things like that.

Aloud, she said: 'Well, it shouldn't be too much to arrange. I mean, normally it's *marrying* princes that's the hard bit.'

'Not for me it isn't,' said Embers. 'It's all *been* arranged. My other godmother says I've got to do it. She says it's my destiny.'

'Other godmother?' said Magrat.

'Everyone gets two,' said Ella. 'The good one and the bad one. You *know* that. Which one are you?'

Magrat's mind raced.

'Oh, the good one,' she said. 'Definitely.'

'Funny thing,' said Ella. 'That's just what the other one said, too.'

Granny Weatherwax sat in her special knees-clenched, elbows-in way that put as little as possible of herself in contact with the outside world.

'By gor', this is good stuff,' said Nanny Ogg, polishing her plate with what Granny could only hope was bread. 'You ought to try a drop, Esme.'

'Another helping, Mrs Ogg?' said Mrs Gogol.

'Don't mind if I do, Mrs Gogol.' Nanny nudged Granny in the ribs. 'It's really good, Esme. Just like stew.'

Mrs Gogol looked at Granny with her head on one side.

'I think perhaps Mistress Weatherwax isn't worried about the food,' she said. 'I think Mistress Weatherwax is worried about the service.'

A shadow loomed over Nanny Ogg. A grey hand took her plate away.

Granny Weatherwax gave a little cough.

'I've got nothing *against* dead people,' she said. 'Some of my best friends are dead. It just don't seem right, though, dead people walking about.'

Nanny Ogg looked up at the figure even now ladling a third helping of mysterious liquid on to her plate.

'What d'*you* think about it, Mr Zombie?'

'It's a great life, Mrs Ogg,' said the zombie.

'There. See, Esme? He don't mind. Better than being shut up in a stuffy coffin all day, I'll be bound.'

Granny looked up at the zombie. He was – or,

technically, had *been* – a tall, handsome man. He still was, only now he looked like someone who had walked through a room full of cobwebs.

'What's your name, dead man?' she said.

'I am called Saturday.'

'Man Saturday, eh?' said Nanny Ogg.

'No. Just Saturday, Mrs Ogg. Just Saturday.'

Granny Weatherwax looked into his eyes. They were more sentient than most eyes she had seen that belonged to people who were, technically, alive.

She was vaguely aware that there were things you had to do to a dead person to turn them into a zombie, although it was a branch of magic she'd never wanted to investigate. Yet you needed more than just a lot of weird fish innards and foreign roots – the person had to *want* to come back. They had to have some terrible dream or desire or purpose that would enable them to overcome the grave itself . . .

Saturday's eyes *burned*.

She reached a decision. She held out a hand.

'Very pleased to meet you, Mister Saturday,' she said. 'And I'm sure I'd enjoy your lovely stew.'

'It's called gumbo,' said Nanny. 'It's got lady's fingers in it.'

'I know well enough that lady's fingers is a kind of plant, thank you very much,' said Granny. 'I'm not entirely ignorant.'

'All right, but make sure you get a helping with snakes' heads in it as well,' said Nanny Ogg. 'They're the best part.'

'What kind of plant is snakes' heads?'

'Best if you just eat up, I reckon,' said Nanny.

They were sitting on the warped wood veranda round the back of Mrs Gogol's shack, overlooking the swamp. Mossy beards hung from every branch. Unseen creatures buzzed in the greenery. And everywhere there were v-shaped ripples cutting gently through the water.

'I expect it's really nice here when the sun's out,' said Nanny.

Saturday trudged into the shack and returned with a makeshift fishing pole, which he baited and cast over the rail. Then he sort of switched off; no one has more patience than a zombie.

Mrs Gogol leaned back in her rocking-chair and lit her pipe.

'This used to be a great ole city,' she said.

'What happened to it?' said Nanny.

Greebo was having a lot of trouble with Legba the cockerel.

For one thing, the bird refused to be terrorized. Greebo could terrorize most things that moved upon the face of the Discworld, even creatures nominally much bigger and tougher than he was. Yet somehow none of his well-tried tactics – the yawn, the stare and above all the slow grin – seemed to work. Legba merely looked down his beak at him, and pretended to scratch at the ground in a way that brought his two-inch spurs into even greater prominence.

That only left the flying leap. This worked on nearly every creature. Very few animals remained calm in the face of an enraged ball of whirring claws in the face. In the case of this bird, Greebo suspected, it might well result in his becoming a furry kebab.

But this had to be resolved. Otherwise generations of cats would laugh at him.

Cat and bird circled through the swamp, each apparently paying the other no attention whatsoever.

Things gibbered in the trees. Small iridescent birds barrelled through the air. Greebo glared up at them. He would sort them out later.

And the cockerel had vanished.

Greebo's ears flattened against his head.

There was still the birdsong and the whine of insects, but they were elsewhere. Here there was silence – hot, dark and oppressive – and trees that were somehow much closer together than he remembered.

Greebo looked around.

He was in a clearing. Around its sides, hanging from bushes or tied to trees, were things. Bits of ribbon. White bones. Tin pots. Perfectly ordinary things, anywhere else.

And in the centre of the clearing, something like a scarecrow. An upright pole with a crosspiece, on which someone had put an old black coat. Above the coat, on the tip of the pole, was a top hat. On top of the hat, watching him thoughtfully, was Legba.

A breeze blew through the stifling air, causing the coat to flap gently.

Greebo remembered a day when he'd chased a rat into the village windmill and had suddenly found that what had seemed merely a room with odd furniture in it was a great big machine which would, if he put a paw wrong, crush him utterly.

The air sizzled gently. He could feel his fur standing on end.

Greebo turned and stalked away haughtily, until he judged himself out of sight, whereupon his legs spun so fast that his paws skidded.

Then he went and grinned at some alligators, but his heart wasn't in it.

In the clearing, the coat moved gently again and then was still. Somehow, that was worse.

Legba watched. The air grew heavier, just as it does before a storm.

'This used to be a great old city. A happy place. No one *tried* to make it happy. It just happened, all by itself,' said Mrs Gogol. 'That was when the old Baron was alive. But he was murdered.'

'Who done it?' said Nanny Ogg.

'Everyone knows it was the Duc,' said Mrs Gogol.

The witches looked at one another. Royal intrigues were obviously a bit different in foreign parts.

'Pecked to death, was he?' said Nanny.

'A foul deed?' said Granny.

'The Duc is a title, not a bird,' said Mrs Gogol patiently. 'The Baron was poisoned. It was a terrible night. And, in the morning, the Duc was in the palace. Then there was the matter of the will.'

'Don't tell me,' said Granny. 'I bet there was a will leaving everything to this Duc. I bet the ink was still wet.'

'How did you know that?' said Mrs Gogol.

'Stands to reason,' said Granny loftily.

'The Baron had a young daughter,' said Mrs Gogol.

'She'd be still alive, I reckon,' said Granny.

'You surely know a lot of things, lady,' said Mrs Gogol. 'Why'd you think that, then?'

'Well . . .' said Granny. She was about to say: because I know how the stories work. But Nanny Ogg interrupted.

'If this Baron was as great as you say, he must have had a lot of friends in the city, right?' she said.

'That is so. The people liked him.'

'Well, if I was a Duc with no more claim on things than a smudgy will and a little bottle of ink with the cork still out, I'd be lookin' for any chance to make things a bit more official,' said Nanny. 'Marryin' the real heir'd be favourite. He could thumb his nose at everyone, then. I bet she don't know who she really is, eh?'

'That's right,' said Mrs Gogol. 'The Duc's got friends, too. Or keepers, maybe. Not people you'd want to cross. They've brought her up, and they don't let her out much.'

The witches sat in silence for a while.

Granny thought: no. That's not quite right. That's how it'd appear in a history book. But that's not the *story*.

Then Granny said, ''Scuse me, Mrs Gogol, but where do you come in all this? No offence, but I reckon that out here in the swamp it'd be all the same whoever was doing the rulin'.'

For the first time since they'd met her, Mrs Gogol looked momentarily uneasy.

'The Baron was . . . a friend of mine,' she said.

'Ah,' said Granny understandingly.

'He wasn't keen on zombies, mark you. He said he thought the dead should be allowed their rest. But he never insisted. Whereas this new one . . .'

'Not keen on the Interestin' Arts?' said Nanny.

'Oh, I reckon he is,' said Granny. 'He'd have to be. Not *your* magic, maybe, but I bet he's got a lot of magic around him.'

'Why d'you say that, lady?' said Mrs Gogol.

'Well,' said Nanny, 'I can see that you, being a lady o' spirit, wouldn't put up with this if you didn't have to. There's lots of ways to sort matters out, I 'spect. I 'spect, if you dint like someone, their legs might unexpectedly drop off, or they might find mysterious snakes in their boots . . .'

'Alleygators under their bed,' suggested Granny.

'Yes. He's got protection,' said Mrs Gogol.

'Ah.'

'Powerful magic.'

'More powerful'n you?' said Granny.

There was a long and difficult pause.

'Yes.'

'Ah.'

'For now,' Mrs Gogol added.

There was another pause. No witch ever liked admitting to less than near-absolute power, or even hearing another witch doing so.

'You're biding your time, I expect,' said Granny kindly.

'Wifing your strength,' said Nanny.

'It's powerful protection,' said Mrs Gogol.

Granny sat back in her chair. When she spoke next, it was as a person who has certain ideas in their mind and wants to find out what someone else knows.

'What sort?' she said. 'Exactly?'

Mrs Gogol reached into the cushions of her rocking-chair and, after some rummaging, produced a leather bag and a pipe. She lit the pipe and puffed a cloud of bluish smoke into the morning air.

'You look in mirrors a lot these days, Mistress Weatherwax?' she said.

Granny's chair tipped backwards, almost throwing her off the veranda and into the inky waters. Her hat flew away into the lily pads.

She had time to see it settle gently on the water. It floated for a moment and then—

—was eaten. A very large alligator snapped its jaws shut and gazed smugly at Granny.

It was a relief to have something to shout about.

'My hat! It *ate* my hat! One of your alleygators *ate* my *hat*! It was my *hat*! Make it give it back!'

She snatched a length of creeper off the nearest tree and flailed at the water.

Nanny Ogg backed away.

'You shouldn't do that, Esme! You shouldn't do that!' she quavered. The alligator backed water.

'I can hit cheeky lizards if I want!'

'Yes, you can, you can,' said Nanny soothingly, 'but not . . . with a . . . snake . . .'

Granny held up the creeper for inspection. A medium-sized Three-Banded Coit gave her a frightened look, considered biting her nose for a moment, thought better of it, and then shut its mouth very tightly in the hope she'd get the message. She opened her hand. The snake dropped to the boards and slithered away quickly.

Mrs Gogol hadn't stirred in her chair. Now she half turned. Saturday was still patiently watching his fishing line.

'Saturday, go and fetch the lady's hat,' she said.

'Yes, m'm.'

Even Granny hesitated at that.

'You can't make him do that!' she said.

'But he's dead,' said Mrs Gogol.

'Yes, but it's bad enough being dead without bein' in bits too,' said Granny. 'Don't you go in there, Mr Saturday!'

'But it was your *hat*, lady,' said Mrs Gogol.

'Yes, but . . .' said Granny, '. . . a . . . hat was all it was. I wouldn't send anyone into any alligators for any hat.'

Nanny Ogg looked horrified.

No one knew better than Granny Weatherwax that hats were important. They weren't just clothing. Hats defined the head. They defined who you *were*. No one had ever heard of a wizard without a pointy hat – at least, no wizard worth speaking of. And you certainly never heard of a witch without one. Even Magrat had one, although she hardly ever wore it on account of being a wet hen. That didn't matter too much; it wasn't the wearing of the hats that counted so much as having one to wear. Every trade, every craft had its hat. That's why kings had hats. Take the crown off a king and all you had was someone good at having a weak chin and waving to people. Hats had power. Hats were important. But so were people.

Mrs Gogol took another puff at her pipe.

'Saturday, go and get my best hat for holidays,' she said.

'Yes, Mrs Gogol.'

Saturday disappeared into the hut for a moment, and came out with a large and battered box securely wrapped with twine.

'I can't take that,' said Granny. 'I can't take your best hat.'

'Yes you can,' said Mrs Gogol. 'I've got another hat. Oh, yes. I've got another hat all right.'

Granny put the box down carefully.

'It occurs to me, Mrs Gogol,' she said, 'that you ain't everything you seem.'

'Oh yes I is, Mistress Weatherwax. I never bin nothing else, just like you.'

'You brought us here?'

'No. You brought yourselves here. Of your own free will. To help someone, ain't that right? You decided to do it, ain't that right? No one forced you, ain't that right? 'Cept yourselves.'

'She's right about all that,' said Nanny. 'We'd have felt it, if it was magic.'

'That's right,' said Granny. 'No one forced us, except ourselves. What's your game, Mrs Gogol?'

'I ain't playing no game, Mistress Weatherwax. I

just want back what's mine. I want justice. And I wants *her* stopped.'

'Her who?' said Nanny Ogg.

Granny's face had frozen into a mask.

'Her who's behind all this,' said Mrs Gogol. 'The Duc hasn't got the brains of a prawn, Mrs Ogg. I mean *her*. Her with her mirror magic. Her who likes to control. Her who's in charge. Her who's tinkering with destiny. Her that Mistress Weatherwax knows all about.'

Nanny Ogg was lost.

'What's she talking about, Esme?' she said.

Granny muttered something.

'What? Didn't hear you,' Nanny said.

Granny Weatherwax looked up, her face red with anger.

'She means my *sister*, Gytha! Right? Got that? Do you understand? Did you hear? My sister! Want me to repeat it again? Want to know who she's talking about? You want me to write it down? My sister! That's who! My *sister*!'

'They're sisters?' said Magrat.

Her tea had gone cold.

'I don't know,' said Ella. 'They look . . . alike. They keep themselves to themselves most of the time. But I can feel them watching. They're very good at watching.'

'And they make you do *all* the work?' she said.

'Well, I only have to cook for myself and the outside staff,' said Ella. 'And I don't mind the cleaning and the laundry all that much.'

'Do they do their own cooking, then?'

'I don't think so. They walk around the house at night, after I've gone to bed. Godmother Lilith says I must be kind to them and pity them because they can't talk, and always see that we've got plenty of cheese in the larder.'

'They eat nothing but cheese?' said Magrat.

'I don't think so,' said Ella.

'I should think the rats and mice get it, then, in an old place like this.'

'You know, it's a funny thing,' said Ella, 'but I've never seen a mouse anywhere in this house.'

Magrat shivered. She felt *watched*.

'Why don't you just walk away? *I* would.'

'Where to? Anyway, they always find me. Or they send the coachmen and grooms after me.'

'That's horrible!'

'I'm sure they think that sooner or later I'll marry anyone to get away from laundry,' said Ella. 'Not that the Prince's clothes get washed, I expect,' she added bitterly. 'I expect they get burned after he's worn them.'

'What you want to do is make a career of your own,' said Magrat encouragingly, to keep her spirits up. 'You want to be your own woman. You want to emancipate yourself.'

'I don't think I want to do that,' said Ella, speaking with caution in case it was a sin to offend a fairy godmother.

'You do really,' said Magrat.

'Do I?'

'Yes.'

'Oh.'

'You don't have to marry anyone you don't want to.'

Ella sat back.

'How good are you?' she said.

'Er . . . well . . . I suppose I—'

'The dress arrived yesterday,' said Ella. 'It's up in the big front room, on a stand so it doesn't get creased. So that it stays *perfect*. And they've polished up the coach specially. They've hired extra footmen, too.'

'Yes, but perhaps—'

'I think I'm going to have to marry someone I don't want to,' said Ella.

Granny Weatherwax strode up and down the drift-wood balcony. The whole shack trembled to her stamping. Ripples spread out as it bounced on the water.

'Of course you don't remember her!' she shouted. 'Our mam kicked her out when she was thirteen! We was both tiny then! But *I* remember the rows! I used to hear them when I was in bed! She was *wanton*!'

'You always used to say *I* was wanton, when we was younger,' said Nanny.

Granny hesitated, caught momentarily off balance. Then she waved a hand irritably.

'You was, of course,' she said dismissively. 'But you never used magic for it, did you?'

'Din't have to,' said Nanny happily. 'An off-the-shoulder dress did the trick most of the time.'

'Right off the shoulder and on to the grass, as I recall,' said Granny. 'No, *she* used magic. Not just ordinary magic, neither. Oh, she was *wilful*!'

Nanny Ogg was about to say: What? You mean not compliant and self-effacing like what you is, Esme? But she stopped herself. You didn't juggle matches in a fireworks factory.

'Young men's fathers used to come round to complain,' said Granny darkly.

'They never came round to complain about *me*,' said Nanny happily.

'And always looking at herself in mirrors,' said Granny. 'Prideful as a cat, she was. Prefer to look in a mirror than out of a window, she would.'

'What's her name?'

'Lily.'

'That's a nice name,' said Nanny.

'It isn't what she calls herself now,' said Mrs Gogol.

'I bet it isn't!'

'And she's, like, in charge of the city?' said Nanny.

'She was *bossy*, too!'

'What'd she want to be in charge of a city for?' said Nanny.

'She's got plans,' said Mrs Gogol.

'And vain? Really *vain*!' said Granny, apparently to the world in general.

'Did you know she was here?' said Nanny.

'I had a feelin'! Mirrors!'

'Mirror magic isn't bad,' protested Nanny. 'I've done all kinds of stuff with mirrors. You can have a lot of fun with a mirror.'

'She doesn't just use one mirror,' said Mrs Gogol.

'Oh.'

'She uses two.'

'Oh. That's different.'

Granny stared at the surface of the water. Her own face stared back at her from the darkness.

She hoped it was her own face, anyway.

'I've felt her watchin' us, the whole way here,' she said. 'That's where she's happiest, inside mirrors. Inside mirrors, making people into stories.'

She prodded the image with a stick. 'She even got a look at me in Desiderata's house, just before Magrat came in. It ain't nice, seeing someone else in your reflection—'

She paused. 'Where is Magrat, anyway?'

'Out fairy godmothering, I think,' said Nanny. 'She said she didn't need any help.'

Magrat was annoyed. She was also frightened, which made her even more annoyed. It was hard for people when Magrat was annoyed. It was like being attacked by damp tissue.

'You have my personal word on it,' she said. 'You don't have to go to the ball if you don't want to.'

'You won't be able to stop them,' said Ella darkly. 'I know how things work in this city.'

'Look, I said you won't have to go!' said Magrat.

She looked thoughtful.

'There isn't someone else you'd rather marry, is there?' she said.

'No. I don't know many people. I don't get much chance.'

'Good,' said Magrat. 'That makes it easier. I suggest we get you out of here and – and take you somewhere else.'

'There isn't anywhere else. I told you. There's just swamp. I tried once or twice, and they sent the coachmen after me. They weren't unkind. The coachmen, I mean. They're just afraid. Everyone's afraid. Even the Sisters are afraid, I think.'

Magrat looked around at the shadows.

'What of?' she said.

'They say that people disappear. If they upset the Duc. Something happens to them. Everyone's very *polite* in Genua,' said Ella sourly. 'And no one steals and no one raises their voice and everyone stays indoors at night, except when it's Fat Tuesday.' She sighed. 'Now *that's* something I'd like to go to. To the carnival. They always make me stay in, though. But I hear it passing through the city and I think: that's what Genua ought to be. Not a few people dancing in palaces, but everyone dancing in the streets.'

Magrat shook herself. She felt a long way from home.

'I think perhaps I might need a bit of help with this one,' she said.

'You've got a wand,' said Ella.

'I think there's times when you need more than a wand,' said Magrat. She stood up.

'But I'll tell you this,' she said. 'I don't like this house. I don't like this city. Emberella?'

'Yes?'

'You *won't* go to the ball. I'll make sure of that—'

She turned around.

'I told you,' murmured Ella, looking down. 'You can't even hear them.'

One of the sisters was at the top of the steps leading into the kitchen. Her gaze was fixed immovably on Magrat.

They say that everyone has the attributes of some kind of animal. Magrat possibly had a direct mental link to some small furry creature. She felt the terror of all small rodents in the face of unblinking death. Modulated over the menace of the gaze were all sorts of messages: the uselessness of flight, the stupidity of resistance, the inevitability of oblivion.

She knew she could do nothing. Her legs weren't under her control. It was as if commands were coming straight down that stare and into her spinal cord. The sense of helplessness was almost peaceful . . .

'Blessings be upon this house.'

The sister spun around much faster than any human should be able to move.

Granny Weatherwax pushed open the door. 'Oh deary me,' she thundered, 'and lawks.'

'Yeah,' said Nanny Ogg, crowding through the doorway behind her. 'Lawks too.'

'We're just a couple of old beggar women,' said Granny, striding across the floor.

'Begging from house to house,' said Nanny Ogg. 'Not coming directly here by any manner o' means.'

They each caught one of Magrat's elbows and lifted her off her feet.

Granny turned her head.

'What about you, Miss?'

Ella shook her head without looking up.

'No,' she said, 'I mustn't come.'

Granny's eyes narrowed. 'I suppose not,' she said. 'We all have our path to walk, or so it is said, although not by me. Come, Gytha.'

'We're just off,' said Nanny Ogg, brightly.

They turned.

Another sister appeared in the doorway.

'Ye gods,' said Nanny Ogg. 'I never saw her move!'

'We was just going out,' said Granny Weatherwax loudly. 'If it's all the same with you, m'lady?'

She met the stare head-on.

The air tingled.

Then Granny Weatherwax said, between gritted teeth, 'When I say run, Gytha—'

'I hear you,' said Nanny.

Granny groped behind her and found the teapot Magrat had just used. She weighed it in her hands, keeping the movements slow and gentle.

'Ready, Gytha?'

'Waitin', Esme.'

'Run!'

Granny hurled the teapot high into the air. The heads of both sisters snapped around.

Nanny Ogg helped the stumbling Magrat out of the door. Granny slammed it shut as the nearer sister darted forward, mouth open, too late.

'We're leaving the girl in there!' shouted Nanny, as they ran down the drive.

'They're guarding her,' said Granny. 'They're not going to harm her!'

'I ain't seen teeth like those on anyone before!' said Nanny.

'That's 'cos they ain't anyone! They're snakes!'

They reached the comparative security of the roadway and leaned against the wall.

'Snakes?' Nanny wheezed. Magrat opened her eyes.

'It's Lily's doing,' said Granny. 'She was good at that kind of thing, I remember.'

'*Really* snakes?'

'Yeah,' said Granny darkly. 'She made friends easily.'

'Blimey! *I* couldn't do that.'

'She didn't used to be able to either, for more'n a few seconds. That's what using mirrors does for you.'

'I -I—' Magrat stuttered.

'You're all *right*,' said Nanny. She looked up at Esme Weatherwax.

'We shouldn't leave the girl, whatever you say. In a house with snakes walking around thinking they're human,' she said.

'It's worse than that. They're walking around thinking they're snakes,' said Granny.

'Well, whatever. *You* never do that sort of thing. The worst you ever did was make people a bit confused about what they was.'

'That's because I'm the good one,' said Granny bitterly.

Magrat shuddered.

'So are we going to get her out?' said Nanny.

'Not yet. There's going to be a proper time,' said Granny. 'Can you hear me, Magrat Garlick?'

'Yes, Granny,' said Magrat.

'We've got to go somewhere and talk,' said Granny. 'About stories.'

'What about stories?' said Magrat.

'Lily is using them,' said Granny. 'Don't you see that? You can feel it in this whole country. The stories collect round here because here's where they find a way out. She *feeds* 'em. Look, she don't want your Ella to marry that Duc man just because of politics or something. That's just an . . . explanation. 'S not a *reason*. She wants the girl to marry the prince because that's what the story demands.'

'What's in it for her?' said Nanny.

'In the middle of 'em all, the fairy godmother or the wicked witch . . . you remember? That's where Lily is putting herself, like . . . like . . .' she paused, trying to find the right word. 'Remember that time last year when the circus thing came to Lancre?'

'I remember,' said Nanny. 'Them girls in the spangly tights and the fellows pourin' whitewash down their trousers. Never saw a elephant, though. They said there'd be elephants and there wasn't any. It had elephants on the posters. I spent a whole tuppence and there wasn't a single ele—'

'Yes, but what I'm *sayin*',' said Granny, as they hurried along the street, 'is there was that man in the middle, you remember. With the moustache and the big hat?'

'Him? But he didn't do anything much,' said

Nanny. 'He just stood in the middle of the tent and sometimes he cracked his whip and all the acts just went on round him.'

'That's why he was the most important one there,' said Granny. 'It was the things going on around him that made him important.'

'What's Lily feeding the stories?' said Magrat.

'People,' said Granny. She frowned.

'Stories!' she said. 'Well, we'll have to see about that . . .'

Green twilight covered Genua. The mists curled up from the swamp.

Torches flared in the streets. In dozens of yards shadowy figures moved, pulling the covers off floats. In the darkness there was a flash of sequins and a jingle of bells.

All year the people of Genua were nice and quiet. But history has always allowed the downtrodden one night somewhere in any calendar to restore temporarily the balance of the world. It might be called the Feast of Fools, or the King of the Bean. Or even Samedi Nuit Mort, when even those with the most taxing and responsible of duties can kick back and have fun.

Most of them, anyway . . .

The coachmen and the footmen were sitting in their shed at one side of the stable yard, eating their dinner and complaining about having to work on Dead Night. They were also engaging in the time-honoured rituals that go therewith, which largely consist of finding out what their wives have packed for them today and envying the other men whose wives obviously cared more.

The head footman raised a crust cautiously.

'I've got chicken neck and pickle,' he said. 'Anyone got any cheese?'

The second coachman inspected his box. 'It's boiled bacon again,' he complained. 'She always gives me boiled bacon. She knows I don't like it. She don't even cut the fat off.'

'Is it thick white fat?' said the first coachman.

'Yeah. Horrible. Is this right for a holiday feast or what?'

'I'll swap you a lettuce and tomato.'

'Right. What *you* got, Jimmy?'

The underfootman shyly opened his perfect package. There were four sandwiches, crusts cut off. There was a sprig of parsley. There was even a napkin.

'Smoked salmon and cream cheese,' he said.

'*And* still a bit of the wedding cake,' said the first coachman. 'Ain't you et that all up yet?'

'We have it every night,' said the underfootman.

The shed shook with the ensuing laughter. It is a universal fact that any innocent comment made by any recently-married young member of any workforce is an instant trigger for coarse merriment among his or her older and more cynical colleagues. This happens even if everyone concerned has nine legs and lives at the bottom of an ocean of ammonia on a huge cold planet. It's just one of those things.

'You make the most of it,' said the second coachman gloomily, when they'd settled down again. 'It starts off kisses and cake and them cutting the crusts off, and next thing you know it's down to tongue pie, cold bum and the copper stick.'

'The way I see it,' the first coachman began, 'it's all about the way you—'

There was a knocking at the door.

The underfootman, being the junior member, got up and opened it.

'It's an old crone,' he said. 'What do you want, old crone?'

'Fancy a drink?' said Nanny Ogg. She held up a jug over which hung a perceptible haze of evaporating alcohol, and blew a paper squeaker.

'What?' said the footman.

'Shame for you lads to be working. It's a holiday! Whoopee!'

'What's going on?' the senior coachman began, and then he entered the cloud of alcohol. 'Gods! What is that *stuff*?'

'Smells like rum, Mr Travis.'

The senior coachman hesitated. From the streets came music and laughter as the first of the processions got under way. Fireworks popped across the sky. It wasn't a night to be without just a sip of alcohol.

'What a nice old lady,' he said.

Nanny Ogg waved the jug again. 'Up your eye!' she said. 'Mud in your bottom!'

What might be called the *classical* witch comes in two basic varieties, the complicated and the simple, or, to put it another way, the ones that have a room full of regalia and the ones that don't. Magrat was by inclination one of the former sort. For example, take magical knives. She had a complete collection of magical knives, all with the appropriate coloured handles and complicated runes all over them.

It had taken many years under the tutelage of Granny Weatherwax for Magrat to learn that the common kitchen breadknife was better than the most ornate of magic knives. It could do all that the magical knife could do, plus you could also use it to cut bread.

Every established kitchen has one ancient knife, its handle worn thin, its blade curved like a banana, and so inexplicably sharp that reaching into the drawer at night is like bobbing for apples in a piranha tank.

Magrat had hers stuck in her belt. Currently she was thirty feet above the ground, one hand holding on to her broomstick, the other on to a drainpipe, both legs dangling. Housebreaking ought to be easy, when you had a broomstick. But this did not appear to be the case.

Finally she got both legs around the pipe and a firm grip on a timely gargoyle. She waggled the knife in between the two halves of the window and lifted the latch. After a certain amount of grunting, she was inside, leaning against the wall and panting. Blue lights flashed in front of her eyes, echoing the fireworks that laced the night outside.

Granny had kept on asking her if she was sure she wanted to do this. And she was amazed to find that she *was* sure. Even if the snake women were already wandering around the house. Being a witch meant going into places you didn't want to go.

She opened her eyes.

There was the dress, in the middle of the floor, on a dressmaker's dummy.

A Klatchian Candle burst over Genua. Green and red stars exploded in the velvet darkness, and lit up the gems and silks in front of Magrat.

It was the most beautiful thing she had ever seen.

She crept forward, her mouth dry.

Warm mists rolled through the swamp.

Mrs Gogol stirred the cauldron.

'What are they doing?' said Saturday.

'Stopping the story,' she said. 'Or . . . maybe not . . .'

She stood up.

'One way or another, it's our time now. Let's go to the clearing.'

She looked at Saturday's face.

'Are you frightened?'

'I . . . know what will happen afterwards,' said the zombie. 'Even if we win.'

'We both do. But we've had twelve years.'

'Yes. We've had twelve years.'

'And Ella will rule the city.'

'Yes.'

In the coachmen's shed Nanny Ogg and the coachmen were getting along, as she put it, like a maison en flambé.

The underfootman smiled vaguely at the wall, and slumped forward.

'That's youngpipple today,' said the head coachman, trying to fish his wig out of his mug. 'Can't hold their drin . . . their drine . . . stuff . . .'

'Have a hair of the dog, Mr Travis?' said Nanny, filling the mug. 'Or scale of the alligator or whatever you call it in these parts.'

'Reckon,' said the senior footman, 'we should be gettin' the coesshe ready, what say?'

'Reckon you've got time for one more yet,' said Nanny Ogg.

'Ver' generous,' said the coachman. 'Ver' generous. Here's lookin' at you, Mrsrsrs Goo . . .'

Magrat had dreamed of dresses like this. In the pit of her soul, in the small hours of the night, she'd danced with princes. Not shy, hardworking princes like Verence back home, but real ones, with crystal blue eyes and white teeth. And she'd *worn* dresses like this. And they had *fitted*.

She stared at the ruched sleeves, the embroidered bodice, the fine white lace. It was all a world away from her . . . well . . . Nanny Ogg kept calling them 'Magrats', but they were trousers, and very practical.

As if being practical mattered at all.

She stared for a long time.

Then, with tears streaking her face and changing colour as they caught the light of the fireworks, she took the knife and began to cut the dress into very small pieces.

*　　　*　　　*

The senior coachman's head bounced gently off his sandwiches.

Nanny Ogg stood up, a little unsteadily. She placed the junior footman's wig under his slumbering head, because she was not an unkind woman. Then she stepped out into the night.

A figure moved near the wall.

'Magrat?' hissed Nanny.

'Nanny?'

'Did you see to the dress?'

'Have you seen to the footmen?'

'Right, then,' said Granny Weatherwax, stepping out of the shadows. 'Then there's just the coach.'

She tiptoed theatrically to the coachhouse and opened the door. It grated loudly on the cobbles.

'Shsss!' said Nanny.

There was a stub of candle and some matches on a ledge. Magrat fumbled the candle alight.

The coach lit up like a glitter ball.

It was excessively ornate, as if someone had taken a perfectly ordinary coach and then gone insane with fretwork and gold paint.

Granny Weatherwax walked around it.

'A bit showy,' she said.

'Seems a real shame to smash it up,' said Nanny sadly. She rolled up her sleeves and then, as an afterthought, tucked the hem of her skirt into her drawers.

'Bound to be a hammer somewhere around here,' she said, turning to the benches along the walls.

'Don't! That'd make too much noise!' hissed Magrat. 'Hang on a moment . . .'

She pulled the despised wand out of her belt, gripped it tightly, and waved it towards the coach.

There was a brief inrush of air.

'Blow me down,' said Nanny Ogg. 'I never would have thought of that.'

On the floor was a large orange pumpkin.

'It was nothing,' said Magrat, risking a touch of pride.

'Hah! That's one coach that'll never roll again,' said Nanny.

'Hey . . . can you do that to the horses too?' said Granny.

Magrat shook her head. 'Um, I think that would be very cruel.'

'You're right. You're right,' said Granny. 'No excuse for cruelty to dumb animals.'

The two stallions watched her with equine curiosity as she undid the loose-box gates.

'Off you go,' she said. 'Big green fields out there somewhere.' She glanced momentarily at Magrat. 'You have been em-horse-sipated.'

This didn't seem to have much effect.

Granny sighed. She climbed up onto the wooden wall that separated the boxes, reached up, grabbed a horse ear in either hand, and gently dragged their heads down level with her mouth.

She whispered something.

The stallions turned and looked one another in the eye.

Then they looked down at Granny.

She grinned at them, and nodded.

Then . . .

It is impossible for a horse to go instantly from a standing start to a gallop, but they almost managed it.

'What on earth did you say to them?' said Magrat.

'Mystic horseman's word,' said Granny. 'Passed down to Gytha's Jason, who passed it up to me. Works every time.'

'He told you it?' said Nanny.

'Yes.'

'What, all of it?'

'Yes,' said Granny, smugly.

Magrat tucked the wand back into her belt. As she did so, a square of white material fell on to the floor.

White gems and silk glimmered in the candlelight as she reached down hurriedly to pick it up, but there wasn't a lot that escaped Granny Weatherwax.

She sighed.

'Magrat Garlick . . .' she began.

'Yes,' said Magrat meekly. 'Yes. I know. I'm a wet hen.'

Nanny patted her gently on the shoulder.

'Never mind,' she said. 'We've done a good night's work here. That Ella has about as much chance of being sent to the ball tonight as I have of . . . of becoming queen.'

'No dress, no footmen, no horses and no coach,' said Granny. 'I'd like to see *her* get out of *that* one. Stories? Hah!'

'So what're we going to do now?' said Magrat, as they crept out of the yard.

'It's Fat Lunchtime!' said Nanny. 'Hot diggety pig!' Greebo wandered out of the darkness and rubbed against her legs.

'I thought Lily was trying to stamp it out,' said Magrat.

'May as well try to stamp out a flood,' said Nanny. 'Kick out a jam!'

'I don't agree with dancing in the streets,' said Granny. 'How much of that rum did you drink?'

'Oh, come *on*, Esme,' said Nanny. 'They say if you can't have a good time in Genua you're probably dead.' She thought about Saturday. 'You can probably have a bit of quiet fun even if you *are* dead, in Genua.'

'Hadn't we better stay here, though?' said Magrat. 'Just to make sure?'

Granny Weatherwax hesitated.

'What do you think, Esme?' said Nanny Ogg. 'You think she's going to be sent to the ball in a *pumpkin,* eh? Get a few mice to pull it, eh? Heheh!'

A vision of the snake women floated across Granny Weatherwax's mind, and she hesitated. But, after all, it had been a long day. And it was ridiculous, when you came to think about it . . .

'Well, all right,' she said. 'But I'm not going to kick any jam, you understand.'

'There's dancing and all sorts,' said Nanny.

'And banana drinks, I expect,' said Magrat.

'It's a million to one chance, yes,' said Nanny Ogg happily.

*   *   *

Lilith de Tempscire smiled at herself in the double mirror.

'Oh deary me,' she said. 'No coach, no dress, no horses. What *is* a poor old godmother to do? Deary me. And probably lawks.'

She opened a small leather case, such as a musician might use to carry his very best piccolo.

There was a wand in there, the twin of the one carried by Magrat. She took it out and gave it a couple of twists, moving the gold and silver rings into a new position.

The clicking sounded like the nastiest pump-action mechanism.

'And me with nothing but a pumpkin, too,' said Lilith.

And of course the difference between sapient and non-sapient things was that while it was hard to change the shape of the former it was not actually impossible. It was just a matter of changing a mental channel. Whereas a non-sapient thing like a pumpkin, and it was hard to imagine anything less sapient than a pumpkin, could not be changed by any magic short of sourcery.

Unless its molecules remembered a time when they weren't a pumpkin . . .

She laughed, and a billion reflected Liliths laughed with her, all around the curve of the mirror universe.

Fat Lunchtime was no longer celebrated in the centre of Genua. But in the shanty town around the high white buildings it strutted its dark and torchlit stuff.

There were fireworks. There were dancers, and fire-eaters, and feathers, and sequins. The witches, whose idea of homely entertainment was a Morris dance, watched open-mouthed from the crowded sidewalk as the parades strutted by.

'There's dancing skeletons!' said Nanny, as a score of bony figures whirred down the street.

'They're not,' said Magrat. 'They're just men in black tights with bones painted on.'

Someone nudged Granny Weatherwax. She looked up into the large, grinning face of a black man. He passed her a stone jug.

'There you go, honey.'

Granny took it, hesitated for a moment, and then took a swig. She nudged Magrat and passed on the bottle.

'Frgtht!! Gizeer!' she said.

'What?' shouted Magrat, above the noise of a marching band.

'The man wants us to pass it on,' said Granny.

Magrat looked at the bottle neck. She tried surreptitiously to wipe it on her dress, despite the self-evident fact that germs on it would have burned off long ago. She ventured a brief nip, and then nudged Nanny Ogg.

'Kwizathugner!' she said, and dabbed at her eyes.

Nanny up-ended the bottle. After a while Magrat nudged her again.

'I think we're meant to pass it on?' she ventured.

Nanny wiped her mouth and passed the now rather lighter jug randomly to a tall figure on her left.

'Here you go, mister,' she said.

THANK YOU.

'Nice costume you got there. Them bones are painted on really good.'

Nanny turned back to watch a procession of juggling fire-eaters. Then a connection appeared to be made somewhere in the back of her mind. She looked up. The stranger had wandered off.

She shrugged.

'What shall we do next?' she said.

Granny Weatherwax was staring fixedly at a group of ground-zero limbo dancers. A lot of the dances in the parades had this in common: they expressed explicitly what things like maypoles only hinted at. They covered it with sequins, too.

'You'll never feel safe in the privy again, eh?' said Nanny Ogg. At her feet Greebo sat primly watching some dancing women wearing nothing but feathers, trying to work out what to do about them.

'No. I was thinkin' of something else. I was thinkin' about . . . how stories work. And now . . . I think I'd like something to eat,' said Granny weakly. She rallied a bit. 'And I mean some proper food, not somethin' scraped off the bottom of a pond. And I don't want any of this *cuisine* stuff, neither.'

'You ought to be more adventurous, Granny,' said Magrat.

'I ain't against adventure, in moderation,' said Granny, 'but not when I'm eatin'.'

'There's a place back there that does alligator sandwiches,' said Nanny, turning away from the parade. 'Can you believe that? Alligators in a sandwich?'

'That reminds me of a joke,' said Granny Weather-wax. Something was nagging at her consciousness.

Nanny Ogg started to cough, but it didn't work.

'This man went into an inn,' said Granny Weather-wax, trying to ignore the rising uneasiness. 'And he saw this sign. And it said "We serve all kinds of sand-wiches." And he said, "Get me an alligator sandwich – and I want it right away!"'

'I don't think alligator sandwiches is very kind to alligators,' said Magrat, dropping the observation into the leaden pause.

'I always say a laugh does you good,' said Nanny.

Lilith smiled at the figure of Ella, standing forlornly between the snake women.

'And such a raggedy dress, too,' she said. 'And the door to the room was locked. Tut-tut. However can it have happened?'

Ella stared at her feet.

Lilith smiled at the sisters. 'Well,' she said, 'we'll just have to do the best we can with what we've got. Hmm? Fetch me . . . fetch me two rats and two mice. I *know* you can always find rats and mice. And bring in the big pumpkin.'

She laughed. Not the mad, shrill laughter of the bad fairy who's been defeated, but the rather pleasant laughter of someone who's just seen the joke.

She looked reflectively at the wand.

'But first,' she said, transferring her gaze to Ella's pale face, 'you'd better bring in those *naughty* men who let themselves get so drunk. That's not respectful.

And if you haven't got respect, you haven't got anything.'

The clicking of the wand was the only sound in the kitchen.

Nanny Ogg poked at the tall drink in front of her.

'Beats me why they puts an umbrella in it,' she said, sucking the cocktail cherry off the stick. 'I mean, do they want to stop it getting wet or something?'

She grinned at Magrat and Granny, who were both staring gloomily at the passing celebrations.

'Cheer up,' she said. 'Never seen such a pair of long faces in all my puff.'

'That's neat rum you're drinking,' said Magrat.

'You're telling me,' said Nanny, taking a swig. 'Cheers!'

'It was too easy,' said Granny Weatherwax.

'It was only easy 'cos *we* done it,' said Nanny. 'You want something done, we're the girls to do it, eh? You show me anyone else who could have nipped in there and done all that in the nick of time, eh? Especially the coach bit.'

'It doesn't make a good story,' said Granny.

'Oh, bugger stories,' said Nanny loftily. 'You can always change a story.'

'Only at the right places,' said Granny. 'Anyway, maybe they could get her a new dress and horses and a coach and everything.'

'Where? When?' said Nanny. 'It's a holiday. And there's no *time*, anyway. They'll be starting the ball at any moment.'

Granny Weatherwax's fingers drummed on the edge of the café table.

Nanny sighed.

'Now what?' she said.

'It doesn't happen like this,' said Granny.

'Listen, Esme, the only kind of magic that'd work right now is wand magic. And Magrat's got the wand.' Nanny nodded at Magrat. 'Ain't that so, Magrat?'

'Um,' said Magrat.

'Not lost it, have you?'

'No, but—'

'There you are, then.'

'Only . . . um . . . Ella said she'd got *two* godmothers . . .'

Granny Weatherwax's hand thumped down on the table. Nanny's drink flew into the air and overturned.

'That's *right*!' roared Granny.

'That was nearly full. That was a nearly full drink,' said Nanny reproachfully.

'Come on!'

'Best part of a whole glass of—'

'Gytha!'

'Did I say I wasn't coming? I was just pointing out—'

'*Now!*'

'Can I just ask the man to get me ano—'

'*Gytha!*'

The witches were halfway up the street when a coach rattled out of the driveway and trundled away.

'That can't be it!' said Magrat. 'We got rid of it!'

'We ort to have chopped it up,' said Nanny. 'There's good eating on a pumpk—'

'They've got us,' said Granny, slowing down to a stop.

'Can't you get into the minds of the horses?' said Magrat.

The witches concentrated.

'They ain't horses,' said Nanny. 'They feel like . . .'

'Rats turned into horses,' said Granny, who was even better at getting into people's minds than she was at getting under their skins. 'They feel like that poor old wolf. Minds like a firework display.' She winced at the taste of them in her own head.

'I bet,' said Granny, thoughtfully, as the coach skidded around the corner, 'I bet I could make the wheels fall right off.'

'That's not the way,' said Magrat. 'Anyway, Ella's in there!'

'There may be another way,' said Nanny. 'I know someone who could get inside them minds right enough.'

'Who?' said Magrat.

'Well, we've still got our brooms,' said Nanny. 'It should be easy to overtake it, right?'

The witches landed in an alleyway a few minutes ahead of the coach.

'I don't hold with this,' said Granny. 'It's the sort of thing Lily does. You can't expect me to like this. Think of that wolf!'

Nanny lifted Greebo out of his nest among the bristles.

'But Greebo's nearly human anyway,' she said.

'Hah!'

'And it'll only be temp'ry, even with the three of us doing it,' she said. 'Anyway, it'll be int'resting to see if it works.'

'Yes, but it's *wrong*,' said Granny.

'Not for these parts, it seems,' said Nanny.

'Besides,' said Magrat virtuously, 'it can't be bad if *we*'re doing it. We're the good ones.'

'Oh yes, so we is,' said Granny, 'and there was me forgetting it for a minute there.'

Nanny stood back. Greebo, aware that something was expected of him, sat up.

'You must admit we can't think of anything better, Granny,' said Magrat.

Granny hesitated. But under all the revulsion was the little treacherous flame of fascination with the idea. Besides, she and Greebo had hated one another cordially for years. Almost human, eh? Give him a taste of it, then, and see how he likes it . . . . She felt a bit ashamed of the thought. But not much.

'Oh, all right.'

They concentrated.

As Lily knew, changing the shape of an object is one of the hardest magics there is. But it's easier if the object is alive. After all, a living thing already knows what shape it is. All you have to do is change its mind.

Greebo yawned and stretched. To his amazement he went on stretching.

Through the pathways of his feline brain surged a tide of belief. He suddenly believed he was human. He wasn't simply under the *impression* that he was human; he believed it implicitly. The sheer force of the unshakeable belief flowed out into his morphic field, overriding its objections, rewriting the very blueprint of his self.

Fresh instructions surged back.

If he was human, he didn't need all this fur. And he ought to be bigger . . .

The witches watched, fascinated.

'I *never* thought we'd do it,' said Granny.

. . . no points on the ears, the whiskers were too long . . .

. . . he needed more muscle, all these bones were the wrong shape, these legs ought to be longer . . .

And then it was finished.

Greebo unfolded himself and stood up, a little unsteadily.

Nanny stared, her mouth open.

Then her eyes moved downwards.

'Cor,' she said.

'I think,' said Granny Weatherwax, 'that we'd better imagine some clothes on him *right now*.'

That was easy enough. When Greebo had been clothed to her satisfaction Granny nodded and stood back.

'Magrat, you can open your eyes,' she said.

'I hadn't got them closed.'

'Well, you should have had.'

Greebo turned slowly, a faint, lazy smile on his scarred face. As a human, his nose was broken and a black patch covered his bad eye. But the other one glittered like the sins of angels, and his smile was the downfall of saints. Female ones, anyway.

Perhaps it was pheromones, or the way his muscles rippled under his black leather shirt. Greebo broadcast a kind of greasy diabolic sexuality in the megawatt range. Just looking at him was enough to set dark wings fluttering in the crimson night.

'Uh, Greebo,' said Nanny.

He opened his mouth. Incisors glittered.

'Wrowwwwl,' he said.

'Can you understand me?'

'Yessss, Nannyyy.'

Nanny Ogg leaned against the wall for support.

There was the sound of hooves. The coach had turned into the street.

'Get out there and stop that coach!'

Greebo grinned again, and darted out of the alley.

Nanny fanned herself with her hat.

'Whoo-eee,' she said. 'And to think I used to tickle his tummy . . . No wonder all the lady cats scream at night.'

'Gytha!'

'Well, *you've* gone very red, Esme.'

'I'm just out of breath,' said Granny.

'Funny, that. It's not as if you've been running.'

The coach rattled down the street.

The coachmen and footmen were not at all sure what they were. Their minds oscillated wildly. One moment they were men thinking about cheese and bacon rinds. And the next they were mice wondering why they had trousers on.

As for the horses . . . horses are a little insane anyway, and being a rat as well wasn't any help.

So none of them were in a very stable frame of mind when Greebo stepped out of the shadows and *grinned* at them.

He said, 'Wrowwwl.'

The horses tried to stop, which is practically impossible with a coach still piling along behind you. The coachmen froze in terror.

'Wrowwwl?'

The coach skidded around and came up broadside against a wall, knocking the coachmen off. Greebo picked one of them up by his collar and bounced him up and down while the maddened horses fought to get out of the shafts.

'Run awayy, furry toy?' he suggested.

Behind the frightened eyes man and mouse fought for supremacy. But they needn't have bothered. They would lose either way. As consciousness flickered between the states it saw either a grinning cat or a six-foot, well-muscled, one-eyed grinning bully.

The coachmouse fainted. Greebo patted him a few times, in case he was going to move . . .

'Wake up, little mousey . . .'

. . . and then lost interest.

The coach door rattled, jammed, and then opened. 'What's happening?' said Ella.

'Wrowwwwl!'

Nanny Ogg's boot hit Greebo on the back of his head.

'Oh no you don't, my lad,' she said.

'Want to,' said Greebo sulkily.

'You always do, that's your trouble,' said Nanny, and smiled at Ella. 'Out you come, dear.'

Greebo shrugged, and then slunk off, dragging the stunned coachman after him.

'What's *happening*?' complained Ella. 'Oh. Magrat. Did you do this?'

Magrat allowed herself a moment's shy pride.

'I *said* you wouldn't have to go to the ball, didn't I?'

Ella looked around at the disabled coach, and then back to the witches.

'You ain't got any snake women in there with you, have you?' said Granny. Magrat gripped the wand.

'They went on ahead,' said Ella. Her face clouded as she recalled something.

'Lilith turned the real coachmen into beetles,' she whispered. 'I mean, they weren't that bad! She made them get some mice and she made them human and then she said, there's got to be balance, and the sisters dragged in the coachmen and she turned them into beetles and then . . . she *trod* on them . . .'

She stopped, horrified.

A firework burst in the sky, but in the street below a bubble of terrible silence hung in the air.

'Witches don't kill people,' said Magrat.

'This is foreign parts,' muttered Nanny, looking away.

'I think,' said Granny Weatherwax, 'that you ought to get right away from here, young lady.'

'They just went crack—'

'We've got the brooms,' said Magrat. 'We could *all* get away.'

'She'd send something after you,' said Ella darkly. 'I know her. Something from out of a mirror.'

'So we'd fight it,' said Magrat.

'No,' said Granny. 'Whatever's going to happen's going to happen here. We'll send the young lady off somewhere safe and then . . . we shall see.'

'But if I go away *she'll* know,' said Ella. 'She's expecting to see me at the ball right now! And she'll come looking!'

'That sounds right, Esme,' said Nanny Ogg. 'You want to face her somewhere you choose. I don't want her lookin' for us on a night like this. I want to see her coming.'

There was a fluttering in the darkness above them. A small dark shape glided down and landed on the cobbles. Even in the darkness its eyes gleamed. It stared expectantly at the witches with far too much intelligence for a mere fowl.

'That's Mrs Gogol's cockerel,' said Nanny, 'ain't it?'

'Exactly what it is I might never exactly decide,' said Granny. 'I wish I knew where she stood.'

'Good or bad, you mean?' said Magrat.

'She's a good cook,' said Nanny. 'I don't think anyone can cook like she do and be *that* bad.'

'Is she the woman who lives out in the swamp?' said Ella. 'I've heard all kinds of stories about her.'

'She's a bit too ready to turn dead people into zombies,' said Granny. 'And that's not right.'

'Well, we just turned a cat into a person – I mean, a *human* person' – Nanny, inveterate cat lover, corrected herself – 'and that's not strictly right either. It's probably a long way from strictly right.'

'Yes, but we did it for the right reasons,' said Granny.

'We don't know what Mrs Gogol's reasons are—'

There was a growl from the alleyway. Nanny scuttled towards it, and they heard her scolding voice.

'No! Put him down this minute!'

'Mine! Mine!'

Legba strutted a little way along the street, and then turned and looked expectantly at them.

Granny scratched her chin, and walked a little way away from Magrat and Ella, sizing them up. Then she turned and looked around.

'Hmm,' she said. 'Lily is expecting to see you, ain't she?'

'She can look out of reflections,' said Ella nervously.

'Hmm,' said Granny again. She stuck her finger in her ear and twiddled it for a moment. 'Well, Magrat, you're the godmother around here. What's the most important thing we have to do?'

Magrat had never played a card game in her life.

'Keep Ella safe,' she said promptly, amazed at Granny suddenly admitting that she was, after all, the one who had been given the wand. 'That's what fairy godmothering is all about.'

'Yes?'

Granny Weatherwax frowned.

'You know,' she said, 'you two are just about the same size . . .'

Magrat's expression of puzzlement lasted for half a second before it was replaced by one of sudden horror.

She backed away.

'Someone's got to do it,' said Granny.

'Oh, no! No! It wouldn't work! It really wouldn't work! No!'

'Magrat Garlick,' said Granny Weatherwax, triumphantly, 'you *shall* go to the ball!'

The coach cornered on two wheels. Greebo stood on the coachman's box, swaying and grinning madly and cracking the whip. This was even better than his fluffy ball with a bell in it . . .

Inside the coach Magrat was wedged between the two older witches, her head in her hands.

'But Ella might get lost in the swamp!'

'Not with that cockerel leading the way. She'll be safer in Mrs Gogol's swamp than at the ball, I know that,' said Nanny.

'Thank *you*!'

'You're welcome,' said Granny.

'Everyone'll know I'm not her!'

'Not with the mask on they won't,' said Granny.

'But my hair's the wrong *colour*!'

'I can tint that up a treat, no problem,' said Nanny.

'I'm the wrong *shape*!'

'We can—' Granny hesitated. 'Can you, you know, puff yourself out a bit more?'

271

'No!'

'Have you got a spare handkerchief, Gytha?'

'I reckon I could tear a bit off my petticoat, Esme.'

'Ouch!'

'There!'

'And these glass shoes don't *fit*!'

'They fit me fine,' said Nanny. 'I gave 'em a try.'

'Yes, but I've got smaller feet than you!'

'That's all right,' said Granny. 'You put on a couple of pairs of my socks and they'll fit real snug.'

Bereft of all further excuses, Magrat struck out in sheer desperation.

'But I don't know how to *behave* at balls!'

Granny Weatherwax had to admit that she didn't, either. She raised her eyebrows at Nanny.

'You used to go dancin' when you were young,' she said.

'Well,' said Nanny Ogg, social tutor, 'what you do is, you tap men with your fan – got your fan? – and say things like "La, sir!" It helps to giggle, too. And flutter your eyelashes a bit. And pout.'

'How am I supposed to *pout*?'

Nanny Ogg demonstrated.

'Yuk!'

'Don't worry,' said Granny. 'We'll be there too.'

'And that's supposed to make me feel *better*, is it?'

Nanny reached behind Magrat and grabbed Granny's shoulder. Her lips formed the words: Won't work. She's all to pieces. No *confidence*.

Granny nodded.

'Perhaps I ought to do it,' said Nanny, in a loud

voice. 'I'm experienced at balls. I bet if I wore my hair long and wore the mask and them shiny shoes and we hemmed up the dress a foot no one'd know the difference, what do you say?'

Magrat was so overawed by the sheer fascinating picture of this that she obeyed unthinkingly when Granny Weatherwax said, '*Look at me, Magrat Garlick.*'

The pumpkin coach entered the palace drive at high speed, scattering horses and pedestrians, and braked by the steps in a shower of gravel.

'That was *fun*,' said Greebo. And then lost interest.

A couple of flunkies bustled forward to open the door, and were nearly thrown back by the sheer force of the arrogance that emanated from within.

'Hurry up, peasants!'

Magrat swept out, pushing the major-domo away. She gathered up her skirts and ran up the red carpet. At the top, a footman was unwise enough to ask her for her ticket.

'You impertinent *lackey*!'

The footman, recognizing instantly the boundless bad manners of the well-bred, backed away quickly.

Down by the coach, Nanny Ogg said, 'You don't think you might have overdone it a little bit?'

'I had to,' said Granny. 'You know what she's like.'

'How are we going to get in? We ain't got tickets. And we ain't dressed properly, either.'

'Get the broomsticks down off the rack,' said Granny. 'We're going straight to the top.'

They touched down on the battlements of a tower overlooking the palace grounds. The strains of courtly music drifted up from below, and there was the occasional pop and flare of fireworks from the river.

Granny opened a likely-looking door in the tower and descended the circular stairs, which led to a landing.

'Posh carpet on the floor,' said Nanny. 'Why's it on the walls too?'

'Them's *tapestries*,' said Granny.

'Cor,' said Nanny. 'You live and learn. Well, I do anyway.'

Granny stopped with her hand on a doorknob.

'What do you mean by that?' she said.

'Well, I never knew you had a sister.'

'We never talked about her.'

'It's a shame when families break up like that,' said Nanny.

'Huh! *You* said *your* sister Beryl was a greedy ingrate with the conscience of an oyster.'

'Well, yes, but she *is* my sister.'

Granny opened the door.

'Well, well,' she said.

'What's up? What's up? Don't just stand there.' Nanny peered around her and into the room.

'Coo,' she said.

* * *

Magrat paused in the big, red-velvet ante-room. Strange thoughts fireworked around her head; she hadn't felt like this since the herbal wine. But struggling among them like a tiny prosaic potato in a spray of psychedelic chrysanthemums was an inner voice screaming that she didn't even know how to dance. Apart from in circles.

But it couldn't be difficult if ordinary people managed it.

The tiny inner Magrat struggling to keep its balance on the surge of arrogant self-confidence wondered if this was how Granny Weatherwax felt *all the time*.

She raised the hem of her dress slightly and looked down at her shoes.

They couldn't be real glass, or else she'd be hobbling towards some emergency first aid by now. Nor were they transparent. The human foot is a useful organ but is not, except to some people with highly specialized interests, particularly attractive to look at.

The shoes were mirrors. Dozens of facets caught the light.

Two mirrors on her feet. Magrat vaguely recalled something about . . . about a witch never getting caught between two mirrors, wasn't it? Or was it never trust a man with orange eyebrows? Something she'd been taught, back when she'd been an ordinary person. Something . . . like . . . a witch should never stand between two mirrors because, because, because the person that walked away might not be the same person. Or something. Like . . . you were spread out among the images, your whole soul was pulled out thin, and somewhere in the distant images a dark part of you would get out and come looking for you, if you weren't very careful. Or something.

She overruled the thought. It didn't matter.

She stepped forward, to where a little knot of other guests were waiting to make their entrance.

'Lord Henry Gleet and Lady Gleet!'

The ballroom wasn't a room at all, but a court-yard open to the soft night airs. Steps led down into it. At the far end, another much wider staircase, lined with flickering torches, led up into the palace itself. On the far wall, huge and easily visible, was a clock.

'The Honourable Douglas Incessant!'

The time was a quarter to eight. Magrat had a vague recollection of some old woman shouting something about the time, but . . . that didn't matter either . . .

'Lady Volentia D'Arrangement!'

She reached the top of the stairs. The butler who was announcing the arrivals looked her up and down and then, in the manner of one who had been coached carefully all afternoon for this very moment, bellowed:

'Er . . . Mysterious and beautiful stranger!'

Silence spread out from the bottom of the steps like spilled paint. Five hundred heads turned to look at Magrat.

A day before, even the mere thought of having five hundred people staring at her would have melted Magrat like butter in a furnace. But now she stared back, smiled, and raised her chin haughtily.

Her fan snapped open like a gunshot.

The mysterious and beautiful stranger, daughter of Simplicity Garlick, granddaughter of Araminta Garlick, her self-possession churning so strongly that it was crystallizing out on the sides of her personality . . .

. . . stepped out.

A moment later another guest stalked past the butler.

The butler hesitated. Something about the figure worried him. It kept going in and out of focus. He wasn't entirely certain if there was anyone else there at all.

Then his common sense, which had temporarily gone and hidden behind something, took over. After all, it was Samedi Nuit Mort – people were *supposed to* dress up and look weird. You were *allowed* to see people like that.

'Excuse me, er, sir,' he said. 'Who shall I say it is?'

I'M HERE INCOGNITO.

The butler was sure nothing had been said, but he was also certain that he had heard the words.

'Um . . . fine . . .' he mumbled. 'Go on in, then . . . um.' He brightened. 'Damn good mask, sir.'

He watched the dark figure walk down the steps, and leaned against a pillar.

Well, that was about it. He pulled a handkerchief out from his pocket, removed his powdered wig, and wiped his brow. He felt as though he'd just had a narrow escape, and what was even worse was that he didn't know from *what*.

He looked cautiously around, and then sidled

into the ante-room and took up a position behind a velvet curtain, where he could enjoy a quiet roll-up.

He nearly swallowed it when another figure loped silently up the red carpet. It was dressed like a pirate that had just raided a ship carrying black leather goods for the discerning customer. One eye had a patch over it. The other gleamed like a malevolent emerald. And no one that big ought to be able to walk that quietly.

The butler stuck the dog-end behind his ear.

'Excuse me, milord,' he said, running after the man and touching him firmly yet respectfully on the arm. 'I shall need to see your tic . . . your . . . tic . . .'

The man transferred his gaze to the hand on his arm. The butler let go hurriedly.

'Wrowwwl?'

'Your . . . ticket . . .'

The man opened his mouth and hissed.

'Of course,' said the butler, backing away with the efficient speed of someone who certainly isn't being paid enough to face a needle-toothed maniac in black leather, 'I expect you're one of the Duc's friends, yes?'

'Wrowwl.'

'No problem . . . no problem . . . but Sir has forgotten Sir's mask . . .'

'Wrowwl?'

The butler waved frantically to a side-table piled high with masks.

'The Duc requested that everyone here is masked,'

said the butler. 'Er. I wonder if Sir would find something here to his liking?'

There's always a few of them, he thought to himself. It says 'Masque' in big curly letters on the invite, in gold yet, but there's always a few buggers who thinks it means it's from someone called Maskew. This one was quite likely looting towns when he should have been learning to read.

The greasy man stared at the masks. All the good ones had been taken by earlier arrivals, but that didn't seem to dismay him.

He pointed.

'Want that one,' he said.

'Er . . . a . . . very good choice, my lord. Allow me to help you on—'

'Wrowwl!'

The butler backed away, clutching at his own arm.

The man glared at him, then dropped the mask over his head and squinted out through an eyehole at a mirror.

Damn odd, the butler thought. I mean, it's not the kind of mask the men choose. They go for skulls and birds and bulls and stuff like that. Not *cats*.

The odd thing was that the mask had just been a pretty ginger cat head when it was on the table. On its wearer it was . . . still a cat head, only a lot more so, and somehow slightly more feline and a lot nastier than it should have been.

'Aaalwaaays waanted to bee ginger,' said the man.

'On you it looks good, sir,' trilled the butler.

The cat-headed man turned his head this way and that, clearly in love with what he was seeing.

Greebo yowled softly and happily to himself and ambled into the ball. He wanted something to eat, someone to fight, and then . . . well, he'd have to see.

For wolves and pigs and bears, thinking that they're human is a tragedy. For a cat, it's an experience.

Besides, this new shape was a lot more fun. No one had thrown an old boot at him for over ten minutes.

The two witches looked around the room.

'Odd,' said Nanny Ogg. 'Not what I'd expect in, you know, a royal bedroom.'

'Is it a royal bedroom?'

'There's a crown on the door.'

'Oh.'

Granny looked around at the decor.

'What do you know about royal bedrooms?' she said, more or less for something to say. 'You've never been in a royal bedroom.'

'I might have been,' said Nanny.

'You never have!'

'Remember young Verence's coronation? We all got invited to the palace?' said Nanny. 'When I went to have a – to powder my nose I saw the door open, so I went in and had a bit of a bounce up and down.'

'That's treason. You can get put in prison for that,' said Granny severely, and added, 'What was it like?'

'Very comfy. Young Magrat doesn't know what

she's missing. And it was a lot better than this, I don't mind saying,' said Nanny.

The basic colour was green. Green walls, green floor. There was a wardrobe and a bedside table. Even a bedside rug, which was green. The light filtered in through a window filled with greenish glass.

'Like being at the bottom of a pond,' said Granny. She swatted something. 'And there's flies everywhere!' She paused, as if thinking very hard, and said, 'Hmm . . .'

'A Duc pond,' said Nanny.

There *were* flies everywhere. They buzzed on the window and zigzagged aimlessly back and forth across the ceiling.

'Duc pond,' Nanny repeated, because people who make that kind of joke never let well alone, 'like duck—'

'I heard,' said Granny. She flailed at a fat bluebottle.

'Anyway, you'd think there wouldn't be flies in a royal bedroom,' muttered Nanny.

'You'd think there'd be a bed, in fact,' said Granny.

Which there wasn't. What there was instead, and what was preying somewhat on their minds, was a big round wooden cover on the floor. It was about six feet across. There were convenient handles.

They walked around it. Flies rose up and hummed away.

'I'm thinking of a story,' said Granny.

'Me too,' said Nanny Ogg, her tone slightly

shriller than usual. 'There was this girl who married this man and he said you can go anywhere you like in the palace but you mustn't open *that* door and she did and she found he'd murdered all his other . . .'

Her voice trailed off.

Granny was staring hard at the cover, and scratching her chin.

'Put it like this,' said Nanny, trying to be reasonable against all odds. 'What could we possibly find under there that's worse than we could imagine?'

They each took a handle.

Five minutes later Granny Weatherwax and Nanny Ogg stepped outside the Duc's bedroom. Granny closed the door very quietly.

They stared at one another.

'Cor,' said Nanny, her face still pale.

'Yes,' said Granny. 'Stories!'

'I'd heard about . . . you know, people like him, but I never believed it. Yuk. I wonder what he looks like.'

'You can't tell just by lookin',' said Granny.

'It explains the flies, at any rate,' said Nanny Ogg.

She raised a hand to her mouth in horror.

'And our Magrat's down there with him!' she said. 'And you know what's going to happen. They're going to meet one another and—'

'But there's hundreds of other people,' said Granny. 'It's hardly what you'd call *intimate*.'

'Yes . . . but even the thought of him, you know,

even *touching* her . . . I mean, it'd be like holding a—'

'Does Ella count as a princess, d'you think?' said Granny.

'What? Oh. Yeah. Probably. For foreign parts. Why?'

'Then that means there's more than one story here. Lily's letting several happen all at the same time,' said Granny. 'Think about it. It's not touching that's the trick. It's *kissing*.'

'We've got to get down there!' said Nanny. 'We've got to stop it! I mean, you know me, I'm no prude, but . . . yuk . . .'

'I say! Old woman!'

They turned. A small fat woman in a red dress and a towering white wig was peering haughtily at them from behind a fox mask.

'Yes?' snapped Granny.

'Yes, *my lady*,' said the fat woman. 'Where are your manners? I demand that you direct me to the powder room this instant! *And what do you think you're doing?*'

This was to Nanny Ogg, who was walking around her and staring critically at her dress.

'You're a 20, maybe a 22?' said Nanny.

'What? What is this *impertinence*?'

Nanny Ogg rubbed her chin thoughtfully. 'Well, I dunno,' she said, 'red in a dress has never been *me*. You haven't got anything in blue, have you?'

The choleric woman turned to strike Nanny with her fan, but a skinny hand tapped her on the shoulder.

She looked up into Granny Weatherwax's face.

As she passed out dreamily she was aware of a voice, a long way off, saying, 'Well, that's me fitted. But she's never a size 20. And if I had a face like that *I'd* never wear red . . .'

Lady Volentia D'Arrangement relaxed in the inner sanctum of the ladies' rest room. She removed her mask and fished an errant beauty spot from the depths of her décolletage. Then she reached around and down to try and adjust her bustle, an exercise guaranteed to produce the most ridiculous female gymnastics on every world except those where the panty girdle had been invented.

Apart from being as well-adapted a parasite as the oak bracket fungus Lady Volentia D'Arrangement was, by and large, a blameless sort of person. She always attended events for the better class of charity, and made a point of knowing the first names of nearly all her servants – the cleaner ones, at least. And she was, on the whole, kind to animals and even to children if they had been washed and didn't make too much noise. All in all, she didn't deserve what was about to happen to her, which was the fate Mother Nature had in store for any woman in this room on this night who happened to have approximately the same measurements as Granny Weatherwax.

She was aware of someone coming up beside her.

'S'cuse me, missus.'

It turned out to be a small, repulsive lower-class woman with a big ingratiating smile.

'What do you want, old woman?' said Lady Volentia.

'S'cuse me,' said Nanny Ogg. 'My friend over there would like a word with you.'

Lady Volentia looked around haughtily into . . .

. . . icy, blue-eyed, hypnotic oblivion.

'What's this thing like an extra bu . . . hobo?'

'It's a bustle, Esme.'

'It's damn uncomfortable is what it is. I keep on feeling someone's following me around.'

'The white suits you, anyway.'

'No it don't. Black's the only colour for a proper witch. And this wig is too hot. Who wants a foot of hair on their heads?'

Granny donned her mask. It was an eagle's face in white feathers stuck with sequins.

Nanny adjusted some unmentionable under-pinning somewhere beneath her crinoline and straightened up.

'Cor, look at us,' she said. 'Them feathers in your hair really look good.'

'I've never been vain,' said Granny Weatherwax. 'You know that, Gytha. No one could ever call *me* vain.'

'No, Esme,' said Nanny Ogg.

Granny twirled a bit.

'Are you ready then, Dame Ogg?' she said.

'Yes. Let's *do* it, Lady Weatherwax.'

The dance floor was thronged. Decorations hung from every pillar, but they were black and silver, the colours of the festival of Samedi Nuit Mort. An orchestra was playing on a balcony. Dancers whirled. The din was immense.

A waiter with a tray of drinks suddenly found that he was a waiter without a tray of drinks. He looked around, and then down to a small fox under a huge white wig.

'Bugger off and get us some more,' said Nanny pleasantly. 'Can you see her, your ladyship?'

'There's too many people.'

'Well, can you see the Duc?'

'How do I know? Everyone's got masks on!'

'Hey, is that food over there?'

Many of the less energetic or more hungry of the Genua nobility were clustered around the long buffet. All they were aware of, apart from sharp digs with a pair of industrious elbows, was an amiable monotone at chest height, on the lines of '. . . mind your backs . . . stand aside there . . . comin' through.'

Nanny fought her way to the table and nudged a space for Granny Weatherwax.

'Cor, what a spread, eh?' she said. 'Mind you, they have tiny chickens in these parts.' She grabbed a plate.

'Them's quails.'

'I'll 'ave three. 'Ere, charlie chan!'

A flunkey stared at her.

'Got any pickles?'

'I'm afraid not, ma'am.'

Nanny Ogg looked along a table which included roast swans, a roasted peacock that probably wouldn't have felt any better about it even if it *had* known that its tail feathers were going to be stuck back in afterwards, and more fruits, boiled lobsters, nuts, cakes, creams and trifles than a hermit's dream.

'Well, got any relish?'

'No, ma'am.'

'Tomato ketchup?'

'*No*, ma'am.'

'And they call this a gormay paradise,' muttered Nanny, as the band struck up the next dance. She nudged a tall figure helping himself to the lobster. 'Some place, eh?'

VERY NICE.

'Good mask you've got there.'

THANK YOU.

Nanny was spun around by Granny Weatherwax's hand on her shoulder.

'There's Magrat!'

'Where? Where?' said Nanny.

'Over there . . . sitting by the potted plants.'

'Oh, yes. On the chassy longyew,' said Nanny. 'That's "sofa" in foreign, you know,' she added.

'What's she doing?'

'Being attractive to men, I think.'

'What, *Magrat*?'

'Yeah. You're really getting good at that hypnotism, ain't you.'

Magrat fluttered her fan and looked up at the Compte de Yoyo.

'La, sir,' she said. 'You may get me another plate of lark's eggs, if you *really* must.'

'Like a shot, dear lady!' The old man bustled off in the direction of the buffet.

Magrat surveyed her empire of admirers, and then extended a languorous hand towards Captain de Vere of the Palace Guard. He stood to attention.

'*Dear* captain,' she said, 'you may have the pleasure of the next dance.'

'Acting like a hussy,' said Granny disapprovingly.

Nanny gave her an odd look.

'Not really,' she said. 'Anyway, a bit of hussing never did anyone any harm. At least none of those men look like the Duc. 'Ere, what you doing?'

This was to a small bald-headed man who was trying surreptitiously to set up a small easel in front of them.

'Uh . . . if you ladies could just hold still for a few minutes,' he said shyly. 'For the woodcut?'

'What woodcut?' said Granny Weatherwax.

'You *know*,' said the man, opening a small penknife. 'Everyone likes to see their woodcut in the broadsheets after a ball like this? "Lady Thing enjoying a joke with Lord Whatsit", that sort of thing?'

Granny Weatherwax opened her mouth to reply, but Nanny Ogg laid a gentle hand on her arm. She relaxed a little and sought for something more suitable to say.

'I knows a joke about alligator sandwiches,' she volunteered, and shook Nanny's hand away. 'There was a man, and he went into an inn and he said "Do you sell alligator sandwiches?" and the other man said "Yes" and he said, "Then give me an alligator sandwich – and don't be a long time about it!"'

She gave him a triumphant look.

'Yes?' said the woodcutter, chipping away quickly, 'And then what happened?'

Nanny Ogg dragged Granny away quickly, searching for a distraction.

'Some people don't know a joke when they hear it,' said Granny.

As the band launched into another number Nanny Ogg rumbled in a pocket and found the dance card that belonged to an owner now slumbering peacefully in a distant room.

'This is,' she turned the card round, her lips moving wonderingly, 'Sir, Roger the Coverley?'

'Ma'am?'

Granny Weatherwax looked around. A plump military man with big whiskers was bowing to her. He looked as though he'd enjoyed quite a few jokes in his time.

'Yes?'

'You promised me the honour of this dance, m'lady?'

'No I didn't.'

The man looked puzzled. 'But I assure you, Lady D'Arrangement . . . your card . . . my name is Colonel Moutarde . . .'

Granny gave him a look of deep suspicion, and then read the dance card attached to her fan.

'Oh.'

'Do you know how to dance?' hissed Nanny.

'Of course.'

'Never *seen* you dance,' said Nanny.

Granny Weatherwax had been on the point of giving the colonel as polite a refusal as she could manage. Now she threw back her shoulders defiantly.

'A witch can do anything she puts her mind to, Gytha Ogg. Come, Mr Colonel.'

Nanny watched as the pair disappeared into the throng.

''Allo, foxy lady,' said a voice behind her. She looked around. There was no one there.

'Down here.'

She looked down.

A very small body wearing the uniform of a captain in the palace guard, a powdered wig and an ingratiating smile beamed up at her.

'My name's Casanunda,' he said. 'I'm reputed to be the world's greatest lover. What do you think?'

Nanny Ogg looked him up and down or, at least, down and further down.

'You're a dwarf,' she said.

'Size isn't important.'

Nanny Ogg considered her position. One colleague known for her shy and retiring nature was currently acting like that whatshername, the heathen queen who was always playing up to men and bathing in asses' milk and stuff, and the *other* one was acting very odd and dancing with a *man* even though she didn't know one foot from the other. Nanny Ogg felt she was at least owed a bit of time in which to be her own woman.

'Can you dance as well?' she said wearily.

'Oh yes. How about a date?'

'How old do you think I am?' said Nanny.

Casanunda considered. 'All right, then. How about a prune?'

Nanny sighed, and reached down for his hand. 'Come on.'

Lady Volentia D'Arrangement staggered limply along a passageway, a forlorn thin shape in complicated corsetry and ankle-length underwear.

She wasn't at all sure what had happened. There had been that *frightful* woman, and then this feeling of absolute *bliss* and then . . . she'd been sitting on the carpet with her *dress* off. Lady Volentia had been to enough balls in her dull life to know that there were occasions when you woke up in strange rooms with your dress off, but that tended to be later in the evening and at least you had some idea of why you were there . . .

She eased her way along, holding on to the wall. Someone was definitely going to get told off about this.

A figure came around a bend in the corridor, idly tossing a turkey leg into the air with one hand and catching it with the other.

'I say,' said Lady Volentia, 'I wonder if you would be so good as to – oh . . .'

She looked up at a leather-clad figure with an eyepatch and a grin like a corsair raider.

'Wroowwwwl!'

'Oh. I say!'

*   *   *

Nothing to this dancing, Granny Weatherwax told herself. It's just moving around to music.

It helped to be able to read her partner's mind. Dancing is instinctive, after you've got past that stage of looking down to see what your feet are doing, and witches are good at reading resonating instincts. There was a slight struggle as the colonel tried to lead, but he soon gave in, partly in the face of Granny Weatherwax's sheer refusal to compromise but mainly because of her boots.

Lady D'Arrangement's shoes hadn't fitted. Besides, Granny was attached to her boots. They had complicated iron fixtures, and toecaps like battering rams. When it came to dancing, Granny's boots went exactly wherever they wanted to go.

She steered her helpless and slightly crippled partner towards Nanny Ogg, who had already cleared quite a space around her. What Granny could achieve with two pounds of hobnailed syncopation Nanny Ogg could achieve merely with her bosom.

It was a large and experienced bosom, and not one that was subject to restraint. As Nanny Ogg bounced down, it went up; when she gyrated right, it hadn't finished twirling left. In addition, Nanny's feet moved in a complicated jig step regardless of the actual tempo, so that while her body actually progressed at the speed of a waltz her feet were doing something a bit nearer to a hornpipe. The total effect obliged her partner to dance several feet away, and many surrounding couples to stop dancing just to watch in fascination, in case the build-up of harmonic vibrations dropped her into the chandeliers.

Granny and her helpless partner whirled past.

'Stop showin' off,' Granny hissed, and disappeared into the throng again.

'Who's your friend?' said Casanunda.

'She's—' Nanny began.

There was a blast of trumpets.

'That was a bit off the beat,' she said.

'No, that means the Duc is arriving,' said Casanunda.

The band stopped playing. The couples, as one, turned and faced the main staircase.

There were two figures descending in stately fashion.

My word, he's a sleek and handsome devil, Nanny told herself. It just goes to show. Esme's right. You can never tell by lookin'.

And her . . .

. . . that's Lily Weatherwax?

The woman wasn't masked.

Give or take the odd laughter line and wrinkle, it was Granny Weatherwax to the life.

Almost . . .

Nanny found she was turning to find the white eagle head in the crowd. All heads were turned to the staircase, but there was one staring as if her gaze was a steel rod.

Lily Weatherwax wore white. Until that point it had never occurred to Nanny Ogg that there could be different colours of white. Now she knew better. The white of Lily Weatherwax's dress seemed to radiate; if all the lights went out, she felt, Lily's dress would glow. It had style. It gleamed, and had puffed sleeves and was edged with lace.

And Lily Weatherwax looked – Nanny Ogg had to admit it – younger. There was the same bone structure and fine Weatherwax complexion, but it looked . . . less worn.

If that's what bein' bad does to you, Nanny thought, I could of done with some of that years ago. The wages of sin is death but so is the salary of virtue, and at least the evil get to go home early on Fridays.

The eyes were the same, though. Somewhere in the genetics of the Weatherwaxes was a piece of sapphire. Maybe generations of them.

The Duc was unbelievably handsome. But that was understandable. He was wearing black. Even his eyes wore black.

Nanny surfaced, and pushed her way through the throng to Granny Weatherwax.

'Esme?'

She grabbed Granny's arm.

'Esme?'

'Hmm?'

Nanny was aware that the crowd was moving, parting like a sea, between the staircase and the chaise-longue at the far end of the hall.

Granny Weatherwax's knuckles were as white as her dress.

'Esme? What's happening? What are you *doing*?' said Nanny.

'Trying . . . to . . . stop . . . the story,' said Granny.

'What's *she* doing, then?'

'Letting . . . things . . . happen!'

The crowd was pulling back past them. It didn't seem to be a conscious thing. It was just happening that a sort of corridor was forming.

The Duc walked slowly along it. Behind Lily, faint images hung in the air so that she appeared to be followed by a succession of fading ghosts.

Magrat stood up.

Nanny was aware of a rainbow hue in the air. Possibly there was the tweeting of bluebirds.

The Prince took Magrat by the hand.

Nanny glanced up at Lily Weatherwax, who had remained a few steps up from the foot of the stairs and was smiling beneficently.

Then she tried to put a focus on the future.

It was horribly easy.

Normally the future is branching off at every turn and it's only possible to have the haziest idea of what is likely to happen, even when you're as temporally sensitive as a witch. But here there were stories coiled around the tree of events, bending it into a new shape.

Granny Weatherwax wouldn't know what a pattern of quantum inevitability was if she found it eating her dinner. If you mentioned the words 'paradigms of space-time' to her she'd just say 'What?' But that didn't mean she was ignorant. It just meant that she didn't have any truck with words, especially gibberish. She just knew that there were certain things that happened continually in human history, like three-dimensional clichés. Stories.

'And now we're part of it! And I can't stop it,' said Granny. 'There's got to be a place where I can stop it, and I can't find it!'

The band struck up. It was playing a waltz.

Magrat and the Prince whirled around the dance floor once, never taking their eyes off each other. Then a few couples dared to join them. And then, as if the whole ball was a machine whose spring had been wound up again, the floor was full of dancing couples and the sounds of conversation flowed back into the void.

'Are you going to introduce me to your friend?' said Casanunda, from somewhere near Nanny's elbow. People swept past them.

'It's all got to happen,' said Granny, ignoring the low-level interruption. 'Everything. The kiss, the clock striking midnight, her running out and losing the glass slipper, everything.'

'Ur, yuk,' said Nanny, leaning on her partner's head. 'I'd rather lick toads.'

'She looks just my type,' said Casanunda, his voice slightly muffled. 'I've always been very attracted to dominant women.'

The witches looked at the whirling couple, who were staring into one another's eyes.

'I could trip them up, no trouble,' said Nanny.

'You can't. That's not something that can happen.'

'Well, Magrat's sensible . . . more or less sensible,' said Nanny. 'Maybe she'll notice something's wrong.'

'I'm good at what I do, Gytha Ogg,' said Granny.

'She won't notice nothing until the clock strikes midnight.'

They both turned to look up. It was barely nine.

'Y'know,' said Nanny Ogg. 'Clocks don't strike midnight. Seems to me they just strike twelve. I mean, it's just a matter of bongs.'

They both looked up at the clock again.

In the swamp, Legba the black cockerel crowed. He always crowed at sunset.

Nanny Ogg pounded up another flight of stairs and leaned against the wall to catch her breath.

It had to be somewhere round here.

'Another time you'll learn to keep your mouth shut, Gytha Ogg,' she muttered.

'I expect we're leaving the hurly-burly of the ball for an intimate tête-à-tête somewhere?' said Casanunda hopefully, trotting along behind her.

Nanny tried to ignore him and ran along a dusty passage. There was a balcony rail on one side, looking down into the ballroom. And there . . .

. . . a small wooden door.

She rammed it open with her elbow. Within, mechanisms whirred in counterpoint to the dancing figures below as if the clock was propelling them, which, in a metaphorical sense, it was.

Clockwork, Nanny thought. Once you know about clockwork, you know about *everything*.

I wish I bloody well knew about clockwork.

'Very cosy,' said Casanunda.

She squeezed through the gap and into the clock space. Cog-wheels clicked past her nose.

She stared at them for a moment.

Lawks. All this just to chop Time up into little bits.

'It might be just the teensiest bit cramped,' said Casanunda, from somewhere near her armpit. 'But needs must, ma'am. I remember once in Quirm, there was this sedan chair and . . .'

Let's see, thought Nanny. This bit is connected to that bit, this one turns, that one turns *faster*, this spiky bit wobbles backwards and forwards . . .

Oh, well. Just twist the first thing you can grab, as the High Priest said to the vestal virgin.*

Nanny Ogg spat on her hands, gripped the largest cogwheel, and twisted.

It carried on turning, pulling her with it.

Blimey. Oh, well . . .

Then she did what neither Granny Weatherwax nor Magrat would have dreamed of doing in the circumstances. But Nanny Ogg's voyages on the sea of inter-sexual dalliance had gone rather further than twice around the lighthouse, and she saw nothing demeaning in getting a man to help her.

She simpered at Casanunda.

'Things would be a lot more comfortable in our little *pie-de-terre* if you could just push this little wheel around a bit,' she said. 'I'm sure *you* could manage it,' she added.

'Oh, no problem, good lady,' said Casanunda. He

*This is the last line of a Discworld joke lost, alas, to posterity.

reached up with one hand. Dwarfs are immensely strong for their size. The wheel seemed to offer him no resistance at all.

Somewhere in the mechanism something resisted for a moment and then went *clonk*. Big wheels turned reluctantly, little wheels screamed on their axles. A small important piece flew out and pinged off Casanunda's small bullet head.

And, much faster than nature had ever intended, the hands sped round the face.

A new noise right overhead made Nanny Ogg look up.

Her self-satisfied expression faded. The hammer that struck the hours was swinging slowly backwards. It struck Nanny that she was standing right under the bell at the same time as the bell, too, was struck.

Bong . . .

'Oh, bugger!'

. . . *bong* . . .

. . . *bong* . . .

. . . *bong* . . .

Mist rolled through the swamp. And shadows moved with it, their shapes indistinct on this night when the difference between the living and the dead was only a matter of time.

Mrs Gogol could feel them among the trees. The homeless. The hungry. The silent people. Those forsaken by men and gods. The people of the mists and the mud, whose only strength was somewhere on the other side of weakness, whose beliefs were as rickety and homemade as their homes. And the people from the city – not the ones who lived in the big white houses and went to balls in fine coaches, but the other ones. They were the ones that stories are never about. Stories are not, on the whole, interested in swineherds who remain swineherds and poor and humble shoe-makers whose destiny is to die slightly poorer and much humbler.

These people were the ones who made the magical kingdom work, who cooked its meals and swept its floors and carted its night soil and were its faces in the crowd and whose wishes and dreams, undemanding as they were, were of no consequence. The *invisibles*.

And me out here, she thought. Building traps for gods.

There are various forms of voodoo in the multiverse, because it's a religion that can be put together from any ingredients that happen to be lying around. And all of them try, in some way, to call down a god into the body of a human being.

That was stupid, Mrs Gogol thought. That was dangerous.

Mrs Gogol's voodoo worked the other way about. What was a god? A focus of belief. If people believed, a god began to grow. Feebly at first, but if the swamp taught anything, it taught patience. Anything could be the focus of a god. A handful of feathers with a red ribbon around them, a hat and coat on a couple of sticks . . . anything. Because when all people had was practically nothing, then anything could be almost everything. And then you fed it, and lulled it, like a goose heading for pâté, and let the power grow very slowly, and when the time was ripe you opened the path . . . backwards. A human could ride the god, rather than the other way around. There would be a price to pay later, but there always was. In Mrs Gogol's experience, everyone ended up dying.

She took a pull of rum and handed the jug to Saturday.

Saturday took a mouthful, and passed the jug up to something that might have been a hand.

'Let it begin,' said Mrs Gogol.

The dead man picked up three small drums and began to beat out a rhythm, heartbeat fast.

After a while something tapped Mrs Gogol on the shoulder and handed her the jug. It was empty.

Might as well begin . . .

'Lady Bon Anna smile on me. Mister Safe Way protect me. Stride Wide Man guide me. Hotaloga Andrews catch me.

'I stand between the light and the dark, but that no matter, because I *am* between.

'Here is rum for you. Tobacco for you. Food for you. A home for you.

'Now you listen to me good . . .'

. . . *bong.*

For Magrat it was like waking from a dream into a dream. She'd been idly dreaming that she was dancing with the most handsome man in the room, and . . . she was dancing with the most handsome man in the room.

Except that he wore two circles of smoked glass over his eyes.

301

Although Magrat was soft-hearted, a compulsive daydreamer and, as Granny Weatherwax put it, a wet hen, she wouldn't be a witch if she didn't have certain instincts and the sense to trust them. She reached up and, before his hands could move, tweaked the things away.

Magrat had seen eyes like that before, but never on something walking upright.

Her feet, which a moment before had been moving gracefully across the floor, tripped over themselves.

'Er . . .' she began.

And she was aware that his hands, pink and well-manicured, were also cold and damp.

Magrat turned and ran, knocking the couples aside in her madness to get away. Her legs tangled in the dress. The stupid shoes skittered on the floor.

A couple of footmen blocked the stairs to the hall.

Magrat's eyes narrowed. Getting out was what mattered.

'Hai!'

'Ouch!'

And then she ran on, slipping at the top of the stairs. A glass slipper slithered across the marble.

'How the hell's anyone supposed to *move* in these things?' she screamed at the world in general. Hopping frantically on one foot, she wrenched the other shoe off and ran into the night.

The Prince walked slowly to the top of the steps and picked up the discarded slipper.

He held it. The light glittered off its facets.

Granny Weatherwax leaned against the wall in the shadows. All stories had a turning point, and it had to be close.

She was good at getting into other people's minds, but now she had to get into hers. She concentrated. Down deeper . . . past everyday thoughts and minor concerns, *faster, faster* . . . through layers of deep cogitation . . . deeper . . . past things sealed off and crusted over, old guilts and congealed regrets, but there was no time for them now . . . down . . . and there . . . the silver thread of the story. She'd been part of it, was part of it, so it had to be a part of her.

It poured past. She reached out.

She hated everything that predestined people, that fooled them, that made them slightly less than human.

The story whipped along like a steel hawser. She gripped it.

Her eyes opened in shock. Then she stepped forward.

'Excuse me, Your Highness.'

She snatched the shoe from the Duc's hands, and raised it over her head.

Her expression of evil satisfaction was terrible to behold.

Then she dropped the shoe.

It smashed on the stairs.

A thousand glittering fragments scattered across the marble.

* |*   *

Coiled as it was around the length of turtle-shaped space-time known as the Discworld, the story shook. One broken end flapped loose and flailed through the night, trying to find any sequence to feed on . . .

In the clearing the trees moved. So did the shadows. Shadows shouldn't be able to move unless the light moves. These did.

The drumming stopped.

In the silence there was the occasional sizzle as power crackled across the hanging coat.

Saturday stepped forward. Green sparks flew out to his hands as he gripped the jacket and put it on.

His body jerked.

Erzulie Gogol breathed out.

'You are here,' she said. 'You are still yourself. You are exactly yourself.'

Saturday raised his hands, with his fists clenched. Occasionally an arm or leg would jerk as the power inside him squirrel-caged around in its search for freedom, but she could see that he was riding it.

'It will become easier,' she said, more gently now.

Saturday nodded.

With the power flowing inside him he had, she thought, the fire he'd had when he was alive. He had not been a particularly good man, she knew. Genua had not been a model of civic virtue. But at least he'd never told people that they wanted him to oppress them, and that everything he did was for their own good.

Around the circle, the people of New Genua – the *old* New Genua – knelt or bowed.

He hadn't been a kind ruler. But he'd fitted. And when he'd been arbitrary or arrogant or just plain wrong, he'd never suggested that this was justified by anything other than the fact that he was bigger and stronger and occasionally nastier than other people. He'd never suggested that it was because he was *better*. And he'd never told people they ought to be happy, and imposed a kind of happiness on them. The invisible people knew that happiness is not the natural state of mankind, and is never achieved from the outside in.

Saturday nodded again, this time in satisfaction. When he opened his mouth, sparks flashed between his teeth. And when he waded through the swamp, the alligators fought to get out of his way.

It was quiet in the palace kitchens now. The huge trays of roast meat, the pigs' heads with apples in their mouths, the multi-layered trifles had long ago been carried upstairs. There was a clattering from the giant sinks at the far end, where some of the maids were making a start on the washing up.

Mrs Pleasant the cook had made herself a plate of red stripefish in crawfish sauce. She wasn't the finest cook in Genua – no one got near Mrs Gogol's gumbo, people would almost come back from the dead for a taste of Mrs Gogol's gumbo – but the comparison was as narrow as that between, say, diamonds and sapphires. She'd done her best to cook up a good banquet, because she had her professional pride, but there wasn't much she felt she was able to do with lumps of meat.

Genuan cooking, like the best cooking every-where in the multiverse, had been evolved by people who had to make desperate use of ingredients their masters didn't want. No one would even try a bird's nest unless they had to. Only hunger would make a man taste his first alligator. No one would eat a shark's fin if they were allowed to eat the rest of the shark.

She poured herself a rum and was just picking up the spoon when she felt herself being watched.

A large man in a black leather doublet was staring at her from the doorway, dangling a ginger cat mask from one hand.

It was a very direct stare. Mrs Pleasant found herself wishing she'd done something about her hair and was wearing a better dress.

'Yes?' she said. 'What d'you want?'

'Waaant foood, Miss-uss Pleassunt,' said Greebo.

She looked him up and down. There were some odd types in Genua these days. This one must have been a guest at the ball, but there was something very . . . *familiar* about him.

Greebo wasn't a happy cat. People had made a fuss just because he'd dragged a roast turkey off the table. Then the skinny female with the teeth had kept simpering at him and saying she'd see him later in the rose garden, which wasn't at all the cat way of doing things, and that'd got him confused, because this wasn't the right kind of body and nor was hers. And there were too many other males around.

Then he'd smelled the kitchen. Cats gravitate to kitchens like rocks gravitate to gravity.

'I seen you somewhere before?' said Mrs Pleasant.

Greebo said nothing. He'd followed his nose to a bowl on one of the big tables.

'Waaant,' he demanded.

'Fish heads?' said Mrs Pleasant. They were technically garbage, although what she was planning with some rice and a few special sauces would turn them into the sort of dish kings fight for.

'Waant,' Greebo repeated.

Mrs Pleasant shrugged.

'You want raw fish heads, man, you take 'em,' she said.

Greebo lifted the bowl uncertainly. He wasn't too good with fingers. Then he looked around conspiratorially and ducked under the table.

There were the sounds of keen gurgitation and the bowl being scraped around on the floor.

Greebo emerged.

'Millluk?' he suggested.

Fascinated, Mrs Pleasant reached for the milk jug and a cup—

'Saaaaucerrr,' Greebo said.

—and a saucer.

Greebo took the saucer, gave it a long hard look, and put it on the floor.

Mrs Pleasant stared.

Greebo finished the milk, licking the remnant off his beard. He felt a lot better now. And there was a big fire over there. He padded over to it, sat down, spat on his paw and made an attempt to clean his ears, which didn't work because inexplicably neither ears nor paw were the right shape, and then curled up as best he could. Which wasn't very well, given that he seemed to have the wrong sort of backbone, too.

After a while Mrs Pleasant heard a low, asthmatic rumble.

Greebo was trying to purr.

He had the wrong kind of throat.

In a minute he was going to wake up in a bad temper and want to fight something.

Mrs Pleasant got on with her own supper. Despite the fact that a hulking great man had just eaten a bowl of fish heads and lapped a saucer of milk in front of her, and was now stretched out uncomfortably in front of the fire, she found she didn't feel the least bit afraid. In fact she was fighting down an impulse to scratch his tummy.

Magrat wrenched off the other slipper as she ran down the long red carpet towards the palace gateway and freedom. Just getting away, that was the important thing. *From* was more urgent than *to*.

And then two figures drifted out of the shadows and faced her. She raised the slipper pathetically as they approached in absolute silence, but even in the twilight she could feel their gaze.

The crowds parted. Lily Weatherwax glided through, in a rustle of silk.

She looked Granny up and down, without any expression of surprise.

'All in white, too,' she said, dryly. 'My word, aren't you the *nice* one.'

'But I've stopped you,' said Granny, still panting with the effort. 'I've *broken* it.'

Lily Weatherwax looked past her. The snake sisters were coming up the steps, holding a limp Magrat between them.

'Save us all from people who think literally,' said Lily. 'The damn things come in pairs, you know.'

She crossed to Magrat and snatched the second slipper out of her hand.

'The clock was interesting,' she said, turning back to Granny. 'I was impressed with the clock. But it's no good, you know. You can't stop this sort of thing. It has the momentum of inevitability. You can't spoil a good story. I should know.'

She handed the slipper to the Prince, but without taking her eyes off Granny.

'It'll fit her,' she said.

Two of the courtiers held Magrat's leg as the Prince wrestled the slipper past her protesting toes.

'There,' said Lily, still without looking down. 'And do stop trying that hedge-witch hypnotism on me, Esme.'

'It fits,' said the Prince, but in a doubtful tone of voice.

'Yes, anything would fit,' said a cheerful voice from somewhere towards the back of the crowd, 'if you were allowed to put two pairs of hairy socks on first.'

Lily looked down. Then she looked at Magrat's mask. She reached out and pulled it off.

'Ow!'

'Wrong girl,' said Lily. 'But it still doesn't matter,

Esme, because it *is* the right slipper. So all we have to do is find the girl whose foot it fits—'

There was a commotion at the back of the crowd. Courtiers parted, revealing Nanny Ogg, oil-covered and hung with spider webs.

'If it's a five-and-a-half narrow fit, I'm your man,' she said. 'Just let me get these boots off . . .'

'I wasn't referring to you, old woman,' said Lily coldly.

'Oh, yes you was,' said Nanny. 'We know how this bit goes, see. The Prince goes all round the city with the slipper, trying to find the girl whose foot fits. That's what you was plannin'. So I can save you a bit of trouble, how about it?'

There was a flicker of uncertainty in Lily's expression.

'A *girl*,' she said, 'of *marriageable* age.'

'No problem there,' said Nanny cheerfully.

The dwarf Casanunda nudged a courtier proudly in the knees.

'She's a very close personal friend of mine,' he said proudly.

Lily looked at her sister.

'*You're* doing this. Don't think I don't know,' she said.

'I ain't doing a thing,' said Granny. 'It's real life happening all by itself.'

Nanny grabbed the slipper out of the Prince's hands and, before anyone else could move, slid it on to her foot.

Then she waggled the foot in the air.

It was a perfect fit.

'There!' she said. 'See? You could have wasted the whole day.'

'Especially because there must be hundreds of five-and-a-half—'

'—narrow fit—'

'—narrow fit wearers in a city this size,' Granny went on. 'Unless, of course, you happened to sort of go to the right house right at the start. If you had, you know, a lucky guess?'

'But that'd be *cheatin*',' said Nanny.

She nudged the Prince.

'I'd just like to add,' she said, 'that I don't mind doin' all the waving and opening things and other royal stuff, but I draw the line at sleepin' in the same bed as sunny jim here.'

'Because he doesn't sleep in a bed,' said Granny.

'No, he sleeps in a pond,' said Nanny. 'We had a look. Just a great big indoor pond.'

'Because he's a frog,' said Granny.

'With flies all over the place in case he wakes up in the night and fancies a snack,' said Nanny.

'I thought so!' said Magrat, pulling herself out of the grip of the guards. 'He had clammy hands!'

'Lots of men have clammy hands,' said Nanny. 'But this one's got 'em because he's a frog.'

'I'm a prince of blood royal!' said the Prince.

'And a frog,' said Granny.

'I don't mind,' said Casanunda, from somewhere down below. 'I enjoy open relationships. If you want to go out with a frog, that's fine by me . . .'

Lily looked around at the crowd. Then she snapped her fingers.

Granny Weatherwax was aware of a sudden silence.

Nanny Ogg looked up at the people on either side of her. She waved a hand in front of a guard's face.

'Coo,' she said.

'You can't do that for long,' said Granny. 'You can't stop a thousand people for long.'

Lily shrugged. 'They're not important. Whoever will remember who was at the ball? They'll just remember the flight and the slipper and the happy ending.'

'I've told you. You can't start it again. And he's a frog. Even you can't keep him in shape the whole day long. He turns back into his old shape at night. He's got a bedroom with a *pond* in it. He's a frog,' said Granny flatly.

'But only inside,' said Lily.

'Inside's where it counts,' said Granny.

'Outside's quite important, mind,' said Nanny.

'Lots of people are animals inside. Lots of animals are people inside,' said Lily. 'Where's the harm?'

'He's a frog.'

'Especially at night,' said Nanny. It had occurred to her that a husband who was a man all night and a frog all *day* might be almost acceptable; you wouldn't get the wage packet, but there'd be less wear and tear on the furniture. She also couldn't put out of her mind certain private speculations about the length of his tongue.

'And you killed the Baron,' said Magrat.

'You think he was a particularly nice man?' said

Lily. 'Besides, he didn't show me any respect. If you've got no respect, you've got nothing.'

Nanny and Magrat found themselves looking at Granny.

'He's a frog.'

'I found him in the swamp,' said Lily. 'I could tell he was pretty bright. I needed someone . . . amenable to persuasion. Shouldn't frogs have a chance? He'll be no worse a husband than many. Just one kiss from a princess seals the spell.'

'A lot of men are animals,' said Magrat, who'd picked up the idea from somewhere.

'Yes. But he's a frog,' said Granny.

'Look at it my way,' said Lily. 'You see this country? It's all swamps and fogs. There's no *direction*. But I can make this a great city. Not a sprawling place like Ankh-Morpork, but a place that works.'

'The girl doesn't want to marry a frog.'

'What will that matter in a hundred years' time?'

'It matters now.'

Lily threw up her hands. 'What do you want, then? It's your choice. There's me . . . or there's that woman in the swamp. Light or dark. Fog or sunshine. Dark chaos or happy endings.'

'He's a frog, and you killed the old Baron,' said Granny.

'You'd have done the same,' said Lily.

'No,' said Granny. 'I'd have *thought* the same, but I wouldn't have done it.'

'What difference does that make, deep down?'

'You mean you don't *know*?' said Nanny Ogg.

Lily laughed.

313

'Look at the three of you,' she said. 'Bursting with inefficient good intentions. The maiden, the mother and the crone.'

'Who are you calling a maiden?' said Nanny Ogg.

'Who are you calling a mother?' said Magrat.

Granny Weatherwax glowered briefly like the person who has discovered that there is only one straw left and everyone else has drawn a long one.

'Now, what shall I do with you?' said Lily. 'I really am against killing people unless it's necessary, but I can't have you running around acting stupidly . . .'

She looked at her fingernails.

'So I think I shall have you put away somewhere until this has run its course. And then . . . can you guess what I'm going to do next?

'I'm going to expect you to escape. Because, after all, I am the good one.'

Ella walked cautiously through the moonlit swamp, following the strutting shape of Legba. She was aware of movement in the water, but nothing emerged – bad news like Legba gets around, even among alligators.

An orange light appeared in the distance. It turned out to be Mrs Gogol's shack, or boat, or whatever it was. In the swamp, the difference between the water and the land was practically a matter of choice.

'Hallo? Is there anyone there?'

'Come along in, child. Take a seat. Rest up a little.'

Ella stepped cautiously on to the rocking veranda.

Mrs Gogol was sitting in her chair, a white-clad raggedy doll in her lap.

'Magrat said—'

'I know all about it. Come to Erzulie.'

'Who are you?'

'I am your – friend, girl.'

Ella moved so as to be ready to run.

'You're not a godmother of any kind, are you?'

'No. No gods. Just a friend. Did anyone follow you?'

'I . . . don't think so.'

'It's no matter if they did, girl. No matter if they did. Maybe we ought to move out into the river for a spell, even so. We'll be a lot safer with water all round.'

The shack lurched.

'You better sit down. The feets make it shaky until we get into deep water.'

Ella risked a look, nevertheless.

Mrs Gogol's hut travelled on four large duck feet, which were now rising out of the swamp. They splashed their way through the shallows and, gently, sculled out into the river.

Greebo woke up and stretched.

And the wrong sort of arms and legs!

Mrs Pleasant, who had been sitting watching him, put down her glass.

'What do you want to do now, Mr Cat?' she said.

Greebo padded over to the door into the outside world and scratched at it.

'Waant to go *owwwt*, Miss-uss Pleas-unt,' he said.

315

'You just have to turn the handle there,' she said.

Greebo stared at the door handle like someone trying to come to terms with a piece of very advanced technology, and then gave her a pleading look.

She opened the door for him, stood aside as he slunk out, and then shut it, locked it and leaned against it.

'Ember's bound to be safe with Mrs Gogol,' said Magrat.

'Hah!' said Granny.

'I quite liked her,' said Nanny Ogg.

'I don't trust anyone who drinks rum and smokes a pipe,' said Granny.

'Nanny Ogg smokes a pipe and drinks *anything*,' Magrat pointed out.

'Yes, but that's because she's a disgustin' old baggage,' said Granny, without looking up.

Nanny Ogg took her pipe out of her mouth.

'That's right,' she said amiably. 'You ain't nothing if you don't maintain an image.'

Granny looked up from the lock.

'Can't shift it,' she said. 'It's octiron, too. Can't magic it open.'

'It's daft, locking us up,' said Nanny. 'I'd have had us killed.'

'That's because you're basically good,' said Magrat. 'The good are innocent and create justice. The bad are guilty, which is why they invent mercy.'

'No, I know why she's done this,' said Granny, darkly. 'It's so's we'll know we've lost.'

'But she said we'd escape,' said Magrat. 'I don't understand. She must know the good ones always win in the end!'

'Only in stories,' said Granny, examining the door hinges. 'And she thinks she's in charge of the stories. She bends them round herself. She thinks she's the good one.'

'Mind you,' said Magrat, 'I don't like swamps. If it wasn't for the frog and everything, I'd see Lily's point—'

'Then you're nothing but a daft godmother,' snapped Granny, still fiddling with the lock. 'You can't go around building a better world for people. Only people can build a better world for people. Otherwise it's just a cage. Besides, you don't build a better world by choppin' heads off and giving decent girls away to frogs.'

'But progress—' Magrat began.

'Don't you talk to me about progress. Progress just means bad things happen faster. Anyone got another hatpin? This one's useless.'

Nanny, who had Greebo's ability to make herself instantly at home wherever she happened to be, sat down in the corner of the cell.

'I heard this story once,' she said, 'where this bloke got locked up for years and years and he learned amazin' stuff about the universe and everythin' from another prisoner who was incredibly clever, and then he escaped and got his revenge.'

'What incredibly clever stuff do *you* know about the universe, Gytha Ogg?' said Granny.

'Bugger all,' said Nanny cheerfully.

'Then we'd better bloody well escape right now.'

Nanny pulled a scrap of pasteboard out of her hat, found a scrap of pencil up there too, licked the end and thought for a while. Then she wrote: *Dear Jason unt so witer (as they say in foreign parts),*

Well here's a thing yore ole Mum doin Time in prison again, Im a old lag, youll have to send me a cake with a phial in it and I shall have little arrows on my close just my joke. This is a Sketch of the dunjon. Im putting a X where we are, which is Inside. Magrat is shown wering a posh dress, she has been acting like a Courgette. Also inc. Esme getting fed up becaus she can't get the lock to work but I expect it will all be OK because the good ones win in the end and that's US. And all because some girl don't want to marry a Prince who is a Duck who is really a Frog and I cant say I blame her, you don't want descendants who have got Jenes and start off living in a jamjar and then hop about and get squashed . . .

She was interrupted by the sound of a mandolin being played quite well, right on the other side of the wall, and a small but determined voice raised in song.

'—*si consuenti d'amoure, ventre dimo tondreturo-ooo*—'

'How I hunger my love for the dining-room of your warm maceration,' said Nanny, without looking up.

'—*della della t'ozentro, audri t'dren vontari-eeeeee*—'

'The shop, the shop, I have a lozenge, the sky is pink,' said Nanny.

Granny and Magrat looked at one another.

'—*guarunto del tari, bella pore di larientos*—'

'Rejoice, candlemaker, you have a great big—'

'I don't believe any of this,' said Granny. 'You're making it up.'

'Word for word translation,' said Nanny. 'I can speak foreign like a native, you know that.'

'Mrs Ogg? Is that you, my love?'

They all looked up towards the barred window. There was a small face peering in.

'Casanunda?' said Nanny.

'That's me, Mrs Ogg.'

'My love,' muttered Granny.

'How did you get up to the window?' said Nanny, ignoring this.

'I always know where I can get my hands on a step-ladder, Mrs Ogg.'

'I suppose you don't know where you can get your hands on a key?'

'Wouldn't do any good. There's too many guards outside your door, Mrs Ogg. Even for a famous swordsman like me. Her ladyship gave strict orders. No one's to listen to you or look at you, even.'

'How come you're in the palace guard, Casanunda?'

'Soldier of fortune takes whatever jobs are going, Mrs Ogg,' said Casanunda earnestly.

'But all the rest of 'em are six foot tall and you're – of the shorter persuasion.'

'I lied about my height, Mrs Ogg. I'm a world-famous liar.'

'Is that true?'

'No.'

'What about you being the world's greatest lover?'

There was silence for a while.

'Well, maybe I'm only No. 2,' said Casanunda. 'But I try harder.'

'Can't you go and find us a file or something, Mr Casanunda?' said Magrat.

'I'll see what I can do, Miss.'

The face disappeared.

'Maybe we could get people to visit us and then we could escape in their clothes?' said Nanny Ogg.

'Now I've gone and stuck the pin in my finger,' muttered Granny Weatherwax.

'Or maybe we could get Magrat to seduce one of the guards,' said Nanny.

'Why don't *you*?' said Magrat, as nastily as she could manage.

'All right. I'm game.'

'Shut up, the pair of you,' said Granny. 'I'm trying to think—'

There was another sound at the window.

It was Legba.

The black cockerel peered in between the bars for a moment, and then fluttered away.

'Gives me the creeps, that one,' said Nanny. 'Can't look at him without thinking wistfully of sage-and-onion and mashed potatoes.'

Her crinkled face crinkled further.

'Greebo!' she said. 'Where'd we leave him?'

'Oh, he's only a cat,' said Granny Weatherwax. 'Cats know how to look after themselves.'

'He's really just a big softie – ' Nanny began, before someone started pulling down the wall.

A hole appeared. A grey hand appeared and grasped another stone. There was a strong smell of river mud.

Rock crumbled under heavy fingers.

'Ladies?' said a resonant voice.

'Well, Mister Saturday,' said Nanny, 'as I live and breathe – saving your presence, o'course.'

Saturday grunted something and walked away.

There was a hammering on the door and someone started fumbling with keys.

'We don't want to hang around here,' said Granny. 'Come on.'

They helped one another out through the hole.

Saturday was on the other side of a small courtyard, striding towards the sound of the ball.

And there was something behind him, trailing out like the tail of a comet.

'What's that?'

'Mrs Gogol's doing,' said Granny Weatherwax grimly.

Behind Saturday, widening as it snaked through the palace grounds to the gate, was a stream of deeper darkness in the air. At first sight it seemed to contain shapes, but closer inspection indicated that they weren't shapes at all but a mere suggestion of shapes, forming and reforming. Eyes gleamed momentarily in the swirl. There was the chittering of crickets and the whine of mosquitoes, the smell of moss and the stink of river mud.

'It's the swamp,' said Magrat.

'It's the *idea* of the swamp,' said Granny. 'It's what you have to have first, before you have the swamp.'

'Oh, dear,' said Nanny. She shrugged. 'Well, Ella's got away and so have we, so this is the part where we escape, yes? That's what we're supposed to do.'

None of them moved.

'They aren't very nice people in there,' said Magrat, after a while, 'but they don't deserve alligators.'

'You witches stand right there,' said a voice behind them. Half a dozen guards were crowded around the hole in the wall.

'Life's certainly busier in the city,' said Nanny, pulling another hatpin from her hat.

'They've got crossbows,' warned Magrat. 'There's not much you can do against crossbows. Projectile weapons is Lesson Seven and I haven't had that yet.'

'They can't pull triggers if they think they've got flippers,' said Granny menacingly.

'Now,' said Nanny, 'let's not have any of that, eh? Everyone knows the good ones always win *specially* when they're outnumbered.'

The guards emerged.

As they did so a tall black shape dropped noise-lessly from the wall behind them.

'There,' said Nanny, 'I said he wouldn't go far from his mummy, didn't I?'

One or two of the guards realized that she was staring proudly past them, and turned.

As far as they were concerned, they confronted a

tall, broad-shouldered man with a mane of black hair, an eyepatch and a very wide grin.

He stood with his arms casually folded.

He waited until he had their full attention, and then Greebo let his lips part slowly.

Several of the men took a step backwards then.

One of them said, 'Why worry? It's not as if he's got a weap—'

Greebo raised one hand.

Claws make no noise as they slide out, but they *ought* to. They ought to make a noise like 'tzing'.

Greebo's grin widened.

Ah! *These* still worked . . .

One of the men was bright enough to raise his crossbow but stupid enough to do it with Nanny Ogg standing behind him with a hatpin. Her hand moved so swiftly that any wisdom-seeking saffron-clad youth would have started the Way of Mrs Ogg there and then. The man screamed and dropped the bow.

'Wrowwwl . . .'

Greebo leapt.

Cats are like witches. They don't fight to kill, but to win. There is a difference. There's no point in killing an opponent. That way, they won't know they've lost, and to be a real winner you have to have an opponent who is beaten and knows it. There's no triumph over a corpse, but a beaten opponent, who will remain beaten every day of the remainder of their sad and wretched life, is something to treasure.

Cats do not, of course, rationalize this far. They

just like to send someone limping off minus a tail and a few square inches of fur.

Greebo's technique was unscientific and wouldn't have stood a chance against any decent swordsmanship, but on his side was the fact that it is almost impossible to develop decent swordsmanship when you seem to have run into a food mixer that is biting your ear off.

The witches watched with interest.

'I think we can leave him now,' said Nanny. 'I think he's having fun.'

They hurried towards the hall.

The orchestra was in the middle of a complicated number when the lead violinist happened to glance towards the door, and then dropped his bow. The cellist turned to see what had caused this, followed his colleague's fixed stare, and in a moment of confusion tried to play his instrument backwards.

In a succession of squeaks and flats, the orchestra stopped playing. The dancers continued for a while out of sheer momentum, and then stopped and milled about in confusion. And then, one by one, they too looked up.

Saturday stood at the top of the steps.

In the silence came the drumming, making the music that had gone before seem as insignificant as the chittering of crickets. This was the real blood music; every other music that had ever been written was merely a pitiful attempt to sing along.

It poured into the room, and with it came the heat and the warm, vegetable smell of the swamp.

There was a suggestion of alligator in the air – not the presence of them, but the promise.

The drumming grew louder. There were complex counter-rhythms, much more felt than heard.

Saturday brushed a speck of dust off the shoulder of his ancient coat, and reached out an arm.

The tall hat appeared in his hand.

He reached out his other hand.

The black cane with the silver top whirred out of the empty air and was snatched up triumphantly.

He put the hat on his head. He twirled the cane.

The drums rolled. Except that . . . maybe it wasn't drums now, maybe it was a beat in the floor itself, or in the walls, or in the air. It was fast and hot and people in the hall found their feet moving of their own accord, because the drumming seemed to reach the toes via the hindbrain without ever passing near the ears.

Saturday's feet moved too. They beat out their own staccato rhythms on the marble floor.

He danced down the steps.

He whirled. He leapt. The tails of his coat whipped through the air. And then he landed at the foot of the step, his feet striking the ground like the thud of doom.

And only now was there a stirring.

There was a croak from the Prince.

'It can't be him! He's *dead*! Guards! *Kill* him!'

He looked around madly at the guards by the stairs.

The guard captain went pale.

'I, uh, *again*? I mean, I don't think . . .' he began.

'Do it now!'

The captain raised his crossbow nervously. The point of the bolt wove figures-of-eight in front of his eyes.

'I said *do* it!'

The bow twanged.

There was a thud.

Saturday looked down at the feathers buried in his chest, and then grinned and raised his cane.

The captain looked up with the certain terror of death in his face. He dropped his bow and turned to run, and managed two steps before he toppled forward.

'No,' said a voice behind the Prince. 'This is how you kill a dead man.'

Lily Weatherwax stepped forward, her face white with fury.

'You don't belong here any more,' she hissed. 'You're not part of the story.'

She raised a hand.

Behind her, the ghost images suddenly focused on her, so that she became more iridescent. Silver fire leapt across the room.

Baron Saturday thrust out his cane. The magic struck, and coursed down him to earth, leaving little silver trails that crackled for a while and then winked out.

'No, ma'am,' he said, 'there ain't *no* way to kill a dead man.'

The three witches watched from the doorway.

'*I* felt that,' said Nanny. 'It should have blown him to bits!'

'Blown what to bits?' said Granny. 'The swamp? The river? The world? He's all of them! Ooh, she's a clever one, that Mrs Gogol!'

'What?' said Magrat. 'What do you mean, all of them?'

Lily backed away. She raised her hand again and sent another fireball towards the Baron. It hit his hat and burst off it like a firework.

'Stupid, stupid!' muttered Granny. 'She's seen it doesn't work and she's still trying it!'

'I thought you weren't on her side,' said Magrat.

'I ain't! But I don't like to see people being stupid. That kind of stuff's no use, Magrat Garlick, even you can . . . oh, no, surely not again . . .'

The Baron laughed as a third attempt earthed itself harmlessly. Then he raised his cane. Two courtiers tumbled forward.

Lily Weatherwax, still backing away, came up against the foot of the main staircase.

The Baron strolled forward.

'You want to try anything else, lady?' he said.

Lily raised both hands.

All three witches felt it – the terrible suction as she tried to concentrate all the power in the vicinity.

Outside, the one guard remaining upright found that he was no longer fighting a man but merely an enraged tomcat, although this was no consolation. It just meant that Greebo had an extra pair of claws.

The Prince screamed.

It was a long, descending scream, and ended in a croak, somewhere around ground level.

Baron Saturday took one heavy, deliberate step forward, and there was no more croak.

The drums stopped abruptly.

And then there was a real silence, broken only by the swish of Lily's dress as she fled up the stairs.

A voice behind the witches said, 'Thank you, ladies. Could you step aside, please?'

They looked around. Mrs Gogol was there, holding Embers by the hand. She had a fat, gaily-embroidered bag over her shoulder.

All three watched as the voodoo woman led the girl down into the hall and through the silent crowds.

'That's not right either,' said Granny under her breath.

'What?' said Magrat. 'What?'

Baron Saturday thumped his stick on the floor.

'You know me,' he said. 'You *all* know *me*. You know I was killed. And now here I am. I was murdered and what did you do – ?'

'How much did *you* do, Mrs Gogol?' muttered Granny. 'No, we ain't having this.'

'Ssh, I can't hear what he's saying,' said Nanny.

'He's telling them they can have him ruling them again, or Embers,' said Magrat.

'They'll have Mrs Gogol,' muttered Granny. 'She'll be one o' them *eminences greases.*'

'Well, she's not too bad,' said Nanny.

'In the swamp she's not too bad,' said Granny. 'With someone to balance her up she's not too bad. But Mrs Gogol tellin' a whole city what to do . . . that's not right. Magic's far too important to be used for rulin' people. Anyway, Lily only had people killed – Mrs Gogol'd set 'em to choppin' wood and doin' chores afterwards. I reckon, after you've had a busy life, you ort to be able to relax a bit when you're dead.'

'Lie back and enjoy it, sort of thing,' said Nanny.

Granny looked down at the white dress.

'I wish I had my old clothes on,' she said. 'Black's the proper colour for a witch.'

She strode down the steps, and then cupped her hands around her mouth.

'Coo-ee! Mrs Gogol!'

Baron Saturday stopped speaking. Mrs Gogol nodded at Granny.

'Yes, Miss Weatherwax?'

'*Mistress*,' snapped Granny, and then softened her voice again.

'This ain't right, you know. She's the one who ought to rule, fair enough. And you used magic to help her this far, and that's all right. But it stops right here. It's up to her what happens next. You can't make things right by magic. You can only stop making them wrong.'

Mrs Gogol pulled herself up to her full, impressive height. 'Who's you to say what I can and can't do here?'

'We're her godmothers,' said Granny.

'That's right,' said Nanny Ogg.

'We've got a wand, too,' said Magrat.

'But you *hate* godmothers, Mistress Weatherwax,' said Mrs Gogol.

'We're the other kind,' said Granny. 'We're the

kind that gives people what they know they really need, not what we think they ought to want.'

Among the fascinated crowd several pairs of lips moved as people worked this out.

'Then you've done your godmothering,' said Mrs Gogol, who thought faster than most. 'You did it very well.'

'You didn't listen,' said Granny. 'There's all sorts of things to godmotherin'. She might be quite good at ruling. She might be bad at it. But she's got to find out for herself. With no interference from anyone.'

'What if I say no?'

'Then I expect we'll just have to go on god-motherin',' said Granny.

'Do you know how long I worked to win?' said Mrs Gogol, haughtily. 'Do you know what I *lost*?'

'And now you've won, and there's the end of it,' said Granny.

'Are you looking to challenge me, Mistress Weatherwax?'

Granny hesitated, and then straightened her shoulders. Her arms moved away from her sides, almost imperceptibly. Nanny and Magrat moved away slightly.

'If that's what you want.'

'My voodoo against your . . . headology?'

'If you like.'

'And what's the stake?'

'No more magic in the affairs of Genua,' said Granny. 'No more stories. No more godmothers. Just people, deciding for themselves. For good or bad. Right or wrong.'

'Okay.'

'And you leave Lily Weatherwax to me.'

Mrs Gogol's intake of breath was heard around the hall.

'Never!'

'Hmm?' said Granny. 'You don't think you're going to lose, do you?'

'I don't want to hurt you, Mistress Weatherwax,' said Mrs Gogol.

'That's good,' said Granny. 'I don't want you to hurt me either.'

'I don't want there to be any fighting,' said Ella.

They all looked at her.

'She's the ruler now, ain't she?' said Granny. 'We've got to listen to what she says.'

'I'll keep out of the city,' said Mrs Gogol, ignoring her, 'but Lilith is mine.'

'No.'

Mrs Gogol reached into her bag, and flourished the raggedy doll. 'See this?'

'Yes. I do,' said Granny.

'It was going to be her. Don't let it be you.'

'Sorry, Mrs Gogol,' said Granny firmly, 'but I see my duty plain.'

'You're a clever woman, Mistress Weatherwax. But you're a long way from home.'

Granny shrugged. Mrs Gogol held up the doll by its waist. It had sapphire blue eyes.

'You know about magic with mirrors? This is *my* kind of mirror, Mistress Weatherwax. I can make it be *you*. And then I can make it *suffer*. Don't make me do that. Please.'

'Please yourself, Mrs Gogol. But I'll deal with Lily.'

'I should box a bit clever if I was you, Esme,' muttered Nanny Ogg. 'She's good at this sort of thing.'

'I think she could be very ruthless,' said Magrat.

'I've got nothing but the greatest respect for Mrs Gogol,' said Granny. 'A fine woman. But talks a bit too much. If I was her, I'd have had a couple of big nails right through that thing by now.'

'You would, too,' said Nanny. 'It's a good thing you're good, ain't it.'

'Right,' said Granny, raising her voice again. 'I'm going to find my sister, Mrs Gogol. This is *family*.'

She walked steadfastly towards the stairs.

Magrat took out the wand.

'If she does anything bad to Granny, she's going to go through the rest of her life bright orange and round, with seeds in,' she said.

'I don't think Esme would like it if you did something like that,' said Nanny. 'Don't worry. She doesn't believe all that stuff about pins and dolls.'

'She doesn't believe *anything*. But that doesn't matter!' said Magrat. 'Mrs Gogol does! It's *her* power! It's what *she* thinks that matters.'

'Don't you reckon Esme knows that too?'

Granny Weatherwax reached the foot of the stairs.

'Mistress Weatherwax!'

Granny turned.

Mrs Gogol had a long sliver of wood in her hand. Shaking her head desperately, she jabbed it into the doll's foot.

Everyone saw Esme Weatherwax wince.

Another sliver was thrust into a raggedy arm.

Slowly, Granny raised her other hand and shuddered when she touched her sleeve. Then, limping slightly, she continued to climb the stairs.

'I can do the heart next, Mistress Weatherwax!' shouted Mrs Gogol.

'I'm sure you can. You're good at it. You know you're good at it,' said Granny, without looking around.

Mrs Gogol stuck another sliver into a leg. Granny sagged, and clutched at the banister. Beside her, one of the big torches flamed.

'Next time!' said Mrs Gogol. 'Right? Next time. I can do it!'

Granny turned around.

She looked at the hundreds of upturned faces.

When she spoke, her voice was so quiet that they had to strain to hear.

'I know you can too, Mrs Gogol. You really believe. Just remind me again – we're playin' for Lily, right? And for the city?'

'What does that matter now?' said Mrs Gogol. 'Ain't you going to give in?'

Granny Weatherwax thrust a little finger into her ear and wiggled it thoughtfully.

'No,' she said. 'No, I don't reckon that's what I do now. Are you watchin', Mrs Gogol? Are you watchin' real close?'

333

Her gaze travelled the room and rested for just a fraction of a second on Magrat.

Then she reached over, carefully, and thrust her arm up to the elbow into the burning torch.

And the doll in Erzulie Gogol's hands burst into flame.

It went on blazing even after the witch had screamed and dropped it on to the floor. It went on burning until Nanny Ogg ambled over with a jug of fruit juice from the buffet, whistling between her teeth, and put it out.

Granny withdrew her hand. It was unscathed.

'*That's* headology,' she said. 'It's the only thing that matters. Everything else is just messin' about. Hope I didn't hurt you, Mrs Gogol.'

She went on up the stairs.

Mrs Gogol kept on staring at the damp ashes. Nanny Ogg patted her companionably on the shoulder.

'How did she do that?' said Mrs Gogol.

'She didn't. She let *you* do it,' said Nanny. 'You got to watch yourself around Esme Weatherwax. I'd like to see one of them Zen buggers come up against *her* one day.'

'And she's the *good* one?' said Baron Saturday.

'Yeah,' said Nanny. 'Funny how things work out, really.'

She looked thoughtfully at the empty fruit juice jug in her hand.

'What this needs,' she said, in the manner of one reaching a conclusion after much careful consideration, 'is some bananas and rum and stuff in it—'

Magrat grabbed her dress as Nanny strode determinedly dak'rywards.

'Not now,' she said. 'We'd better get after Granny! She might need us!'

'Shouldn't think so for one minute,' said Nanny. 'I wouldn't like to be in Lily's shoes when Esme catches up with her.'

'But I've never seen Granny so agitated,' said Magrat. 'Anything could happen.'

'Good job if it does,' said Nanny. She nodded meaningfully at a flunkey who, being quick on the uptake, leapt to attention.

'But she might do something – dreadful.'

'Good. She's always wanted to,' said Nanny. 'Another banana dak'ry, mahatma coat, chopchop.'

'No. It wouldn't be a good idea,' Magrat persisted.

'Oh, *all* right,' said Nanny. She handed the empty jug to Baron Saturday, who took it in a kind of hypnotic daze.

'We're just going to sort things out,' she said. 'Sorry about this. On with the motley . . . if anyone's got any left.'

When the witches had gone Mrs Gogol reached down and picked up the damp remains of the doll.

One or two people coughed.

'Is that it?' said the Baron. 'After twelve years?'

'The Prince is dead,' said Mrs Gogol. 'Such as he was.'

'But you promised that I would be revenged on *her*,' the Baron said.

'I think there will be revenge,' said Mrs Gogol. She tossed the doll on to the floor. 'Lilith has been fighting me for twelve years and she never got through. This one didn't even have to sweat. So I think there will be revenge.'

'You don't have to keep your word!'

'I do. I've got to keep something.' Mrs Gogol put her arm around Ella's shoulder.

'This is it, girl,' she said. 'Your palace. Your city. There isn't a person here who will deny it.'

She glared at the guests. One or two of them stepped backwards.

Ella looked up at Saturday.

'I feel I should know you,' she said. She turned to Mrs Gogol. 'And you,' she added. 'I've seen you both . . . before. A long time ago?'

Baron Saturday opened his mouth to speak. Mrs Gogol held up her hand.

'We promised,' she said. 'No interference.'

'Not from *us*?'

'Not even from us.' She turned back to Ella. 'We're just people.'

'You mean . . .' said Ella, 'I've slaved in a kitchen for years . . . and now . . . I'm supposed to rule the city? Just like that?'

'That's how it goes.'

Ella looked down, deep in thought.

'And anything I say people have to do?' she said innocently.

There were a few nervous coughs from the crowd.

'Yes,' said Mrs Gogol.

Ella stood looking down at the floor, idly biting a thumbnail. Then she looked up.

'Then the first thing that's going to happen is the end of the ball. Right now! I'm going to find the carnival. I've always wanted to dance in the carnival.' She looked around at the worried faces. 'It's not compulsory for anyone else to come,' she added.

The nobles of Genua had enough experience to know what it means when a ruler says something is not compulsory.

Within minutes the hall was empty, except for three figures.

'But . . . but . . . I wanted *revenge*,' said the Baron. 'I wanted *death*. I wanted our daughter in power.'

TWO OUT OF THREE ISN'T BAD.

Mrs Gogol and the Baron turned around. Death put down his drink and stepped forward. Baron Saturday straightened up. 'I am ready to go with you,' he said.

Death shrugged. Ready or not, he seemed to indicate, was all the same to him.

'But I held you off,' the Baron added. 'For twelve years!' He put his arm around Erzulie's shoulders. 'When they killed me and threw me in the river, we stole life from you!'

YOU STOPPED LIVING. YOU NEVER DIED. I DID NOT COME FOR YOU THEN.

'You didn't?'

I HAD AN APPOINTMENT WITH YOU TONIGHT.

The Baron handed his cane to Mrs Gogol. He removed the tall black hat. He shrugged off the coat.

Power crackled in its folds.

337

'No more Baron Saturday,' he said.

PERHAPS. IT'S A NICE HAT.

The Baron turned to Erzulie.

'I think I have to go.'

'Yes.'

'What will you do?'

The voodoo woman looked down at the hat in her hands.

'I will go back to the swamp,' she said.

'You could stay here. I don't trust that foreign witch.'

'I do. So I will go back to the swamp. Because some stories have to end. Whatever Ella becomes, she'll have to make it herself.'

It was a short walk to the brown, heavy waters of the river.

The Baron paused at the edge.

'Will she live happily ever after?' he said.

NOT FOREVER. BUT PERHAPS FOR LONG ENOUGH.

And so stories end.

The wicked witch is defeated, the ragged princess comes into her own, the kingdom is restored. Happy days are here again. Happy ever after. Which means that life stops here.

Stories *want* to end. They don't care what happens next . . .

Nanny Ogg panted along a corridor.

'Never seen Esme like that before,' she said. 'She's in a very funny mood. She could be a danger to herself.'

'She's a danger to everyone else,' said Magrat. 'She—'

The snake women stepped out into the passage-way ahead of them.

'Look at it like this,' said Nanny, under her breath, 'what can they do to us?'

'I can't stand snakes,' said Magrat quietly.

'They've got those teeth, of course,' said Nanny, as if conducting a seminar. 'More like fangs, really. Come on, girl. Let's see if we can find another way.'

'I hate them.'

Nanny tugged at Magrat, who did not move.

'Come *on*!'

'I really hate them.'

'You'll be able to hate them even better from a long way off!'

The sisters were nearly on them. They didn't walk, they glided. Perhaps Lily wasn't concentrating now, because they were more snake-like than ever. Nanny thought she could see scale patterns under the skin. The jawline was all wrong.

'Magrat!'

One of the sisters reached out. Magrat shuddered.

The snake sister opened its mouth.

Then Magrat looked up and, almost dreamily, punched it so hard that it was carried several feet along the passage.

It wasn't a blow that featured in any Way or Path. No one ever drew this one as a diagram or practised it in front of a mirror with a bandage tied round their head. It was straight out of the lexicon of inherited, terrified survival reflexes.

'Use the wand!' shouted Nanny, darting forward.

'Don't ninj at them! Use the wand! That's what it's for!'

The other snake instinctively turned to follow the movement, which is why instinct is not always the keynote to survival, because Magrat clubbed it on the back of the head. With the wand. It sagged, losing shape as it fell.

The trouble with witches is that they'll never run away from things they really hate.

And the trouble with small furry animals in a corner is that, just occasionally, one of them's a mongoose.

Granny Weatherwax had always wondered: what was supposed to be so special about a full moon? It was only a big circle of light. And the dark of the moon was only darkness.

But half-way between the two, when the moon was between the worlds of light and dark, when even the moon lived on the edge . . . maybe *then* a witch could believe in the moon.

Now a half-moon sailed above the mists of the swamp.

Lily's nest of mirrors reflected the cold light, as they reflected everything else. Leaning against the wall were the three broomsticks.

Granny picked up hers. She wasn't wearing the right colour and she wasn't wearing a hat; she needed *something* she was at home with.

Nothing moved.

'Lily?' said Granny softly.

Her own image looked out at her from the mirrors.

'It can all stop now,' said Granny. 'You could take my stick and I'll take Magrat's. She can always share with Gytha. And Mrs Gogol won't come after you. I've fixed that. And we could do with more witches back home. And no more godmothering. No more getting people killed so their daughters are ready to be in a story. I know that's why you did it. Come on home. It's an offer you can't refuse.'

The mirror slid back noiselessly.

'You're trying to be *kind* to me?' said Lily.

'Don't think it don't take a lot of effort,' said Granny in a more normal voice.

Lily's dress rustled in the darkness as she stepped out.

'So,' she said, 'you beat the swamp woman.'

'No.'

'But you're here instead of her.'

'Yes.'

Lily took the stick out of Granny's hands, and inspected it.

'Never used one of these things,' she said. 'You just sit on it and away you go?'

'With *this* one you have to be running quite fast before it takes off,' said Granny, 'but that's the general idea, yes.'

'Hmm. Do you know the symbology of the broomstick?' said Lily.

'Is it anything to do with maypoles and folksongs and suchlike?' said Granny.

'Oh, yes.'

'Then I don't want to hear about it.'

'No,' said Lily. 'I imagine you don't.'

She handed the stick back.

'I'm staying here,' she said. 'Mrs Gogol may have come up with a new trick, but that doesn't mean she has won.'

'No. Things have come to an end, see,' said Granny. 'That's how it works when you turn the world into stories. You should never have done that. You shouldn't turn the world into stories. You shouldn't treat people like they was *characters*, like they was *things*. But if you *do*, then you've got to know when the story ends.'

'You've got to put on your red-hot shoes and dance the night away?' said Lily.

'Somethin' like that, yes.'

'While everyone else lives happily ever after?'

'I don't know about that,' said Granny. 'That's up to them. What *I'm* sayin' is, you're not allowed to go round one more time. You've *lost*.'

'You know a Weatherwax never loses,' said Lily.

'One of 'em learns tonight,' said Granny.

'But *we're* outside the stories,' said Lily. 'Me because I . . . am the medium through which they happen, and you because you fight them. We're the ones in the middle. The free ones—'

There was a sound behind them. The faces of Magrat and Nanny Ogg appeared over the top of the stairwell.

'You need any help, Esme?' said Nanny cautiously.

Lily laughed.

'Here's *your* little snakes, Esme.'

'You know,' she added, 'you're really just like me.

Don't you know that? There isn't a thought that's gone through my head that you haven't thought, too. There isn't a deed I've done that you haven't contemplated. But you never found the courage. That's the difference between people like me and people like you. *We* have the courage to *do* what you only dream of.'

'Yes?' said Granny. 'Is that what you think? You think I dream?'

Lily moved a finger. Magrat floated up out of the stairwell, struggling. She waved her wand frantically.

'That's what I like to see,' said Lily. 'People wishing. I never wished for anything in my life. I always *made* things happen. So much more rewarding.'

Magrat gritted her teeth.

'I'm sure I wouldn't look good as a pumpkin, dear,' said Lily. She waved a hand airily. Magrat rose.

'You'd be surprised at the things I can do,' said Lily dreamily, as the younger witch drifted smoothly over the flagstones. 'You should have tried mirrors yourself, Esme. It does wonders for a soul. I only let the swamp woman survive because her hate was invigorating. I do like being hated, you know. And you *do* know. It's a kind of respect. It shows you're having an effect. It's like a cold bath on a hot day. When stupid people find themselves powerless, when they fume in their futility, when they're beaten and they've got nothing but that yawning in the acid pit of their stomachs – well, to be honest, it's like a prayer. And the *stories* . . . to *ride* on stories . . . to borrow the strength of them . . . the *comfort* of them . . . to be in the hidden centre of them . . . Can you understand that? The sheer pleasure of seeing the patterns repeat themselves? I've always loved a pattern. Incidentally, if the Ogg woman continues to try to sneak up behind me I shall really let your young friend drift out over the courtyard and then, Esme, I might just lose interest.'

'I was just walkin' about,' said Nanny. 'No law against it.'

'You changed the story your way, and now I'm going to do it mine,' said Lily. 'And once again . . . all you have to do is go. Just go away. What happens here doesn't matter. It's a city far away of which you know little. I'm not totally certain I could out-trick you,' she added, 'but these two . . . they haven't got the right stuff in them. I could make jam of them. I hope you know that. So tonight, I suggest, a Weatherwax learns to lose?'

Granny stood silent for a while, leaning on her useless broom.

'All right. Put her down,' she said. 'And then I'll say you've won.'

'I wish I could believe that,' said Lily. 'Oh . . . but you're the nice one, aren't you? You have to keep your word.'

'Watch me,' said Granny. She walked to the parapet and looked down. The two-faced moon was still bright enough to illuminate the billowing fogs that surrounded the palace like a sea.

'Magrat? Gytha?' she said. 'Sorry about this. You've won, Lily. There ain't nothing I can do.'

She jumped.

Nanny Ogg rushed forward and stared over the

edge, just in time to see a dim figure vanish in the mists.

All three figures left on the tower took a deep breath.

'It's a trick,' said Lily, 'to get me off guard.'

'It isn't!' screamed Magrat, dropping to the stones.

'She had her broomstick,' said Lily.

'It don't work! It won't start!' shouted Nanny. '*Right*,' she said, menacingly, striding towards the slim shape of Lily. 'We'll soon wipe that smug look off your face—'

She halted as silver pain shot through her body.

Lily laughed.

'It's true, then?' she said. 'Yes. I can see it in your faces. Esme was bright enough to know she couldn't win. Don't be stupid. And don't point that silly wand at me, Miss Garlick. Old Desiderata would have defeated me long ago if she could. People have no understanding.'

'We ought to go down there,' said Magrat. 'She might be lying there—'

'That's it. Be good. It's what you're good at,' said Lily, as they ran to the stairwell.

'But we'll be back,' snarled Nanny Ogg. 'Even if we have to live in the swamp with Mrs Gogol and eat snakes' heads!'

'Of course,' said Lily, arching an eyebrow. 'That's what I said. One needs people like you around. Otherwise one is never quite sure one is still working. It's a way of keeping score.'

She watched them disappear down the steps.

A wind blew over the tower. Lily gathered up her skirts and walked to the end, where she could see the shreds of mist streaming over the rooftops far below. There were the faint strains of music from the distant carnival dance as it wound its way through the streets.

It would soon be midnight. Proper midnight, not some cut-price version caused by an old woman crawling around in a clock.

Lily tried to see through the murk to the bottom of the tower.

'Really, Esme,' she murmured, 'you did take losing hard.'

Nanny reached out and restrained Magrat as they ran down the spiral stairs.

'Slow down a bit, I should,' she said.

'But she could be hurt – !'

'So could you, if you trip. Anyway,' said Nanny, 'I don't reckon Esme is lyin' in a crumpled heap somewhere. That's not the way she'd go. I reckon she did it just to make sure Lily forgot about us and wouldn't try anything on us. I reckon she thought we were – what was that Tsortean bloke who could only be wounded if you hit 'im in the right place? No one ever beat 'im until they found out about it. His knee, I think it was. We're her Tsortean knee, right?'

'But we know you have to run really fast to get her broomstick going!' shouted Magrat.

'Yeah, I know,' said Nanny. 'That's what I thought. And now I'm thinking . . . how fast do you go when you're dropping? I mean, straight down?'

'I . . . don't know,' said Magrat.

'I reckon Esme thought it was worth findin' out,' said Nanny. 'That's what I reckon.'

A figure appeared around the bend in the stairs, plodding upwards. They stood aside politely to let it pass.

'Wish I could remember what bit of him you had to hit,' Nanny said. 'That's going to be nagging at me all night, now.'

THE HEEL.

'Right? Oh, thanks.'

ANY TIME.

The figure continued onwards and upwards.

'He had a good mask on, didn't he,' said Magrat, eventually.

She and Nanny sought confirmation in each other's face.

Magrat went pale. She looked up the stairs.

'I think we should run back up and—' she began.

Nanny Ogg was much older. 'I think we should walk,' she said.

Lady Volentia D'Arrangement sat in the rose garden under the big tower and blew her nose.

She'd been waiting for half an hour and she'd had enough.

She'd hoped for a romantic tête-à-tête: he'd seemed such a nice man, sort of eager and shy at the same time. Instead, she'd nearly been hit on the head when an old woman on a broom and wearing what looked, as far as she could see through the blur of speed, like Lady Volentia's own dress, had screamed

347

down out of the mist. Her boots had ploughed through the roses before the curve of her flight took her up again.

And some filthy smelly tomcat kept brushing up against her legs.

And it had started off as such a nice evening . . .

''ullo, your Ladyship?'

She looked around at the bushes.

'My name's Casanunda,' said a hopeful voice.

Lily Weatherwax turned when she heard the tinkle of glass from within the maze of mirrors.

Her brow wrinkled. She ran across the flagstones and opened the door into the mirror world.

There was no sound but the rustle of her dress and the soft hiss of her own breathing. She glided into the place between the mirrors.

Her myriad selves looked back at her approvingly. She relaxed.

Then her foot struck something. She looked down and saw on the flagstones, black in the moonlight, a broomstick lying in shards of broken glass.

Her horrified gaze rose to meet a reflection.

It glared back at her.

'Where's the pleasure in bein' the winner if the loser ain't alive to know they've lost?'

Lilith backed away, her mouth opening and shutting.

Granny Weatherwax stepped through the empty frame. Lily looked down, beyond her avenging sister.

'*You broke my mirror!*'

'Was this what it was all for, then?' said Granny.

'Playin' little queens in some damp city? Serving stories? What sort of power is that?'

'You don't understand . . . you've broken the mirror . . .'

'They say you shouldn't do it,' said Granny. 'But I reckoned: what's another seven years' bad luck?'

Image after image shatters, all the way around the great curve of the mirror world, the crack flying out faster than light . . .

'You have to break *both* to be safe . . . you've upset the *balance* . . .'

'Hah! *I* did?' Granny stepped forward, her eyes two sapphires of bitterness. 'I'm goin' to give you the hidin' our Mam never gave you, Lily Weatherwax. Not with magic, not with headology, not with a stick like our Dad had, aye, and used a fair bit as I recall – but with skin. And not because you was the bad one. Not because you meddled with stories. Everyone has a path they got to tread. But because, and I wants you to understand this prop'ly, after you went *I had to be the good one.* You had all the fun. An' there's no way I can make you pay for that, Lily, but I'm surely goin' to give it a try . . .'

'But . . . I . . . I . . . *I'm* the good one,' Lily murmured, her face pale with shock. 'I'm the good one. I can't lose. I'm the godmother. You're the wicked witch . . . and you've broken the mirror . . .'

. . . moving like a comet, the crack in the mirrors reaches its furthest point and curves back, speeding down the countless worlds . . .

'You've got to help me put . . . the images must

be balanced . . .' Lily murmured faintly, backing up against the remaining glass.

'Good? Good? Feeding people to stories? Twisting people's lives? That's *good*, is it?' said Granny. 'You mean you didn't even have *fun*? If I'd been as bad as you, I'd have been a whole lot worse. Better at it than you've ever dreamed of.'

She drew back her hand.

. . . the crack returned towards its point of origin, carrying with it the fleeing reflections of all the mirrors . . .

Her eyes widened.

The glass smashed and crazed behind Lily Weatherwax.

And in the mirror, the image of Lily Weatherwax turned around, smiled beatifically, and reached out of the frame to take Lily Weatherwax into its arms.

'Lily!'

All the mirrors shattered, exploding outwards in a thousand pieces from the top of the tower so that, just for a moment, it was wreathed in twinkling fairy dust.

Nanny Ogg and Magrat came up onto the roof like avenging angels after a period of lax celestial quality control.

They stopped.

Where the maze of mirrors had been were empty frames. Glass shards covered the floor and, lying on them, was a figure in a white dress.

Nanny pushed Magrat behind her and crunched forward cautiously. She prodded the figure with the toe of her boot.

'Let's throw her off the tower,' said Magrat.

'All right,' said Nanny. 'Do it, then.'

Magrat hesitated. 'Well,' she said, 'when I said let's throw her off the tower, I didn't mean me personally throwing her off, I meant that if there was any justice she ought to be thrown off—'

'Then I shouldn't say any more on that score, if I was you,' said Nanny, kneeling carefully on the crunching shards. 'Besides, I was right. *This* is Esme. I'd know that face anywhere. Take off your petti-coat.'

'Why?'

'Look at her arms, girl!'

Magrat stared. Then she raised her hands to her mouth.

'What has she been *doing*?'

'Trying to reach straight through glass, by the looks of it,' said Nanny. 'Now get it off and help me tear it into strips and then go and find Mrs Gogol and see if she's got any ointments and can help us, and tell her if she can't she'd better be a long way away by morning.' Nanny felt Granny Weatherwax's wrist. 'Maybe Lily Weatherwax could make jam of us but I'm damn sure I could knock Mrs Gogol's eye out with the fender if it came to it.'

Nanny removed her patent indestructible hat and fished around inside the point. She pulled out a velvet cloth and unwrapped it, revealing a little cache of needles and a spool of thread.

She licked a thread and held a needle against the moon, squinting.

'Oh, Esme, Esme,' she said, as she bent to her sewing, 'you do take winning hard.'

Lily Weatherwax looked out at the multi-layered, silvery world.

'Where am I?'

INSIDE THE MIRROR.

'Am I dead?'

THE ANSWER TO THAT, said Death, IS SOMEWHERE BETWEEN NO AND YES.

Lily turned, and a billion figures turned with her.

'When can I get out?'

WHEN YOU FIND THE ONE THAT'S REAL.

Lily Weatherwax ran on through the endless reflections.

A good cook is always the first one into the kitchen every morning and the last one to go home at night.

Mrs Pleasant damped down the fires. She did a quick inventory of the silverware and counted the tureens. She—

She was aware of being stared at.

There was a cat in the doorway. It was big and grey. One eye was an evil yellow-green, the other one pearly white. What remained of its ears looked like the edge of a stamp. Nevertheless, it had a certain swagger, and generated an I-can-beat-you-with-one-paw feel that was strangely familiar.

Mrs Pleasant stared at it for a while. She was a close personal friend of Mrs Gogol and knew that shape is merely a matter of deeply-ingrained personal habit, and if you're a resident of Genua around Samedi Nuit Mort you learn to trust your judgement rather more than you trust your senses.

'Well now,' she said, with barely a trace of a tremor in her voice, 'I expect you'd like some more fish legs, I mean heads, how about that?'

Greebo stretched and arched his back.

'And there's some milk in the coolroom,' said Mrs Pleasant.

Greebo yawned happily.

Then he scratched his ear with his back leg. Humanity's a nice place to visit, but you wouldn't want to live there.

It was a day later.

'Mrs Gogol's healing ointment really seems to work,' said Magrat. She held up a jar that was half-full of something pale green and strangely gritty and had a subtle smell which, you could quite possibly believe, occupied the whole world.

'It's got snakes' heads in it,' said Nanny Ogg.

'Don't you try to upset me,' said Magrat. 'I know the Snake's Head is a kind of flower. A fritillary, I think. It's amazing what you can do with flowers, you know.'

Nanny Ogg, who had in fact spent an instructive if gruesome half-hour watching Mrs Gogol make the stuff, hadn't the heart to say so.

'That's right,' she said. 'Flowers. No getting anything past you, I can see that.'

Magrat yawned.

They had been given the run of the palace, although no one felt like running anywhere. Granny had been installed in the next room.

'Go and get some sleep,' said Nanny. 'I'll go and take over from Mrs Gogol in a moment.'

'But Nanny . . . Gytha . . .' said Magrat.

'Hmm?'

'All that . . . stuff . . . she was saying, when we were travelling. It was so . . . so *cold*. Wasn't it? Not wishing for things, not using magic to help people, not being able to do that fire thing – and then she went and did all those things! What am I supposed to make of that?'

'Ah, well,' said Nanny. 'It's all according to the general and the specific, right?'

'What does that mean?' Magrat lay down on the bed.

'Means when Esme uses words like "Everyone" and "No one" she doesn't include herself.'

'You know . . . when you think about it . . . that's terrible.'

'That's witchcraft. Up at the sharp end. And now . . . get some sleep.'

Magrat was too tired to object. She stretched out and was soon snoring in a genteel sort of way.

Nanny sat and smoked her pipe for a while, staring at the wall.

Then she got up and pushed open the door.

Mrs Gogol looked up from her stool by the bed.

'You go and get some sleep too,' said Nanny. 'I'll take over for a spell.'

'There's something not right,' said Mrs Gogol. 'Her hands are fine. She just won't wake up.'

'It's all in the mind, with Esme,' said Nanny.

'I could make some new gods and get everyone to believe in 'em real good. How about that?' said Mrs Gogol. Nanny shook her head.

'I shouldn't think Esme'd want that. She's not keen on gods. She thinks they're a waste of space.'

'I could cook up some gumbo, then. People'll come a long way to taste that.'

'It might be worth a try,' Nanny conceded. 'Every little helps, I always say. Why not see to it? Leave the rum here.'

After the voodoo lady had gone Nanny smoked her pipe some more and drank a little rum in a thoughtful sort of way, looking at the figure on the bed.

Then she bent down close to Granny Weatherwax's ear, and whispered:

'You ain't going to *lose*, are you?'

Granny Weatherwax looked out at the multi-layered, silvery world.

'Where am I?'

INSIDE THE MIRROR.

'Am I dead?'

THE ANSWER TO THAT, said Death, IS SOMEWHERE BETWEEN NO AND YES.

Esme turned, and a billion figures turned with her.

'When can I get out?'

WHEN YOU FIND THE ONE THAT'S REAL.

'Is this a trick question?'

No.

Granny looked down at herself.

'This one,' she said.

And stories just want *happy* endings. They don't give a damn who they're *for*.

Dear Jason eksetra,

Well so much for Genua but I learned about Mrs Gogol's zombie medicin and she gave me the ~~fesipe~~ ~~fesatpy~~ told me how to make banananana dakry and gave me a thing call a banjo youll be amazed and all in all is a decent soul I reckon if you keeps her where you can see her. It looks like we got Esme back but I don't know shes actin funny and quiet not like herself normally so Im keepin an Eye on her just in case Lily puled a farst one in the mirror. But I think shes geting better because when she woke up she arsked Magrat for a look at the wand and then she kind of twidled and twisted them rings on it and turned the po into a bunch of flowers and Magrat said she could never make the wand do that and Esme said no because, she wasted time wishing for thinges instead of working out how to make them happen. What I say is, what a good job Esme never got a wand when she was young, Lily would have bin a Picnic by comparisen. Enclosed is a picture of the cemtry here you can see folks are buried in boxes above ground the soil being so wet because you dont want to be dead and drownded at the same time, they say travelin brordens the mind, I reckon I could pull mine out my

*ears now and knot it under my chin, all the best,
MUM.*

In the swamp Mrs Gogol the voodoo witch draped
the tail coat over its crude stand, stuck the hat on the
top of the pole and fastened the cane to one end of
the crosspiece with a bit of twine.

She stood back.

There was a fluttering of wings. Legba dropped
out of the sky and perched on the hat. Then he
crowed. Usually he only crowed at nightfall, because
he was a bird of power, but for once he was inclined
to acknowledge the new day.

It was said afterwards that, every year on Samedi
Nuit Mort, when the carnival was at its height and
the drums were loudest and the rum was nearly all
gone, a man in a tail coat and a top hat and with the
energy of a demon would appear out of nowhere and
lead the dance.

After all, even stories have to start somewhere.

There was a splash, and then the waters of the river
closed again. Magrat walked away.

The wand settled into the rich mud, where it
was touched only by the feet of the occasional passing crawfish, who don't have fairy godmothers and
aren't allowed to wish for anything. It sank down
over the months and passed, as most things do, out
of history. Which was all anyone could wish for.

The three broomsticks rose over Genua, with the
mists that curled towards the dawn.

The witches looked down at the green swamps around the city. Genua dozed. The days after Fat Lunchtime were always quiet, as people slept it off. Currently they included Greebo, curled up in his place among the bristles. Leaving Mrs Pleasant had been a real wrench.

'Well, so much for *la douche vita*,' said Nanny philosophically.

'We never said goodbye to Mrs Gogol,' said Magrat.

'I reckon she knows we're going right enough,' said Nanny. 'Very knowin' woman, Mrs Gogol.'

'But can we trust her to keep her word?' said Magrat.

'Yes,' said Granny Weatherwax.

'She's very honest, in her way,' said Nanny Ogg.

'Well, there's that,' Granny conceded. 'Also, I said I might come back.'

Magrat looked across at Granny's broomstick. A large round box was among the baggage strapped to the bristles.

'You never tried on that hat she gave you,' she said.

'I had a look at it,' said Granny coldly. 'It don't fit.'

'I reckon Mrs Gogol wouldn't give anyone a hat that didn't fit,' said Nanny. 'Let's have a look, eh?'

Granny sniffed, and undid the lid of the box. Balls of tissue paper tumbled down towards the mists as she lifted the hat out.

Magrat and Nanny Ogg stared at it.

They were of course used to the concept of fruit on a hat – Nanny Ogg herself had a black straw hat with wax cherries on for special family feuding occasions. But this one had rather more than just cherries. About the only fruit not on it somewhere was a melon.

'It's definitely very . . . *foreign*,' said Magrat.

'Go on,' said Nanny. 'Try it on.'

Granny did so, a bit sheepishly, increasing her apparent height by two feet, most of which was pineapple.

'Very colourful. Very . . . stylish,' said Nanny. 'Not everyone could wear a hat like that.'

'The pomegranates suit you,' said Magrat.

'And the lemons,' said Nanny Ogg.

'Eh? You two ain't laughing at me, are you?' said Granny Weatherwax suspiciously.

'Would you like to have a look?' said Magrat. 'I have a mirror somewhere . . .'

The silence descended like an axe. Magrat went red. Nanny Ogg glared at her.

They watched Granny carefully.

'Ye-ess,' she said, after what seemed a long time, 'I think I should look in a mirror.'

Magrat unfroze, fumbled in her pockets and produced a small, wooden-framed hand-mirror. She passed it across.

Granny Weatherwax looked at her reflection. Nanny Ogg surreptitiously manoeuvred her broomstick a bit closer.

'Hmm,' said Granny, after a while.

'It's the way the grapes hang over your ear,' said

Nanny, encouragingly. 'You know, that's a hat of authority if ever I saw one.'

'Hmm.'

'Don't you think?' said Magrat.

'Well,' said Granny, grudgingly, 'maybe it's fine for foreign parts. Where I ain't going to be seen by anyone as knows me. No one important, anyway.'

'And when we get home you can always eat it,' said Nanny Ogg.

They relaxed. There was a feeling of a hill climbed, a dangerous valley negotiated.

Magrat looked down at the brown river and the suspicious logs on its sandbanks.

'What I want to know is,' she said, 'was Mrs Gogol really good or bad? I mean, dead people and alligators and everything . . .'

Granny looked at the rising sun, poking though the mists.

'Good and bad is tricky,' she said. 'I ain't too certain about where people stand. P'raps what matters is which way you face.

'You know,' she added, 'I truly believe I can see the edge from here.'

'Funny thing,' said Nanny, 'they say that in some foreign parts you get elephants. You know, I've always wanted to see an elephant. And there's a place in Klatch or somewhere where people climb up ropes and disappear.'

'What for?' said Magrat.

'Search me. There's prob'ly some cunnin' foreign reason.'

'In one of Desiderata's books,' said Magrat, 'she says that there's a very interesting thing about seeing elephants. She says that on the Sto plains, when people say they're going to see the elephant, it means they're simply going on a journey because they're fed up with staying in the same place.'

'It's not staying in the same place that's the problem,' said Nanny, 'it's not letting your mind wander.'

'*I'd* like to go up towards the Hub,' said Magrat. 'To see the ancient temples such as are described in Chapter One of *The Way of the Scorpion*.'

'And they'd teach you anything you don't know already, would they?' said Nanny, with unusual sharpness.

Magrat glanced at Granny.

'Probably not,' she said meekly.

'Well,' said Nanny. 'What's it to be, Esme? Are we going home? Or are we off to see the elephant?' Granny's broomstick turned gently in the breeze.

'You're a disgustin' old baggage, Gytha Ogg,' said Granny.

'That's me,' said Nanny cheerfully.

'And, Magrat Garlick—'

'I know,' said Magrat, overwhelmed with relief, 'I'm a wet hen.'

Granny looked back towards the Hub, and the high mountains. Somewhere back there was an old cottage with the key hanging in the privy. All sorts of things were probably going on. The whole kingdom was probably going to rack and ruin without her around to keep people on the right track. It was her job. There was no telling what stupidities people would get up to if she wasn't there . . .

Nanny kicked her red boots together idly.

'Well, I suppose there's no place like home,' she said.

'No,' said Granny Weatherwax, still looking thoughtful. 'No. There's a billion places like home. But only one of 'em's where you live.'

'So we're going back?' said Magrat.

'Yes.'

But they went the long way, and saw the elephant.

THE END

INTERESTING TIMES
Terry Pratchett

'Funny, delightfully inventive and refuses to lie
down in its genre'
Observer

'A foot in the neck is nine points of the law.'

THERE are many who say that the art of diplomacy is
an intricate and complex dance between two
informed partners, determined by an elaborate set of
elegant and unwritten rules. There are others who
maintain that it's merely a matter of who carries the
biggest stick. Like when a large, heavily fortified and
armoured empire makes a faintly menacing request of a
much smaller, infinitely more cowardly neighbour. It
would be churlish, if not extremely dangerous, not to
comply – particularly if all they want is a wizard, and
they don't specify whether competence is an issue...

'Imagine a collision between Jonathan Swift at his
most scatological and J.R.R. Tolkien on speed...
This is the joyous outcome'
Daily Telegraph

'Like Dickens, much of Pratchett's appeal lies in his
humanism, both in a sentimental regard for his
characters' good fortune, and in that his writing is
generous-spirited and inclusive'
Guardian

9780552153218

SOUL MUSIC
Terry Pratchett

'Classic English humour, with all the slapstick,
twists and dry observations you could hope for'
The Times

*'Be careful what you wish for. You never know who
might be listening.'*

THERE'S no getting away from it. From whichever
angle, Death is a horrible, inescapable business. But
someone's got to do it. So if Death decides to take a
well-earned moment to uncover the meaning of life and
discover himself in the process, then there is going to be
a void of specific dimensions that needs to be occupied,
particularly so when there is trouble brewing in
Discworld. There aren't too many who are qualified to
fill Death's footsteps and it certainly doesn't help the
imminent cataclysm that the one person poised
between the mortal and the immortal is only sixteen
years old...

'Very clever madcap satire which has universal
appeal. If you haven't tried him, this is a fun one
to start with'
Today

'Pratchett lures classical themes and popular
mythologies into the dark corners of his
imagination, gets them drunk and makes them
do things you wouldn't dream of doing with
an Oxford don'
Daily Mail

9780552153195

MASKERADE
— Terry Pratchett —

'As funny as Wodehouse and as witty as Waugh'
Independent

'I thought: opera, how hard can it be? Songs. Pretty girls dancing. Nice scenery. Lots of people handing over cash. Got to be better than the cut-throat world of yoghurt, I thought. Now everywhere I go there's…'

DEATH, to be precise. And plenty of it. In unpleasant variations. This isn't real life. This isn't even cheesemongering. It's opera. Where the music matters and where an opera house is being terrorised by a man in evening dress with a white mask, lurking in the shadows, occasionally killing people, and most worryingly, sending little notes, writing maniacal laughter with five exclamation marks. Opera can do that to a man. In such circumstances, life has obviously reached that desperate point where the wrong thing to do **has** to be the right thing to do…

'Cracking dialogue, compelling illogic and unchained whimsy…Pratchett has a subject and a style that is very much his own'
Sunday Times

'Entertaining and gloriously funny'
Chicago Tribune

9780552153232

FEET OF CLAY
Terry Pratchett

'The work of a prolific humorist at his best'
Observer

'Sorry?' said Carrot. 'If it's just a thing, how can it commit murder? A sword is a thing' – he drew out his own sword; it made an almost silken sound – 'and of course you can't blame a sword if someone thrust it at you, sir.'

For members of the City Watch, life consists of troubling times, linked together by periods of torpid inactivity. Now is one such troubling time. People are being murdered, but there's no trace of anything alive having been at the crime scene. Is there ever a circumstance in which you can blame the weapon not the murderer? Such philosophical questions are not the usual domain of the city's police, but they're going to have to start learning fast...

'Like most true originals, Pratchett defies categorization... Deliciously and amiably dotty... Driven by Swiftian logic and equally intellectually inventive'
The Times

'Fantastical, inventive and finally serious... It's enjoyable as crime fiction, but the real attraction is the laughter waiting to be uncovered on every page'
Observer

'An explosion of imaginative lunacy'
Daily Express

9780552153256

JINGO

Terry Pratchett

'Generous, amusing and the ideal boarding point for those who have never visited Discworld'
Sunday Telegraph

'Neighbours...hah. People'd live for ages side by side, nodding at one another amicably on their way to work, and then some trivial thing would happen and someone would be having a garden fork removed from their ear.'

THROUGHOUT history, there's always been a perfectly good reason to start a war. Never more so if it is over a 'strategic' piece of old rock in the middle of nowhere. It is after all every citizen's right to bear arms to defend what they consider to be their own. Even if it isn't. And in such pressing circumstances, you really shouldn't let small details like the absence of an army or indeed the money to finance one get in the way of a righteous fight with all the attendant benefits of out-and-out nationalism...

'Pratchett's writing is a constant delight. No one mixes the fantastical and the mundane to better comic effect or offers sharper insights into the absurdities of human endeavour'
Daily Mail

'One of those very rare writers who appeals to everyone...He satisfies the need for fast-moving, breathtaking plots with entirely satisfying endings, and the equally primitive desire for an alternative world, full of thrills but benign, into which one can step for pleasure and enlivenment'
Daily Express

'Vintage Pratchett...Perennially funny...A sharp satire on the futility of war'
Metro

9780552154161

Visit

www.**terrypratchett**.co.uk

to discover everything you need to know
about Terry Pratchett and his writing, plus all
manner of other things you may find interesting, such as
videos, competitions, character profiles and games.

 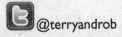